TERRA ROSSA

TERRA ROSSA

BY

DEREK TRUEMAN

White Falcon
Publishing
www.whitefalconpublishing.com

Terra Rossa
Derek Trueman

www.whitefalconpublishing.com

All rights reserved
First Edition, 2019
© Derek Trueman, 2019
Cover design © White Falcon Publishing, 2019
Cover image © Derek Trueman

Requests for permission should be addressed to
pipkrake@yahoo.com

ISBN - 978-93-88459-96-9

PASQUALE'S ITALY

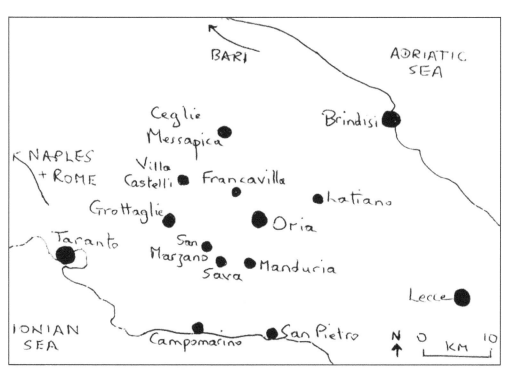

1

LUCKY STRIKE

1 9 5 2

He put down his metal detector and jabbed down with the metal tool he pulled from his waist belt.

...clunk.

Rock or metal?

How can anyone see anything in this accursed heat? he thought, as his eyes stung from perspiration.

Siesta or not, Pasquale thrust another wrist-jarring stab of his vanga into the baked, red soil. Nothing.

OK, a bit to the left, he muttered. Try again.

...clang.

Oh metal, surely? Yes, please let it be metal! Three hours walking and stabbing into this blasted patch of ground on the edge of a desolate field, in the middle of a desiccating hot day, has to yield some reward, surely? And a timely escape from today's sirocco wind *would* certainly be some kind of reward too.

Reward. His wandering thoughts returned to the job in hand. Gently now, on all fours, finally using the little piece of old metal he had found earlier, the nearest thing he had to a trowel, he prodded gently all around his 'clang'.

It had to be; this *was* the spot. He had judiciously measured all the distances around the site, as accurately as his olive-tree measuring stick would allow anyway, give or take a few gnarled twists and turns along its abrasive grey wood.

And then, yes, there it was: dull, blackened and imperfectly rounded, but certainly a coin. He relaxed, smiled a part-toothless grin, eased his aching back and arms, and rubbed his stinging eyes with the now dust-spattered, grimy vest. Rolling the coin gently between thumb and finger he soon realised it was not unique, nor that valuable, and he had damaged it too with his vanga, but depending on how many more were scattered around, quite a pleasing return for a morning's work in this summer-semi-desert.

Later, returning along the pot-holed dirt track he glanced again at the cloth bag bouncing on his handlebars. Its contents would keep Mario happy for a few days at least and certainly yield Pasquale a few thousand lira to boot. But he must go easier with the vanga and have more patience, he committed to memory with a smile.

Oh, a good day indeed, made better immediately by the sudden emergence of a tree ahead on the roadside, a tree literally bursting with fresh, sweet, juicy figs -- his favourite thirst quencher in such emergencies.

***

2

GOODBYE FATHER

1 9 3 9

"That's it, finito!" screamed Eduardo vehemently. He glared at the pale watery soup and bread Isabella had placed on the table yet again. No meal for a toiling breadwinner in this appetite-sapping heat, he thought. I can't do this any longer, there has to be something better after sweating blood all morning in the fields to come home to three cloying children and an abrasive wife completely under the thumb of her mother. Springing to his feet, he sent the table and its liquid contents flying. Amidst panic-stricken faces he stormed to the front door. Taking his last look at the cramped, dirty stone house, with its high-arched tufa ceilings and tiny windows, he stepped out into the glaring midday sun. The searing heat almost knocked him back into the relative cool of the room, but he managed somehow to continue his dramatic exit and walk as upright as possible down the narrow stone-paved street which wound through the old centre.

"Tell Andrea to find me at Cosimo's next week and I'll see if there is any money to spare", he shouted back at Isabella as she frantically screened the doorway of his house.

My house? He thought. No, not my house anymore; their ugly little house and welcome to it! The sudden feeling of release so overcame him that he continued on his way whistling, something he rarely did or ever felt like doing in his limited circumstances.

"Has Papa gone without pranzo, Mama?"

"Of course, but he'll be back." He always comes back, she mused.

"Can I have his then, Mama? Please?"

"Papa will come running back hungry, you'll see. If not, Andrea needs it more. We'll give it to her."

"It's all right, Mama, I'm not that hungry, it's too hot, and anyway Pasquale needs it more than I," said Andrea.

"Well, he'd better start learning to wash-up afterwards then and give us a break," Mama laughed.

Andrea pleaded, "no Mama, Pasquale's a boy, don't insult him, boys mustn't do housework, Mama, you know that!"

"And look where it gets us when you let men get away with everything. He'll be at that bar now, drinking away the little money we've got and leering at that bodice behind the counter."

"But he will be back tonight, Mama, won't he?" mumbled a slightly worried little boy. Pasquale was seven but often mistaken for four or five because he was so short in height. Not short in stature though - a most stocky, wiry little chap. Andrea, on the other hand, was six years older than her brother and already starting to blossom into the classic southern beauty ---long black curled hair, twinkling eyes and a glowing satin sheen complexion. And her subtle, seductive, swinging gait was already attracting the town boys, even under the shapeless dresses handed down from her Mama's 'teenage trunk'.

Perhaps it was also the motherly image she projected that attracted them too, because most of her time she would only be seen out in the streets watching and carrying baby Maria as she crawled and toddled about happily on the smooth polished stones that had repelled thousands upon thousands of cartwheels and hooves.

Avetrana was a very small provincial town cleverly positioned two miles inland of the Ionian Sea. Between it and these glittering waters lay a long, low, asymmetric ridge of barren tufa rock. Although it was only good enough to support scrub and a few sheep without water, the creamy coloured tufa was a useful building stone and had supplied all the blocks for the surrounding areas from its small handcut quarries. Cunningly therefore, Avetrana could not be seen by an enemy approaching from the sea, but once the soldiers had toiled and sweated over the ridge they would still have to capture the little town laid out before them before they could advance inland. And in the centre of all the twisting, jumbled, old stone streets was an imposing albeit small castello, with requisite domed chiesa, to further arrest their progress.

The castello, surrounded by a deep moat and with only one drawbridge and portcullis for entry, had both a round tower and a square keep, with a central courtyard sufficiently spacious to house in olden times the 500 or so residents of the town under attack. The chiesa had been rebuilt later in 1660 after the original had been burned down in a dispute between the lord and the priest. Indeed, historians swear that Avetrana castle had never been breached in over 800 years and the only real damage done, ironically, was from the 1861 earthquake that shook the whole centre of Puglia. But today the streets around the centre only echoed the children's giggles of glee, not the soldiers' boots and grunts, and the castello's former glory had long since evaporated in the mists of time.

Pasquale's Avetrana was now merely one of many tiny towns scattered about the Salento Plain, serving only to accommodate farmers and labourers toiling the surrounding land. Unlike northern Europe, where farmers actually lived on their farms in farmhouses and labourers huddled in thousands of villages no more than half a day's walk from the fields in which they toiled, here practically no-one lived on the farmland and there were next to no villages. There was simply no need because the produce was, and always had been, so different. In Britain, France, Germany and so on, workers needed to attend to cows, pigs, horses and vegetables on a daily basis. However, in Puglia the wheat fields, olive groves and vineyards only needed a few visits a year.

So people huddled in small towns for protection and the countryside was devoid of buildings, except for the odd square stone hut where a worker might shelter from the heat of the siesta sun or occasionally overnight during peak times. Consequently, farms were also smaller and tracks fewer, while dry stone walls were everywhere as no wild vegetation would mature into a hedge, except cacti. Even the farm equipment was kept in the towns for safety but then clogged up the roads on carts en route to the farms on those few days of the year when needed.

Although the muted green of the olive tree blended pleasingly with the more verdant green of the vines and the soft gold of the wheat, Pasquale's favourite time of the year was April when all the Spring flowers burst forth, especially after a heavy, air-clearing rainstorm, to paint a riot of colour. They danced between the tolerant, unmoved, gnarled olive trees – some over a thousand years old -- and across the stringy grass fields of yellow daisies, blood-red poppies, blue violets and pink peonies, sweeter than even a Monet scape.

Eduardo did *not* return that evening, contrary to Isabella's prediction, or the next lunchtime or the next evening. Therefore, the Carones were indeed forced to send Andrea down to Cosimo's shop a week later, only to find their father had in fact truly moved on with no intention of returning. He had not just left his friend's house but the town, his labouring job in the fields and all his responsibilities.

"Tell Andrea I have gone and do not attempt to trace me", he had said to Cosimo.

Cosimo was shocked, but knowing Eduardo of old he was not that surprised. After all, how many times in the last year was he forced to stagger out of his bed in the early hours to let Eduardo in? Indeed, he was surprised this had not happened sooner. As he saw it, Eduardo sweated all day for a tragic minimum wage, breaking his back and his bones for an early grave. There was hardly enough to buy food, let alone firewood or candles or a night out for the family at the bar, or a chicken once a month. Furthermore, he could see no light at the end of the tunnel with the War fast approaching, although desperate times had been known to create desperate results. Although he did not condone his best friend's infidelity to his family, he could understand why he was going away. So many were these days, but not all in such a dramatic fashion. Most fathers who were heading north merely told their families they were seeking better work with more money to send home, not that they were walking out on them and never returning. Even in 1939 there was already a great rift between the richer North and the poorer South of Italy and this North-South divide was never going to improve.

Indeed, Cosimo had tackled Eduardo on that very subject but he had received stonewall treatment: sometimes his friend was impossible to reach and could even become violent. All Cosimo knew was that Eduardo still simmered over Cosimo being chosen over him for the comfortable job in the little village shop, just because Cosimo had completed one more year of elementary school and could actually add '19 and a half and 12' in his head. Eduardo needed more than ten fingers and nearly a minute to complete such a sum!

But I'll show them, thought Eduardo, as he dreamt of finding a decent job in nearby Brindisi, perhaps down at the docks counting in and out the trays of fresh prawns, calamari and spigola moving from the boats into the trains and lorries. Surely some fish can wriggle into my pocket too, he chuckled, as he bounced along in the rickety bus that plied its trade twice a week to the fishing and packet port of south-east Italy.

The main road, still dirt, was much busier than usual. It seemed the whole country was mobilising. Why shouldn't he? War was coming and Mussolini was invoking every fit man to join his army to create a glorious future for Europe. Eduardo might have been an insignificant peasant from a tiny town, but his brain was not. He could see no fortune in becoming cannon-fodder for a pompous little leader with a big mouth and feathers for a hat, but he could see vast potential in a protracted war for anyone willing to work cunningly and risk a few lira outlay. But the latter was his immediate problem-- no cash -- so initially he would have to try to find and work he could in the port and a bed at his cousin's, then see what progressed.

* * *

3

BREADWINNER

1 9 4 0

No such dreams of work for Pasquale, like his father. What could he do at eight years of age, but still technically the bread winner, in such a traditional backwater as Avetrana? He had never seen the inside of a school room in his entire life - his father could not afford to pay the teaching board's small monthly fee. Everything he knew he had gleaned second-hand from his sister, and his mama, or occasionally his papa when he had bothered to take him out into the fields. These trips had become more frequent in the past couple of years as he had become strong enough to do more than just stand and watch his father pruning vines, gathering olives or hoeing melon rows. He had soon realised too that a giggling game of hide and seek, or trotting off to explore some secret nook, was not what his father required; the lesson sealed with a resounding slap or a brief belt-whipping. But he had learned some useful strategies out in the campagna --- he had memorised where each farm was, what each farm grew, what delightful little fruit delicacies concealed themselves behind walls and outhouses, and when each crop came to fruition in its rightful season. The Northern Europe three course or four course rotations did not exist here under the hot Mediterranean climate so crops changed little from year to year, and remembering all this was subsequently made easier for the little boy.

So on 3 September 1940 Pasquale was huffing and puffing along the main dirt road out of Avetrana on his ancient little pushbike his father had found for him "behind a wall". Rusty and mud-encased it may have been, but to Pasquale it had been the most precious moment of his life when his father had led him out, eyes closed, into the blinding sun and said 'see what I've got for you. Don't ever say I don't give you presents!'

Pasquale had set to, with brush and cloth, to make it sparkle nearly as much as his little eyes. Andrea had helped with the stubborn sun-hardened mud and rust, but even so he reckoned *he* had done a great job. Then, surprisingly, Cosimo had found a little paint left from a job in the shop and he'd given it a sparkling new coat. The solid tyres needed little repair, the one brake a little oil (they only had olive oil but just as good!), and soon he was the envy of his poverty-stricken street.

Each day he would peddle a little further afield, once he had received the seal of approval from the ever-watchful Andrea. In siesta time nothing moved, except his bike, so he was even allowed to go past the last houses and into the nearby farm tracks. Oh, what freedom! Oh, what excitement, even though Andrea sat in the shade of a fig tree and supervised his progress. Soon he became so sensibly trustworthy that she no longer bothered to go out with him.

Unfortunately, however, while under the tree Andrea had found the time to complete her beloved sewing, but now that she stayed at home she seemed to be given more and more chores instead. Inevitably both the sewing output and the enthusiasm suffered. There was no doubt Andrea had a gift for fine sewing and simple weaving: everyone knew it and regularly placed small orders with her for handkerchiefs, shawls and doilies. There was little profit to be made, especially as most of her 'customers' were friends, but every lira helped in this time of crisis.

Pasquale loved these afternoons in the fields, heat or no heat, and far quicker than his street-bound friends he started to unravel the secrets of the campagna. In his freedom he quickly learned how to ride with a tiny bag on his back, and as it quickly became such a common sight no-one ever gave it a second glance.

'There goes Pasquale again, off for his ride into the country, bag on back, huffing and puffing. Strange lad'.

But in just one four-hour siesta Pasquale found, to his delight, that he could make four, or sometimes even five, mini trips out and return with what his mama called his 'most precious cargo'.

With great concern they had to explain one day to the fuel man that they needed less firewood because Eduardo had left for work elsewhere, so they were only four to feed and warm. The resigned peddlar merely shrugged and smiled, not realising that Pasquale was fuelling their domestic supplies from fallen sticks from the trees. Incidentally, the fuel man was a good person to tell this too because he was the village, and inter-village, gossip so news of Eduardo would be mooted quickly by the broadcasting of it. Unfortunately, they still ended up paying him the same amount each week because everything, not just fuel, was steadily rising in price with the impending war.

Not that such problems concerned little Pasquale; he felt most important. When his mama hugged him and said, 'I don't know how we'd manage without you now,' his scrawny chest swelled with pride because he was fast becoming the little "man about the house".

However, after a while, sourcing dead olive branches, snapping them with his boot on the hypotenuse of soil and a stone, and laying them neatly in his back-sack for maximum packaging, became a rather mundane task.

So, there he was, on 3ʳᵈ September 1940, about to initiate his first serious mission. Two pm with not a soul stirring, he cautiously parked his bicycle behind the small, square stone shelter. It was the correct shelter because right behind it, almost beckoning him, were the objects of his mission - a fig tree and a lemon bush! Within two minutes he had garnered enough figs and lemons to make his back-sack bulge alarmingly. He had meant to take fewer, but you know how it is the first time, flushed with success and excitement. How can you possibly stop? he told himself. Away he peddled as fast as he could. No, no, no, slow down, act normal, don't be silly! and he eased back into the Pasquale pace that everyone waved at and ciao-ed. But there was no 'everyone' today, this was deep siesta time and thirty minutes later he was gently shaking his mama's shoulder and whispering excitedly, 'wake up, wake up, look what I have found for you!'

Now, to Pasquale 'found' was the operative word, because in his opinion he had just been cycling along innocently and had come across this delicious fruit dangling over the wall of the track. 'Common property' his father had instilled into him, whenever he had reached for a fresh juicy fig. Pasquale had had no idea what he had meant, but from the outright audacious way his father had plucked them he assumed it must have been fine.

Pasquale had lain his treasures in a bowl as Isabella stirred in the relative coolness of their one bedroom - the one-third metre thick stone walls certainly kept out much of the heat. But the heat rose in her eyes, and her breath, as she screamed at Pasquale, "you bad boy, fiacco…wicked, wicked little boy…you thief! Oh, how could you ever do this thing, Pasquale?"

"But Mama, what? What have I done?" Ignoring him, she slapped him soundly across the head and continued her tirade. "You wake me up out of a beautiful slumber to tell me you are a thief and you have stolen fruit…oh, fiacco, fiacco!" and as she burst into tears Andrea also woke from the mattress on the floor and joined in the general wailing.

"But Mama, Andrea, I haven't stolen them…"

"…You must have. Where from? Who? Tell me now or I will beat you harder than even your Papa did!"

"Mama, please, I f…f…f…found them," pouted poor little Pasquale as his bottom lip started to tremble and his eyes watered. This was certainly not the reaction he had expected. Five minutes ago he had triumphantly marched through the front door and had preened at the thought of the hero's welcome. 'Prince Pasquale, champion of fruit gatherers, accept your reward!'

* * *

4

BIGGER BREADWINNER

1 9 4 0

Isabella had received nothing from Eduardo, not even a word; nor had Cosimo, more to her surprise. The few lira notes she had left in her purse were dwindling rapidly and on no account did she intend to break into her little pot of savings, hidden behind the bucket under the sink in the kitchen. The children were, as ever, hungry and grumpy yet all she had to offer was the interminable wild artichoke and fare (swede) soup with a few morsels of grainy, rough bread.

"OK Pasquale, you win, if you must. If you promise you did not steal the fruit, then go! Go and find some more, as quick as you can, otherwise we might starve at this rate."

Pasquale sprang out of his chair, all hunger and grumpiness forgotten, and was about to launch himself onto the commercial world when Mama called, "wait, let me see if I can find you a bigger, sturdier bag". Pasquale beamed, Maria gurgled and even Andrea could not resist a sly smirk to her brother, plus one raised eyebrow for good measure.

But as Pasquale reached the door and looked out into the magical Mediterranean Hour he suddenly realised the problem. "But mama, siesta is already over, it's nearly 6 o'clock, there will be people everywhere".

"No, not in the fields, if that is where you found it all. That's what you said, right? In the fields?"

"Of course, Mama, but it will be dark soon and I might get attacked."

"A little, unassuming boy such as you, brother, how could you think so?" chimed in Andrea. "Dark? All the better to not see you. Be off with you before we all die of hunger here!"

So Pasquale found himself anxiously pedaling off, smiling and waving to all he knew. He certainly understood the seriousness of the situation. All these other families had some money coming in at least. Not much, but enough to scrape by on. We had nothing, he thought. Was it Papa's fault or…? He did not want to ponder that further so he switched his brain to ways of camouflaging the booty on his return trip.

Then he suddenly realised how hungry he really was, and that made him realise the gnawing would not be assuaged by lemons and figs: he needed to find vegetables, yes, fat juicy vegetables.

One hour later, with dusk wrapping its milky September coat around everything, he slunk back into town, his little bag bursting with green beans and zucchini. As luck would have it, most folk were now indoors preparing or eating cena, and he easily contended with the few residue children left playing in the gutter.

"Oh, Pasqua, what a bonanza," giggled Andrea, "where did you get these? Or perhaps I shouldn't ask. Mama, come, look!"

"Oh, Pasquale, what can I say? Except perhaps that I hope our need is greater than who these belonged to!"

"Mama, tonight shall we have beans and bread? Tomorrow I could try to sell two or three more handkerchiefs and buy a little spaghetti and pomodoro. Yes?"

Pasquale and tiny Maria clapped their hands and skipped around the overcrowded little room. Oh, how they had missed their fortnightly treat of canned tomatoes and spaghetti these past few months. The staple food at this time in Puglia for the working class was in fact bread not spaghetti, and spaghetti was a treat from the North only afforded two or three times a month. Similarly, tomatoes consumed in the South were usually canned, unless you were rich, because fresh tomatoes only grew in the cooler, wetter North. Fresh were expensive, and meat of any description was a luxury, of course.

"If I have any lira left, Pasqua, as a reward I will try to get you some of your favourite sweets, the dried fig ones, yes?"

"Oh thank you, thank you, Andrea. I love you, I love you!"

"No, big breadwinner, I love *you*!"

***

5

EDUARDO IN BRINDISI

1 9 4 3

Eduardo had been fortunate. There *had* been work in the port and he had flourished. There had been many trays of fish and some had indeed fallen into his pockets, metaphorically. Following the initial tongue-lashing from his cousin over his questionable morality, he and his wife had looked after him well. So well that his poverty-stricken past in the countryside soon became a distant memory.

However, Eduardo was not all bad and he did have some wistful memories of his little Maria and of course Pasquale, trapped in their tiny tufa rectangle of a house in that awful, backward Avetrana, probably half starving most of the time. But what more could he do? He sent the odd postal order for a few lira to Cosimo when he could, but he wondered if it ever arrived, or if it did whether the scheming Isabella kept it all to herself. He had no news of them and they none of him. Avetrana, then, was almost forgotten.

Brindisi, on the other hand, was the place to be. After a long early morning and part afternoon at the fishing port, followed by a siesta and dinner at home, he could take his pick of the evening's entertainment. The town was a busy packet port -- fish, passengers to and from Greece and Yugoslavia, cargoes from all over the Mediterranean -- a bustling and cosmopolitan place. Not a place for nervous little sardines but a place for braggart swashbucklers with bulging muscles and much derring-do. Ideal for Eduardo.

Dotted around the old cobbled streets of the centro storico were many bars, cafes and restaurants, all with attendant attractions that only large town centres could usually offer. The shops stocked items which left

Eduardo's mouth agape, while two cinemas and a new 'live' teatro were bringing the world to this heel of Italy, albeit in celluloid or stage paint.

Unfortunately, although Eduardo believed his pay to be fantastic it certainly did not stretch far after a Friday and a Saturday night on the town, especially if assignations were kept with work colleagues or the occasional 'better-than-the-one-night' lady but still the 'need-to-be-paid' lady. With both groups he was immensely popular, with the former for his side-splitting tales of poverty in Avetrana and with the latter for his persisting rugged good looks and swarthy debonair disposition. After all, as he kept reminding himself, I'm still only 37 and a handsome lady-killer.

To be sure, he had seldom visited the ladies of the night along the pungent streets abutting the harbour, and only when he had first arrived, had known no-one, but had sought some kind of comfort. However, his regular appearance around the town bars and his physical attractions had not only made him a leader of his band of dockers but also very noticeable to women. With so many of their boyfriends and husbands heading North for better work, not only was their work vacancy being filled by men from the countryside but also the vacant spaces in their girlfriend's and wives' beds.

However, not all was pleasure. The War was rumbling on, and Italy, after entering it one year before, was already sinking into depression, deprivation and despair, with most not wanting Mussolini anyway, or so the radio reported. In Puglia, the heel, so far away from these northern theatres of war, the impact was watered down by the friction of distance, so that life continued very much as it always had in such a rural backwater, well at least three quarters of normality.

This Saturday night was little different to any other: Eduardo was relaxing in the Acropolis Bar with his usual gang of cronies. They had already consumed sufficient bottles of Peroni to take them past the gossip and the stories of the day's work to the point of making that compulsory light-headed conversation only too much beer can create. This is where Eduardo always shone because he had been born with a quick wit and a sharp tongue which enabled him to quip far faster than the next man or seven. He was always 'amusing', regularly 'very funny' and occasionally 'a little gem' – all valid reasons for his obvious popularity. At a party, in a crowded social circle, Eduardo was the man you needed, he'd never let you down, he'd always keep the chat alive and he'd always entertain. Consequently, it also went without saying that he seldom had to buy many rounds of drinks either!

The usual girls were seated at the usual stools along the bar --- stool pigeons just waiting to be winged, though who they could be decoy to no-one ever knew. They sat half-swivelled to half-look at the men in mock propriety. The evening looked extra promising, considered Eduardo, because the girls were still all there. A couple of them, Meira and Helena, were actually quite pretty, perhaps even beneath the half inch of foundation and paint, who knows? It must have been a slow evening because they were still balanced quite cheerfully on their perches, unbothered by the limited preening and muscle-flexing going on in the shadows. They could certainly have their pick of this bunch but, oddly enough, never Eduardo...yet. His mates had also considered that and always thought it odd whenever the conversation had come up, which of course was nearly every night owing to the limited heights men can raise their level of chat to beyond work, women, sport and beer. So is this my night? thought Eduardo. If so, which one? They're both equally attractive, although Helena is slightly more humorous and, I hear, raunchier. But they're not cheap and I have to be careful with my cash. His thoughts rumbled on, becoming ever so slightly more befuddled by the thickening fog of alcohol as the night wore on.

Eventually he turned to his good friend and confidante, Dino, and asked which he fancied. Dino could never hold his beer as well as the rest, smiled, clicked his tongue and muttered, "Whoever you leave for me, Casanova, I'm past fussy!"

Typical Dino, thought Eduardo, as he watched his other friends already tuning in to the same wavelength and dividing the imaginary spoils. The problem was Meira and Helena should not have been in the mix, they should have been long gone, so they were upsetting the numbers' balance somewhat.

As if to mock Eduardo further both Meira and Helena slid gracefully, oh so gracefully, off their perches and started swaying towards him. Well, not actually swaying - that would have reflected a certain level of alcohol at work - but more the swaying of their voluminous skirts as one slender foot placed itself in front of the other in a sequence only women and gay men understood. Eduardo stiffened, he hoped not visibly, as he prepared for their attack. Unsure of their true intentions he turned away and continued to chat with Dino, or in this case pretend to chat, because Dino was by now far away on a Peroni planet. It must look ridiculous to the ladies, he thought, but what the hell, what is a boy to do, and a smile creased his visage. The ladies took that as a prompt and bore down on him slightly faster.

"Hi, Eduardo," they chimed chirpily, or was it a bell ringing in his ear and stirring his consciousness?

"Hi ladies, beautiful as ever!" replied Eduardo, trying to form each and every word as clearly and as unambiguously as his trembling lips could manage. He was convinced the wobbly lips were due to alcohol not trepidation, but at this moment he could not be sure of anything.

"Ed, can we call you Ed? Ed, we've thought for ages what a gorgeous man you are and…"

"Really? As I remember you've always avoided me, disappearing quickly without so much as an hello."

"Well, you see, we've always been shy of you, you are so much more of a man than all the rest of these losers in this bar, so…"

"Losers? Who is calling my friends losers? Angrily Eduardo made to stand.

"Sorry, Ed, so sorry, look, sit down, please be calm…" Helena had gently pushed him back down, but not without first noticing his interest, something she'd had years of experience noticing. She leaned gently over him in the process so he could intoxicate himself in her cheap scent, then in one graceful movement she had turned sideways and slithered onto his lap, thus confirming her earlier visual check. "Ed, we've come up with a lovely plan, well lovely for you but unfortunately only lovely for one of us. So what we suggest is that there's no need for you to choose, you can sleep with both of us. Er… I don't mean at the same time, although…"

"…Ladies, very flattered 'n all that, but…"

"Ed, let me finish, you can have both of us to try us out, and the one who pleases you the more you can keep. She could be your lady, your permanent girlfriend, or even if you want, your wife. That's our plan!"

"Unless you're already married, of course!" laughed Meira.

"What?" shouted Eduardo, slowly realising the proposition laid out before him. "You want me to…er…er… with both of you and then choose? Are you crazy?"

"Yes, we are both crazy, crazy for you Ed, and we can't think of a better or fairer way to sort it out" pleaded Meira.

"Who'd have guessed?" butted in Dino, overhearing the last few exchanges.

"And if this fantasy of yours were ever to take place, my darlings, when might it be?"

"No time like the present, eh? We can get away from all these losers now, if you like," purred Helena, slightly adjusting her exquisite frame to a more comfortable position on Eduardo. But it certainly was not so comfortable for Eduardo who was beginning to feel the heat of not only Helena on top, or Meira's shoulders on the side, but also the heat of the situation. Inside he did feel somewhat tempted, who wouldn't after all, and the thought of these two naked in his arms, yes two at once even, was many a man's biggest fantasy. So why was he hesitating? A prostitute for a wife? Was that it? Or was it that both had already known many men, some of dubious pedigree? Could such a lady ever be faithful too? Once a hooker, always a hooker? But these *were* unusual circumstances, difficult times, and people did the most base things to stay afloat. Maybe after the War they would be normal again. They? No, only one. He could only choose one. And then, he had only seen them in the context of this dingy bar, performing one sole function. Would they be able to be a good wife? Even mother? Oh, this is just too much. He jumped to his feet, throwing off the startled Helena.

The ladies misread his intention. They thought he'd agreed. They smiled at each other. "Yes," they giggled.

"No!" boomed Eduardo, just as the door was flung open... and just as quickly slammed shut. Even above the Greek music the crash was audible. A wisp of heady perfume cleansed the bar immediately, as if an angel had floated through. All heads slowly rotated towards the counter and each head's mouth started to drop as the creator of the noise and scent became apparent. Eduardo, and no doubt all the other men, witnessed the most stunning vision float across the room, until it glided onto a stool. The stool pigeons grudgingly yielded, whispering and peeping to themselves instead of chatting to the men they were supposed to accost. 'Such bearing and class, what the hell is she doing in here?' they muttered in annoyance.

The vision had chosen to visit these poor folk in this grimy bar in a gossamer, silky, strapless dress, the azure accentuating even more her dark eyes and honeyed shoulders. Perching upright on the stool also accentuated her slender straight back and perfectly formed front. In elegance she half stared up to the ceiling, trying to read a notice high behind the bar.

Suddenly another crash echoed around the stunned, silent bar. This announced the arrival of two further, but lesser visions, obviously the ladies-in-waiting, and they rushed over to the vision's side, gushing apologies. Eduardo could just about make out their giggly conversation - 'night out...fun...that'll teach him...who cares...'

The three ladies ordered cocktails of a sort, or the best simulation possible in such a bar at such a time, and sat to survey the scene, swivelling on their perches with far more grace and elegance than the warm-up act earlier. The vision noddingly agreed with her friends, "I know, there is no way I would ever dare to enter such a place normally, but just this once, eh? It could be great fun."

Eduardo gave them enough time to increasingly giggle their way through a couple more cocktails and fortunately Meira and Helena had sensed this was no longer the right moment to further their proposition. Finally he could wait no longer. The visions seemed in no hurry to leave but he was not going to risk losing the chance to speak to the most amazing woman he had ever seen in his narrow life. And what better chance than this? She was obviously becoming the worse for the drink and his timing had to be impeccable. Too early and risk rebuttal, too late and be beyond knowing. It was now or never.

He walked to the bar from the scrutinising table he had earlier retreated to, pretending to fetch another drink. Meira and Helena seemed to know what would transpire and they did not wish to lose too much face with his cronies, so they quietly slunk away into a corner as all the knowing and available eyes homed in on Eduardo's quest. Certainly no other of the males assembled would dare to go on the doomed adventure he was about to embark upon.

"Ciao bella!" he brazened, directly at the vision's face. Lord, even more beautiful close up, he thought.

"Ciao yourself," she slurred slightly, and everyone giggled some more.

"Eduardo Carone at your service, bella, escorting and protection my speciality!"

"Hmmm, I might need that later, if you're still around", she quipped.

"I'd be around forever for you, bella," he retorted, instantly regretting his beer tongue taking over his brain. But he was in luck this time, she had not heard him owing to her giggling entourage, and if she had...

"I do believe your motives somewhat fishy, young man..."

"Damn, how could you know I work at the port?" he laughed, again regretting his lack of tact. Why would she want to talk to a lowly fish porter? he thought.

But fortunately the cocktails made her roar with laughter and her head flew back exposing an endless, creamy, unblemished neck. Eduardo wobbled at the sight of it, but again he was in luck because suddenly on impulse she slid off the stool, grasped him and whisked him off to the jukebox where a few couples were starting to entwine. Eduardo was in Heaven. He could not believe his good fortune as she started to delicately and demurely gyrate against him, albeit not totally steady on her feet. Keep calm, he thought, the panic slowly rising, along with his manhood. This is one special fish, must reel her in slowly and steadily, he laughed inside. She quickly tired, or the alcohol did, and she placed her head gently on his chest. He tightened his grip around her back as he sensed her starting to slide downwards towards the floor. Exquisite joy!

Sensing the worrying situation worsening, the ladies-in-waiting drifted across the room to gently entice her away, muttering 'we should be going now'. But Eduardo pulled her back, "Heh, I don't even know your name."

"Don't answer, Valeria, come away," one whispered.

"But he's nice," Valeria muttered, now obviously the worse for wear.

"Leave him, he's just port scum!" the other screamed, more paranoid than her sister.

"Heh, who you calling port scum, lady? Take that back. Now!"

"I'm so, so sorry," sighed Valeria, "my friend has had far too much to drink, I think. Valeria Pinto, Via Manzoni, Eduardo. Visit me sometime and..."

At that, her friends literally dragged her away, at the same time scolding her for giving so much information to a perfect stranger, and a swarthy port worker at that. Oh so humiliating.

Perfect stranger, hmm, how true...possibly, she mused as they bundled her out of the door.

Next day, after work, Eduardo found no trouble discovering where Valeria Pinto lived. He quickly staked out the imposing 4-storey terrace in the fashionable part of town. Even changed into his best he felt totally out of place, totally out of his league. But he was on a mission, a mission to conquer love, to conquer all despite their differences, and he believed himself sufficiently confident to carry it off. He had hung on to that last look she had given him and he had believed her feelings to be clear, even through the fog created by alcohol.

For four nights he waited, patience slowly soaking thinner with every visit, as well as his clothes soaking once following the inevitable night rains that the cauldron of heat cooked up. But his declining patience operated in inverse proportion to his determination, which steeled with every hour's stake-out. It merely followed the truism that the more something is taken away or made more difficult the more one wants it or is determined to fight for it. He had something to prove, as well as the obvious desire to take her out. He *was* going to see her again even if it cost him dear. And, sure enough, on the fifth night he *was* rewarded because there she was, coming out of her door with a man, both beautifully dressed for a presumed dinner assignation. He tailed them to Le Travolta, an extremely expensive trattoria, and watched as they fine dined through the window, he unseen like some waif child desperate for a morsel.

His accidental bumping into them as they tumbled out laughing onto the street worked perfectly, but no spark lit her eyes, only a flash of anger as he stepped on her exquisitely-encased toe.

"Valeria?"

"Yes? And who am I addressing?"

"Eduardo. It's Eduardo. Carone? We met in the bar last week?"

"Bar? What bar?" exclaimed her escort, who thought it time to start interjecting, even though the braggart bully looked far more than a match for him if it came to a physical challenge for Valeria's hand.

"I do not frequent bars, sir, so I'll trouble you to leave us alone," she ventured, and started to walk off, leaving a gaping, bemused and crestfallen Eduardo in her wake.

But he did not flinch from his quest. He continued to stake her out and two nights later she approached her door alone from a taxi.

"Valeria, please, I am not mistaken. How could I confuse such a beauty with any other lady. You danced in my arms and we were magical. It was the most wonderful mo…"

"I know," she whispered, as if every brick in the street would soak up her words.

"You know?"

"Yes, of course I remember. How could I admit it, silly boy! As it was we had such a row afterwards, and he says if I dare to cavort with any low-class ruffians, ever, he would never want to be seen in my presence again!"

"So you won't be seeing him again," stated Eduardo extremely coolly and calculatingly.

"Is that a question or a statement?" she giggled.

"Oh, the latter, most definitely. But you knew that. Tomorrow evening, 8pm then?"

"Well, I'm not…I'm unable…mmm… Well, if you just happen to be standing on that corner down there at 8pm I might just happen to stroll past casually…perhaps."

And so it was. As they strolled that magical next evening she learned something of his history, minus the obvious wife and three children in Avetrana, and he learned that she was the daughter of an ageing count from a country castello, in this case a cross between a very large farmhouse complex and a small castle, and she was living with her aunt in Brindisi to avoid her father's painful, dangerous demise.

They met secretly to avoid the aunt but they could not avoid everyone. Eduardo considered it best to take Valeria to the bar where they'd first met because he thought he, and perhaps she, would feel most comfortable in such convivial surroundings and, perhaps more important, it was certainly not a place her circle would ever frequent. At first Valeria found it difficult to adjust, as did Eduardo's friends, who were not used to females invading their male territory, but after a while an arrangement naturally developed to suit all. Obviously, there would be those unhappy with this arrangement, to be precise, the ladies, but they stayed true to their word and never said anything about Eduardo's past peccadilloes. No-one knew about Isabella anyway, and as he had permanently shut her out of his mind on arrival in Brindisi, not even when he had become blind-drunk had her visions reappeared to lubricate his tongue.

Valeria's old flame had reappeared at her door though, several times, to plead with her to take him back. From arrogant to pleading to crying, he had tried everything, but all to no avail. Valeria was done with these society fops; she wanted a real, genuine, down-to-earth man. Eduardo had caught him just the once, when he was still in the pleading phase, and had effortlessly sent him packing with one wave of his tanned, muscular arm.

And so it was that within a year they were blissfully married and living back in the near derelict masseria, trying to restore it to its former glory with what little her father had bequeathed her. Valeria cared little what the rest of her prejudiced family thought of her totally unsuitable husband; she was besotted with his rural looks, charm and honesty, as well as his rampant manhood, something she had never unfortunately encountered before in her own social circle. Whenever anyone in the family complained her one argument always silenced them: where else would I find someone so good looking and so strong to be able to repair this old pile of tufa blocks, she would jest.

* * *

6

INTERMEDIATE TECHNOLOGY

1 9 4 4

Pasquale always made sure he never 'stole' from the farms of the folk in his village. But that was not always easy to achieve as a number of the families had some kind of plot to supplement their rural, subsistence lifestyle. A typical plot would have 70 to 700 olive trees, some fig trees, a few lemon and orange bushes and some vegetables. However, he had found that if he stuck to his 'four-kilometre rule' none of the farms outside that would conflict with his conscience. Fortunately too one lemon looked like any other lemon. Neighbour C did not grow X lemons and neighbour D grow Y lemons: a lemon was a lemon, so unless he was actually seen helping himself at the point of production he was in the clear. But four kilometres there and four kilometres back was eight kilometres, a very long distance to pedal just to carry such a small bounty back on one's back.

So one night found him in San Marzano, a fairly nearby town, and in the dead of night he finally ditched his old baby bike, the one his long-gone daddy had given him. Now he was 12 it was impossibly painful to ride any longer anyway, even though he was very small for his age, and because he was looking very silly perched on this tiny metal contraption he was now doing the opposite of what had let him get away with his 'stealing' for so long –drawing attention to himself. Regular shouts from passers-by such as 'you'd be quicker walking' or 'take pity on that poor contraption' were not really what he needed right now.

It was a carefully manoeuvred military operation, because 15 minutes after ditching the bike he was pedalling sedately out of town on a grown-up bike he had spotted leaning against a wall near a bar. Too drunk to miss it or want to ride it home, anyway, he considered, as the guilt threatened to choke him: and after all it *is* wartime and these *are* extenuating circumstances. Maybe God will even bless me for donating a little charity as, after all, what I am doing is that by helping myself I am actually helping those who cannot help themselves. Hmmm, that's actually very droll, he considered, smiling his way along the moonlit road towards home. Now, if a juicy fig tree appeared in the darkness that would be a further miracle, wouldn't it, surely a sign from above? And, as if to prove his point, a heavily-laden fig tree duly emerged out of the inkiness, so that his bag was soon filled and his mission fully completed.

His mother never ever asked any questions of Pasquale, too fearful of the galling truth.

Pasquale perfected his collection system. He found derelict stone shelters everywhere, deserted by farmers moving North, and he utilised them more efficiently as temporary holding centres for his rich hauls. This enabled travelling time to be decreased and picking time to be increased. He never went to the same area two nights running and never picked the same fruit. Soon he was able to construct a crude map of the area, on which he gave each plot or farm a number. On the reverse he drew up columns and under the headings 'plot number', 'date', 'fruit', he recorded every 'collection'. Soon a pattern became very clear and, although he continually increased the length of return to a particular plot in order to ease suspicion or to stop a farmer catching him in the act because he too might have also spotted a temporal pattern, his job was made considerably easier by such regimented organisation.

Eventually, however, everyone in Avetrana got to know what Pasquale was doing somehow. They understood too that he never raided their own plots and soon the Four-Kilometre Rule became famous locally, folk chuckling whenever it was mentioned. They all kept quiet over his activities and not one gave him away, not even to the local greengrocer. Pasquale's prices were half the greengrocer's and the produce twice as fresh. So it was not long before the poor greengrocer had to close down, believing the War had made business bad and supplies erratic. Everyone except him knew the real reason. Pasquale had found a captive market and he capitalised on it very quickly and very efficiently. Picking by night, sleeping by morning, selling by teatime. No overheads, all pure profit. Soon his secret stone cache behind the loose tufa block in the kitchen was bursting with lira coins and notes. Owing to this lack of storage space Pasquale asked his customers to round off prices to accommodate only notes because coins were bulky and heavy. They minded little as rounding up one day and rounding down the next evened out over time and, anyway, his prices were ridiculous to the extreme.

Pasquale saw it more as a service to the struggling community rather than as 'theft'. He saw it as a means of transferring a 'good' --- the farmer had, the poor townsfolk had not, simple. What was that fable he had once been told about from England? Robin someone, was it? Robin? Great name, he laughed to himself. And after all, there *was* a War on, everyone was suffering. He never 'took' that much, just enough, and he was sure it would never be noticed. He only took when the target was plentiful and hence his small acquisition would not be missed. If he'd thought otherwise there would have been no way he would have carried on.

One old villager was so proud of him, thinking him like a son he'd never had, that he offered storage space in his back yard. More important, Cosimo started selling Pasquale's produce in his village shop at a nice little profit for Cosimo, but still much cheaper than the erstwhile greengrocer. On Pasquale's 12th birthday Cosimo presented him with the temporary loan of his horse and cart. Pasquale was truly on his way, it would seem. He had saved all of 85,000 lira through his fastidious business practices and he thus decided he could start to risk putting some of it to use. As yet another field went begging when the owner moved North to find work, so did little Pasquale move in on the wife and plead that if she would let him 'borrow' the field he would pay her in produce. No problem. Simple as that.

Two days later he was peddling home at dusk when he heard in the distance a strange roaring noise. It became louder and louder very quickly and was coming from the rear. Suddenly he heard a great 'whooshing' noise and he was knocked off his bike by the force of the air itself as some huge, blue, metallic monster sailed past him. Whatever it was it was doing a great speed and left a huge billowing trail of dust behind, dust that choked the breath out of poor Pasquale lying with twisted ankle in a shallow ditch by the roadside. To add insult to injury he had fallen in a patch of nettles and wild flowers and the two itches he now suffered did not cancel each other out. He winced as he moved his damaged ankle, and after a few sideway inches it met an obstacle that prohibited it from moving further. He yanked his foot back, as hard as he could stomach the pain, which wasn't much, and a long black tube appeared from amidst the thorns.

Eventually he found it to be a huge coil of rubber piping, stamped with a German factory's name all over it, lying at the bottom of the ditch and nearly overgrown with weeds. Presumably a retreating army lorry had lost it, or more likely had thrown it off and dumped it to aid in the speed of retreat northwards. Then he saw another, a few metres away, its end peeping out of the weeds. And another. His search continued all the way to the end of the ditch, but no more. However, battling thicker weeds the other way he found 3 more. What a haul, six huge coils. He knew immediately what had to be done with them. His prayers had been answered, well, at least once. If only another prayer, the one about his father someday returning, could be dealt with similarly!

Pasquale knew the field he had borrowed had an old water tap at the road end, and soon enough he was in business. He took Cosimo's horse and cart to the ditch where the pipes were, released the horse and tied a rope to the coil. He then threaded the rope through the side of the cart and tied the other end to the horse. By walking the horse away from the cart it pulled the coil up onto the cart, with a bit of huff and puff thrown in, but it took all of a siesta to manage the six coils and he was exhausted by the end of it all.

In the field he used a similar method, positioning the cart at one end, getting the horse to pull off the coil at the back with the tailgate down, then attaching the end of the coil to the horse by rope and walking it down the field away from the cart. The tubing was now laid out in lines across the field, but next he had to think of a way to puncture holes all along it. This turned out to be the most gruelling part because he had to use an old shortened pitchfork and physically punch the tube every few centimetres along its course. It cost him the best part of two weeks and many blistered fingers. Attaching the tubing to the tap he finally held his Grand Irrigation Opening Ceremony for a crowd of one, not counting the horse, but it worked, after a fashion, and soon water was trickling into the field and onto the dry, bare soil. Now, all he hoped was that the water kept coming and wasn't noticed by whoever was, or was not, paying for it. The other problem was that it could take many hours before the areas at the far end of the pipe system received any water so he would have to take that into consideration when planting out his seedlings. And throughout all this lengthy process not a single person had seen him, so secluded was this field, or so empty of people was the countryside.

Therefore, he had created what was so needed in the South, but so difficult to achieve – an irrigated field. He now had the soil, he had the water, he had the hot sunny weather, so all he needed next was a suitable crop. He knew one or two farms that grew water melons in this way, but melons were not a profit-intensive crop and were too heavy. Nor were oranges or lemons - too slow to form bushes. What he needed was a vegetable, and one which was easy to grow. Something like beans, yes stick beans, he thought. He only knew of one farm growing these, but what he had seen had been poor quality ---wizened, small, dry and tasteless. These were the beans he had 'transferred' on that now memorable first day five years ago when his mama had scolded him so severely. They had improved little over that five years. The farmer did not have irrigation.

He started to make regular transference raids on that farm and he stored the booty in one of his little tufa buildings, waiting for the pods to dry out. When he had enough he had to 'shell' each pod and plant the seeds out, by hand, after watering the rows well beforehand. This also made it easier to make a little hole in the softened soil to place them in. It was backbreaking work and enervating, because it always had to be done in siesta time, the hottest part of the day, but what in life is not worth doing if it isn't difficult to achieve?

The long, hot summer of the Mediterranean, combined with the wetter spring and autumn, was ideal for two, or perhaps even three, crops to be produced per year. Sure enough, within a few days the beans had sprouted and after seven weeks he found himself harvesting more fat, juicy beans than he could cope with.

The citizens of Avetrana were ecstatic, of course. Fresh green vegetables at a ridiculous price in wartime? Celestiale!

Soon Pasquale had to chip out another tufa block in the kitchen wall when Mama and Andrea went out. Still, the noise of prising open the stone echoed way down the street so he had to use little Maria as a guard and make it a game to spot their return as they turned the corner. However, he was always cautious to never let her see what he was doing, otherwise Mama would have been the first to hear from the little tell-tale sister burgeoning with nascent independence.

One day, an unaccustomed rest day, he plucked up courage to hitch a ride to Brindisi. He had never been there before, and indeed he had never been to such a big town before, but he needed to find some kind of shop or merchant selling seeds. After an hour of dusty travel and another hour following various peoples' conflicting opinions on where he would discover such an item in wartime he eventually chanced on a merchant who had seed. Pasquale took all the bean and tomato seeds the man had to his counter and dropped them down with hard cash.

"Big garden then, lad?" smiled the old man, considerably surprised and slightly baffled.

"Oh no, sir, buying for the whole village."

"And they trust you with all that money in a big town?"

"Yes sir."

"And what village might want so many beans and tomatoes, lad?"

"Please sir, I am in a great hurry. Please take my money. Don't you know there's a war on?"

Fortunately a queue was starting to form behind Pasquale and they found his last little joke highly amusing, so somewhat embarrassed the shopkeeper hurriedly bagged up his purchase and let him on his way. He wondered where a boy that young would get all that money and what village would allow it. Must be a desperate village, he thought.

Ecstatic, Pasquale could not wait for the bus home and a start on his big project. Dreaming, he suddenly heard "You boy, what have you got?"

Damn, it was a town policeman and he was carrying out his regular check at the bus station. If only I had been more alert, Pasquale thought, I could have concealed things a bit better. In wartime port towns like Brindisi had to be monitored carefully for movement of illegals, spies and the like, especially in the bus station, train station and the docks.

"Just a bit of shopping, sir, nothing really."

It was the 'nothing really' that persuaded the policeman. Oh, little Pasquale still had a lot to learn.

"If its 'nothing really' you won't mind me having a look then, eh boy?" smirked the uniform. He'd had a boring day and needed something positive to report back to his police post. And anyway, the enemy was increasingly cunning; why not use boys?

He snatched the large sack that threatened to topple Pasquale if he didn't find a seat soon.

"Bully!"

"What?" shouted uniform. Someone in the queue had witnessed the scene and had felt sorry for the boy. After all, he was a rosy-faced innocent looking boy. "Keep your nose out of this, whoever you are," shouted uniform, darting glances this way and that but not making any impact on the sea of faces.

"Leave him alone, he's only a boy. Why pick on him?"

Uniform was truly angry now. He could not locate the voice and that was really annoying him. More of the crowd were now also beginning to take an interest, always a problem for discrete searches. And he was beginning to feel over-exposed. Eduardo stayed well and truly hidden. Oh, how he hated these uniformed poppycocks, all kitted out in extravagant uniforms while the rest of us are suffering through the privations of war.

"I'll bet he's getting rich on kickbacks, while here is a poor lad desperate to make ends meet," he shouted in a deliberate attempt to incite the crowd. The mumblings grew and the uniform looked concerned.

Suddenly their bus arrived, puffing diesel smoke everywhere. People forgot the interesting, developing stand-off and scrambled to be first in the queue and get a seat, pushing and kicking at the door. In wartime services were not reliable but were always overcrowded, so when the door finally gave way under the human pressure there was a mad surge forward, all hopes of an orderly queue quite forgotten.

Seeing his chance, Pasquale wriggled free of uniform and made a dash for the door. He squeezed through a narrow gap between two old ladies but his bundle didn't. Tugging it through forced a number of packets of seeds to squeeze out of the top and cascade all over the floor. He swore. He swore so loud an old lady castigated him severely as she plumped herself down next to him in a front seat. He inwardly cursed himself for being such an idiot, but wait, surely he had escaped uniform, hadn't he? He prayed for the bus to get moving quickly, as more and more people bumped and jostled down the aisle. If uniform did manage to squeeze on he'll surely catch me, I'm so near the front. How stupid can I be? What was I thinking? Why didn't I move down to the back? Oh!

Uniform had got a foot up on the first step, then the second. The bus revved up, more clouds of smoke burst through the still open front door, the driver shouted something like "no more passengers! I want to get home tonight before Town Curfew", and they were off. Uniform was almost thrown to the roadside as the bus shuddered forward, groaning under its overloaded cargo.

Tap, tap. Tap, tap.

What was that noise? thought Pasquale.

He looked out of the window. As the bus was trying to pick up speed someone outside was trying to thrust something through the open slit. Packets of seeds! Gratefully he grabbed them and in an instant caught a glimpse of the man. Do I know him? Fleeting images flashed in front of him. Is that...?

Goodbye Pasquale. I don't have a clue what you are up to with all these packets, but good luck. It suddenly dawned on him how much he did really miss the boy, especially now he was more grown up and sensible. I do miss you so, really, mouthed Eduardo, but his silent words were whisked away on the air as the bus gathered speed.

Could that be Papa? No, surely not. And then the corner arrived and the old lady crashed into him and his senses, nearly sending him flying off his precious seat.

"Eh, are these yours? They hit me! What a stupid man, throwing packets through a window like that!"

* * *

7

GOODBYE ANDREA

1 9 4 5

"Do you have any fresh vegetables, please? I forgot to buy them for my wife and the maid has deserted us yet again." Why is it that wealth always needs to justify un-wealth actions? thought Massimo.

"You are in luck sir, we have plenty left. My brother has just replenished us. Tomatoes? Beans? Potatoes?"

"Yes, yes, a little of everything then", he gabbled, obviously slightly out of his depth and embarrassed.

"Yes, sir. How much of everything is a little, sir?" asked Andrea.

"Oh, whatever, I don't really know. A bag of each, I suppose." Was his fluster just because he hated being in such a miserable little shop or was it something else? And was his driver, leaning against the car outside, cigarette in hand, smirking or just smiling at the warm spring afternoon? Stop thinking and pay her, damn it! But she is rather pretty. "How old are you?" he blurted out without realising his thoughts had engaged his mouth.

Taken aback but not wishing to appear ill-mannered to a customer, Andrea said, "16, but I'll soon be 17, sir."

"Ah, lovely age, enjoy it, dear girl," he replied, starting to calm down a little and recover his composure somewhat.

"Looks like I'll be able to, signore, the War has gone away."

"Yes, yes, indeed. We are indeed fortunate." Hmm, he thought, she seems to bear herself well and answer politely. Not an introverted village girl at all.

"Thank you, signore, 300 lira please."

"300? Is that all? My, I shall have to come again!" he joked.

No chance of that, she thought, looking out of the door to the fine car he owned. How many cars do we ever see through this place in a year, and how many like that? And a driver too, he must be really rich. Oh well, la dolce vita, not for the likes of me.

"Goodbye, er..."

"Yes, goodbye. Is there something else, signore?"

"Your name, young lady, your name!" he replied, rather impatiently.

"Oh, sorry, Andrea." He asked my name, no less. What a refined way to behave, she considered, and such quality clothes. Rich city type, no doubt, just passing through. They all just pass through, don't they, but they never stop, that's the pity.

A few days later a big black car was parked outside Pasquale's little house when she arrived home from work. The same driver was leaning on that same car door and she could hear muffled voices inside. Then she heard her mother giggle and light up half the street.

Quickly Andrea entered and heard "...3000 lira a week."

"Oh my," her mother exclaimed, "that's a king's ransom!"

"It may be round here, Madame Carone, but not in Taranto. But we would give her a nice room and, of course, feed her well."

"Feed who well, mama?" enquired Andrea as heads turned towards her entry.

"You, of course, silly! Signore...er...Signore"

"Massimo Starsi, madame."

"Signore Starsi has offered you a job, would you believe? Curtsy to him then, ungrateful girl!"

Curtsy? Andrea nearly fainted on the spot, but recovered enough on reaching the nearest chair to ask what kind of job.

"As I just explained to your Mother, I run a chain of high-class ladies' gown shops and..."

"Starsi and Son, Signore?"

"Yes, Andrea, that's right. Have you heard of them then?"

"Oh yes. Mama, you know, those famous shops you see the adverts for..."

"Er, oh, er, yes, yes of course. Oh my!" feigning cognition. Unfortunately, poor Mama knew very little about almost anything, but how could anyone be critical of someone so lovely and devoted to her family?

"So, when I met you in the village shop I was most impressed with your efficiency and most of all your polite manner and deference.

That's what my lady customers expect but do not always receive, and so I thought you'd fit the bill perfectly. I got Stefano outside to do a bit of checking and observing and he gave you a clean bill of health, so here we are. What do you say?"

"Signore, I am so flattered that you think I could take on such an important job, but I cannot leave my Mama to look after Pasquale and Maria, it is too much."

"But Andrea, I am giving you this fantastic opportunity. You would work in our Taranto store and live above it in a pretty little flat. Please agree."

"Signore, thank you, but I might be frightened, I'm only 16 and living alone is…"

"… hardly alone, dear, above a shop and quite safe. After all, you are nearly 17, you said so yourself."

"But I don't know, Signore, I might…"

"…shush, piccolo, you'd be silly not to go, it's a chance of a lifetime."

"But Mama, Taranto is a big city, Avetrana is little more than a village. I could never cope."

"Silly girl" Be quiet! Signore Sarsi, she *will* go. When do you want her to start, please?"

"Well, really as soon as possible, if she can. Look, if my driver takes me for lunch somewhere I can return in an hour and take Andrea with me if you like?"

"Mama? Please?"

"Shush, go and pack. Not that you have that much to pack. Oh, don't forget your sewing things, they might come in useful there, eh? Oh, Signore Sarsi, I don't know about lunch, we have no restaurant here. There's a kind of café in the centre if you don't mind that, or there's always Branetti, 7 kilometres away, I think they have a proper café."

"Never mind, Signore Carone, we can manage. One hour then?" He left the cramped tiny house as fast as he could before the rural odours started him gagging. How can people live couped up like that? he wondered.

Andrea busied herself as fast as she could, packing her best dress, well, her only dress, one pair of stockings she had been saving for the Natale Fiesta, and of course her precious sewing kit. I won't have much time for that, she thought, although just what will I do at night, all alone, no Mama, no Pasquale, no Maria to cook for, wash for, tell stories to. The more she considered this the closer she came to tears.

Isabella came in silently and saw her, "get on, girl, you've not long left," she ordered.

"Mama, I shall be so lonely."

"Shush, piccolo, you will be so tired you'll go straight to sleep. Just think, they'll feed you, probably proper food, you'll be beautiful. And anyway, the money will be wonderful. Just think, if we save it all up, we'll be rich! Well, rich by Avetrana standards at least!"

"But Mama, I shall have to buy things, clothes, underwear and so on.

"Yes, yes, I know. I don't mean save everything, but just as much as you can…and you be careful with your money!"

"Of course, Mama."

"And no going out!"

"No going out? What? Never?"

"No silly, I don't mean never. Obviously, you will go to church on Sunday, maybe with Mr Sarsi's family. Heh, they might even take you out and treat you to an excursion…"

"Oh, that would be lovely. He seems a nice man."

"Now you be careful, girl. Seeming nice men are not always nice…"

"But will they give me any holiday, Mama? I mean, will I get to come home to see you often?"

"Yes, I'm sure they will and we will love it when you come to see us. But you are a big girl now and must make your own start in the world. The War is nearly ending and they'll be a lot of changes. There always are after wars. They'll be a great need for clever young ladies everywhere, mark my words, lots of opportunities."

"But Mama, I can't read or write, or even do anything more than simple arithmetic. How will I cope?"

"You will be fine, Andrea," said Isabella more sternly, "you can learn!"

Just then a car horn tooted. It was time to leave.

"But Mama, I have not said goodbye to Pasquale. I can't leave without seeing him. He will be so angry."

"Too late, he will have to suffer. Never mind. Come here and give your old mother a hug. Then kiss Maria and go!"

And that was it, another Carone left the old stone house to find their way in the world, but the difference this time was that it was a happy departure, full of promise, in the best car any Carone was ever likely to see, let alone sit in.

* * *

8

YANKIE BONANZA

1 9 4 5

"Heh kid, how's it going?" smiled the American sergeant.

Pasquale looked bemused but returned the smile and assumed all was well as the sergeant was smiling too. He had grown to like the sergeant's quirky disposition over these last few days, even though he hadn't a clue what he was saying unless someone translated.

"What you got for us today, then?" pointing at Pasquale's sacks. Pasquale beckoned him over, his smile still encased in facial concrete.

The sergeant prised open the bulging sacks, "Phew, where the hell do you get all this stuff, around this desert wasteland, when my men can't find a solitary bean in a coffee jar?"

Pasquale's smile was truly hardened by now and he stood his ground.

"You don't understand a frigging thing I'm saying to you, do you boy. Soreno, get over here, now, pronto!"

"Yes, Sarge?"

"Ask him how he can manage to get this booty when no-one else can, eh?"

"OK, Sarge, but ain't no word in Italian for 'booty'. I'll do my best."

Soreno, one of the *new* Italian American immigrants, proceeded to translate question and answer between Pasquale and the sergeant, smiling faintly at the boy's answers.

"He reckons he's found an empty field and grows it all himself, with holes in some damn drainage pipes for the water from some tap, Sarge. Whaddya reckon?"

"Reckon? Grows it himself? I don't care to reckon, I just care to keep this damn army moving in this shit-hot country. It's fantastic, the boys will just love some fresh tomatoes. Tell the cooks to do spaghetti with some of that cheese Pasquale got us yesterday. Now, all we need is some of that local wine, what's it called?"

"Primitivo, Sarge".

"Yeh, that's the stuff. Some of that red vino and we'll all be in Heaven, not in this shit war chasing I-don't-know-who up this where-I-don't-know, damn peninsula. Ask him his price for some bottles, quick. Calm me down."

Soreno duly translated.

Sergeant Bush had to sit down. More from the shock than the heat. "The boy's crazy, gotta be! He's giving it away. Ah, he's a nice lad, very reliable and obviously desperate, like most of these peasants down here. Give him double that, Soreno, and heh, throw in a bottle of whisky gratis. And tell him we'll have twice as many sacks of those tomorrow, OK?" And with that he wheeled away, whistling happy. The better these boys are fed, the better they'll fight, the quicker we'll win and the sooner we'll go home, he thought. Brilliant logic, if I say so myself, he laughed to himself.

"Here you go, kid, 80,000 lira and a bottle of the best. Take care with these, there's an army of thieves about", he laughed, and Pasquale soon saw the joke.

"Domani, double, OK?"

Pasquale, almost unable to contain his joy, could only nod 'si'. He knew from experience that advancing armies were always more cheerful and accommodating than retreating armies, but what he didn't know was that both usually raped and plundered the land, taking for free whatever they wanted. But in his case he supposed the Yanks had decided it was cheaper to pay his pitiful price than spend time looking for his field.

Instantly he swivelled round as his horse and cart moved slowly away, checking for anyone following him. If they do, he thought, laughing, I'll lead them a merry dance.

Double? Mama Mia, I'll have to go straight back to the field and start picking now. It will take me all night at this rate. But who cares? 160,000 lira for a night's work? Totally unbelievable!

An hour later he pulled up the old cart alongside a large field. Enclosed by stone walls and scatterings of fruit trees it looked very much like any other field around Torre Santa Susanna, but at least it lay at the bottom of a narrow, shallow valley and wasn't immediately obvious. The one big difference, however, was that the field was covered with parallel rows of black lines, thick rubber piping laid out right across the field longways, about 30 feet apart. And between each pair of pipes grew five rows of green plants about two feet tall, covered in tiny, rosy red tomatoes, the pomodoro famous in North Italy.

Immediately Pasquale got to work on row 24, where he had just left off this morning, and started gently filling the first of many sacks before tomorrow morning. There was no-one he could ask anyway. A week more of this and I'll be rich, he chuckled to himself, God bless those soldiers, God bless America!

* * *

9

GANG THREATS

1 9 4 6

"Heh, Carone, we know what you are doing, you know. You think you're so clever, eh? We know all about your little scam!"

Pasquale was happily riding out to where he kept his supplies and nearly fell off in shock at the boy's bellowing voice. Just one problem though: a voice but no head. Then, right on cue, a tousled mop suddenly popped up from behind the stone wall, then another, and then another. Late-teenage heads, curly-haired, stubbly-chinned, one even with pubescent beard. Oh no, thought Pasquale, this could be trouble. Trouble indeed. I've managed this so long without problems, I suppose it just had to happen one day, he reasoned.

What poor Pasquale did not seem to understand, behind all his youthful exuberance, was that people *had* known, and known for ages, but being the beneficiaries of the 'transfers' they had done nothing about it, obviously.

But these youths did not seem to be locals, he thought. As they stood up from behind the wall, one by one, he realised he didn't recognise any of them. One had a belt in his hand and started to crack it, like a cowboy, not menacingly at first but the intention was clear. Another pulled out his comb and instead of running it through his tousled mop, which he probably couldn't anyway because it was so tangled, dragged it across his throat instead, not touching the skin but an obvious gesture of intent. So who are they? fretted Pasquale.

They must have read his mind because suddenly the biggest and scruffiest announced himself with a bellow. "Damiano Malone at your service, Carone!"

This meant nothing to poor Pasquale, but from the tone he knew it sounded decidedly problematic. He considered it would be extremely unwise to even open his mouth or dignify the announcement with any kind of reply, so he just kept staring straight ahead from his dismounted bicycle. Fortunately I'm going *to* my supplies, not *from* them, so at least I have a small chance of getting away from all this.

"Where you going, Carone?" menaced the leader boy, as if reading his mind.

"Oh, just cycling around for fresh air and exercise," Pasquale replied as cheerily and non-committal as he could.

"What?" bellowed mop-head, "mess with us? How dare you!" He leapfrogged the wall most adroitly, followed in sequence one after the other by his band of merry men-boys. In a flash they had half-circled Pasquale, almost in show formation sequence it was so efficient. They stood there, hands on hips, leering as menacingly as they could manage with broken, blackened or missing teeth.

"I'm sorry, I wouldn't dream of messing with men as big and strong and menacing as you," replied Pasquale with a genuine, honest smile on his still-sweet, fourteen year old face. He watched them flick sly glances to each other, as if to say, is this boy genuine or is he winding up our clocks?

Mop-head tried again, refusing any victory to Pasquale, "Carone, we know what you're doing and have done for a long time", he repeated.

"Yes, and you said that a long time ago too," chirped Pasquale, immediately cursing himself for overstepping the mark, for overstepping he surely had. Mop-head was not going to tolerate such a blatant attack on himself and let Pasquale get away with it in front of all his gang. He never lost face, knowingly, by anyone.

"Look, cut the cheek, boy, before I cut the cheek!" threatened Mop-head, backed by a cacophony of howling laughter, backslapping and general rolling about.

"Great joke, Dami, you show him!" one shouted out. "Yeah, yeah," cried the others, pulling their hands across each other's cheeks and grimacing.

"I give you no cheek, Dami," calmed Pasquale, resisting the real and insistent urge to turn his face sideways and protrude his cheek forward.

"Heh, you don't call me Dami, ever. Only my friends call me Dami."

"Can we be friends then, Dami, or is it Damiano?"

Pasquale had cleverly quelled the tension and moved the episode on adroitly.

"Maybe there *is* a way we could one day become slightly less than enemies, little snot boy, but the transition would need to be oiled by money."

"Money? I don't have any money. How could I, a poor little snot boy from a poor little snot village?" Careful again, he thought, don't overdo the sarcasm.

But Mop-head let it go because there was money on the table, metaphorically anyway, and that was his favourite topic.

"You make a good living from your vegetables, Carone snot, and of course we would not want to stop you. Quite the reverse in fact, we would want you to continue helping as many people as you can. But this is a very dangerous world and as more and more people start to learn about your success some are going to want to benefit unfairly from it. Do you follow my meaning so far, dumb snot?"

"Well, if I do do what you say I do, do you not do..."

A number of the gang thought that was a highly amusing sentence construction opener and immediately broke out laughing, as if against their leader. With one swipe of his arm Damiano cut them off. Pasquale noted the amount of power this boy wielded over his gang and compartmentalised it into the 'dangerous foe' mental cupboard.

"Cut the nonsense, snot boy, do you follow me?"

"I think so, Damiano. You're saying you want some of my hard-earned money and this is a robbery. Right?"

Damiano laughed. "Heh, not so fast, knob snot, we ain't no robbers, we don't want to take money off you. Well, we do, but what I am trying to say is that we are trying to offer you a service, a much needed valuable service, and for that we would need to be compensated."

"A service?"

"Yes, a service. You need protection from these bad people."

"You mean, protection from you, right?"

"Look, I have taken just about enough of your cheek." Mop-head took a couple of paces forward, swinging his belt. Time to end the fun, thought Pasquale.

"OK, I need protection. But why? Who wants to hurt me?"

"You still don't get it, do you. No-one wants to hurt you, they just want your money, but they might want to hurt you to force you to give them your money."

"Oh, I see. But for that to happen I would need to have money, and I keep telling you I don't have any money."

"We know you do, so let's not argue that any more. I repeat, we protect you from your enemies and you pay us a little each week for the service. Deal?"

"Would you let me think about it, please?"

Surprisingly, to Pasquale anyway, Mop-head said, "OK, you think about it. I'll give you a week".

"But how will you find me?"

"How did we find you today, dumb snot? Really, you are just a silly little boy!"

Yes, but a rich silly little boy, mused Pasquale, unlike you, and from gotten gains not ill-gotten ones. He was obviously still foggy on how the Law would interpret 'transference of a good'.

"That was today, but what about next time?"

"Oh, I hate dealing with stupid little snot knobs like you. Don't you get it, some of my associates are at your house now, paying your mother a neighbourly visit, ha-ha!"

* * *

10

JOINING THE GANG

1 9 4 6

Pasquale rushed home as fast as he could. The gang had petrified him, although he had done his best not to show it, and he wanted to check that his dear Mama and family were ok, as well as move the money as quickly as possible. Or was that exactly what Damiano wanted him to do? Watching him as well, no doubt. With his wartime earnings and present large-scale production profits he estimated about 440,000 lira, give or take. The problem here was that he never had a convenient moment to count it, or even organise it better into denominational bundles, as either his family was around or he was out working, or he was just too plain exhausted.

"Some boys were looking for you," his Mama said as he rushed in.

"Really? Who?" Pasquale pretended to be cheerful but vague.

"Don't know, but I do know one thing, I hope they are not boys you've made friends with".

"Oh, why is that then? Equally upbeat but non-committal.

"I didn't like the looks of them, for one. And at one point one of them pulled out a nasty-looking knife and pretended to clean his nails. I told him in no uncertain terms they certainly needed it. He got very upset and tried to frighten me. I told him I'd put him over my knee if he didn't shut up. The others laughed so he stopped. If I knew who his mother was I'd pay her a..." She laughed.

"His nails?"

"Yes, trying to make a point, certainly. Another had two gold fillings which flashed a bit ominously in the sunlight, even though it was setting."

"Hmmm, gold, setting suns, all very strange. Anyway, what's for dinner, Mama?"

"Nothing special. Well, don't you want to know what they wanted?"

"No, I know what they wanted."

"What then?"

"Me, of course!"

"How did you know?"

"You just told me, Mama!"

"I told you? When did I tell you?" Mama was angry now because she was mystified.

"When I walked in! "

"Eh?"

"When I walked in just now, you said, 'some boys were looking for me'." He laughed, "Silly Mama, let's not worry about that now. Look what I've got you."

"But I do," Mama grumbled as she slouched off to check on the chicken casserole.

Filled with relief, Pasquale had a long wait till late afternoon and he could hear no more sounds in the house or the street as the siesta matured. Removing one of the two tufa blocks, he hastily stuffed some of the money into a small, dirty sack, leaving plenty for 'ready money'. His heart thumped as he crept through the house. Luckily the floors were stone and could not creak like timber, but the front door could, and usually did on opening. He'd sworn for ages to rub some olive oil down the hinges to stop the squeaking but he always forgot after his tiring days of work. One slight creak later he was mounted on his trusty bike and away, certain he was being watched and followed. So he went a different way to a different place, all the time wondering just when he would be set upon. They were good, though, he thought admiringly, not a sound so far, nor a glimpse of movement......professional almost. He stifled an inner smile irritatingly. Will they accost me openly, so I'll know who they are, or will they stay hidden, hit me over the head and let me think I never knew who did it? The former, most likely, he considered solemnly.

He was right. Three kilometres out of Avatrana he took a side track that he knew like the back of his hand and followed it down to an enormous old olive tree with its split trunk. In the hollow gap, on the inside of the trunk, it was soft enough to carve a hole with a sharp knife, and just as he had finished and was getting up to leave the four boys suddenly appeared out of nowhere in the gathering darkness of the cloudy sky

"Hello there, Carone, out picking fruit?"

Pasquale did not reply.

"Olives aren't your style, are they? Perhaps there's better fruit inside?" Two of the boys darted in and quickly retrieved Pasquale's sack. "Mm, a good haul of fruit here, I'd say!" he laughed.

"Leave it alone, it's all my savings…"

"…All your savings?"

"Yes, all the money I have accumulated over the years."

"So why isn't it at home then? Not safe enough for you?" he laughed.

"True. After your visit today I thought it best. But I don't understand, you never said you would rob me of all my money; you said you'd protect it for a small fee."

"Correction. We said we would protect *you* for a small fee, not your money!" he roared merrily. He was seriously enjoying his evening out.

"But…"

"Not to worry, this will come in very useful for our operations, comrade! We do have surprising overheads, you know. Consider it a contribution to the cause, the great cause we are fighting for."

"Which is?"

"Ah, not for young boys like you to know…"

"But old enough so you can take all my earnings. What will I do?"

"Do? Do? It's obvious what you'll do, isn't it? You will go back to your fields and your thieving and start again, that's what you will do."

"What, just so you can come along again in six months and take it all away again? You think I'm stupid?"

"Do you have any choice?" he laughed. "What do you think…" he paused, "heh, boys, did you see that light over there?"

"Where?" they whispered in sequence.

"It's gone out again but I think someone is there, let's go!"

Pasquale had seen nothing and quickly realised the gang was merely making an easy escape to keep face. What do I do? What choice have I got? He muttered to himself as all went very quiet very quickly in the inky night.

And then it came to him, in a flash, like a shooting star in that ink. He still had about 300,000 lira left and now it was probably in the safest place. They would never think of looking there and, anyway, they already think they have got all the money. Let them carry on thinking that and I'll play along with their game.

Two days later he signalled to one of them in the street. He knew they were still checking on him but this time either he was ready and looking, or they weren't being so cunning, or he'd learned to recognise some of the gang individually. Whichever, he hailed him over.

"I want to see your boss Damiano, please," asked Pasquale gently.

"Any reason, village snot?"

"Yes, I have a proposition for him."

"Hmm, OK, I'll tell him, I'll say snot boy has a proposition", imitating Pasquale's still squeaky, unbroken little boy's voice.

"How will I know, Toni?"

With slightly more respect, because he was shocked the snot even knew his name, he retorted, "don't worry, you'll know!"

Next afternoon Pasquale found himself being led blindfolded through the back streets of the neighbouring small town. He knew which town it was as he had been told the name of it to walk to. Why no bike, he wondered, it is very strange. The walk had been exhausting in the siesta heat and perhaps Damiano had deliberately planned it that way to tire him out.

Suddenly he heard a door bang open and he was bundled roughly through the gaping portal. "Ah, Carone, welcome, take a seat. Someone get that hood off him, it must be unbearably hot under there!"

It was. He felt very wobbly as he was manhandled onto the chair, but he had to pursue his chosen course now he had come so far.

"I want to join your gang," stated Pasquale so quietly it was almost inaudible. But there was purpose and no emotion: he knew what he was doing.

"You...what?" spluttered the leader.

"I want to join your gang, Damiano, I really really do." Urgency too, now.

"But...but why? Such a good boy as you, hardworking, looking after your mama and sisters since your papa left, feeding the town like a Good Samaritan..."

"...you've hardly been the Good Samaritan, eh? You have taken all my money, I am totally dejected and rudderless now. Do you not understand what that has done to me, here, inside? I have no will to go back to that backbreaking work and to be the town saviour, you have shown me there are much easier ways to make money, and I want my share."

"Your share?"

"Yes, my share, what's rightfully mine. You had no right to rob me like that but I am willing to forgive you if you let me in."

"You are willing to forgive me?" Damiano roared, "oh funny, you are very, very funny!"

"And I am also very clever, very innovative and very creative. Before you die of laughing, think seriously. I could be quite an acquisition to you…"

"Acquisition? Well, certainly not brawn, that's for sure. But maybe brains…perhaps."

"Yes, I…"

"…but do I want brains? I'm not the brightest around but even I can recognise you might be too…"

"Damiano, Luigi's returned and needs you to come", interrupted one of the gang, shouting through the open doorway.

"Damn! I don't need him here now. Pasquale, let me think…er…yes, OK, perhaps we'll give you a try. Talk to Paolo in there about our latest operation, OK? I've gotta go, quick."

Pasquale leapt through another door, looking for Paolo. Here's my chance, don't blow it now, he thought, vengeance is mine, and all that, ha!

＊＊＊

11

THE TRY-OUT

1 9 4 6

Damiano had talked to Paulo, who'd talked to Giuliano, who'd broached the others, and although they all had this or that reservation about Pasquale joining them, they had to admit that what he had said about himself was all very true. How good or useful he'd be in a fight was very debateable but there was no doubt he could think things through and organise well. After all, how else could he have accumulated all that lira so young?

So they had decided to take him on their next little sortie, a gentle break-in for the new boy (not literally burglarising a house, mind you!). A new shop had opened in a neighbouring village, owing to the upturn in the local economy, and to date it was under no-one's 'protection'. Pasquale was therefore delegated to be the first 'envoy', whose job it was to explain politely to the shopkeeper that apart from official insurance he should also consider unofficial insurance; insurance for those occurrences that an insurance company may not pay out for.

"What occurrences?" asked the wily shopkeeper.

"Er...for a broken shop front window, perhaps?" volunteered Pasquale.

"Huh, my policy covers broken front windows," replied the shopkeeper smugly.

"Yes, but maybe not more than once or twice a year!" smiled Pasquale, trying to look both as polite but as menacing as he could.

"But that's..."

"...quite. Imagine the most unlikely scenario that a broken window could happen, say nearly every month. It's possible, you know, times being what they are."

"Every month? Impossible!" laughed the shopkeeper, his rolls of fat reverberating as he rocked.

"Oh, I don't know, accidents happen. And I hear there are some very naughty bored young boys in this village… I am thinking that a window your size would cost at least a week's profits to keep replacing, sir. And such a shame too, when obviously this village is crying out for such a lovely shop as yours. I can see you making a handsome living here…with protection".

Suddenly the shopkeeper stopped laughing and began to realise the sinister message that this innocent-looking, polite youth was trying to relay.

"Oh, I see, if I pay your contacts something less than the cost of replacing a window each month they will ensure that such naughty boys never get close enough to throw a rock through my window?"

"Well done, sir, how sensible you are! I can see you will make a successful shopkeeper very quickly. My contact will return soon then. Goodbye!" And Pasquale cheerfully walked out the shop, leaving the blustering shopkeeper open-mouthed.

Pasquale triumphantly reported the success of his mission to the boys waiting at the end of the street. Although not amazed they *were* impressed that he had persuaded the man on his very first visit, and without the assistance of a little gentle violence. "Not bad, Pasquale, now try to persuade that farmer over there that his tractor could be in danger from a gang of tractor thieves!" they laughed.

"Seriously?" asked Pasquale.

"Yes, serious, deadly serious, and from experience farmers are far more difficult to persuade than shopkeepers. You might have to drop 'Sacra Corona Unita' gently into the conversation, by the way. That will help no end."

"Sacra Corona Unita?" asked Pasquale fearfully, "isn't that the Mafioso organisation of Puglia?"

"Yes, stupid, that's us!"

"Us? You mean we are they? It is us? We are them?"

"Certainly! Who do you think we are then, an aimless bunch of youths with insufficient brains to find jobs?"

"Well, no," smile Pasquale, "no, but…"

"…no 'but's, off you go!"

An hour later Pasquale had to admit he'd failed, and the farmer had almost marched him off his land at the end of a shotgun. He had not taken kindly to Pasquale's polite pleadings, and he had described in the most graphic anatonomical detail what he would do to the lad should he ever return.

"OK lads!" shouted Damiano, "your evening's social activities tonight are cancelled. Meet back here at midnight, sober and ready to pull."

"Pull what?" some muttered.

"A tractor, of course, stupid!"

And so, at one a.m. they discovered that the farmer had felt confident enough not to return his tractor to the village that night but to choose to keep it in the field for the next day's ploughing. The tractor was calmly moved off the field by nine youths pulling on three ropes, after first noiselessly picking the padlock on the wheel. When the farmer returned in the morning the first thing he saw was the note pinned to the gatepost, "your tractor back when you promise to put 4000 lira in a brown envelope in the box at the foot of this post every last Friday of the month at 4pm." And so Sacra Corona Unita, Youth Branch Puglia, added yet another poor farmer to their newly-formed 'Round 14' collection.

The following night Pasquale helped break in to a builders' supply yard and 'requisition' an old Yankie supply trucks-worth of valuable timber, cement and tools, which ended up all around west Puglia before the week was out.

But better than that, Pasquale now knew where he could guarantee himself a free gelato whenever he minded to call in that village shop!

* * *

12

ANDREA'S NEW LIFE

1 9 4 6

As the limousine swished her through the suburbs of Taranto Andrea realised she had never ever been to a large town. Dismay welled up increasingly as kilometre after kilometre of houses, shops and factories whizzed past. Just the noise of the cars made her frightened too; she had seldom seen cars in Avetrana, let alone something as voluminous and classily-appointed as Signore Starsi's. Then the road would suddenly open out into a piazza lined with grand palazzos and villas behind high stone walls and billowy trees. Trees --- there was another delight. Avetrana had incipid, puny trees compared to these, constantly fighting for any drops of water that might come their way along unkempt roadsides. These were beautifully manicured and regularly pruned to improve their bushiness and colour.

Another piazza, even grander. And another. How long would this go on, she thought, how big is this place? Will I cope or will I be lost?

The car slowed, gates ahead started to open and they crept silently into an exquisite mini poplar-lined drive. Andrea never caught a glimpse of the house as the next thing she saw were the steps. The car pulled up with a perfunctory crunch on the gravel at the foot of gleaming white marble stairs leading up through pillars and portico to magnificent black double doors. They were edged in gold paint and even the door knocker looked like gold. Immediately they swung open to reveal a butler who regally walked down the steps to open the front car door. Massimo Starsi stepped out gracefully and began his climb, never looking back. Indeed, he had not spoken a word to the girl the whole journey and had closed the curtains between himself and her in the rear seat. This in no way worried her: she did not expect or even hope that someone of Signore Starsi's importance would stoop so low as to make chatty conversation with a village girl in a car. No, more important to Andrea was the fear that she would begin to 'smell' in the close confines of the car, because she had been given no time to wash at home after coming straight from the shop after handling onions and cheese!

Andrea shifted across the seat to follow but was hit full on by a booming voice. "Heh, where do you think you're going, girl? Sit still, this is not for you," Stefano grunted curtly.

"Oh, is this where Signore Starsi lives then?"

"Of course it is! Does it look like a shop, stupid girl?"

"Are we going to the shop then?" enquired Anthea as the car again pulled away.

"Where do you think we'd be going then? The theatre, the cinema, dinner, bed?" Stefano said menacingly.

This confirmed her fears; she definitely did not like this cruel-mouthed man, and never had. She vowed to be more careful and play things closer to her heart and less on her sleeve. But there was also no doubt she had a lot to learn about sensible chit chat. Her chit chat was totally naïve and laughable and she would not go far in a top gown shop talking to customers in that manner.

Fifteen minutes later they stopped in a back alley. Andrea, for some reason, panicked and thought something terrible was going to happen, but Stefano merely got out and beckoned her to follow. True to his fashion he could not even be bothered to carry her small case, which she nearly forgot in her nervousness, and she had to drag it up the airy, light stairs he beckoned her to. At the top a cheerfully painted blue door was unlocked by Stefano with gusto, as if he knew it well, and inside it opened into a charming living room with beautifully appointed furniture and imposing draped curtains masking a large old-fashioned window.

"Oh, how beautiful," she squealed, "is this where the ladies try on their gowns?"

"Too good for the likes of you, village slut!" he hissed. Perhaps he thought he had cause to insult her as, once, after one of the girls had been moved on, he had asked if he could take these rooms for himself and his family. The response angered him no end, but he continued working for Starsi because the money was good and no-one asked questions about the 'extras'.

"Really, this room is for me, then?"

"And the bedroom here," walking through French doors to wave his arm, "and the bathroom over there, and that little kitchen next to it!"

What? All this? A bath? A real cooker? A double bed? She could not believe it.

"Bit of a jump up from your village hovel, eh! Agh, you don't deserve none of this!"

"Oh Signore," said Andrea so politely, "please do not be so unkind. Village folk cannot aspire to anything better. It is not our fault we have to live like that. Most people in the South live like that, as I am sure you know." She gave him a telling look but his face registered no response.

Instead, he shouted "Don't you ever speak to me again like that, and in such a tone, you ungrateful little whore!" and he swiped the back of his hand across her face before she realised it or could flinch away.

"Ah!" she cried and collapsed on the bed, holding her cheek. As he snatched her hand away he immediately saw the blood. Oh God, have I cut her? Damn, it's that ring again. He grabbed her face and saw only a trickle. Only a trickle, thank heavens, he thought as he strolled nonchalantly to the bathroom and returned with a wet cloth. He dabbed it as she winced, watching him warily but saying nothing. Oh please, let it be nothing, Starsi will feed me to the dogs if I've cut her and it scars. She'll be useless, my job will be finished and no more money or perks. Damn my temper!

Fortunately it *was* only a nick, the ring had barely touched her skin. "Come on," he said soothingly, "it's OK, really it is, just a little scratch. Come to the mirror and see. Look, it's stopped bleeding already. No harm done, eh?"

He made light of it and busied himself around the rooms, checking all was as it should be. She could not wait for his departure, but she had to play the game. After all, who was the boss here? He returned and said, "Yes, everything is as it should be. Look, there is even some cold food in the kitchen which you can heat for your dinner. Tomorrow at 8 a.m. you must go down the stairs into the alley, take the door immediately to your left and go into the back of the shop. Look for Madame Fano, the manageress, who will discuss your duties. Ok?"

"So the shop is right underneath, is it?"

"Of course."

And with that he was gone, leaving Andrea flooded with so many emotions she just keeled over onto the bed and fell into a deep troubled sleep.

* * *

13

ISABELLA

1 9 4 7

Isabella, are you OK?"

"Yes thanks. Is that you Cosimo?" she replied from deep inside the house.

"Sure it is. Who else do you think it might be then? Eduardo? Ha!" He roared with laughter.

"Oh, Cosimo, do not be so cruel." Isabella appeared at the door looking sad.

"Still so sad, Izzie? I thought you still hated him for walking out like that. How long is it now? Eight years? Eight years already?"

"Oh, is it really? Oh dear, I do seem to have lost track of time...oh, and do not call me Izzie!"

"Sorry. Yes, remember, little Maria could only have been two when he left... bastardo, and now look at her. Ten last week, right?"

"Yes, and you should not have brought her such a lovely present, we don't expect it, you know. Oh, and by the way, do not blaspheme in my house!"

"Sorry, Izz...Isabella. Expect it? Maybe not, but dear Isabella, you have had such a hard life and the little one has so few joys, I thought it might bring her some cheer."

"Cheer? She was over the moon. Who else is ever going to find enough money to buy a bike like that?"

"It was nothing. Things like that get cheaper and cheaper nowadays. The War is over and life is returning to normal. Anyway, I got it in a special sale down at Brindisi Dock. Some import-export company going broke. Had an auction. I only paid a few thousand for it, honestly!"

"Well, it was a kindness we did not expect. Thank you," replied Isabella, who not wanting to sound too familiar and obliged suddenly added, "anyway, it was much more than all the other help you've given us over these past eight years!"

"Help?"

"Well, apart from sending us the shop leftovers and paying a little to get Pasquale through some schooling, there's not been much, has there? And anyway, I assume that the school money came from Eduardo, right?"

"Eduardo?"

"Yes, he said he would give you something every month for us, right?"

Cosimo roared with laughter, "Eduardo? Give me money? I haven't seen Eduardo since he left! He's long gone, could be anywhere now, doing anything, that one. Even dead maybe?"

Isabella shuddered, surprising even herself, "oh, don't say such horrible things!"

"And he didn't do horrible things to you, leaving like that, eh?"

"I expect he had his reasons, man reasons..."

"...oh Isabella, listen to you. Please don't continue to defend him like this. Eduardo was rotten, through and through. He was never right for you," pleaded Cosimo in a heartfelt manner which surprised even himself. It sure was a morning for surprises, he thought. I must change the subject, and quickly. "Er... it was worth sending Pasquale for those two days a week then?"

"Yes, he is so blessed he can read and write quite well now, if only with simple..."

"...and how is dear Andrea these days, has she recovered yet? How awful," he interrupted, intent on getting the conversation back onto a truly even keel.

"Oh, Cosimo, please, I'd rather not speak of it, if you don't mind."

"Certainly, my dear, I quite understand."

"And I am not your 'dear'! Certainly not! So what brings you here today?" asked Isabella, trying to cheer herself up. Not that it did much good: there was little cheer in her life these days, she thought.

"Oh, nothing special, just the usual. A few vegetables and bread ends from the shop, if you want them?"

"God bless you, Cosimo!" As she reached out to take the bag with one hand she lightly touched his arm with the other. Cosimo quickly handed over the bag and instantly placed his hand on top of hers. It all happened so quickly, in a flash.

"Isabella, I've been meaning to ask this for ages." She panicked, yearned, feared, mellowed all in one instant, wondering what he was going to ask. "Would you do me the honour of accompanying me to the annual Regional Shopkeepers' Federation Dance in Brindisi next month?"

"The what?"

"A dance, Isabella." His nervousness showed badly for all to see, if there had been anyone else around. He tried to smile but it materialised inappropriately and he thought perhaps it looked more like a leer. He immediately started to redden and he dropped his hand. Isabella was quite taken aback; this must have been her first invitation to do anything, by a man, since Ed had left. What should she do? What would her children think? What would the neighbours say? In the absence of sense, her mouth beat her brain to it, "a dance? Brindisi? Me? Shopkeepers?"

Cosimo saw her confusion and felt her panic. He started to panic too. This was his first time inviting a lady out in many years too, all his life consumed by the shop. He had no idea what the dances were like, he'd never been, but he started to bluster his way through, "yes, dancing, food, dressing up, shopkeepers and their wives..."

"...but I'm not your wife. And I cannot dance, Cosimo. And I cannot get to Brindisi. How do I afford the bus?"

"I will take you, silly..."

"...but, Maria, how can I leave Maria?" She had become totally irrational now and even Cosimo could see that. He could no longer suppress a tiny smile, and soon it became a small laugh. Suddenly Isabella too realised how silly she was being, like a nervous schoolgirl being asked out on her first date, and she smiled too. Laughed. Soon both were laughing uncontrollably.

"I'll assume that means 'yes', then?" Cosimo finally inquired.

"Er... no, I mean yes...yes, alright. Do you think it will be alright? I have nothing to wear, what about Maria, the neighbours, how late will it be? I don't think..."

"...hush, Isabella, please stop!" bellowed Cosimo. "It's OK, everything will be fine. Honestly. I promise. There's lots of time to sort it all out. No problem. It's only a dance with a bar and a buffet, you'll have a great..."

Just then Maria breezed in, ten-year old tresses bouncing, wide eyes sparkling, muddy as sin. "Hello Mama, I'm home. Oh, Signore Patisso, sorry, I didn't see you."

"Hello Maria," replied Cosimo, looking a little sheepish.

"And look at the state of you, child, what have you been doing?

"Mama, nothing, honest. Thank you again for the lovely bike, Signore Patisso."

"Well, go on then, give him a hug for it. Oh no, you'd better not, look at the mess you're in. Off you go, go and get cleaned up, but don't waste water, I am not going to the village tap again today!"

Maria still looked suspiciously at the two of them and wondered why, and how, she'd escaped a scolding, and probably extra household jobs.

"OK, Isabella, I'd better go now. Thank you so much for agreeing to accompany me. You won't change your mind, will you? Female prerogative and all that?"'

"No, Cosimo, it's really kind of you to ask. Cheer an old lady up, at least?"

"Old lady? Heh, what's that all about? You're a fine lady and lovely looking, in your prime, Isabella, don't let anyone say you're not!" Realising he had finally overshot the mark and outstayed his welcome he began to make his exit, again reddening with acute embarrassment.

"I don't know about that, but what about all those other 'fine ladies' you could ask?"

"None left, Izzie, bye!" he joked, and hastily skipped out, leaving poor Isabella with a lot of thinking to do. Obviously Cosimo had already accomplished that task. It was true she'd had a miserable eight years since Eduardo had departed. Eight years? It had actually been a lot more; he'd been awful to her for years before that too. But at least she'd still been able to go to church of a Sunday until he'd left, now she hadn't been able to show her face for at least five years, the excuse that 'Eduardo had moved up North for work' finally running thin. It was true too that she still had some girlishness and good looks to spare. And it was also true she had not had a man for eight years. Perhaps that was what worried her most? Fear of intimacy after so long. Suddenly she felt hot flushes rising and she grasped her neck almost defensively. 'Oh my,' she uttered.

"Oh my what, Mama?" Maria had re-entered the room holding a small bunch of beans. "Do you like beans that much, Mama?" she asked innocently.

"What, my precious?"

Precious? thought Maria. What has just happened here? Is this Heaven on Earth? What is wrong with Mama?

"The fagioli, Mama, the beans I have grown."

"Beans? Grown? You, you grow beans? What are you talking about, silly head?"

"Mama, I admit have kept it a secret, but now that I have the proof I can finally tell you. Look. I've grown them myself. Aren't I clever?"

Mystified and still burning up Isabella tried to re-focus, "Well, yes Maria, well done. But where?"

"Ah, that's the secret really, Mama. I have grown them where Pasquale used to grow them," she announced triumphantly.

"What?"

"Yes, I never told you this before but I used to follow Pasquale sometimes when none of you were taking notice of me. He never ever saw me either, I was too small to be seen, ha! But it did use to exhaust me, running to keep up with his bike."

"Maria, you ran behind Pasquale into the campagna all alone?"

"Yes. Actually, now I think about it perhaps it was a bit silly."

"Silly? Silly? You stupid girl, how could you have taken such a risk?"

"What risk Mama, Pasquale was always there if I needed help."

"And was there...trouble, ever?"

"No, Mama, it was easy. I only went on his picking days. On his cultivating days it would have been too long and I'd have got bored, and thirsty, and hungry, I reckon!"

"Thirsty? You could have got seriously ill all day without water, you silly girl!"

"Yes, that's why I only went when he was picking in the cool of the morning. I even picked up the odd piece of frutta or fagioli he dropped along the way home so no-one would be suspicious."

"And he never saw you? Mm, thoughtful child, even if a bit silly. So you now grow some beans where he used to?"

"Yes, I've just started this Spring. These are my first crop."

"A bit skinny, aren't they?"

"Well, yes, but you see, I can't turn the tap on where the water comes out into the pipes; it's much too stiff for my little hands. And it has been so dry this Spring, they became desperately thirsty."

"So you won't be able to grow any more in the summer?"

"Not unless you come and loosen the tap for me..."

"Well, well, well, I just do not know what to say." So Isabella didn't. Her brain was already in total turmoil over Cosimo's invitation. Two major revelations in the space of minutes was beyond the realms of possibility in Isabella's tiny world. She needed time, time to think, but as ever there was no time. Work to be done, always work to be done.

"Right, Maria, we'll talk about this later. Please go and get on with your jobs. Oh, and well done, clever little thing!" she smiled.

* * *

14

A STITCH IN TIME

1 9 4 7

Andrea found Signora Faro with little ado as she, with one other girl, was already in the shop by 8 a.m.

"How do you do?" said Signora Faro in a most urbane and stately manner. At 52, with two husbands exhausted, she had seen much of the world Taranto had to offer, but she had stopped in her tracks, tracks which had just been transporting her from opening the front door of the shop to the counter and till. It was Andrea's blossoming beauty, enhanced by its innocence and honesty, that had stopped her. Starsi has hired a number of pretty girls over the years but where did he find this peasant beauty, she mused.

"Hello," replied Andrea nervously, with a hint of a smile and a curtsy.

The signora glared darkly, "oh no, no, no, Andrea, please. 'Hello' will just not do". The other girl started to turn away and snigger, relieved that her competition was not completely perfect then. "You are to be a young lady now, not a village girl, in one of the most fashionable and respected ladies' outfitters in the south of Italy, so 'hello' will just not do." The signora was already puffing up with pride, almost entirely believing what she was saying.

That's overdoing it a bit, thought Fantella, but how typical of this place. Still, you've got a long way to go, my girl, to get to this shop's norm.

"So what will do, Signora Fano?" interrupted Andrea.

"You...girl...never interrupt a lady when she is addressing you," replied the signora in a powerful voice which remarkably had not raised its volume one notch. "And you, Fantella, stop gawping at our new employee and get on with your work!"

"And what will that work be, now that she's here, madame?" asked Fantella sweetly and innocently enough, but the signora knew her of old and how much mocking was concealed in those words.

The signora replied in almost the same saccharine-sweet manner, with her super-false smile, "your work will be to show dear Andrea what goes on in this shop, initially, until she has learned the ropes."

"Well, I cannot really get on with my work then, until you stop nagging her about saying 'hello' instead of 'a good morning to you too, signora', can I?" she smiled back.

For a second the signora considered this rudeness, then thought about exploding, but quickly realised that Andrea had only been here five minutes and what kind of impression it would give her. So instead she broke out into a broad grin and started to laugh heartily. Her medium to heavy frame started to vibrate in a rolling motion that looked more in place on an ocean liner in heavy seas, and the two girls sheepishly took their cue and started to laugh too. "Too true, too true," the signora muttered, "and the correct response would be, Fantella, 'I am very well, thank you'!"

Andrea, being the astute girl she was, realised that the potentially tricky situation had been defused but she could see too that this was no ordinary signora who was going to be her superior, and she wistfully thought she was totally ill-equipped to deal with such city folk.

"Now, Andrea, you are going to be my assistant along with the lovely Fantella here, in this famous and busy shop. She will teach you all you need to know. You will take lunch in the café across the road and come home with me for dinner each evening until you are settled. Here is an allowance to get you started, I am sure you do not have much money with you." She walked over to a mannequin in the window, yanked a chiffon scarf off it and wrapped it round Andrea's neck. "And cover your awful dress up with this for today. I'll see if I can find you something at home or in the back of the shop to make you presentable. That dress will just not do, my dear, you are in Taranto now, not your village." And at that she swirled away to the office at the back in a purposeful yet elegant gait befitting the long-time manageress of a gown shop.

Oh, and by the way, in this shop in front of customers you will address me as 'Madame'. It is French you know, befitting the high class of this establishment.

Andrea stood transfixed, staring at the two 2000 lira notes, while Fantella continued to snigger. She had never been given so much money in one transaction in her life, not even in Cosimo's village shop, and for a moment she began to panic. But Fantella's sarcastic, almost cynical tone brought her back to normality. "I was never given money like that. Why are you so special, eh, eh?"

"Please, Fantella, I do not know. I was brought here in a limousine, I have been given lovely rooms above here, and now this. I just don't know."

"Someone obviously likes you," she said jealously, "likes you a lot!"

Fantella's sarcastic laughing gave Andrea a moment, at last, to cast her eyes around the shop. What a heavenly sight it was, row upon row of exquisite gowns, mannequins elegantly posing in the windows, an accessories counter to match, and more rails of day wear and even sporting outfits. Fantella quickly sensed Andrea had never seen the likes of all this before, but took no pity on her at all. All she could think about was why this peasant girl from a totally obscure village was receiving such regal treatment and whether she was in fact her replacement employee. She knew for a fact that although business was steadily growing now the War had ended there was just not enough profit to sustain three staff like this. Could she be in for a nice surprise soon? Maybe they would transfer her, perhaps to something better, leaving this upstart to pick up the pieces of all her corner-cutting? Could there be anywhere better, save perhaps Bari or Naples? Time would tell, she considered.

And so it was. Within three days Andrea had got to understand how to welcome, address and serve the upper-class ladies who were their main clientele and who thought nothing of spending a year of Andrea's salary on just one dress. She was a fast learner and was even beginning to understand how to pamper them, preen with them and patronise them (without their realising, of course) as they tried on gown after gown just for the experience of it. She learned how to work the till, how to display the goods and, most of all, how to make the signora's cappucci just the way she liked it on the little machine in the office. Both the signora and Fantella had to agree, grudgingly in the latter's case, that Andrea was a truly excellent worker -conscientious, diligent and polite. Why, one lady had even been in twice in the same week, buying two dresses no less, and rewarding Andrea with 'a little something for your trouble, my dear'. Andrea had been in a quandary about this tip and had asked Signora Fano what to do with it. On the other hand Fantella had had no doubts, "just pocket it and say nothing" she'd recommended. Signora Fano had been slightly more circumspect and had admitted that it was certainly not normal procedure in this shop.

However, if the lady had liked her and had been given excellent service there was no reason Andrea couldn't have taken it, but she should not make a habit of it. A 'tips pot' was not the kind of thing that such a sophisticated, high-class shop as theirs would have, she stressed.

Every night at 9pm, after work, Signore Fano would pick them both up in his car and drive them home to a sumptuous dinner prepared by the servants. Afterwards, Signora Fano would educate Andrea on the ways of the business world, the ways of the Taranto world and the ways to convert her into a high-class young lady. Although the signora remained calmly detached Andrea sensed a certain level of warmth between them, whether artificial or natural she cared not. She missed Mama, Pasquale and Maria so any substitute was welcome. She wondered too if perhaps it was like the signora having another growing-up daughter needing advice on womanhood, until she discovered one day by accident that she'd never been able to have children and she was past regretting it now.

One day Fantella did not appear for work. The signora said she was not feeling well. One day soon turned into one week so Andrea enquired again.

"Oh, Signore Sarsi has transferred her. I should have told you, sorry, I forgot because we have been so busy. It's just you and me now." Andrea thought that strange, both that Fantella had been transferred and that the signora had not found time to tell her. After dinner each evening would have been an obvious time. Things did not seem right.

Two days later, as Andrea was crossing the road for her lunch, which she could now easily afford as the little gratuities kept rolling in regularly beyond the usually watchful eye of the signora, a bus fumed its way past her at high speed. Expect the driver wants to get home for siesta, thought Andrea, looking up. A girl was hanging out of a window waving at her and shouting "watch out, they'll…" And the sound drifted away on the wind. Andrea stared, horrified, for she was sure it was Fantella. Signore Starsi had no other shops in Taranto, to her knowledge, so if it was Fantella then what was going on? she considered. She ate little lunch that day. She did enquire later of the signora exactly where Fantella had been transferred but she said she did not rightly know. She seldom saw Signore Starsi or his driver, she added.

The shop was very busy for just two people to run and neither had a moment to communicate on non-business matters. To make things worse, a batch of dresses came in with varying degrees of faulty stitching, and from Turin no less. Quite a number of customers were having to return them. The first lady that day was singularly unimpressed and Andrea heard her arguing with the signora.

"Look, I must have this dress for tomorrow evening, my husband is taking me to the Mayor's private dinner party."

"I am so sorry, signora, but our repairer could not possibly have that finished by tomorrow and…"

"…what! You employ a repairer then? Does that mean that shoddy clothes such as these are common here, eh?"

"Signora, please let me assure you that we do not…", but the customer was no longer listening.

"… perhaps I should no longer bring my custom here if that is the case. And I thought Sarsi and Son had a fine reputation. Well, it won't after I reveal this tomorrow night at the Mayor's table. Good day, madame."

"But I merely meant I would not be able to find a seamstress in such a short time prepared to tackle such a task for the Mayor's dinner," pleaded Signora Fano, attempting to offer some face to the departing customer.

"Signora Fano, perhaps I could help?" Everyone turned to the origin of the voice, for by now the whole shop was hanging on baited breath.

"You? Help? Please, no. Keep out of this, I will handle it, Andrea."

"But I can get it mended by tomorrow, for certain."

"How? Who do you know who can do this? You have only been in Taranto a couple of weeks," the signora sneered.

"But can you, girl?" enquired the customer eagerly.

"Yes, madame, just show me what needs doing."

Again Signora Fano imposed, "Andrea, I said I would handle it, please."

"Well, you do not seem to be handling it at the moment and this sweet young thing has offered to help. Look, I have little choice in the matter with such a time constraint so let your girl deal with it. I must go, the beauty parlour awaits. Six p.m. tomorrow." And with that she made her dramatic exit, being no stranger to a show of drama, leaving all and sundry in a humdrum of chatter. Andrea calmly took the dress to the office and continued her serving. The signora was likewise busy the rest of the evening and had no chance to take up the matter again until after closing.

"Andrea," she barked haughtily, "I think tonight you had better not come home for dinner. You can surely get your own, can't you?"

"Yes, madame."

"And I have no idea what you are up to with that dress repair, but mark my words, if you do not find someone to do it tonight you will be out of a job tomorrow. I do not take kindly to being made to look foolish in my shop, do you understand?"

Before Andrea could answer the signora had spun on her heels and stormed off, obviously very angry but also very embarrassed. Andrea grabbed a snack across the road, ran up to her rooms and pulled out the sewing kit that had lain unused for weeks. Just the feel of the box, the threads, the click of needle point against thimble made her feel all warm inside. She had forgotten just how much she had missed sewing.

Next evening at six the customer returned, looking hesitant but expectant. Andrea produced the dress from under the counter and Signora Fano was amazed. "What beautiful workmanship. Please try it on, madame."

Madame reappeared with a blissful look on her face, at last, "it is perfect, just perfect! How could you have found someone so quickly to do such lovely work, my dear? Normally I would not pay for something like this, after all the dress was faulty and not merely requiring alteration, but here is 500 lira for your trouble, girl. Andrea, isn't it?"

"Yes, madame, please madame, I do not need anything…"

"…but someone has to pay the seamstress, right?"

The signora coughed exquisitely. "Starsi and Son will cover the cost, madame, for all your trouble and inconvenience."

"Hmmm! Andrea, you keep it anyway, for your trouble. I think you deserve it. A stitch in time, and all that," laughed the delighted customer, and she swept regally out of the shop still chuckling to herself over something about her husband and the mayor.

"Right my girl," said the signora, bemused and irate, "just who did you get to repair it so quickly? I will need to pay them for their excellent service."

"No-one, signora."

"No-one? How? That is impossible!"

"Actually, no it isn't," smiled Andrea, really starting to enjoy the baiting now.

"Stop talking in riddles, girl, I'm far too busy for this. For the last time, who did it?"

"Actually, I did," said Andrea triumphantly. And secretly relieved the game was over.

"You?"

"Yes, me, signora."

"Well I never," puffed Signora Fano. "In all my years… quite remarkable." She was about to scold the silly girl for annoying her when suddenly it dawned on her what was happening here. "Look, let's put the 'taking a break' notice on the door and slip over the road for refreshment. I will buy you anything you like, my dear. In exchange you must tell me all about how you learned to sew like that." She didn't need to guide Andrea across the road; the arm around her shoulder was far more interactive.

One week later Andrea's handmade lace handkerchiefs were being held by all the mannequins in the window, while her siesta times and evenings were no longer her own --- lace-making and dress alterations put paid to that!

*** *** ***

15

SENIORITY

1 9 4 8

By attrition and gang stupidity Pasquale quickly ascended the ranks of the SCU Youth Group. Giuliano suddenly disappeared after a late-evening raid on his home by the polizia municipale and was later heard to be residing in a youth detention centre near Bari. Demizzo fell victim to the delights of bootleg whisky and once too often spoke too much and too loudly in a local bar. Unfortunately for him he chose the moment two regional detectives decided to stop for a cappuccino. Fortunately for the gang members he had uttered no-one's individual name, but it was enough to compromise the movement as a whole. A few weeks later he suffered a fall down some steep steps in the self-same detention centre and unfortunately joined the angels in Heaven, or more likely the beasts in Hell. Tomaso's family had to move unexpectedly quickly to avoid the tax inspector closing in fast on his father's illegal activities, and being only fourteen Tomaso had had to run with them. He was last heard of in Matera, tricking people out of their cave homes with tales of a spreading malaria epidemic.

That only left Damiano and Paulo at the head of the growing, increasingly-fruitful gang, with Pasquale coming up the rails a close third, only a short-head behind Paulo. And then Paulo got sick and within the month was dead. Consumption, they were told, but they thought that was only for older folk. And so it was, almost overnight Pasquale had become deputy leader of a secretive but notorious gang of young ne'er-do-wells. He felt ambivalent about this because at heart he had always been brought up an honest, hard-working child, even though his father had walked out when he was seven. On the other hand, he and his mother and siblings had consequently suffered great poverty and hardship, therefore he considered he kind of 'deserved' some of the easy pickings the SCU offered. Deep down he knew what they did was not to restore the balance of economic society but was downright illegal, but in these post-war years so many ordinary folk were also having to do illegal things just to stay alive. So where was the justice of War, he thought. At only sixteen even Pasquale could realise that War was not honourable, was not the means to right wrongs, was not the golden chance to set the world straight again. If War was futile then everything was futile, and nothing comes out of futility except greater futility, he surmised.

Yet on that late October day, with the sun an enormous golden orb setting on the impossibly mellow Salento Plain and a strong hint of a mist starting to rise over the orange-tipped leaves of the spent vineyards, how could life be futile? he thought.

The gang was advancing carefully on a farmer's white stone house, one of those who lived just off the edge of town in smallholdings, transitional between town housing and countryside emptiness. Clearly this farmer had failed to hear of, or accept, the growing reputation of this clandestine youth group and he had openly laughed at their initial formal approaches regarding protection money for his tractor, just like a number of foolish farmers before him. When will they ever learn? he thought.

Damiano had indeed heard a number of stories about Signore Lorenzo, some good, some bad, but some downright odd. Hence in view of the last description Lorenzo had always been put near to the end of their 'to do' insurance invitation list. They knew he had moved from Napoli during the War and had taken up farming after his wife had been killed in an air raid. They also knew he shunned banks, assuming he had lost all in Napoli. They certainly knew he was a grumpy recluse. And it was whispered that he had colluded with the Nazis in the war and had been well compensated. So since the day he had refused their 'invitation' to help him protect his tractor they had posted a permanent surveillance on him. They had already issued the 'final warning letter', daring him to sleep easy in his bed of a night, and tonight their patience had been exhausted and they were planning a little mayhem to remind him with whom he was dealing.

They observed the huge red orb as it set behind his house. Darkness follows so quickly in south Italy and within minutes all they could see across his vineyard were the narrow strips of land illuminated by the two lit windows. "Avanti," whispered Damiano, and as the gang fanned out on all sides Damiano led the frontal assault and Pasquale controlled the rear. Slowly they crept forward, ever closer to teaching him a lesson. Suddenly Damiano stretched to full height and lobbed a cobble through a front window. The crash was amplified a hundred times in the still evening air. Fredericio then rose to splatter dog turds all over the front door from a bag he had carefully and complainedly carried all the way from town. But before he could throw the contents the door crashed open and Lorenzo straddled the light, legs planted firmly apart and shotgun in hand.

"Scatter lads, he's got a gun!" screamed Damiano, and they all dived for cover in the natural alleys between the rows of grape bushes. Lorenzo boomed an enormous laugh and scattered both barrels, more into the air than in malice, and then, as if understanding their strategy, reloaded and swaggered round to the rear. Pasquale did not need to tell his troops what to do; they'd scattered in all directions. Pasquale's own flight angled him towards an old out-house and he crouched behind it rather than risk having buckshot prised later out of his rear. The rest of the gang, being younger and more innocent, just kept running in the dark like headless chickens.

After a minute Pasquale could hear someone talking. Oh no, he thought, surely there is not more than one of them? But then he calculated it was actually Lorenzo mumbling to himself. Huh, pathetic stupid boys; at the first sight of trouble they run, just like Mussolini's Elite in Napoli. Pathetic! And then Pasquale heard no more, except footsteps coming perilously close to him. He started to tremble and fought to control any rustling this movement might give away. He was fortunate to be crouched downwind of Lorenzo, otherwise the fragrance of spreading panic sweat would have quickly laced Lorenzo's nostrils and given away his position.

Still muttering, Lorenzo dragged back the old wooden door of the outhouse and entered, only three feet and a wall between him and Pasquale. Through a crack between these old crumbling blocks of tufa stone he could just make out Lorenzo crouched over an old wooden box in the corner which he had dragged out of a hole after throwing back some filthy old tarpaulin. Ah, no problem then, what idiots! mumbled Lorenzo. Suddenly the old man sprang back up, frightening Pasquale so much that he jerked back and whistled in breath. But Lorenzo heard or saw nothing and shuffled back to his house chuckling.

Intrigued, Pasquale sneaked round and pulled out the filthy box, wondering what it could contain. To his amazement he could just make out by feel and the light of the rising moon wads of bank notes and layers of paper. There must be millions here, he thought in a panic, what a find! But wait, this is certainly not a find, this is Lorenzo's not mine. I cannot take these, it's a crime. I am not a criminal. Oh Lord, what should I do? Would he have shot me if he'd seen me, like a stray dog in a street? He would have certainly marched me off to the polizia at least. Still, I'd certainly have deserved it anyway. He felt a cramp coming on so he shifted onto one knee. Hell, there's a fortune here; Lorenzo's fortune, not my fortune though. Perhaps if I repositioned the money in a safer place and then offered to return it for a small commission? Yes, I could manage that and it wouldn't seem so much like a crime after all, more like a business transaction. That could work, and be profitable. So Pasquale scooped up all the money and sheets into his knapsack, replaced the box with a rock in it, peeped out the door, and ran, crouching as low as he could between the vines. He need not have worried: Lorenzo was safely and happily ensconced in his house and clouds encroaching on the moon had turned the night sky inky black.

Once home he crept into bed without anyone noticing and stashed the knapsack under his body, falling asleep almost instantly he touched his pillow. But nightmares raged and they troubled him to wake so many times he eventually gave up on sleep. He knew it was the guilt. He had never done anything so wicked before. He had acted in haste, as perhaps most others would, in an emergency situation, and he realised he had made the wrong decision. It would be obvious who the thieves were. It was, after all, far too coincidental that it was the same night as the raid.

But wait, he considered. Just how often would Lorenzo check his precious hoard? He had already seen it intact after the raid and had mumbled happily to bed. It might perhaps be days, weeks, even months before he checked again, who knows? Suddenly Pasquale breathed easier. And as he started to feel more comfortable inside he thought he might as well have a little peep at the treasure trove. So he sneaked out into the small back courtyard and as luck would have it dawn was breaking. Without being too obvious, though he couldn't for the life of him understand why, as no-one could see in from the street, he opened the knapsack to stare at the money. But was it money?

He did not recognise lira banknotes, the sheets of paper were nothing like banknotes. They were twice the size, each one folded and covered in small type print. But not a language with which he was familiar. He peered closer and began to make out words in German. He knew it was German because he had remembered some of the posters and leaflets left as the German army moved through. He was fairly sure anyway. But there were numbers too, a bit like a banknote, with the word "marks" next to them. Big numbers too, a lot of zeros. He was baffled. There were many, many sheets, mostly new and still crisp, and in a range of colours just like banknotes. At the base of each was a most impressive signature penned in a flourishing, confident, almost arrogant, style with a stamp printed over each one. They certainly looked important but Pasquale fretted in his disappointment: he thought he had in his possession money, lots of money. How could he get value from pieces of paper like this? He knew clearly he was way out of his depth and he would need another person's help one day. That could be a big problem. He even began to regret taking the sheets and wondered that if he put them back would Lorenzo ever guess they had been missing in the first place?

* * *

16

BONDS

Pasquale knew it wouldn't work. But he had to try.

Cosimo was no fool, but he had always been a good family friend, standing by them through thick and thin. And after all, who else could he ask anyway? If indeed they were valuable people would start to ask questions. With persistence they might even threaten him, follow him or even, Heaven forbid, rob him.

He knew it wouldn't work, but he would say he'd found it along a roadside. Ridiculous really, he knew it. What would such a piece of paper be doing lying on a roadside in the campagna?

Cosimo took it eagerly, smiling as Pasquale spun his awful lie. "Good Lord, Pasquale, this is a German bearer bond worth...er...20,000 marks, printed in Napoli in 1943."

"20,000 marks?"

"Yes, well, it would have been then, maybe. But the Germans just printed them to make their own money, really, and maybe its real worth was more like 20,000 lira not marks," he laughed.

"But now, Cosimo?"

Cosimo paused, scratched his chin and ruminated. "Now? Hm... now. Actually I believe they are illegal in Italy and hence utterly worthless. But just how in the name of Mother Mary would one end up here, in a ditch, hundreds of kilometres from Napoli. How strange."

Trying to choke back his anger, misery and tears Pasquale mumbled, "Oh well, perhaps someone was carrying it around, you know, like a souvenir or a memory and just dropped it?"

"True, possible. But I am trying to think if I know anyone around here who came from Napoli or near there. Most people are going the opposite way; can't wait to get out of here and head up North looking for work. How strange."

Pasquale made his exit quickly and also thought it very strange. Worthless paper? Why did I waste all my time and worry so much then? The bright sun hit like the flames of a forest fire as he sauntered down the road. But wait, he considered, why on earth would Lorenzo hang on to these like that Jew he'd heard about in a Dicken's novel, Fagin wasn't it, as if it were precious treasure? Oh dear, does he perhaps not realise they are worthless yet? Does he think he is still sitting on a fortune? And if they are illegal surely he is not going to report them stolen when he finds they're gone? And even if he did, wouldn't the polizia just tell him the same, laugh at their worthlessness and send him packing? So am I in the clear now?

Immediately he cheered up, the disappointment of their worthlessness replaced by the relief of knowing he was now probably off the hook. He started skipping down the road in a manner most unlike him. Still, I'd better hide them quickly, anyway, just in case, he chuckled.

That night he buried them in waterproof canvas in a deep hole beneath his first field of beans, on the edge at the highest point where rain would drain away fastest.

Two days later Cosimo called him into the shop as he was sauntering past. There were customers so Pasquale had to wait. But when were there never customers? Cosimo's store was the only one in the vicinity and extremely popular. But he missed seeing his sister's lovely smile behind the counter and her fresh smell from the lavender soap with which she spoiled herself as she swished round to reach for a tin off the shelf. After browsing and seeing off that batch of customers Pasquale jumped in fright as Cosimo slammed down The Brindisi Star on the counter and muttered, "read page four!"

Pasquale scoured the page until he saw a tiny column entitled 'Local Resident Loses Bonds' but all it said was a local man, unnamed, had lost some bearer bonds and if anyone knew anything to please report it to any police post.

Cosimo said, "looks like whoever got hold of them, by whatever means, must have dropped one, or some, just as you described, Pasquale. Obviously there is no mention of their worth. The newspaper probably wants to remain neutral in the affair and not cause some goldrush-type stampede, so its all a bit cat and mouse really, eh?"

"Yes, true."

"No doubt you'll not be making any visits to any police posts," he smiled.

"Well, I wouldn't like to be labelled a mouse!" Pasquale retorted, bravely trying to match Cosimo's humour. Or was it humour? he thought, Cosimo is no fool. I knew it wouldn't work.

Pasquale waited a week until the commotion had died down. Surely it would in seven days, he thought. So 2 am on the eighth night saw him creeping along the lane-side to old Lorenzo's farm with a canvas bag on his back in a knapsack. He'd deliberated long and hard about this and he had decided he was not a criminal, despite the perceived fortune he could be sitting on. He would take it back, less a couple of bonds he'd keep for himself as a souvenir, as it were, and if nothing else it would give old Lorenzo a real shock to find it back in the same place unharmed. He hoped it would not give him a heart attack instead! As he lay it quietly in its hiding place the thought occurred to him that he could not resist leaving a, not so much a clue, but a statement, inside the box. But what? he thought as this sudden idea had rushed through his mind only at that moment. Searching his pockets he found he still had a few bean seeds left from the last planting, so he hurriedly placed two right at the bottom, under the last bond. Ha! He felt better immediately because there was no doubt he still had qualms about giving up this fortune, now that he was actually physically doing it. Walking back down the lane he could not resist a whistle, safe in the knowledge that the wind was carrying it away from Lorenzo's slumbering frame in the silent farmhouse.

* * *

17
DOWNHILL IN TARANTO
1 9 4 9

"Come here, Andrea, Signora Fano tells me you are an excellent employee."

"Oh thank you, Signore Sarsi, I do try my best."

"And you have hidden talents too, I understand?"

"Well, yes…it helps me send some money home to Mama, Signore."

"Now, my dear, now, now…I think it is somewhat more than 'a little money', isn't it?"

"Well Signore, it is true I have saved some. But I have also spent some, unfortunately. The temptations of Taranto are much greater than tiny Avetrana, Signore," she giggled.

"Hm, I wonder if you have any more hidden talents or other temptations," leered Signore Starsi, with such a slight wink of an eye that it appeared merely like a twitch. Fortunately his specious jibe flew totally over the sweet, innocent head of Andrea, but it certainly did not miss Signora Fano.

"Oh Sarsi, you are a wicked man with such naughty thoughts!" boomed Signora Fano with a hearty, almost lusty laugh. No eavesdropper would have guessed from this innocent bantering that it was anything but innocent. On the contrary, however, it had all been carefully planned and rehearsed by the pair of them.

"Sorry, Bella, I'm sorry but I do become a little flighty and lightheaded in the company of beautiful young ladies!"

"Ladies? Ladies plural, you say Signore? I only see one here," she laughed.

"Yes, and only one 'young' one too," retorted Starsi, obviously warming to the task and beginning to enjoy himself enormously. Let's hope no customer walks in at this moment, it's all going perfectly, he thought.

Poor Andrea watched all this with some amusement and slowly it dawned on her that her seniors were lightly flirting. "I see three 'young', Signore, three 'young at heart'," she laughed, joining in the harmless banter.

"Oh, very droll, Andrea, very droll. Excellent! I can see working in my fashionable store is becoming the making of you."

"Well Signore, the conversation I'll admit is considerably different than Cosimo Patisso's village shop. But I have still much to learn, and…"

"…precisely! Now to the business at hand therefore. I actually came here today to ask you something along those lines. Andrea, would you be interested in furthering your social skills? I mean by the way of learning how to make polite conversation to your betters."

"But Signore, I do try my best, honestly," pleaded Andrea, "if anyone has had cause to complain then I am truly sorry. I will try…"

"…no, no, no, Andrea, no, I do not mean that". He moved to her, seeing it as a wonderful opportunity to put his arm round this beautiful young creature. "No, no-one has complained, quite the opposite, my dear. I understand from Signora Fano that all the customers speak most highly of you."

"Andrea, that is true, very true. They all love you and find you so helpful."

"Oh thank you signora, I am much relieved to hear that."

"No, Andrea," continued Signore Starsi, "what I meant was practise the art of conversation with some of the ladies."

"I'm sorry, Signore, I do not understand what you mean."

"Well…it was actually Signora Fano's idea. Would you like to explain further? Probably better than I."

"Yes, it was my idea. It suddenly came to me one day whilst watching you with a customer. I mentioned it to Signore Starsi, who approved, and then approached one or two of the ladies about it. You see, some of them are actually widows or even spinsters and I have sensed for a while that, although rich, some of them are actually intensely lonely. They actually have few people to talk to, apart from the odd word in the street or in a shop such as ours, and apart from, say, a rather limited maid at home sensible conversation passes them by."

"So how could I possibly help, Signora? Am I not classified in the same category as 'rather limited maid'? I'm from the countryside, with no education, no knowledge of the world…"

"...no education?" argued Signora Fano. "This shop has been your education these past seven months. Look how much you have learned, picked up, discovered. And they would pay..."

"...pay?"

"Oh yes, they would give you a little tip or a treat as a thank you, that's for sure."

"Really?"

"Certainly," agreed Signore Starsi, "maybe even handsomely too!"

"But... how would I manage to do all this?" enquired Andrea nervously.

Signore Starsi was well prepared for this bit and with a comfortable ease to his voice he silkily explained the mechanics, "well, Andrea, what I thought might be a lovely, civilised idea would be for you to entertain them in your pleasing rooms during the afternoon siesta, just for an hour, say, or even half an hour. Can you read?"

"Not well," answered a now concerned Andrea, "I never learned, I never went to school, it's only what I have picked up here in Taranto, looking at the newspaper stands, adverts, pictures in windows and so on..."

"...oh, you will certainly need to keep up with important news somehow. The ladies love nothing better but to dissect the gossip of the day and then when they run out, the big news from far and wide. It is like their meat and drink, their raison d'etre..."

"...their what, Signora? Please excuse my French but what does that mean?" joked Signore Sarsi.

The signora guffawed brightly at his intended humour, "most droll, Signore Starsi, most droll. Perhaps, Andrea, I could give you a brief run-down of the latest scandals in our lunch break, before you go for siesta time with the ladies?"

"That would be really helpful, thank you Signora."

"Good," said Starsi, "so it is all agreed then. I will now..."

"... but what exactly will I have to do, please?" panicked Andrea.

"Do?" repeated Starsi, "just make them some expensive tea, I will give you some, serve them a cake or a biscuit and 'do' polite conversation. Nothing more. That will make them quite happy, I can assure you."

"Will it? Really? How strange are the ways of the rich," Andrea smiled.

And it did make them quite happy... at first, anyway. Initially Andrea was very tense and nervous, having to invite these self-important rich ladies into her humble rooms for such an artificial liason, but when

she found them mostly to be charming, polite and friendly she began
to relax. It was true, they only wanted a little human contact, sensible
conversation and warmth from someone new, enthusiastic and different.
Soon they took to bringing her small gifts as a token of their so-called
friendship, items they could only too readily see Andrea had none of--
whalebone combs, sparkling hairbrushes, nail scissors, pot plants and
the like--but after two or three pleasing visits the gifts started to take
on more value ---- a gold bracelet, a silver cross, a Moroccan fan of
exquisite peacock feathers. Andrea began to become embarrassed by
this attention and this display of opulence, but the ladies tish-toshed
it, mere trinkets for us, my dear, and certainly not a strain on our
husbands' pockets, they laughed.

Andrea had at least six ladies vying for her 'tea siesta' attention
and soon she had to buy a little notebook to keep abreast of their
comings and goings. Entertaining only one at a time and usually only
two per day soon became a permutational nightmare which needed
careful logging. To her knowledge too she didn't think the ladies knew
about each other's visits, or at least not many knew, and she liked to
keep it that way in case any rivalry reared its ugly head. So she had to
allow a good half hour between one lady leaving and the next arriving,
but after a while it became increasingly difficult to get rid of the first
one, she being so relaxed and pleased with Andrea, and so she had to
increase this gap to 45 minutes. The second's departure was never a
problem as Andrea would remind her she had to return to work soon.

Andrea learned that the lady she had helped repair the dress for
the mayor's dinner was Signora Bassano and there was no doubt she
was the youngest and most beautiful of Andrea's 'guests'. Andrea
always felt somewhat indebted to her for starting her off earning all
the considerable extra money she was saving up, so when one siesta
she came swaying into the room in a most light-headed, giggly manner
Andrea did not dare say a word of rebuke but merely smiled and
acquiesced. She slurred, "Andrea, I'm sorry, I took a little too much
wine with my lunch, I do apologise. You see, I had some bad news this
morning and it has quite undone me."

"Oh dear, madame, I do hope the bad news is of a temporary nature."

"Fraid 'tis not," she continued to slur, "shocking news, heartbroken."

"Oh dear, please come and sit down, quickly."

"Mind if I lie on the bed?" was more of a demand than a question,
as Signora Bassano stumbled towards the bedroom.

"Why, certainly, er... if you feel that unwell," shouted Andrea from the kitchen where she was hunting for a bowl, a bucket or any vessel that might be needed to catch the inevitable.

"Please help!" cried the signora, "I feel rather faint." Andrea moved as fast as she could negotiate around the heavy, immovable furniture and found her sprawled all over the outer bedspread and looking less than happy. "Please sit with me, dear, and hold my hand. I am just not used to this unusual sensation." So Andrea obliged, not wanting to upset her good customer, and within a few minutes the signora had passed out, or fallen asleep, whichever happened to be the more correct description in polite circles.

Andrea had been overworked for days with her tea siestas, dress repairs and alterations and lace-making, on top of a normal busy day in the shop, so she too lay gently down beside the signora. 'It's only 2.40pm after all, time for a little nap,' she thought.

Shadows passed over her, goblins danced all around the bed, a huge squashy tomato zoomed at her face and thunderclaps rang out. But over all this came a sweet, fine voice whispering "it's lovely, it's fine, it's alright." Suddenly she felt at peace with the world as the shadows, goblin and tomato departed, leaving her in a cool, blissful garden permeated with birdsong and scents of rose petals. Oh my, how lovely, yes it is fine, it is so fine, answered Andrea's inner thoughts.

A movement next to her. The cool garden faded, the oppressive afternoon heat replacing it. A clock, her clock. The flocked wallpaper, her wallpaper. And then that sweet, calm voice again, "wake up dear Andrea, wake up; it will soon be time for work again." Oh what a sweet, calm voice! She opened her eyes and looked away from her wall. The signora was at the door. As she turned she was doing up her top blouse button. She saw Andrea looking.

"Thank you, my dear, for staying with me and for loosening my blouse. I'm sorry, I was a little tipsy," she smiled and giggled, "are you alright, my dear, my dear little dear? You must have fallen asleep with me. Too much work for such a young beauty as you, you must rest more."

"Yes, thank you, I had the most beautiful rest I can ever remember. It was so strange, yet comforting."

"Mm, you seemed extremely happy. So I too am happy. Tea before we go?"

* * *

18

EVENING WORK

1 9 4 9

"Andrea, there is just nowhere in this shop I can do this. I hope you don't mind if I use your rooms?" asked Massimo.

"Do what, Signore Starsi?" she replied, knowing full well that she was living in relative luxury upstairs, and for no rent, so how could she refuse him.

"I have two new suppliers now, one for dresses and the other for underclothes, but the latter are, how should I put this delicately, at the forefront of fashion!"

"How exciting!" interjected Andrea, as ever trying to both please and impress at the same time.

"Yes, I agree, very exciting, but that is my point, you see. Taranto, as I am sure you know now, is rather a backwater of everything, especially fashion, and I am trying to bring it into the post-war era as quickly as I can. These clothes are, as they say in France, somewhat avant garde." He puffed with pride at this point, pride in both his grasp of another language and his knowledge of international haute couture and fashion trends. "My suppliers are therefore concerned that the Taranto market will be, how shall I say, a little risky, to say the least. Hence they are looking for reassurance that their products will be popular here."

"Yes, Signore, I can understand their concern, but how does this affect me then?"

"Well, they are suggesting that the best approach would be to have small, select, informal viewings of their ranges, but only for our special customers…"

"…do you mean rich, Signore?" Andrea laughed, pleased she was able to create humour such as this.

Obviously her siesta teas are having the desired effect, he thought satisfyingly, and he smiled slightly lasciviously at the beautiful girl. "Quite so, quite so, Andrea, you clever young beauty. I think it an excellent strategy. Now, as you may well know, whenever they show new clothes in Milano, Torino, London or New York they put models on a catwalk. Beautiful girls for beautiful clothes, eh?" He preened at his intelligent linkage.

"But are these clothes for beautiful people too?"

"No, of course not, but that is the whole point of fashion, isn't it? The clothes are to make plain people feel beautiful. We are not selling clothes really, we are selling dreams."

"Anyone can dream, signore, but only the rich can have their dreams come true", she smiled.

"Oh, Andrea, how you are blossoming. What wonderful conversational skills you are developing. Those tea chats are really helping, aren't they."

"Actually, signore, I really wanted to ask you about them. Some of the ladies, particularly Signora Bassano, are starting to get very possessive. They want to see me every day…"

"…what is wrong with that? I'm sure they reward you well?"

"But it is becoming impossible…"

"…we will talk of it another day, Andrea, let us concentrate on this matter at hand, shall we? We need to show our frumpy old ladies that they will not be brutta in our clothes but beautiful, desirable creatures. I know for some it will prove an impossible task but we must try. So, if they see these garments on a beautiful young body they might believe the effect will be the same on them…"

"…and do you have anyone prepared to model these clothes, signore?"

"Ah, now that is the point. I was hoping, to keep down costs, that you might volunteer for the delightful task, my dear Andrea. You would look stunning. And of course, they already know you and are comfortable in your presence, as you in theirs."

"Oh signore, I don't know. Are you sure? I…I…"

"…I think you would do a wonderful job, and of course, I would happily offer you a little bonus for accommodating us."

"But when you say 'clothes and underclothes' what exactly do you mean by the latter, signore? I would be very happy to show off new clothes to the ladies but…"

"...My dear little petal, do not fear, I have seen them and they are not any kind of problem at all. And anyway, there will only be the ladies in the room after all."

"But, but, what would my mama say…"

"Your mama is a long way away, do not fear. And you would be in your own rooms, not some strange place. That would relax you, wouldn't it, the familiarity of your own surroundings?"

"Yes, I suppose so. Well, if you really think…"

"…I do, Andrea, I really do. Thank you, thank you. You will not regret it!" said Starsi, pressing some notes into her hand. "Excellent, next Wednesday, then. Here is a little extra for your greatest kindness towards Starsi and Son, you will need some new makeup and soap, I'm sure, my dear," he smiled. At that he turned and left, carefully obscuring the growing smirk on his face. It was only matched by the smirk on Signora Fano's face as she watched from her office, concealed throughout the exchange behind the door. 'What a wily old fox he is,' she pondered, full of admiration for his technique with the young staff.

Wednesday evening came round quickly, far too quickly for the nervous but excited Andrea. At eight pm the shop closed early and two dapper gentlemen in their 50's entered her apartment, weighed down with expensive looking clothing bags.

'Buona sera!' they unisoned and promptly wisped past to the bedroom. Andrea was to change there and to show in her drawing room. At eight fifteen exactly Massimo Starsi appeared, hustling four late middle-aged ladies into comfortable chairs, and immediately started to serve them a cocktail which he had brought ready-mixed in five silver flasks. The ladies were all very giggly and chatty within minutes of this obvious VIP treatment and Andrea surmised it must be partly because they had not yet had dinner and were consuming on empty stomachs. She recognised Signora Bassano, nodded and smiled, to which the signora replied with an even wider smile on a somewhat knowing face. Andrea had no time to reflect on this greeting and was in truth too innocent anyway. She was called to the bedroom.

"Hurry child," insisted one of the men, "we must get ready quickly. Dresses first, then underclothes, OK?"

"Er…OK. Well, I am not sure. I shall need considerable help with some of these delicate dresses. Where is Signora Fano? Won't she be helping me?"

"No," replied the other man, in a high-pitched voice, "she went home unwell, unfortunately. Anyway, do not fear, my child, we shall be doing this, it is our job and we are very used to it. Oh, and there's no need to be coy, we've seen it all in our lifetimes and, anyway, we have no interest at all in ladies, if you know what I mean." The two men smiled sweetly at each other and caressed hands sparingly, as if to make the point even more obvious. Even the innocent Andrea guessed what they meant and relaxed a little. But she jumped when they clapped hands and said, "let us begin."

Andrea had to admit that it was a wondrous feeling to put on such expensive, delicate dresses and parade in front of the increasingly-pleased and vociferous audience, even if she thought the colours a little too bright and the necklines, and backlines too for that matter, too plunging for her modesty. The way the dresses always fell short of the ankle concerned her too, but that obviously pleased the ladies. She asked the men if she was too tall and they assured her it was all the rage. Before she knew it the dresses were finished. It had all been a bit of a dream as she rushed out of one dress into the next, always hurried by the two gentlemen who she had to admit never impinged upon her form and certainly knew what they were doing with pinning when a dress was too loose and hemming if not short enough. It was all such a whirl and she was loving it. So was her audience, presumably fuelled by Starsi's cocktails. He knocked on the bedroom door, "can I come in please? You are doing a fantastic job, Andrea, do you need refreshment?"

She nodded and he decorously poured her some liquid from the silver flask. "Here, this will help, I'm sure", he said, and sure enough within a few minutes Andrea was feeling more relaxed and at one with the world.

"I think one's enough, Alfredo, get the underwear ready," whispered Starsi, and left the room quietly.

"Andrea, it's time for the underwear now," said Alfredo and he pulled out the second large bag. After rustling around he triumphantly held up two small pieces of white material.

"What?" spluttered Andrea.

"Don't worry, my dear, these are the latest from America…"

"…but where is the pretty one-piece I am used to, the chemise isn't it?"

"Sorry, no chemises tonight, these are called 'brassieres' and these 'pants'. They are all the rage in New York and have spread to London, Paris and now Milano. Be proud: I think I am right in saying you will be the first lady to wear these in the whole of the south of Italy, well south of Napoli at least! What an honour, an honour indeed!

"An honour?"

"Yes, quite so. Massimo has even planned a little surprise next door to mark the occasion." But Andrea felt flushed and sick. This was far too exotic and beyond the borders of her normality. She felt she was fast losing her grip on reality and all she could hear was the growing impatient calls from next door and the two men urging her on. "Listen, dear, your public grows impatient, come on, just take off all your clothes and slip into these."

"But... you'll see..."

"...don't be silly, we will turn our backs, we're not interested in the least anyway. Hurry, put the brassiere on your...er...your bosoms and clip it behind your back. The pants should fit, they are your size, I would judge. Now!"

Poor Andrea had little choice, it seemed, and so she did. Quickly, with great embarrassment and reddening face, she turned her back to the men and undressed. She could not see if they had done the same and, of course, they hadn't, they had only three quarters turned and were squinting happily over their shoulders. She struggled with the back clip and one of them had to come and help. He could hardly conceal his delight. She felt totally naked and stood with each arm crossed, trying to conceal her finest beauty. Finally, when ready, the men turned and were forced to bite their tongues, pretending to be totally nonchalant and unaffected. It was near impossible: Andrea was, and looked, truly beautiful. They could not remember a time of greater delight and thanked the Lord above for such mercies.

"Quick, girl, you cannot stand like that," shouted Alfredo, trying to bring himself back down to Earth, "learn to walk, put some pride in your step! You are not only showing off the underwear, you are showing off south Italy's youthful beauty. Be proud!"

And so she did, or tried to do. Twice round the bedroom and her fears eased slightly, helped by the concoction she had drunk earlier which was starting to have an even greater effect on her. The high heels they made her wear helped to raise her, her body and her confidence, all in one go. A deep breath, a 'here at last' from Alfredo and a plunge through the double doors into the drawing room. There was no going back now, ever.

She was greeted by a hot, suffocating fug and a blast of noise. Was it the smoke in the room or the massive flash of light that made her eyes water? She did not worry, all the less to see them with, she thought. The cheers and clapping deafened her ears; it was obvious the crowd was well stoked by now. But someone has turned off most of the gas lights and she could not make out anyone in the packed room, even if her eyes had not been watering. Maybe it was not all ladies? Maybe Signore Starsi was lurking there? Who had caused the flashing lights? She panicked. Someone shouted 'walk, walk, come on, let's see', and so she tried to pull all her dignity together and start putting one step in front of another. The baying crowd immediately quietened and she could feel her confidence returning. She walked proudly, as Alfredo had asked, to the end and returned even slower and more poised. Another flash. She reached to bedroom door and went to push through. It would not budge. The men must have locked it. She had to turn. 'More, more' the ladies chanted in their increasingly-tipsy lasciviousness, and she walked the length of the room again to thunderous applause. She pushed again at the door and this time it opened. She was unready and stumbled across the room, falling clumsily almost onto the bed. Alfredo's friend caught her, fortunately, but she thought he held her too close and for too long before easing her back upright. His breath smelled like a sewer.

"Now, the next one," demanded Alfredo.

"Another? I have to wear more?" pleaded Andrea.

"Oh yes, my little beauty, the ladies need a wide selection before they buy. We have quite a few here."

"But this will take all night, signore."

"No, no, don't you worry, we'll speed up. After all, it is not like climbing into a huge dress is it?" he sniggered.

"Yeh, only takes a few seconds, eh Alfredo. Heh, turn round, no peeping!" the friend guffawed. "Do you need a drink? You look so hot and flustered."

"Oh yes please," pleaded Andrea. He returned from the room with another cocktail and she could have sworn she saw him wink just before he entered. But she was parched and hardly noticed the heady concoction as it slid through her oh so rosy lips and down, oh so gently. inside her long graceful neck. The two men stared in rapture; this surely was a stunning lady.

She returned to the fray. The raucous crowd again hushed as she moved through the doors, then oohed and aghed when they saw how little she was wearing and cheered when she floated through their midst. One old lady grabbed at the pants, ostensibly to feel the quality of the silk, but she also tried to yank them down. Another smacked her hand and she let go with a 'yelp'. Andrea was glad to get back to the bedroom in one piece, or in two pieces, as it were.

And so the evening rushed on, more underwear, more drinks and more quick changes. Her head was swimming as the party became more out of hand. Finally it was over and all the ladies rushed over to thank her. More likely they wanted to get as close to her as possible and just get a chance to touch her youthful velvet body. As she thanked them she started to swoon. Starsi swooped in, ever on the alert, and tried to shoo them away. He had never seen anything like it either and was also glad it was over. Drunken old ladies are impossible, he thought.

Andrea thought she heard one giggle to Starsi, "Starsi, I would have paid triple that entry fee to have seen what I have seen. What a beauty! When can we do this again, eh?" But a great dizzying fog was descending on her rapidly and she fell back onto the bed, her head spinning and her limbs numbed. She vaguely sensed more of the flashing lights and hands constantly rearranging her limbs, then nothing.

Later she awoke once and thought she vaguely heard Starsi whispering to the men, "OK, I won't bother to use those prints I took through the door crack as they might not come out well with no flashlight. The ones on the bed will be fantastic though."

"No, keep them all, Massimo, men get excited watching women undressing, even if they are poor quality. That will make the photos feel more elicit. It's all about action versus static. Believe me, I should know!"

"OK, if you insist. And you'll have the money next week?"

When Andrea awoke again it was morning and she was wearing her sleepsuit. As the fog slowly cleared she realised who must have dressed her in it. She leapt up, ran to the sink and was violently sick.

※ ※ ※

19
THE LETTER
1 9 4 9

Within a day of receiving the letter Pasquale Carone had made his plan.

Of course, his mother had had to ask who the letter was from, as letters were not the most common item their house received and, after all, it had been she who had been disturbed out of her kitchen by a man calling for her determinedly. She had known it could not have been Cosimo, he never called her Signora Carone, so in her usual worrying manner, like most mothers, she had dispatched herself in some haste to the door.

"Thank you, signora," was all il postino had said, and was away in a trice. She didn't recognise the handwriting, there was no scent or perfume on it, indeed it looked most businesslike. Who did Pasquale know in Taranto? she wondered. Should I open it or wait?

Fortunately wait she did, because Pasquale was just as puzzled as she when he opened it. It was a typed letter, all business-like and formal. 'Dear Signore Carone, it will distress you to hear that someone you know well is in trouble,' it read.

"Heavens," thought Pasquale, it might be one of those contacts I tried to make in Taranto. They might have been caught because of my innocent request to know what to do with that coin I had found in my vegetable field. Perhaps this is a solicitor writing?

"Well, who is it from, Pasquale? Don't keep me in the dark here any longer, you dithering boy. You never get letters like this, ever; what is it?"

"Hold on, Mama, I'm still reading. Someone is in trouble, I think…"

"…you'll be in trouble if you don't tell me soon, my lad!"

"Sorry, Mama, please wait. You know I cannot read very well, and this is all very difficultly worded. Legal talk, you know."

"Hm, sometimes I am very glad I cannot read at all, believe it or not."

Pasquale read on. Without trying to show his shock or horror he learned it was not from any business people, it was from dear Andrea. She had typed it, and the envelope too, presumably on the shop typewriter so that no-one would know it was her. If she had gone to that much trouble there was no way he was going to displace her trust and confidentiality. "Oh," he breathed a false sigh of relief for effect, "it's OK Mama, it's nothing important, it's some businessman down in Taranto I contacted a while ago to see if he was interested in taking any of my vegetables. I've often got far too many to get rid of quickly, they being so perishable."

It seemed a rather lame excuse, but he started to walk away slowly as if his mind had already switched to something else. To allay even more suspicion he asked innocently what was for dinner. In reality, he could not wait to get to his room, the agonising slow motion-ness of it all was crippling. Time seemed to stand still as he shuffled nonchalantly across the floor to his sanctuary. He would be safe in the house's sole bedroom that Mama had so graciously vacated when Andrea left home so that he could have some privacy as he grew up. He would be safe there: Mama never entered anymore, she slept with little Maria in the living room.

Dread with fear he lay on his bed and read on. 'You are required to come as soon as possible, preferably 9 November at 9.30pm, and help this person leave by the rear entrance door next to the labelled shop door. It will be open. Thank you, yours sincerely, A C, pp Sarsi and Sons.'

'Oh no, that's Andrea. She's in trouble. What trouble? Why? Poor girl. Oh Heavens, 9 November is tomorrow!'

He returned to the dinner table where a large steaming bowl awaited eagerly. More eager than he, though. Oh well, his preferences come and go, considered Isabella, he used to love his fave stew, but certainly not tonight.

"What's wrong, Pasquale, you've hardly touched your bowl. In love?" Mama joked. Maria clapped her hands with glee. She certainly loved her brother.

* * *

20

TO THE RESCUE

1 9 4 9

"I've got to go out, Mama," shouted Pasquale.

"Is it to do with that letter you received this morning?"

"No. Crops to tend, people to see. You know."

"Alright, but remember dinner will be late tonight, I have to visit poor Signora Paulti down the road. Her husband left for the North last year and she's just heard he is not coming back."

"Oh, met another woman then?"

"Afraid so. Aren't men just awful?"

"Yes, and I even hear some men keep two families going secretly, so she should be lucky."

"Lucky? Why? All her means of support is gone, like ours was, and she is nearly starving."

"True," replied Pasquale, trying desperately to dig himself out of the rapidly deepening hole of his own making, "but in defence, she does at least know her husband is divorcing her."

"Divorcing? What a stupid boy you can be sometimes."

"Yes, stupid boy!" chimed in Maria.

"Be quiet, you're stupid, Maria. What do you know?" shouted Pasquale, sick that he ever tries to argue with women.

"Yes, be quiet Maria and go and see if the dough has risen yet, otherwise there will be no frittelli for dinner tonight!"

"Ah, tonight, dinner, Mama", answered Pasquale. Sorry, but I'm afraid I shan't be home in time, even if it is later. I have an important meeting tonight."

"You and your meetings! Are you sure everything you do, my boy, is legitimate? Sometimes I worry what you are getting yourself into, you know, and hanging around with those other boys, oh my!"

"Oh Mama, you must have something to worry about, mustn't you?"

"Better than carefree and foolish, like you."

"Oh Mama, that's not fair, not fair at all. Please take that back… now!"

Isabella had to pause, think about it and then finally agree that her mouth had beaten her brain to it, yet again. An increasingly worrying problem she had. There was no doubt Pasquale was a good boy; he had single-handedly kept this family together with his agricultural skills and his derring-do all the years since Eduardo had left. Why, indeed, even Andrea in Taranto sent less money back than he provided every week. And she knew he had managed to put some money away somewhere, but she just could not discover where. "OK, OK, I'm sorry. I was only joking, just trying to annoy you. But I do worry for you, you know that."

"Thanks, Mama. Have you heard from Andrea this week? When do you think we shall see her again? It's been ages."

"Who can tell? She is at the mercy of Signore Starsi, I suppose. We never did discuss home visit arrangements, unfortunately. But you can see how busy she is there."

"Yeah, yeah, yeah!" interjected Maria, "I miss Andrea, no more cuddles or stories or…"

"…be quiet, Maria!" shouted Mama again.

"It's alright, Maria, I'm sure she'll be back soon to give you a cuddle," said Pasquale, knowing full well it might even be the next day if everything went to plan. "You'll just have to have Mama's cuddles in the meantime!" he laughed.

"Mama too rough, Mama too rough!" giggled Maria as she tried to dodge the towel Isabella was wielding at her as she was chased around the kitchen.

Pasquale took the opportunity to slip out while his mother was distracted and he went straight to Damiano's meeting point. There was always a gang member on duty there and he ran straight off to pass the word. The SCU Youth branch had not been operating around Avetrana for long and so they had to be particularly careful. In those days social mobility was extremely low, apart from those departing for work up North, and the average person seldom travelled more than a few kilometres from home most of his life. Telephones were few and far between and newspapers unaffordable to most. So life was very insular and everyone knew everyone else. Strangers were spotted a mile away and even a slight variation in local or regional accent was picked up straight away. Consequently Pasquale did not wait at that rendezvous but moved on to number 3 site to await Damiano. Number 3 site was two kilometres away, in the fields behind a tufa hut, so he had plenty of time to saunter along and not raise any suspicion.

Pasquale discussed the rescue with his leader, who was at first horrified, then dubious, then discouraging, until finally grudgingly accepting. But he needed to voice his concerns, "I still can't understand why your sister needs rescuing. She doesn't say what the problem is or what has happened to her, and certainly not what might…"

"…but that is the point," countered Pasquale, "she would not ask for such a dramatic solution if she were not in danger."

"Has she ever been one to exaggerate, to be over-dramatic?"

"No, never. She has always been the calm and sensible one."

"But this is not an easy thing you ask of me, my friend." Did Pasquale detect a note of concern in Damiano's voice? When with the gang he was always full of bravado and rhetorical fire.

"I know, and I do understand, but it is urgent and if I had time to plan it I could perhaps manage alone. But it has to happen tomorrow or we know not the consequences. Pray nothing happens, but if we tarry and it did, would we want it on our consciences for the rest of our lives, knowing we did not help when we were asked?"

"True, true, dear friend. But it is not just a village down the road either, it is Taranto, you know, 40 kilometres! How in Mary Mother of God's name are we going to get there? And more serious, get back here late at night? Have some sense, it is impossible! Forget it!"

"Forget it? No! How can you, you dog! If you had asked for my help I would always have stood beside you. I have never asked a favour of SCU before, I have been loyal to our gang, I have…"

"… OK, OK, OK, calm down, my friend. I suppose you are right. Let me think." Damiano sat quietly for what seemed to Pasquale an age, and then he suddenly said, "Can you drive any better than the last time you tried?"

"Well, no, not really. What chance would I have had? The car you stole we got rid of a few days later, and you can't count tractors, can you?" Pasquale added sarcastically, "oh, so you are thinking of driving a tractor all the way to Taranto and back then?"

"Now who is being stupid and negative? Look, you've got one day to learn to drive then. I will steal a car tonight. That's as far as I think

I can help on this fool's errand. You will have to drive it all the way to Taranto and back yourself, in the dark. I am not coming."

"Damn it, Damiano, that's impossible. How can I do that?"

"It will be night, and dark, and there's bound to be light traffic in Taranto on a weekday evening."

"But I'll never find the right street or the shop. Taranto is huge, it's a city, I'll get lost. And I'll need to concentrate all my wits on just working the car…"

"….Pasquale, you do not 'work a car'," he laughed.

"Well, what do you do, then, clever?"

"You drive a car, drive a car. Got it?" And with that Damiano started roaring with laughter. How naïve this Pasquale is for a 17-year old. Oh dear, he thought. But, more important, the laughter overcame the fear and sharpened his resolve. "Ok, look, this is what we will do then. You go down to Taranto on the afternoon bus, get your sister at the appointed time and I will drive the car down and meet you. We can meet at the end of the road there and I will bring you back to Avetrana. It will all be over really quickly before anyone has time to draw breath or notice she has gone. They won't find out till the next morning and by then we will be kilometres away. Right?"

"Right, it's a promise. Thank you so much dear friend." They shook on it and smiled over the outcome. "But, how will I know which car?"

"How many cars do you think there will be in the road at 9.30 at night. Silly? I will be looking out for you. I will see you before you see me, OK?"

"Yes, but which end of the street will you be? Which way do we have to run? Away from or towards the Centro? Where…"

"…oh, Pasquale, please be quiet. I'll be there, you'll see me, OK? Just take it easy. Let me work out how I am going to get a car first. Then I'll find a map of Taranto and we can work it all out tomorrow. Meet me here at noon, OK? I'd better get going. Do you think it is easy stealing a car? There aren't that many cars around here, no-one can afford them, haven't you noticed? Then I have got to find somewhere to hide it until tomorrow night while everyone will be out looking for it. Ah, go now before I change my mind," he laughed.

Pasquale ran; ran like Hell was on his tail.

He slept badly that night, obviously. All through those writhing hours he fought bodyguards, monster lorries and evil shopkeepers. But the next noon saw him poring over a map with Damiano at the rendezvous. He said he had been able to 'procure' a safe-looking vehicle, not too flashy and not too bright-coloured, and he remembered to plaster mud over front and rear plate markings. It was going to be all night-driving anyway so he felt confident no-one would spot it was stolen. They arranged a relatively simple meeting point, just down the road from the shop at the next junction, crossed themselves and locked fists in the SCU gesture of solidarity.

Dressed as inconspicuously as possible Pasquale boarded the 4.30pm bus for Taranto and dozed all the slow, bone-jarring way there. Even in early November the late afternoon sun slanted straight through the windows on his side and the ensuing heat made him a little more than drowsy. Alighting clumsily in his sleepy stupor at the centro he banged into a dubious-looking character who proceeded to rant at him with a tirade of abuse: just what Pasquale did not need as more and more people gathered for the entertainment. But it was short-lived because the crowd quickly dispersed when a policeman appeared, and Pasquale melted away with the crowd quite nimbly too, all things considered. He branched out and easily found Starsi's street. But it was only 6pm and he needed something to settle his butterfly stomach. Choosing a café at random and not even remembering what he ate he proceeded to wait nervously. Time stopped still, even though people in the café still seemed able to take a disproportionate amount of interest in him. Perhaps he looked totally out of place, or a country yokel in a sea of sophistication. Whatever, it made him so uncomfortable he had to move to a bar, risking spending more of his dwindling supply of cash to appease his state of mind. Why should anyone be looking at him? He was not about to rob the till. But the customers did not know that for sure, he pondered. Perhaps he was too young for a bar in a city. After all, village bars served anyone, they were family socialising points, but clearly in Taranto bars after work were for businessmen to relax or approach new deals and for richer folk to socialise. He did appear awfully out of place. But in consolation at least the bar was right opposite Starsi's and he only had another hour to wait. He tried to remain impassive and nonchalant but found it very hard not to utter a tiny outcry of joy each time Andrea flitted past a lighted window or opened the glass door for a customer. He thought she too lingered those few seconds longer at the door, her eyes sweeping the street for any possibilities, before bowing her head and retiring inside.

Finally, 9pm saw the window blinds being drawn, lights being dowsed and Signora Fano leaving the shop, padlocking the front door and climbing into her husband's car. Seconds later a light came on above the shop and Pasquale saw his beloved sister drawing her curtains. 'Calm, calm, all is well, a normal evening scene,' he thought as his nerve ends began to jangle, 'just a few minutes more.'

At 9.20 precisely he left the bar, noticing that few eyes could be exercised to follow him now they were well oiled with wine, and he sauntered casually around the block to the road at the back of the shop. The required door was easy to find as it was to the right of the one labelled 'Sarsi & Son, trade entrance'. He tested it nervously and sure enough it was unlocked. Once inside he saw ahead of him a flight of dimly-lit stone steps, so he tiptoed up to the door at the top. A muffled knock, a pause, and Andrea was there, arms open almost ready to sob. "Oh brother, you came, grazie, grazie, grazie!"

"Quick, let's go. No, leave the light on. Have you a bag?" She handed over a medium-sized bag which gave nothing away as to its purpose. "OK, come, quietly."

They turned to leave the doorway and descend the steps. "Oh no," uttered Andrea, staring down the steps. A huge man in aggressive stance was framing the still-open street door.

"Heh you, what are you doing up there? Who are you?" boomed Stefano with enthusiasm. But Pasquale made no reply, quietly quaking with fear. Indeed, he could not even think what to say as panic overtook him. Fortunately, however, it was an extremely dimly-lit stairwell and Stefano could not yet sense his fear. "Andrea, I go for a quick coffee and this is what you get up to, eh?"

"I don't know what you mean, Stefano," stammered Andrea, "Why are you here?"

"Oh, boyfriend, is it?" he laughed. "Here? What do you mean? I'm here every night looking after you, didn't you know?"

"Looking after me? Why? What for? I need no looking after!" she shouted, her anger and astonishment rising by the second. She had never seen him here, not even sensed his presence before.

"Ah, that is where you are very wrong, my little precious. Or should I say Signore Starsi's greatest precious? Don't you realise you are his greatest asset right now? And like any precious asset it must be carefully looked after," he laughed menacingly. Andrea shivered at this thought. How could anyone view another person as an asset? And why should

I be so precious, just for entertaining a few ladies and doing their running repairs. This man must have gone for something far stronger than a coffee. Advancing up the stairs Stefano again bellowed, "I'll say it again, who are you boy?"

"Please do not be rude, Stefano, this is my bro..." at which point Pasquale tried to cover her mouth with his hand, but it was too late.

"Your brother, eh? Yeh, yeh, I'll believe that if you want me to, very funny. Now come here, my lad, you're going back out into the street, now." Stefano ran up the stairs fearlessly and as he reached out to grab the shaking Pasquale the latter had a sudden surge of bravery. He swung his foot forward and caught Stefano fair square in the groin, who immediately doubled up in pain and roared, "bastardo!" Pasquale saw his second chance and pushed the man with all the downward force he could muster in the circumstances. Stefano went crashing and screaming down the steps, landing as crumpled as only a large man could at the bottom, and never having time to recover from the curled-up pose a person naturally assumes as a defence mechanism on falling.

No movement, as still as the dead. The terrified siblings gaped at each other. What had they done? They had defied Starsi's evil minder, for one. And hurt him, for sure. They were going to pay, that was inevitable, but at this moment they could not think of that, or anything at all; they were stunned beyond belief. Pasquale recovered from their stupor first, "come sister, run, run like mad, let's get out of here!"

"But can we get past him?"

"We have too, come on, the longer we wait, the likelier he might recover." So they ran. Down the steps with Andrea's bag, ready to swing at him if he moved, and over his still body. Pasquale swore an arm swung out from its grotesque angle to grab his ankle as they climbed clumsily over him. He stopped to look. No panting noise, no chest rising or falling. No blood either. Was he unconscious or dead? No time to deliberate further, run, run.

They slammed the door on its lock and scurried out into the night, not stopping till they reached the rendezvous. In the distance the Town Hall clock said 9.55pm. Was that all? It seemed like forever. But where was Damiano? This was the spot. Definitely. He had double-checked earlier. No car, no Damiano. Where was that fool? Pasquale pulled Andrea back into the darkness of a shop entrance as a car slowly approached and cruised by. Otherwise, apart from two cars further down the next road there were no other vehicles in sight. Damn,

damn, damn him! They both looked anxiously back, expecting to see a hobbling, angry Stefano bearing down on them, but the street was deathly quiet. And now cold. Pasquale had not realised how cold the night had become and shivered. Or was it released fear, the after-shock of that traumatic escape? Whatever it was, all he wanted to see was a car pull up with Damiano smiling at them.

"Brother, what are we doing standing here? We need to get away as quickly as possible, now." To which Pasquale tried to explain as calmly as he could that his friend was supposed to be there in a car. "But he's not, and we've been here far too long. Please, let us go!"

And at that he realised his precious plan was fast falling apart. "OK, let's go, but try to walk naturally."

"Naturally, at 10 o'clock at night in the centre of Taranto?"

"OK, we must get away without looking guilty. Smile, pretend to laugh, we are having a happy evening walk…"

"…with this bag?"

"Get rid of it then. Smile."

"What? How can I? It has all my precious possessions in…and quite a bit of money."

"Oh Mother of God, if we are robbed now!"

"Pasquale, pull yourself together, think. There are no buses home now, it's too late. And we can hardly go to a hotel, or find a room, as brother and sister. Who would believe us? I have papers but I'll bet you didn't bring yours, did you?"

"I seldom carry my papers. Anyway, it was all going to be so simple…"

"…so we just keep walking, steadily and purposefully. The first bus home I think is 7 am so we'd better find somewhere to shelter and try to keep warm."

As they walked away from the town centre the buildings became slightly more dilapidated and eventually they came across a disused shop with a broken padlock. Although it was filthy inside it took them out of the chill, strong wind that had kicked up and they were glad for small mercies. Sleep was impossible and they sat all night whispering, shivering and worrying as they tried to catch up on all that had befallen Andrea. She could not relate all the wickedness that had transpired, out of sheer embarrassment, but Pasquale built up a sufficient picture to certainly make his anger glow and keep him warm.

Dawn brought some respite, but even more danger. Their escape plan was very limited and Starsi must know that. All he and his henchmen would have to do is turn up at the bus terminus and catch the pair boarding an Avetrana bus. So the siblings grabbed a snack at a roadside bar and avoided the terminus, instead walking out of town along the bus route until they were far enough away to feel safer. They would pick up the bus at any stop along the way.

But surely Stefano would have regained consciousness by now, contacted his boss and they would all go first to the terminus? And then they would have the same thought as Pasquale and then drive along the bus route? Oh Damiano, you wretch! The car plan was so easy, what went wrong? This is frightening.

But the bus came and they saw no-one as they boarded. Andrea dozed instantly but Pasquale's mind was still racing. What if Starsi had cut out the bus plan entirely and had driven straight to their house? He'd be waiting for them to walk straight into his trap. Oh, Mother Mary, he'd obviously not realised all the implications of this rescue. He had just dashed into it without thinking. And it suddenly dawned on him: he could not go home with Andrea. Indeed, it could never be their home any longer, it would never be safe. The whole family is going to have to leave…immediately. What would he tell Mama? Oh Lord, please help!

And what if the reason they had not seen Starsi this morning was because he had actually killed Stefano on the stairs and no-one yet knew Andrea had fled? That makes me a murderer! How could I prove it had been an accident? I had meant it to be an accident, hadn't I? Of course. I never dreamed of killing him. Oh, home… my money, all my money in the kitchen, aah! And my fields, what of my fields? All that effort. And my business? All finished. No more! He started to sob. Andrea awoke as she felt his rhythmic jerking jarring her and she put her hand on his arm to reassure him, thinking he was sobbing out of fear. If only she knew.

And so it was. They got off the bus at Avetrana with trepidation but saw no-one threatening. A shout. Oh no, run. No, it's OK, just a friendly face welcoming Andrea back. Just in case, they took the long way to their house, trying both not to look about suspiciously but also to walk normally, and finally they arrived. Not a soul in sight, perfect.

"Mama, look who's here!" shouted Pasquale excitedly.

"Oh Andrea, my dearest darling Andrea! What are you doing here? A visit? Have they given you some time off? Wonderful, lovely, oh my heart fills with joy. Maria, come here this instant, your sister's home."

"Hello, Mama, how happy I am to see you." All Andrea's emotions which had been volcanically bubbling suddenly burst out in an almighty eruption. She just could not contain them any longer and stood sobbing against her mother's breast.

"Oh my," exclaimed Isabella with a chuckle, "are you this happy to see me, then?" But Andrea would not stop her sobbing. Meanwhile, Pasquale was acting extremely oddly by decamping at the front door and constantly looking one way or the other down the street in a nervous fashion. "This is wonderful, but how long can you stay?"

"Oh, for ever, Mama, please, for ever!" mumbled Andrea.

"Why, what do you mean, child? Are you not happy in Taranto?"

But Pasquale was the one to break the news, seeing the wretched state his sister was now in, "Mama, things have not worked out as well as we might have hoped in Taranto. Last night I had to help Andrea escape. Now we all have to leave, and quickly."

"What do you mean, we must all leave? Where to? Why? This is my home. You cannot just expect me to get up and go. Whatever are you talking about, silly boy?"

"Because if we stay here there may be trouble, well, more like, there *will* be trouble!"

"Trouble? What trouble? Who will give us trouble?"

"Mama, please, just believe us," pleaded Andrea, "pack your precious possessions and let's leave." But Isabella just stood rooted to the spot. She was going nowhere. No-one was going to scare her out of her own house. "Now, Mama!"

"Yes please, Mama, go now, grab what you can. We must leave. Andrea, help little Maria with her bits and pieces."

Isabella finally began to realise they were serious, "oh what have you done, Andrea? And you, Pasquale?"

"Later, Mama, we will explain later, promise. Just go and fill a suitcase, please."

In five minutes they were ready, of a fashion. Pasquale said, "wait round the back, I'll be there in a moment." As they disappeared he ran to the kitchen, pulled out the undisturbed tufa blocks and stuffed all his money in his bag. Quietly he said 'goodbye' to the little old house and locked up.

* * *

21

ORITANIA

1 9 5 0

The ancient, diesel-spewing bus pulled up outside Manfredi Gate. Pasquale and the family dived into the relief of the shade afforded by the attached town wall. It was siesta time and not a creature murmured or moved, except the throaty exhaust of the receding inter-Puglia blue bus. They walked along the 13th century tufa block castle wall and under the stone-arched portal, with its crucifix scene frescoed on the inside crown-piece, and they trudged up to the unimposing small piazza. Even here Oria slept. Not even a mangy stray dog to bark their arrival or a single café to quench their thirst. But fortunately they spotted a municipal water fountain and gulped down the near lukewarm but refreshing water. The Sedile Hall clock chimed, but 1pm not the 3pm it was --- did ever a town clock keep the right time? Behind rose the imposing dome of the Cathedral, ever resplendent in its green and red stained-glass inserts.

Not that way, he thought. Three other narrow cobbled streets ran off from the square. Pasquale chose the opposite direction and soon they were plunged into the long, winding, narrow Via Militia, but even with the sun swooping down from its near-vertical midday-high they could pass, single file, along the edge of the houses and keep shaded. And at least the Sirocco was creating a reasonable draught too, albeit a hot humid draught.

In other ways it was the best time to arrive in a new town: no-one to see the new and homeless family.

On they trudged, slowing commensurately with their heat-tiredness, looking for that all-important sign 'Affittasi'- 'To Rent'. They passed a tiny church built almost into the town wall, a crumbling palazzo trying to remember its former glories, and a simple pizzeria, which of course was 'chiuso' at this time of day. After five minutes the road disgorged out of the ancient 'Centro Storico' through another portal, the Jewish Gate, and into more recent, unappealing streets and houses. So they back-tracked, turned left and soon reached where the tiny street ended in a very small piazza near Vicolo Bainsizza. Exhausted they collapsed onto a set of fairly imposing steps outside the biggest house in the street and rested. Just then an old man came out of the next-door house, spotted them and retreated hastily back in.

"Hostile natives," whispered Pasquale, trying to cheer his tired and despondent family.

"No, on the contrary, dear, look," said Isabella, and the old man reappeared with a bottle of water for them. They thanked him profusely and wished him well.

"Are you lost?" he said, "or just looking for someone?"

"No, not 'someone', signore, somewhere. We seek accommodation to rent. Do you know of any, please?"

"Oh dear, around here? Nothing, as I know of. Even though people keep leaving for the North."

"Sorry to have troubled you then, we'll be on our way," and they wearily arose to return back down the road. The wind was now behind them and with nothing to caress their faces the heat threatened to melt them.

"Wait!" The voice seemed a great distance away, but as they turned they saw it could only have been fifty paces. The old man was hobbling along as fast as he could with a slightly younger man in tow. Breathlessly he explained, "I called on my friend, Signore Bellini, explained your problem and he says he may be able to help, if you want."

"Yes, I live at number 18, right in the corner, and my neighbour in number 12 just died. He gave me a key last year and said if anything happened could I look after the house and contact his son in Torino. Well, I have written now three times to the address he gave me, but with no reply each time. So I wondered, perhaps you could stay there till things get sorted out, yes?"

"Oh thank you, signore, grazie mille. Blessings be upon you. You have saved our lives!" cried Isabella, "yes please!"

They returned and climbed five marble steps, opened the wooden half doors and entered a long, almost tunnel-like, room. Although it was narrow and dark at the far end it did not feel claustrophobic because the high-arched, Puglian stone ceiling lent it splendid grandeur. At the far end, as their eyes adjusted from the bright sunlight, they could now see an Arabic-shaped arch and across it a half-drawn heavy curtain revealed a smaller room, like a bedroom, with its own independent arched ceiling, a ceiling within a ceiling. Its roof only reached halfway up the main room's walls and above it was a mezzanine area reached by a metal ladder cemented vertically into the wall. The mezzanine was fronted by a thin plaster wall which had an opening to climb through.

Maria whooped with joy, scuttled up the ladder and immediately reported back that indeed there were two single beds up there.

To the right they opened a door through to a large kitchen-dining area, with its own stone ceiling, which contained a forno, sink and cold pantry. Another door led them out into a small courtyard. On one side was a bathroom and an outhouse, either for storage or to keep animals in, and on the opposite wall clung a gnarled old grape vine, dripping with readying future fruit. The corner had its own occupant, a lemon tree desperate for radical pruning but still supporting a smattering of fruit.

"That looks like a castle wall, with its castellated top and slits for ancient archers' bows," observed Pasquale.

"Quite right," replied Bellini, "we are built right into the castle's outer wall. Step back to the far side and look up; you can see Oria Castle towering over us."

Obediently they all trooped across, Maria tripping over a stray bucket, and sure enough, between the castle wall and the castle itself only the tops of fruit trees could be seen. "Is that the castle's garden, then?" enquired Pasquale.

"Yes, I believe the narrow lawns were planted in trees about 50 years ago. But don't go getting any ideas, you cannot get into it and even if you did you'd be quickly spotted from any of those rows of windows up there. That's the main banqueting hall, I'm told."

"Have you never been in, then?" Pasquale persisted.

"Heavens no, why would I be invited there?"

"Oh, I don't know, I thought perhaps they might open the castle once a year to the town?"

"How exciting all this is, mama," squealed little Maria.

The old man saw the joy and capitalised on it. "Yes, I know the place is in a bit of a mess but once its cleaned up it will be fun to live right next to a castle, eh, little girl."

"Yes, sir, thank you sir," replied Maria, hastily remembering and retrieving her manners.

"I presume you want to stay now? I will get you some wood for the forno. Try to run the tap and see if the water is OK," said Bellini.

"A tap?" muttered Isabella, "oh what joy, no more trips to the pump!"

"I assume you are from a village, then?" inquired the old man.

"Yes, yes," hurried Pasquale before his mother could speak and land them with more problems. Thinking fast he continued, "we've come from Omanzia. They are building a new road to Taranto and needed to knock down our house for widening. They gave us little money for it or time to evacuate, damn Government!" He had carefully concocted this story coming along in the bus, testing it and re-testing it for loopholes. He thought it sounded plausible and hoped others would. Tonight he would have to teach it to the others so they would be ready when asked the inevitable question.

"So why Oria?" inquired Bellini politely, taking the words from his old friend's breath.

"Um, we heard there were nice shops here and my sister would like to work in one..."

"...why not Taranto, if you want nice shops?" interrupted Bellini, and the Carone family shivered as they felt like they had finally come full circle.

"Too expensive property," Pasquale offered, quickly cutting that subject dead. "And anyway, no work for me there. I like working on the land and am hoping there will be opportunities here now that so many are heading north. Signore Bellini, is there a shop nearby for provisions, please?" Pasquale was pleased that he had managed to change the subject so quickly.

"Yes, sorry, of course. Go straight out of the Jewish Gate and right opposite. Open soon. Oh, I'll get that wood now."

"One more thing, Signore Bellini, why is it called the Jewish Gate?" asked Andrea.

"Porta Ebrei, this was once the Jewish Quarter of the town. It goes right back to the 11th century when some Jews came to live from... well... it's just been created, hasn't it, from Israel."

"Oh really? That long ago."

"Yes, a famous Jewish scribe came with them and I understand the Tel Aviv university is looking in to it. I do know that my old friend here hid two Jewish people up in that mezzanine floor. The curtain pulls right across and it looks like a normal wall behind. There used to be a false trapdoor to get in and out. But I never saw any Germans here as I was away those months they passed through.

"But they bombed this area, didn't they?"

"Ah, now there's a story of faith, if ever there was one. St Barsanofio has now been made our patron saint."

"Really?"

"Yes, we were told to go and light oil drums around the old airstrip south of the town, on the road to Manduria, and St Barsanofio laid his cloak over the town and draped it in darkness. When the German bombers came at night they mistook the airstrip for the town and we were all saved. Praise God!" He crossed himself, felt pleased with his economical explanation of a complex miracle and quietly excused himself. His old friend dutifully followed, muttering, "I have plenty of olive oil should you need it, signora".

"Many thanks, signore."

The two men finally left and in their turn left the Carones to finally look around as well. The house was better than their abode in Avatrana, that's for sure, and it was already furnished too. Comfortably, not elegantly, even down to crockery and cutlery. Although they muttered to each other about using dead people's sheets, beds and the like, they realised also just how well they had fallen on their feet. "God is to be praised for his goodness and mercy," cried Mama, and they all nodded solemnly.

"And he did not even mention rent, did he," chipped in Pasquale, ever the practical businessman, although still so young.

"But do we have enough to live on?" asked Mama. "This is a much bigger and more important town and will cost more to live in."

Please do not worry, Mama, my fields will keep us alive for a long time…"

"…oh yes, how, by some magical distance control? We are here, the fields are there. Or do you intend to commute daily to your fields and after factoring in the travel time have only half an hour a day left to tend them?" she laughed, although it was not a funny matter to her, it was a question of life and death, that eternal struggle to obtain sufficient sustenance to survive, or die.

"Don't be silly! I have made a lot of money from those fields and…"

"…and where is it, pray? In your socks?" laughed Mama, relaxing.

"Never mind that, it is safe, and…"

"...and I managed to save quite a lot in Taranto, dear Mama," added Andrea, who then promptly shuddered and had to sit down. Since her flight there had been absolutely no time to reflect on the experience and this was indeed the first chance she had received to remember those awful ordeals she was forced to endure.

"Oh, you must tell me all about it, dear, but not now, all in good time."

Yes, thought Andrea, it would need a good long time before I tell anyone what I was forced to do.

"Agreed," retorted Pasquale, trying to inject a modicum of cheer into the proceedings. "Now, to the shop, then food. Tonight we'll sleep where we can and tomorrow we wash bedding and clean up the house. It's going to be fine here, I can feel it, really fine!"

And so it was ...for half a year. The Carones kept themselves to themselves, made little noise or fuss, spoke politely when spoken to, contributed an economy of factual information when asked, and stuck to their prearranged script if pressed. But in general people were content to live and let live. The War had upturned society, dumping some haves back to the bottom of the pile and escalating some have-nots to the higher eschelons of society. It was a funny old time indeed and people did not want to open too many skeleton cupboards unless absolutely necessary.

Not that there was a lack of speculation about the Carones around the Jewish-Quarter-which-housed-no-Jews, especially when they were frequently heard and occasionally seen clearing up the appallingly filthy courtyard at the back of their house. The ancient tin lean-to's corrugated roof had so rusted it had collapsed, the grape vine had run riot through lack of husbandry, the east wall was crumbling and the outhouse stank from the presumed animals that had once been corralled there. The soil had overspilled from the narrow border and had been washed by the rain into the cracked and jagged tiles on the floor, while the overflow drain had become so permanently blocked that every time it rained the water banked up until it overflowed as a muddy, stinking sheet flood into the kitchen. So Pasquale and his family band of helpers stripped everything out, pruned the vine, patched the wall, unblocked the drain and gave the whole courtyard a fresh lick of whitewash. Signoree Bellini was understandably ecstatic, of course, and could not sing their praises too highly all around the neighbourhood.

The family then turned their attention to sprucing up the interior. Waiting for warm, sunny October days they washed or aired fabrics, mopped floors, scrubbed walls, cleansed the kitchen and removed dirty, unwanted pieces of furniture. Signoree Bellini was again understandably ecstatic, of course. Rent had still not been discussed and when he saw the gleaming spotless rooms he had no heart to ask more than a few hundred lira a week. Everyone by now was understandably ecstatic, obviously.

Andrea was now a most poised and beautiful young lady, despite her 'Taranto Tragedy', as she began to call it. She had outlined the events to Isabella but had wisely, in her own opinion at least, omitted the worst parts. She felt it would benefit no-one to know the real horrors that had overtaken her, so why even bother to mention them. Pasquale knew; that was enough. But she'd had to give some idea otherwise Mama would have wondered why indeed she had had to be whisked away in the dead of night and then disrupt their whole lives like this. In her turn Isabella had listened to Andrea's abridged Taranto Tragedy with remarkable patience and she had let Andrea pour it all out uninterrupted. At the end Mama had wrung her hands and started to rock in her chair as she let out a deafening wail. Eventually, when she had calmed down, they discovered that Mama had blamed herself for the Tragedy, not Andrea. It was Mama's stupidity, naivety and greed that had caused her to so readily jump at Sarsi's offer. She should have known better, she railed, and she should have realised from the start that nothing comes easy in this life unless it is evil. But the offer had sounded so grand.

"And it was, Mama, for a while," agreed Andrea, "it was a wonderful new life for me and I felt very privileged and needed…"

"…yes, that's how they wanted you to feel, the bastardos," interrupted Pasquale.

"Language, boy!" shouted Mama.

"Sorry. But they were bastardos…and still are. Who knows, they could be just round the corner, now, this minute, looking for us. Do you think they'd just let us go, having all that knowledge of what was going on above that shop?"

"But what if the chief of police's wife was in the audience?" laughed Andrea, attempting to lighten the tone in the house. "I know the mayor's was, at least."

"Look, seriously, they will try to find us, that's for sure, and we must continue to be very cautious in action and economical in chat, OK?" commanded Pasquale, beginning to feel the overly-burdening pressures of being the only male left in the household. He too knew first hand that nothing comes easy in life unless it is evil. Oh, how he missed his fields, his tomatoes and his beans, and he wondered nightly, as he lay on his bed, about all the possibilities that could have befallen them. The permutations made him so sad he had to stop before he wept silent buckets. He was in Oria now, a totally different kettle of fish, and he needed to adapt quickly to town life and emerging adulthood. His one relief was that he had escaped, temporarily or permanently he knew not, the clutches of the SCU gang. But he wondered if they too were now looking for him because he had disappeared and left a sizeable hole in their ranks, as well as holding intimate knowledge of their modus operandi.

In turn, Andrea felt she carried the full guilt of all the family's misfortune and so she felt she must endeavour to put it right immediately.

❋ ❋ ❋

22
FOUND OUT

Andrea had faced no problem at all in securing employment in Bar Sedile in Piazza Manfredi, what with her looks and her new-found confidence in dealing with customers, especially customers who had far out-ranked these ruffians from a public drinking establishment. And soon her fame began to spread - the "dark beauty of Manfredi" they called her. At the weekend men and boys alike would find any transport available to reach Oria, just to catch a glimpse of her curly black hair reaching down to her waist. Alberto, the owner, merely rubbed his hands with glee as his takings soared by the week. He could even start floating offers similar to modern "happy hours" – '3 Peroni for the price of 2 before 9pm' and so on. Andrea had to start wearing a concealed type of money belt to collect all the tips every weekend and Alberto had to personally escort her out the back door and half way up Via Militia before regretfully parting company. But fortunately by closing time most of the men were so intoxicated they could think of little more than how to put one foot in front of the other, rather than advancing any amorous thoughts of trailing after the fast-walking Andrea.

This was exactly what the Carones did not want, of course. The money, yes, but the publicity, no. More than once a hot-blooded young man had tempered his alcohol intake enough to become wise to the backdoor escape routine. Andrea, therefore, needed to lead him on a circuitous route through the narrow, cobbled, rabbit warren of streets in order to give him the slip, which she usually managed, before reaching Porta Ebrei and home. If all else failed it was fortunate that their house was right in a corner, and from the synagogue house at the entrance to the tiny piazza their door could hardly be seen. Likewise, the front wall of number 8 jutted out somewhat and afforded further concealment in the dimly-lit street as she stood pressed hard against the warm whitewashed wall. And the punters thought she always wore white to appear pure and innocent, she joked to herself. If only they knew a thing or two about night camouflage and walls!

But it was obvious it would only be a matter of time before she met a real problem alone in the dark, so with regret she had to give her notice and leave the bar. The customers were devastated, Alberto mortified. He had overstretched his budget, buying in extra crates of beer for the predicted continued onrush of custom, but now they no longer came he found himself caught in a financial bind, to put it mildly. Even improved promotions and offers did not clear the backlog, but he was eventually saved by discovering Andrea's new place of employment and selling on his stock to the next bar owner, to whom he wished better luck in hanging on to the now "Dark beauty of Lama".

Andrea had approached Bar Caro in Piazza Lama, Oria's second square, and her fame had preceded her. So Deni, the owner, jumped at the money-spinning opportunity, even doubling her previous wages at a stroke, no argument, and giving her two evenings off per fortnight. This was an admirable arrangement for Andrea, especially as Lama was much closer to her house and a less formidable walk up over Cathedral Hill. But it was little more than a few days before word had spread, the boys started arriving in droves and the whole cycle began all over again.

Meanwhile, Pasquale looked for casual farm work, but as winter approached there was less and less available once the grapes had been picked, the vines tended and pruned and the intervening soil weeded and hoed. By Natale he found himself sitting at home all day vegetating. It was so unlike him: he was an active person with an active brain. Although deep down he knew he should not have run with the SCU he had to admit it was a thrill and it had certainly got his adrenalin flowing. And anyway, how many young men had not given in to a "naughty lad phase"? His fields had also exercised both his mind and his body and he really did miss them, and of course the money. He missed Cosimo too, in an odd sort of a way. Perhaps because Cosimo had been the only real father figure he had remembered, because his real father had coldly and wickedly left him at seven. He needed to get his teeth into something; this domestic sojourn was really disturbing his mind. It gave him too much time to reflect on past events. Had he killed Stefano or not? Why did the wretched Damiano never turn up with the car? Was Starsi still looking for them? And the SCU? He squirmed, ill at ease. Would he ever discover the truth? Would his family ever be able to live without constantly looking over their shoulders? It was affecting them all, except little Maria of course, and on some days nerves were taut and tension became frayed. It hadn't helped that for obvious reasons they had not been able to get too friendly with the neighbours. The latter, in turn, had extended the hands of both friendship and kindness, but once bitten the hands thought twice about re-extending themselves. So the Carones bungled on, living a kind of lie in a vacuum of perpetual fear.

And then it happened. One Saturday night in Bar Caro. A group of men had been drinking all evening, becoming more and more raucous as the hours ticked away. They kept shooting leering glances at Andrea and mumbling obscene comments, followed by knowing laughter. Finally they became so drunk the owner and the barman had to hustle them out into the street, but as they struggled to get up from their table one hastily tried to fold some pages of a magazine together. In his haste and stupor he did not realise he had dropped one and Andrea saw it first as she was clearing the table and sweeping up off the floor all the crumbs of small taralli biscuits they had eaten with their Primitivo wine. She put the sheet on her tray of glasses and was carrying it back to the bar, but looking down she suddenly understood what all the obscenity had been about---the page contained a photo of a woman, near naked, lying on a bed, draped delicately with a silk sheet. The face was not totally distinct, partly hidden by long hair, but as she looked closer she realised there was no doubt at all...it was her! She almost dropped the tray of glasses in her shock and horror, but she had enough courage to make it safely to the bar. She quickly put down the tray, carefully folded the page into four and forced it into her tip belt and carried on without batting an eyelid. Fortunately the barman was still in the street dealing with the drunks and Andrea had carefully positioned her body between the bar and the rest of the customers, so no-one saw her sleight of hand with the paper.

Moments later the owner and barman returned and she asked for a break, feigning a dizzy spell in the heat and smoke, and rushed to the rear of the property. A quick look back, remembering her coat, and she was out into the street behind, running like the wind, running free. No drunks waiting for her, it was too early, so no need for the circuitous route; she ran straight home, so fast that the wind almost washed away the tears brimming over her eyelids.

"You're early, dear, are you OK?" asked Mama.

"Not feeling well, Mama, they let me come home. I think I'll go to bed now."

"Sure it's nothing serious?"

"No, it's OK Mama, probably the Curse".

"OK, so wrap up warm then. Go, I'll bring you a hot drink in a minute."

"Oh thank you so much, Mama," smiled Andrea falsely. It was so hard to be calm, yet she needed to be calm, especially now.

But Andrea could only lie on her bed and quake with fear and embarrassment. How can I live this down, she thought. I must leave Oria, I cannot be seen here again. Oh Lord, that is why I was so popular. Ugh! She shivered and wept. But where can I go? Every man in Puglia will have seen me. Naked and taunting, like some devilish siren. I may as well kill myself. And she sobbed on.

Maria slept through the wailing, it would take an earthquake to wake her, but Pasquale had come home and heard her. "Mama, why is Andrea home so early, and crying so?"

"Something happened at the bar? She won't say. Tells me it's the Curse. Never is, that visited her only 2 weeks ago, hah!"

Pasquale crept into her room and gently sat beside her, "dear sis, what ails you? You can tell me."

"No I can't!"

"You can, you know you can. You told me all about the Taranto Tragedy, what could be worse?"

"Oh brother, there could be worse, believe me!"

"Surely not? That was awful, a never-to-be-repeated nightmare."

"Well, it is repeating, and a far worse nightmare it is too."

"So please share it with me, sis, and the nightmare will be halved."

She lay and thought about it and Pasquale kept as quiet and as still as possible, for he knew she was calming down and weighing up the situation. Please don't come in now, Mama, thought Pasquale, please. She didn't and Andrea realised that she did indeed need to share the pain and humiliation, and her brother was the only one she felt she could share it with. So she poured out the whole catalogue of events of that evening, but embarrassingly refused to let him see the folded photo.

"Oh you poor, poor thing," purred Pasquale in his best commiseratory voice. He was no expert at this but Andrea didn't mind, it just felt better telling someone. "Although it is not essential I see the photo, sis, it might help me realise the gravity of the situation, you know."

"Surely not?"

"Well, half of the male population of Puglia has probably seen you with nothing on, yet I haven't." But immediately he said it he realised what a fool he was, and quickly added, "I'm sorry, sis, that was stupid, please ignore it, of course I don't need to see the photo, you're my sister, how terrible of me."

"OK."

"But we need to dry our eyes quickly and start thinking of the reality of this situation. It is grave, you know, sis, very grave."

"Don't you think I don't know that, stupid!" shouted Andrea angrily. "Surely you know I have a brain as good as yours, if not better. After all, I am older than you!"

"Oh sis, sorry, sorry. I am so sorry, I never meant to insinuate that, or anything else. I'm just trying to stay calm here and consider the implications of all this."

"Implicate on, then!" And they both were forced to laugh.

"Well, it is possible word may travel back through to Starsi. Certainly Damiano will get to know about it. You say it's been going on for weeks without you realising it? They may already know then. So they will certainly be on their way here, well, at least Starsi will. He cannot risk any scandal blowing wide open. Men look at these magazines all the time but seldom does it ever come to light who takes the photos or where. I'll bet the police would desperately like to know. After all, we are a strict Catholic country and I have no doubt such magazines are hardly legal. Starsi knows you know, and to get your revenge he might think you may swallow your humiliation by going to the police to report..."

"...what an excellent idea, brother, let's do that..."

"...all in good time. One thing at a time, eh? He will certainly try to find you and silence you..."

"...silence me? How do you mean? Surely you aren't thinking of a permanent silencing, are you? Heavens, let's get out of here, now!"

"Yes, that's the problem. He will know you are working in Oria if the reports come from Oria and it wouldn't take a day to find us in this small town. People talk. And people will talk plenty for a bit of cash."

"But he doesn't have a photo of me, well not one he can show people for identification," she laughed, "and no-one knows either our real names or where we came from."

"Yes," said Pasquale, "I'm really glad we decided to use false names with Signore Bellini and keep ourselves to ourselves with the neighbours. But they could link the magazine picture to you here, maybe."

"Surely if we stay in this house and don't go out, except for supplies, we could be safe, agreed?"

"Certainly that would be easier to explain to Mama than asking her to run away to another town, yet again. The truth of all this would probably kill her anyway. She has already had to cut all ties with her relatives and friends and that is obviously distressing her as it is, even though she never mentions it," Pasquale offered.

"That's awful, isn't it? Not being able to even tell your relatives where you are living…"

"…and they maybe thinking that we've died or something, our disappearance being as sudden as it was."

"I wonder what poor Cosimo is making of all this?"

"Hm, there's another story," retorted Pasquale.

"I did like Uncle Cosimo, you know. He was so kind to us as well."

So we just tell Mama you're staying home because you got tired of the advances of all those drunken men and you were sometimes scared walking home. And you basically need a rest from all the late nights. OK?"

"OK."

* * *

23

WEATHERING THE STORM

1 9 5 0

"Do we have enough for bread today, Pasquale?" asked Mama.

"Enough? Enough? What talk is this Mama? Are you going patso – mad - woman? Of course we have money for bread; we have enough money to buy the bakery, probably!" he laughed.

"OK, OK, boy, I may be a crazy head but I have enough brain to keep this family going, so there!"

"Yes, alright, Mama, I give in, sorry."

"And I'll tell you more, it's no fun skulking around out there, head covered in a shawl and stinking hot, carrying heavy groceries and looking out for Starsi and his crew popping up from behind a wall!"

"But it's the same for me, you know, when I go to fetch the wood. And for Andrea when she takes some evening air with Maria. Especially Andrea. Oh Mama, she does look si3ly dressed as a boy!"

"Don't blame me, it was her idea not mine. I think it works pretty well, actually, don't you?"

"Yes, it seems to, but did she really have to cut off some of her gorgeous hair?"

"Hair grows, she's not in the market for a husband yet. No problem," laughed Mama.

"She did say the police scrutinised her rather closely last week from a distance. Lucky we do not have to carry papers around with us everywhere anymore and they did not press the matter."

"They would certainly have been in for a big surprise!"

"Pasquale, how much longer do you think we have to go on with this pretence?" asked Isabella, reverting to a serious manner.

"I don't think much longer. It's been 4 weeks, near enough. The excitement should soon die down, I think, especially as Andrea is no longer present to fuel the desire. Men are generally pathetic and if another pretty barmaid appears they'll soon forget Andrea." Of course, what he meant to say, but couldn't, was that every pornographic magazine had lots of pretty girls in, each month or even each week, and pretty girls come and go, especially if the publication was illegal, or it was restricted to many Puglian men by price. It would all blow over soon enough.

"And I'm never really sure who we are hiding from ---Starsi or the men in town?" commented Mama for the umpteenth time.

Now this is where Pasquale had nearly floundered umpteen times before too. Mama'a argument was sound: why should they be hiding so much from someone like Starsi? According to Mama, Andrea's only misdemeanour was to disappear overnight without giving any notice. Although not ideal public relations or work practice, it was also not exactly a crime worth seeking out and punishing. The whole charade became increasingly absurd as the weeks followed until Pasquale, with Andrea's agreement, was forced to offer a slightly juicier morsel of information alluding to possible irregularities in the shop's accounts which had been attributed to her. As Pasquale explained, it was actually Senora Fano who was massaging the accounts and creaming off a nice little extra salary, but when Starsi had finally spotted the errors Fano had cleverly deflected the blame to Andrea to protect herself. Andrea had tried to plead her innocence but Fano was extremely cunning and the poor naïve girl had little chance. So Starsi had threatened to call in the police and hence Andrea's flight. Although running confirmed her guilt it was still better than staying and trying to prove her innocence in a courtroom with the odds loaded against her. "She wouldn't have stood a chance, Mama, quite honestly," Pasquale ended his story triumphantly. Mama was not exactly delighted to hear the real truth of Andrea's flight but at least it made her feel better understanding the reasons for it. Andrea and Pasquale felt rather good too that they had managed to concoct such a convincing tale and keep Mama 'happy'.

So the days passed and the Carones began to breathe easier. They were winning this latest battle in their life. One hiccup after another was overcome with careful planning, but when little Maria fell ill one evening there was panic. Pasquale had to go out looking for a doctor, the one two doors down being absolutely mad and unsafe to practice, in their humble opinion, and not only because he kept 22 barking, stinking dogs in his parlour, as the gossip went. Indeed, the mad doctor was the only neighbour they did not trust. They had already had one or two minor spats with him over these constantly yapping dogs and their anal deposits in the street. Whether it was siesta time or night time they would bark at the most minor of instigations; that high-pitched but air-piercing yapping that only small dogs can successfully manufacture. Regarding the droppings, the less said the better, of course. But under cover of darkness Pasquale managed to get Maria to another doctor, and fortunately medicine, and a further tricky trip to a chemists was not required

What Pasquale could not tell the family was that he was actually more concerned about Damiano than Starsi. He would have been less than pleased that Pasquale had just upped and left, and of course there was the gang law that 'once an SCU member, always an SCU member'. There was no leaving such an organisation. Pasquale would have to be located and 'checked', at the minimum, to ensure that he was not divulging any gang secret, and at the maximum to re-enrol him in that local SCU group. Discovering the whereabouts of Pasquale was compulsory; it was like having a permanent shadow all your life. In fact, Pasquale was most surprised and even more concerned that he had not been located yet. The SCU would have branches in most towns and such a spider-webbed organisation would find no difficulty in passing on the necessary information and visual description to locate him quickly and easily. He could only presume therefore that they had in fact already located him and were merely keeping a watching brief. Perhaps they were surprised about his change from living a fairly normal life in Oria to this hermit's recluse, and that was maybe why they had not yet exposed themselves to him. They were watching, wondering and waiting, basically, he assumed.

The days passed, the weeks slipped away and soon it was New Year's Eve 1950, celebrations for a half century and reaching it safely after two world wars. What a night it was! And what a year it had been for Andrea and the Carone family.

There were street parties, the dancing of Pizzica, the local boy-girl love dance based on Puglia's Greek heredity, and fireworks at midnight. The Carones finally let loose and enjoyed themselves. Not only had the milestone of half a century passed but also the Carones' own milestone of fear too. They breathed easy again. Time washes away and evens out everything, like the rushing backwash of foaming sea on a sandy beach.

In the new year Andrea found a very nice job in a smart ladies' outfitters and she slid straight back into her past role as if she had never been away for over a year. By 1952 she had been promoted twice to Manageress, a great honour indeed. At 25 she was reaching her second peak of beauty, the most beautiful one many argue. She had found she had many admirers, the photograph business was never ever again mentioned by anyone, and she'd even walked out with a few young men around Piazza Lorch, the small, attractive square next to Piazza Manfredi outside the town walls, following an outer concentric circle to avoid the younger giggling couples circumnavigating a narrower inside walking circle. Apart from this promenading positioning she also had one other main difference - she did not need to be tailed by a chaperone. She was considered "safe" enough at her age not to have an elderly grandma in tow, puffing and snorting to keep up with the deliberately speeding couple, anxious to shake her off their tail for at least one snatched kiss behind a statue or a bush.

However the ever-fresh memories of her Taranto Tragedy were enough to cause Andrea to flinch or even recoil from gentlemen when they tried to launch the physical aspects of their relationship, and she soon began to get a new whispered reputation as a cold fish - Signorina Frigido of Oria. When she eventually discovered this she seemed not to care and merely smiled to herself. All will be well, God knows, she thought, I will one day find a sensitive and caring man who will understand.

But unfortunately for Andrea the wrong man found her.

Pasquale, in contrast, had not been so fortunate. Decent work was very hard to find for someone without schooling and qualifications, and after a succession of farm work and casual jobs he realised he had little option but to return to old skills if he were not to be forced to move 'up North'.

Poor Maria was in a similar boat. Already 15 she had never been to a school or had proper schooling at home, and she had spent the whole of her short life helping Mama at home. She now started longing for some independence but in the still-fiercely masochistic society of south Italy she had little chance. The doctor next door had offered her work cleaning but Mama this time said a definite 'no': she had learned her lesson. At least Signore Starsi had *appeared* a proper gentleman though. Andrea had kindly passed on to Maria all she knew about needlework on those long winter nights in Oria and it was now Maria who was starting to take in small commissioned projects from around the Jewish Quarter. She soon gained a reputation for neat work, finished punctually and at a very fair price.

So slowly but surely, by sound neighbourliness, the Carones were beginning to become accepted in Vicolo Bainsizza. More than a year before, Signore Bellini had knocked on their door oh so politely, as he always did, to announce the news that his letters to the new owner of their house were still being shunned. "No news is always good news, then, Signore Bellini," laughed Isabella as she poured him a measure of strong Primitivo her neighbour had just made from his tiny vineyard out in the countryside. "Be careful with this one, it will take you head off!" she joked again. It was so good to see her happy again, thought Bellini.

When she asked him what would happen next, therefore, he threw up his hands in that wonderful Puglian gesture and replied "boo". No-one had a clue where "boo" had come from, like so many street-talk words, but it had now become firmly Oritanian for "don't have a clue". Eventually he even stopped asking them for rent for the simple reason that he had no idea what to do with the money or where to send it! As far as he was concerned they could stay there for as long as they liked. He had managed to discover that the old people who had died in it had left no will. With no traceable relative, and he would testify that he had tried his best over these years to communicate with the family up North, in Italian law the Carones could lay claim to the property after 5 years possession. Bellini was so happy with their tenancy and husbandry of the house that he was also willing, when the time came, to write them a properly signed and witnessed statement as to the date they had arrived.

Consequently the Carones were overjoyed at this news: they might finally actually own property at long last. Isabella had never owned a house and she danced about like a singing schoolgirl all day long. Until Pasquale reminded her and the others of one important snag which they had overlooked in their joy. If Signore Bellini were to write the letter he would have to know one truthful fact, surely? He could not state that in 1949 the house had become occupied by the Fantini family, could he?

After the initial shock and understandable concern, they deliberated for days over how best to solve this problem. But in essence the problem was easily solved in only one way - they would have to come clean and tell the truth; there was no other way. So next they planned all kinds of ways to broach Bellini about it, but when they finally got him into the house, sat him down in the most comfortable chair and started to ply him with their best homemade amoretto biscuits and limoncello he dumfounded them all by calmly saying "it's not a problem, it doesn't bother me!"

Isabella was stunned, "but we have lied to you all these years, Signore."

"People lie every day. There was a war, we all lied and did things we were not proud of. I don't care where you came from and what your real name is, all I know is what I see in front of me, and how you have looked after this house so beautifully these past years. I didn't ask for this task of looking after the property; it was just a promise I made to the old couple when they were still alive. I certainly did not expect all this unnecessary stress in my life. Who cares! Come, another limoncello would be priceless, you are an expert distiller Isabella!"

Although becoming somewhat merry from the alcohol they did decide on two things - that he should keep all the rental money he had carefully put away, as a reward for all his efforts, and they would continue to be known as the Fantini family in the neighbourhood, but when it came to signing official documents later they should use their own names, for after all no officials knew them personally anyway and it was no-one else's business what they were really called. They drank to that! Even Maria took a drop and promptly set about giggling, much to everyone's joy and amusement.

As they laughed and drank some more lemon liquor there was a knock on the front door. They looked one to another in a concerned manner: few people visited them or knocked their door. It was Pasquale first to break the silence, "it didn't sound like an authoritarian kind of knock, you know, like the police; it was more of a hesitant, am-I-sure-the-person-lives-here knock."

It came again, even less certain this time. "Pasquale, you must answer it, you're the man of the house. Go on," whispered Mama.

"OK, are you ready then everyone?"

"Of course we are, silly, do you think we're off to do the washing out the back?"

Signore Bellini sat totally nonplussed by all this secrecy and vacillation and watched with mouth ajar and head spinning from the liquor.

"Pasquale!"

"Oh, what are you doing here?" replied Pasquale in total shock.

"Your Mama wrote and invited me to come anytime. I'm sorry, I've been so busy, but I am here now. Greetings from Avetrana! Pasquale continued to stand across the doorway with mouth open and hands on hips. "May I come in or not? It's very hot out here, you know."

Suddenly Pasquale pulled himself together, "oh, sorry Cosimo, so sorry. Yes, do come in. We're very pleased to see you. Look everyone, look who it is!"

* * *

24
REUNION

"Hello Isabella."

"Oh Cosimo, it *is* you. Er... welcome," replied Mama, somewhat embarrassed to say the least. This out-of-the-blue visit had certainly stirred her emotional cocktail on the spot. Alone it might have tasted delicious, but with present mixed company it was more likely to turn sour.

"Hello Cosimo," exclaimed all the children, more surprised than any to see him, while Signore Bellini rose stiffly to his feet, bowed graciously and muttered, "very pleased to make your acquaintance, signore." Did Mama sense a little hostility maybe, some frisson of anger between them?

"Sorry, Signore Bellini, this is my ex-h...er...*my* very good friend Cosimo from...er...where we used to live." She suddenly realised how difficult it was to hide the past, especially if one was momentarily caught off guard. And at the mention of 'very good friend' did she detect a hint of perhaps jealousy, or even envy, in Signore Bellini? Whatever it was she smiled inwardly and assuredly, as if she had been paid a compliment, despite her advancing years.

"I am very pleased to meet you, Cosimo," said Bellini magnanimously.

"And I too, signore."

"So, you know these wonderful people well?"

"Wonderful? What *have* they been doing?" he laughed. "Seriously, yes, I have known them for, er, 20 years or more, I believe. Good honest folk too, signore."

"Oh indeed. Yes, they have been wonderful here in Bainsizza, helping me and everybody. We are good friends indeed."

"Good, now we have that sorted out, let's ask Cosimo how the old town is," proffered Pasquale.

"Much the same as ever, afraid to say. No great scandals and no major calamities; life just going on as normal." Cosimo had sensed there was an air of caution in the wind and wasn't sure of the status of Bellini, so he kept his comments as vague as possible. Throughout his tiny speech he noticed Isabella was smiling at him - a good sign? But Bellini was still giving him the secret police look - could it be jealousy? Had he interrupted something between them? He desperately hoped not because he had come a long way to say something very short. "And you, you all, are you well? Happy? How is Oria?"

"Yes, fine, we are happy here," responded Andrea and Maria. "We have got jobs now and enjoy life here, thank you."

"Isabella, I have much to tell you, the neighbours and the like, but I fear this is not the best time. Perhaps I should take my leave?"

"Oh no, dear Cosimo, you have come so far..."

"...Cosimo is right. He has come a long way and has much gossip, I am sure. It is I who should take his leave, what am I thinking?" He got up and continued, "many, many thanks for your hospitality, Isabella, and you all. I shall act on what we have agreed. Ciao!"

"No, Signore Bellini, please do not go on my account," pleaded Cosimo, not so falsely that it would be noticed, for he was exceedingly happy at this turn of events.

"No, it is not a problem. I have things to do too. Ciao and grazie."

Pasquale and the girls decided to leave too, at the winking eye of their brother, and soon Isabella and Cosimo were alone at last.

"Izzie, do you realise it is nearly five years, five whole years, since you accompanied me to that dance in Brindisi?"

"Oh Cosimo, is it really? Where have the years gone?"

"More to the point, where did you all go? You upped and left Avetrana without a word, like ghosts in the night, and couldn't even tell me. That hurt."

"I'm so sorry, dear, yes we did leave rather quickly. We had rescued Andrea from Taranto and were in fear of our lives, as I remember it..."

"...yes, but you could have let me know sooner."

"We did discuss it but thought it would be best for you if we did not tell you we were leaving and then later not write to you. We were scared out of our minds, Cosimo, it was no joke! And we thought they might come enquiring and eventually get to you."

"Hmm, I can see your logic. But why so long before you wrote?"

"As I just said, we thought if you were the person who knew us best you would be the one they would concentrate on in trying to elicit where we had gone, even check things like your letters. And we did not want to drag you into it as well. They were dangerous men. Who knows what harm they may have done you to get information."

"Hmm, true, true. But I've missed you so much, Izzie," squeezing her hand.

"I've missed you too, dearest,' putting her head on his shoulder. And then they embraced and Isabella felt tears welling up.

There was a knock at the door.

"Oh dear, what a time to call," muttered Isabella as she extracted herself and got up.

"Hello, dear," chirped Astella from three doors away, "sorry to bother you but we've run out of olive oil, do you have any, please?"

"Of course. Do come in." As soon as she had said it she realised her mistake. It had been a reflex reaction and she had forgotten protocol. "Look, Cosimo, this is our neighbour Astella. Astella, Cosimo, a long time friend of the family."

"A pleasure to meet you, signora, I am just visiting from Avetrana."

"Oh, is that where you Carone's are from then, Isabella?" asked Astella innocently… or not.

"No, not from that way. Cosimo knows some of our distant relatives who live that way, don't you Cosimo!" Isabella demanded, for emphasis.

"Yes, true," picking up quickly on the alibi, "they asked me if I was passing to deliver some things here."

Isabella had hurriedly fetched as much oil as she could spare in an old wine bottle just to get rid of the nosy neighbour. She thought to herself, that is not fair, all neighbours are nosy, and she smiled wryly. "Here you are, should be enough to last you a while!"

Cosimo was no fool and realised that in translation that meant 'don't come back in a hurry, eh!' He too smiled wryly.

But any magic there had been was now broken and, anyway, domestic duties called as well, so he spent the next hour happily helping Isabella prepare the evening meal. The returning Pasquale, Maria and Andrea were happy to see Cosimo still there, and even happier when they all agreed he should stay the night instead of paying unnecessarily for a hotel. Cosimo reckoned that even sleeping rough on the floor was better than a hotel bed if it meant he could stay with this lovely family who he had so taken to over the years. He was overjoyed to see how happy they were and very pleased to learn that Pasquale, amongst other things, was now managing to feed Bainsizza once a week with whatever was in season – free lemons, oranges, beans, cave, figs, grapes, nectarines and occasionally melons, but that was infrequent as they were so heavy to loot and carry.

Indeed, Pasquale had slowly become the saviour of the square and was quietly nicknamed 'the farmer'. Such name was only whispered discretely, and then only out of earshot of the polizia and other administrative meddlers, and he happily allowed his fame to flourish. The neighbours never knew which day of the week it would be but if they heard a discrete knock at the door around 7pm and saw Maria standing there with a bag, they knew. A nod and a simple smile were the passports. On the neighbours' part, an outsider would have considered it rather odd, or extremely neighbourly, that the Carones never went short of firewood or olive oil or flour or wine. Exponents of a cash-free society could have done worse than to visit Piazza Bainsizza!

❋ ❋ ❋

25

CHEATED

1 9 5 2

"I trust you will reward me in the usual manner, Mario", grunted Pasquale, "after all, it did take me all of two days to find these coins."

Mario Gennari's eyes gave nothing away, they hadn't for many years, nor did the smile fixed permanently on his face. He was leaning back on his rickety chair, feet parked on his desk, stroking his finely-penciled chin, in his small, cramped, backstreet office. Beads of sweat were beginning to break out on Pasquale's forehead. Were they because he was not sitting directly under the ailing old ceiling fan, or was it because he sensed something? If it were the latter then it would be a subconscious reaction, most likely. Certainly he had never found coins like this before, unlike the earlier set he had dug up in the heat of the day at the edge of the field. These were from the adjoining field, starting to run up a gentle slope on the hill – a much more likely place to discover such a hoard because the richer folk would have lived there with the view and the breeze. Their pressing was unlike anything he had ever seen. But was he the expert in Romano-Greek archaeology or numismatology? Certainly not. Mario had been a dealer for 20 years. Mario would know. Yet Mario was certainly giving nothing away beyond that grinning façade.

"Pasquale, right? My dear, dear Pasquale, much as I would love to help you it is not easy now. You know, the antiquities division of our dearly-beloved government has recently appointed many more inspectors, spies I call them, to watch our every move. I suspect it was a political move just to create more employment, hence a lot of them,

I hear, are very lazy and do little in their job. But not so here in Taranto, I'm afraid…"

"We have one here then?"

"…and I am sure you know that for the past few years since the War there have actually been fewer rich coin collectors, well any collectors for that matter, and less interest and certainly less money to invest. The old collectors either had their beautiful possessions stolen by the retreating German generals or by the advancing American and British generals, ha!"

"…you mean…?"

Mario continued, immune to any interruption, "…or they just don't have the money to invest in fine arts when huge profits are being made in reorganising and developing our beloved country's economy. I deal less in this stuff now and we have had to diversify…cigarettes, silk stockings, booze. And my costs have risen dramatically too, trying to avoid the new laws and these wretched inspectors".

"This is terrible…"

"…yes, terrible, these wretched inspectors," Mario re-emphasised, at a much higher pitch and volume.

"So you cannot take them at all, Mario, is that what you are trying to tell me?" pleaded Pasquale. "Look, I have toiled so hard to find these, and they are very unusual…"

"…hmm, I must agree, they are different. For you, let me look again. Give them here."

Pasquale gently laid out the twenty-one oval black and red coins on the velvet cloth. Why do they always use velvet? He thought, oddly.

"Mm, a lot of cleaning needed, eh? But quite a strong imprint still. Look, I'll tell you what, I can probably manage something as I might be able to find a buyer."

Pasquale perked up at once when Mario said, "Let me give you 20,000 lira, it's all I can manage".

"Oh, that's fantastic, yes, certainly."

Mario peeled four 5000 lira notes off a stack and handed them over.

"20,000?" asked Pasquale.

"Yes, 20,000, as agreed."

"But you meant 20,000 per coin, right? This is for one coin, right? Do you not want all twenty-one then?"

"Yes, of course I'll take all twenty-one. That's it, 20,000 lira *is* for all the coins."

"What?" screamed Pasquale, "all of them?"

"Yes," said Mario, becoming impatient.

"But that's impossible. The man in the bar down the road said they were worth 20,000 each, at least, and…"

"…what man in what bar?" demanded Mario, leaning forward menacingly.

"I showed a man in a bar the coins when I stopped for a drink. He had spotted the bag and asked me what was in it. I never thought finding coins was illegal so I was quite happy to show off my find."

"Did he know much about old coins then?" asked Mario suspiciously.

"That's true, he did and he seemed to know about you too."

"But who talks about me like this, who knows my business?" shouted Mario.

"I can't remember much about him, really," said Pasquale.

"OK, look, I could perhaps manage 40,000 for the lot, but no more."

"40,000, you must be…" Just then the door crashed open and Mario's hefty accomplice Toni loomed in the frame.

"It's OK, Toni, there's no problem, everything's fine. Sorry I shouted. Thanks for checking."

"No boss, it's not that, some men are outside in the shop asking about you and about coins. They look official-like…"

"Oh no, mio dio, not the inspectors? You see, Pasquale, what talking to men in bars does? You have no idea who they might be, and now you have brought them to my door. If there was time I might have asked Toni to thank you for me personally, with his fists, know what I mean?" He lurched forward menacingly and hung over Pasquale. "But not now. Do you want the deal or not? Hurry. They'll be here in a second. Here's the money, take it or leave it."

Pasquale jumped up in a daze. In a flash Mario had scooped up the coins, put them back in a cosy little velvet bag he just happened to have handy, whipped them into a lower drawer and threw some papers on the desk where they had been lying.

"Yes or no? Now!" shouted Mario. Hastily he peeled the same notes back off the roll from his pocket, added four more, and threw them all at Pasquale. Pasquale muttered, "yes, alright," and as he grabbed the notes he was bundled out of another door through into the back alley.

A minute's silence seemed to last an eternity in the stuffy, crowded room. Finally Toni could contain himself no longer and he spluttered into a roaring laugh, almost causing tears to bubble up in his eyes. "Heh boss, we're getting better every time, eh?"

They sat down, took out glasses and ryegrass whisky stolen from the Yanks and toasted their success.

"Yes," agreed Mario, "about 350,000 lira profit there, give or take. Not bad for 5 minutes play-acting."

Mario could not resist a gloat as he eased back into his chair on this hot, humid afternoon, and replaced his gleaming white spats carefully back onto the desk.

***

26

EDUARDO IN CLOVER

1 9 5 2

"Daddy, where is that new ribbon you bought me?"

"Just like you to lose something precious I bought you, Helena. It's just another proof you do not love me!" replied Eduardo, laughing in pseudo mocking tone.

"Oh, Eddy, please don't tease the child so much. You'll give her an inferiority complex or turn her into a man-hater."

"Don't be silly. Isn't Mummy being silly, Steph?"

"I am not, Eddy. It is a well-known fact that fathers must never tease their daughters otherwise all sorts of terrible things will happen, like they will end up marrying someone like their Daddy!" Valeria shouted from upstairs.

"Oh Mummy!" Helena had finally got the joke.

"OK, OK, OK, enough. I'm sorry."

"You will be sorry if we walk into church late, you know how we cannot be late, we have our honour to uphold"

"Valeria, I'd rather miss church altogether if I had my way."

"No," shouted Valeria, as if she could almost read his mind.

Eduardo was unsure. That 'no' could have referred to a whole number of possibilities so he decided not to pursue the matter now but instead hunt the wretched ribbon. In a trice it was in his hand. It had fallen under the bed exactly where the girl stood. Why are children so hopeless at losing things, he thought. Is it because they throw everything all over the place, drop things whenever and wherever, and are just too busy to remember detail? Certainly, he could not get used to the idea that what might be precious to him may not be precious to a rich, spoiled 8-year old.

But there was no doubt that, with Valeria's legendary beauty and his roguish charm, Helena had turned out to be a really stunning offspring. Everyone said it, not just the two biased and besotted parents.

So it was, ten minutes later out trotted the highly respectable and highly respected Pinto familia, on their way to church in their beautiful open-top Bugatti. Eduardo had gladly accepted Valeria's offer of keeping her family name alive, particularly because by default it also meant the name Carone would never have to be acknowledged where they lived.

Fabrizio loved this moment the best of the week. A hint of heat, detracted by the still-cool, sweetly-perfumed air, brushed past his fresh, rosy-cheeked 6-year old face and his flowing locks. He hung slightly precariously over the side of the sleek limousine and studied the crunching noise of the tyres on the long, stone driveway. Valeria always wanted to shout at him to pull back and sit in properly but she knew Eduardo would castigate her for stopping the lad wanting to be a lad. Again she bit her tongue and shot up a quick prayer above.

Make no mistake, in eight years the Pintos had clawed back much of the position, power and wealth of Valeria's father by determined application. Valeria would call it sheer hard work, but Eduardo's version would add in much more -- ruthlessness, a little bullying and sizeable bribery and corruption.

Year by year he had cunningly turned the screw progressively tighter on the villagers who farmed 'his' land. In just a 30-minute marriage service he had claimed the opportunity, not exactly the 'right', to wreak all the revenge he could ever dream of for all his years as a battered and bruised farm labourer himself at the hands of *his* wicked employers. He even managed to blame most of it on the War or the declining economy, or the price of seed or the cost of temporary labour, or any such fancy he could manufacture. Some saw through him, many did not, but what did it matter, he was their landlord.

And then there was the Black Market. Throughout the War and the aftermath there was a burgeoning exchange of illegal goods liable to make anyone canny extremely rich. With all the contacts Eduardo had made in Brindisi, despite all his desire to forget them and pretend they no longer existed in his new life, he was able to set himself up as an important inland 'centre'. After all, where else better to store huge quantities of plunder with least questions asked than in a run-down outhouse or two on an almost forgotten semi-derelict castello? Lorries could come and go freely all through the night in this lonely place. And if a villager wished to blurt out such information to the authorities, who was going to believe him? And how would he know if Eduardo had not already got to the poorly-paid minor official first with some well-oiled gifts? As a last resort, the lorries could always have been carrying building supplies to help renovate the property. Anyway, what official could be bothered to get up in the dead of night to sit by a roadside waiting for the ghostly silhouette of a lorry perhaps armed by brigands.

These ill-gotten gains had been more than sufficient to renovate and refurbish their home, with plenty left to squirrel away for a rainy day (of which there *were* some in the Heel!). So together with the farm rental profits as well the Pintos were doing very nicely indeed once again. Eduardo seldom appeared grateful to Valeria, and even inside never felt humbled by all his good fortune, because he insisted they had got it all by their own hard work, well, mainly his, he thought.

That was not to say the talk about a secret stash of Valeria's father's fortune had ceased. The intriguing topic was still doing the rounds of the villagers' homes, but as every year passed the interest lessened, and instead of being a 'real possibility' it was slowly downgraded to 'hopeless fantasy'. Valeria, however, was convinced the hoard existed as she knew her father had hidden some of his wealth from, as he called them, the 'enemies of true capitalism', both before and during the War. In other words, he did not want to declare everything for taxation. But in those days there was no sophisticated way of hiding the money like there is nowadays. He would have had to have created a secret place of sizeable proportions to hide everything, probably in the form of physical goods rather than banknotes, and keeping secret a place that size would have been near impossible.

However, for now there was ample money and an opulent lifestyle that Eduardo could only have dreamed about and Valeria had not enjoyed since late teenage days.

✳ ✳ ✳

27

DOWNHILL IN BRINDISI

1 9 5 3

"We have a problem, Ed," muttered Arturo.

"How many times have I told you, not on the phone, Arturo!"

"Yeah, yeah, but this is urgento, real urgento, it's about that…"

"…not on the phone, Arturo! Look, can we meet? Usual place?" demanded Eduardo angrily.

"How long? You see, I'm not sure we have time, this *is* urgent, Ed."

"Give me an hour, I'll be driving. Not much traffic at this time of night but the wet roads are slippery."

"Ok, no more, one hour, max, and, oh, be very careful as you go; this is our big investment so we don't want anything happening to you, do we?" One click and he'd gone.

Whatever now, Eduardo thought, whenever is there *not* a problem? Though this sounds pretty serious. He called to Valeria to say he had got to go out and shouted "goodbye darling."

"Oh Eduardo, surely not now, Flavia will have the dinner ready soon and the children are so looking forward to dining with you, for once."

The sarcasm was not lost on Eduardo even though he was busying himself getting his coat and scarf on. Puglia on a cold, wet winter's night is the antithesis of the perceived Mediterranean climate, though fortunately there are not that many such nights. "Sorry, can't stop, business."

"Business, business, it's always business with you. I just do not understand why you continue to meddle in this business. Business to people like us is oh so demeaning, we are above 'business', my dear Eduardo, we are landed gentry."

"But…"

"…no buts, Eduardo, if we are to dabble in any business then it is solely the business of running the estate. Leave the peddling of wares to the grimy little mercantile courtesans, scratching around in the fish docks and in their shops to make a struggle of a profit. We are rich, we need of no business," pontificated Valeria, but on sensing her husband's darkening visage quickly introduced a little humour into the occasion by adding, "not that it's any of my business, of course!"

Eduardo lightened at that and his loud chuckle defused the situation somewhat. "So, how long this time, Ed dear?" but he had gone, gone out into the foulest of nights, heading towards the garages and outhouses, cursing and shouting for Benito.

Benito stumbled out of the tiny cottage that came with the job. "Benito, get the Bugatti out, quick, like yesterday…now!"

"Yes sir, if you say so, but…"

"…yes, I do say so, no 'buts'. Look, if it's not here in thirty seconds you are fired," he roared.

"But, sir, I haven't finished the upholstery yet and…"

"…sod the upholstery, it's my fastest car, and if you can't notice, I… am… in… a… desperate…hur…ry!"

Eduardo cruised down the Brindisi backstreet, pulled off the street and edged into the front of the garage. A knot was twisting at his stomach and prickles of fear nibbled his neck. Was all well? It seemed to be. Perhaps it was just the freezing wind sliding over the open top of the Bugatti. He had had no time to put the top up in his haste to confront the 'urgent problem'. He whistled his usual tune and a small door opened in the large double gate.

"Were you followed? Quick!"

"Followed? Why would I be followed? Heaven forbid, I live in the middle of nowhere. Who in their right mind would want to stake me out?" As they entered a large, darkly-lit office Eduardo carried on talking, "anyway, what is so urgent, then?"

Suddenly he thought he heard a 'thud'. But as he tried to pick himself up off the floor he realised he *was* the thud! His head was throbbing and he felt nauseatingly dizzy as two pairs of hands dragged him across to a chair. As his eye fog cleared he could make out Arturo and an ugly, scar-faced thug confronting him. The thug was nestling a machine gun on his hip. "Thanks for the friendly welcome, Arturo, so what's the urgent problem again?" he quipped, though his head felt like it was cracking open and he was in no mood for quips. It would be obvious even to a blind man that he was in serious trouble here.

"The problem, Eduardo? The problem? You are the problem, Ed!" sneered Arturo. Thug gave a first lick of his lips, revealing one gold tooth nestling between a rotten row as he smiled.

"Arturo, my friend, I have been a problem my entire life, but who am I the problem to now, and why?"

"Why? You don't know? And by the way, I ain't your friend, never was, huh! So, you pretend you don't know why you are the problem, eh Ed?"

"Nope."

"How about you give us our cut, I mean our proper cut? Before I cut you, asshole!" Arturo was impressed with his own developing level of humour. Thug was over the moon and roared a snorting kind of laugh.

"Now then, Arturo, no need to call names, like a snotty schoolboy. Anyway, have we ever actually stopped to measure assholes to see who has the bigger?" Eduardo laughed, although inside he was not enjoying this one bit and realised that there could only be one end to all this: his end probably. Still, humour always lightens the moment and I may as well end on a humorous note if it is to be my end, he thought.

But Arturo did not seem to see the funny side of it at all and snarled, "you ain't even an arsewipe for my arsehole, you arsehole, you're shit in my …er …your arsehole, arsehole." He was obviously losing the thread of this plot and he knew it, so he did what only a ruffian like Arturo could do when he couldn't win a verbal argument, he stepped forward and punched Eduardo squarely on the jaw. More pain to add to the throb, thought Eduardo, but he continued to smile through the blood.

"Arturo, you and me go back years, well a few anyway. What's all this? We're best buddies. We make a great team, what's wrong, eh?"

"What's wrong, you honey-mouthed asshole? You know exactly what's wrong: you're double-crossing us!"

"What? Oh, and by the way, an arse cannot have a mouth. I'm doing what?"

"You ain't honouring your promises, you're not splitting it fairly. We know, we got proof. Hah, that's caught you out, eh?"

"Caught me out? Caught me out? Heh, you catch this!" As he spoke he bent down and all in one graceful motion whipped out two ankle-strapped knives and flipped them directly into Arturo and thug's hearts, before either of them could even move. Arturo hit the floor first, but not even thug had time to put finger to trigger before he crashed down too. 'Amateurs!' muttered Eduardo, as he set about wrapping up the bodies before too much blood betrayed the spot, 'I know I should have joined the circus with these knife skills,' he chuckled.

But as the adrenalin slowed and his aches returned he began to realise he had not been acting out an American gangster movie, he had really killed two men in an instant. He had crossed the line. By tomorrow, probably, he would know how he truly felt, but he knew one thing now - his black-market career had come to an end. He replaced everything as it had been, he poured oil onto the small bloodstains and he bundled the bodies into his Bugatti. No-one must ever know he had been here. He went to the office, cleared out what little there was in the safe and took the rudimentary bookwork that Arturo enjoyed keeping, as well as the personal knickknacks lying about. It had to look like he had left for pastures new, and in a hurry. As he slipped back out into the forecourt no-one was about: why would they be on a night like this? He loaded his dead cargo, edged the Bugatti back out into the road and disappeared into the inky blackness.

* * *

28

THE CAR

1 9 5 3

"What would you like to eat on your birthday Pasquale? Or should we splash out on that expensive restaurant in Piazza Manfredi?" shouted Isabella, trying to make herself heard over him trying to sharpen a vegetable knife on the screeching grinding wheel.

"Birthday?"

"Yes, silly boy, next Thursday. How could you forget? A very special birthday it is too."

But Pasquale could forget, and forget very easily, because his brain was totally and constantly consumed by his new vegetable business. Already at 20 years and 359 days he was worth a considerable amount, well, a small fortune relative to any village's economy, and still none of it was in the bank. How could he go to a bank? Imagine how suspicious they would be, asking questions about where he had legitimately obtained this fortune. Imagine how loose bank workers' tongues were, even though they were supposedly sworn to secrecy over their customers' business. He would soon have every Tom, Dick and Harry out in the campania looking for his fields and hunting down his little pots of gold at the end of his rainbows. Hmm, if rainbows always end at the same place, then would all the pots be together? he surmised.

It had taken him a long time settling into the town's way of things, certainly a different kettle of fish to tiny Avatrana. Opportunities there were, but they were not so easy to discover because the owners of the fields were scattered throughout a town of over 10,000 people. But slowly he had elicited the necessary information and after a while he now leased five fields from unneedy widows in different neighbourhoods of the town. He always chose only one widow from each neighbourhood so that all of them, or none of them, would know little of Pasquale and his business. Divide and rule, he considered. Consequently, he was again producing enough tomatoes, beans, chicory and melons for at least five villages around Oria and some selected recipients of the town, like restaurants, bars and greengrocers.

And, as if this were not enough to take all Pasquale's waking hours, he had also taken up a new hobby. One day in a bar he had overheard men saying there was much money to be made searching for buried treasure in certain fields, using one of those new fangled machines called a metal detector. They had been very useful in the war and could be obtained cheaply second hand if you knew where to ask, they said. So Pasquale asked, and soon managed to be the proud owner of such a device. Well. 'proud' might be an exaggeration because it was a fairly rudimentary and pernickety one which seemed to only detect to within a few feet of the object, but to Pasquale that made it all the more fun as he then had to scrape and dig around a bit before he triumphed. And he could only detect for a few hours at a time because the machine was very heavy in the Puglian heat. Success had been limited thus far but he befriended the men in the bar who were only too happy to point him in the right direction, literally, after a few rounds of Peroni.

His fruit and vegetable name was already again a household legend for fairness and decency, and he even employed a young man to deliver to the villages every day, plus three permanent pickers bending their backs daily under the unyielding sun. Rather them than me, he thought, somewhat uncharitably, although it was well known he always paid above rates and there was never a shortage of applicants for jobs, and even a steady stream of enquiries when there were none. He paid them more so that they would keep quiet about their labours, and it seemed to work, so far at least.

The War was already a faded memory and life had returned to normal. At worst, in a war-ravaged place the population would forget much of the horror in one generation, but in a place such as Oria where the War never really infringed for long, five years was enough to forget the odd local lad who had been killed fighting for freedom, or whatever he had fought for, or the shortages of food and products, derailed for the War Effort. Of course, to many American and British soldiers moving through the South the war 'effort' was little effort; soldiers sitting round village fountains awash with wine and with a girl, lured by the dramatic uniform, on each knee. Better than home and better than ever dreamed of.

Old feuds were now resurrected, old alliances re-cemented and new ones broached. Some of the men had returned from the War, often with telling injuries, and they spent their days sitting around the piazzas or village squares, unable to perform manual labour ever again. As there was little other work available to suit their downfallen machoes, this meant unemployment forever and no money or hope. Wine sales were brisk, as were cognac, limonchello and menthe.

The remainder had sought to avoid this shame and had stayed up North or joined Camorristi gangs in Napoli and its surrounding towns. There were rich pickings to be had in every illegal trade imaginable and the Allies' withdrawal had led to open season because of the starvation and poverty that ensued.

Thus in 1953 The Heel was in a state of flux and could go either way ---back to more of the same poverty or forward to a brave new dawn of industrialisation, aided by the new Government's initiative – the 'Mezzogiorno' scheme.

But in the gathering evening gloom that follows the magic Mediterranean hour of gentle light and beauty Pasquale was certainly in no state of flux. Rather, he was in a state of dreaming…daydreaming. Riding along he had been so captured by the subtle interplays of shadow and form between the olive trees, the stone walls and the fields, whilst still reflecting on his growing agricultural empire, that he must have taken a different turn by accident. Essentially, therefore, he was now lost! Well, he certainly did not recognise where he was. But to say 'lost' was rather too final for this situation. He knew he would find his way home in time. But wait, I know that silhouette across the road in the field behind the wall, he realised, despite the camouflage of weeds and vines.

There was no mistake, it *was* a car!

He leapt over the wall with an impressive side straddle to investigate further. Sure enough it was a rusty, fairly battered old Fiat 2800. Oh my, this is a real find, thought Pasquale. And that was true. The 2800 was only made between 1938 and 1944 and even so only 624 models were made, by hand. Of those 210 were made only 9 foot 9 inches long, not 10 foot 5 inches, and with strengthened chassis and bigger wheels. They were purpose built for the generals of the Italian military. Indeed, the 2800 was a sure sign of class and dignity as they were extremely expensive top-of-the-range limousines driven by the Italian elite. Pasquale did not know any of this then; all he saw was a battered old beauty which was never likely to ply the roads ever again. Presumably that's what others had seen too, then walked away. After all, there had to be a good reason why it had lain there all these years. The inside was little better either, once he had forced open the stiff rusty door.

Obviously the car had been dumped and left there to rot. But by whom? How many people around here could have afforded such opulence ten years before? Why just dump it? Why not try to sell it, even if it had maybe crashed? It would surely have had a value, even damaged. Perhaps it had been deserted by an Italian general after it had broken down and instant retreat had been necessary. That seemed far more plausible, Pasquale levelled.

Fuelled by his exciting discovery dreamtime was over and he quickly realised where he was. It was in fact merely a parallel road to his usual. So the next day he knocked on the door of the house nearest to the car and enquired its history. 'Bingo!' It *had* been deserted in the depths of night. Yes, about seven years ago, and no, no-one knew what to do with it, they'd just let it rot.

Pasquale was allowed to requisition it and in the few free hours he was able to carve out for himself he started work on the interior, followed by the exterior. He made a passable job of both, despite having to evict the longstanding tenants nesting inside and scraping through great thicknesses of animal deposits. Under the bonnet the battery was moulded and corroded but everything else seemed intact and in reasonable condition. Fiats built for the rich were very different to Fiats built for the toiling class.

Signore Bellini was consulted and he sent his mechanic friend to assess the damage. He returned overawed at Pasquale's discovery, but fortunately he was an honest man. He told Pasquale that cars like that were extremely rare and only for the rich. Why, even King Vittorio Emanuelle II and the Pope had owned 2800's so he was in the best company! However, a car for the rich needed the rich to pay for the car. Overheads were colossal and Pasquale should think carefully about this.

"The repairs will be extensive, that's for sure. A new battery, obviously, plugs, filters, fan belt etc. Fortunately the brakes seem OK, the suspension I can't check yet but might need new rods, the starter motor I won't know till…"

"…oh, spare me the details, how much, please?" interjected the excited and impatient Pasquale.

"Around about 80,000, 80 to 100000 lira, I would reckon."

"Great, just get it running, if you would please".

Pasquale quivered with even more excitement. This was the first really big thing he had ever spent on, apart from farm equipment. It felt wonderful after all these years of toil to be able to hand over a huge sum of money for something. Now people are going to talk, he thought.

And talk they did. A week later Pasquale was no longer seen on bicycles, he was riding his limousine. Well, driving it to be precise. Although his definition of 'drive' would probably not match many others if challenged, he was not just a learner of car driving but also of showing off. He needed a straighter back, a more regal hello wave, a dignified smile not a spoilt childish grin, and better mount/dismount postures. But what the heck! The wind in his hair, the sun on his back, the feeling of brute force in his hands. *And* he could make 30 kph on a straight road if he steered it successfully. What more could a boy of 21 want? What a birthday gift for the emergent adult! His only regret was that the car would not fit, literally, Piazza Bainsizza because of the narrow, single-lane, cobbled streets. Consequently he had to park it outside the city walls of the Jewish Gate and walk the 150 yards to his house. However, on reflection, perhaps that was the best solution, otherwise the nosy neighbours would wonder where he had got the money to buy such a beauty. If only they knew he had found it.

* * *

29

SSUSA DE CASSA

1 9 5 4

Bella needed Andrea's help. She could think of no-one else and, anyway, who better to ask than one's own upright employer. "Madame," she asked, as usual addressing her using the French word because such was the fashion industry, "I would really like it if you could help me, please."

"Yes, certainly. Is it a problem with the labels?" replied Andrea, completely misreading the situation.

"No, no, Madame, I don't mean help me here, not in the shop, but outside."

"Oh really?" replied Andrea, somewhat surprised and a little less than enthusiastic. Over the years she had learned to steer clear of anything to do with the community except, of course, unless it related to the shop and advertising.

"You know that man who waits for me most nights after work?"

"Your brother?"

"Yes, my…well, no, Madame, that's the reason I ask. He is not actually my brother, you see…" she tailed off.

Suddenly it dawned on Andrea. "Oh, I see now," and she smiled a knowing smile.

"Isn't he lovely, Madame," Bella smiled back, "isn't he the best thing since iced coffee?" Before Andrea could answer she continued, "almost as handsome as that man you talked to the other day".

Bella was not the cleverest of girls and that last statement could easily have been taken solely at face value. Certainly it helped Andrea double her smile and relax a little. But in fact Bella had said it cunningly and quite deliberately in an attempt to curry favour with her boss and consequently get her on her side for the battle ahead.

"I could be persuaded to agree, if you put it like that, Bella," she laughed.

"Well, Madame, the simple truth is...I love him!"

"Really?"

"Yes, Madame, I really do. He's the one. We have been walking out for two years now and we want to get married."

"So what is the problem, Bella? Why do you need my help? To twist his arm?" At that last quip she laughed, but really it was more to hide her increasing annoyance at this silly girl and her request.

"No, Madame, you are a figure of importance, a lady of grace and manners, a manageress of an important shop..."

"...Bella, flattery only gets you so far!"

"I know, Madame, but it's true, you have an influential position. My parents are simple folk, honest mind you, but not classy like you..."

"...oh Bella, you don't know everything."

"I know enough. Madame, would you please do me the honour of being my intermediary, my go-between?"

"Between what?"

"Oh Madame, with my parents, to ask them if Luigi can marry me."

Andrea paused before replying, "oh, I see, I'm sorry. I am not totally myself today, apologies. But is not the man supposed to do this, or find someone himself to do this?"

"Yes, normally, but he fears they will say no and he knows no-one as influential as you."

"I see. A strange request indeed. Let me think on it." Bella's face dropped. She had expected an instant answer. She could not bear the waiting.

"Oh, Madame, I..."

As if she had not heard Bella, or perhaps just to play a joke on her, Andrea interrupted, "Yes, OK. I will do it. But there must be promises from you first!"

"Yes, anything! What must I promise?" Bella replied, petrified.

Andrea then bust out laughing, "If you promise I will not be shot at, or attacked, or thrown into the street!"

"Oh no, Madame, of course not!"

"Oh? So how can you be so sure? Have your parents met Luigi? Do they know him or his family then?"

"Yes, yes, they know him, they like him. His family is agreeable and knows my family."

"Seems like I am unnecessary, then!" laughed Andrea.

"Tradition, isn't it, Madame."

"I suppose so."

That night, after work, Andrea accompanied Bella and Luigi to Bella's house and while the couple waited impatiently outside, like children awaiting a treat, Andrea entered and performed the necessary ritual. Minutes later three beaming faces emerged and a succession of double-cheek kiss embraces commenced. Andrea couldn't help being caught up in the joy of it all but she also felt rather ambivalent about the loneliness deep in her heart.

The next night she again had to return to the house. How silly of her to think her job had been done the previous evening! The second round of formalities had to take place this night and when she arrived with Bella they were hastily rushed up to the rooftop terrace where her mother offered refreshments and seats. After a pleasant chat they heard the sound of throats being cleared in the street below. Before they could even get up to see who it was the music started. A professional three-piece band had been hired by Luigi to serenade Bella.

As the lilting love songs progressed Andrea had to admit to both herself and the gathered ladies that it was a most beautiful and romantic occasion. Finally, Luigi bellowed up his protestations of love and proposed to Bella. Smiles all round, whoops of joy, embraces in abundance. The band was invited in to soothe their parched throats and Luigi triumphantly introduced his parents. It was to be a long night, full of mirth and celebration.

Now my job is done, thought Andrea, as she rushed home in the darkness. She had told them she would be late, but not this late: they would be worried.

The next morning Bella did not appear for work. Must have been a wonderful party, thought Andrea, as she wearily threw herself into the busy daily routine, and she did not concern herself too much about it. She hoped Bella would appear for the evening opening after siesta and was admittedly surprised that she did not appear or even send word of the inevitable hangover.

The next morning was the same: no Bella, no word. Andrea quizzed the two other assistants to see if they knew. One didn't but the other nodded her head sheepishly. If that girl is taking this shop's time-off unduly she had better watch out, considered Andrea, somewhat annoyed. There are plenty of girls interested in working here; we are the biggest and best ladies' outfitters in central Puglia. How dare she? "Antonia, are you telling me the truth? Or are you hiding something?"

"No Madame," mumbled Antonia, eyes rolling slightly downwards.

"Not protecting Bella?"

"No, Madame," eyes definitely on the floor now.

"Out with it, girl, now, or else!" shouted Andrea.

"Well, you see…I did hear that Bella had run into a spot of bother, Madame…"

"….yes, yes? About what, pray? Claudia, get on with your work, now!"

"Well, I think Bella's parents found out something about Luigi and they are not happy. They are very traditional parents, you see. I think… er…I think they are keeping Bella locked in her room."

"What?"

"It's only what I've heard, Madame, honest!"

Andrea considered this bombshell. "So, they are stopping her coming to work then. How dare they?" She became angry at Bella's absence and more angry at tradition.

"But they are frightened she might run away."

"Right, I am going there now. Look after the shop!" She grabbed her hat and stormed out into the crisp morning sun. But by the time she had reached the house and knocked the door she had had some time to think about it and she had calmed down somewhat.

The mother opened the door. "Oh, it's you, hello. My husband is working. Will you return this evening please?"

Andrea marvelled at how traditional these folk still were. Why did she think all business had to be transacted through the husband? "No, it is all right. I was just concerned. Bella has not been to work for two days and I wondered if she was unwell?"

"Oh, Bella. No, Bella is fine. I'm sorry she has not been to work, she's been unable to."

"Really? Is there anything wrong, then?"

"As I said, you should really talk to her father, in the evening as …"

"…well, can I have a word with Bella now, if she is home, please?"

"It won't be easy, Signorina."

"Why not? You said she was not unwell? Is she asleep still perhaps?"

"I really can't say, sorry." She began to fidget on the doorstep and she spotted one of her neighbours taking more than a token interest as she swept her front steps.

Andrea sensed the situational change and drove the knife in. "Why not? Really, this is very silly. What is wrong? Tell me now!"

The poor woman began to collapse under the two-pronged pressure. "I shouldn't say it, my husband can be very strict…" She paused.

"…Yes? Please."

"OK, no more secrets. He has locked her in her room!"

"Locked?"

"I'm sorry."

"My word, yes, sorry you should be. Someone should be. How can your husband do such a thing?"

"Yes, I know."

"But how long? Two days and more?"

"Yes."

"But has she food and drink? Can she wash? Toilet?"

"Well, I bring her food, obviously, but I have to give her a pot, we only have one toilet. And a jug of water to wash."

"Oh signora, this is monstrous!" railed Andrea.

More nervously now, "well, my husband says…"

"…your husband should be locked up, not Bella. This is disgraceful!" Andrea's mind raced as she thought of ways to get her out as quickly as possible, but how? And suddenly the perfect idea came to her; luckily while the father was not home. Andrea now smiled at the mother, "you know that my shop is a very important one, don't you?"

"Yes, indeed, the best around…"

"Well then, to keep it important and to offer the best service I do need a minimum number of staff. You understand that, yes?"

"Of course."

"Well, already one of my staff is off sick this week and I have had to leave the shop in the hands of one assistant to come here, as it happens our youngest and newest employee. So if I don't hurry back there might be all sorts of chaos and complaints."

"Oh dear!"

"Yes, oh dear indeed! But that is the measure of importance I have attached to this mission. Bella is an excellent employee and it is quite clear I need her at work, now."

Worried, and considering the gravity of the situation, the mother offered, "I can see that, certainly, but…"

"…I'm sorry, there can be no 'but's', I'm afraid. I am in a desperate hurry here. I truly need Bella at work, now. Do I have to also remind you of how important a job this is for Bella? She learns a lot more than how to fit and sell a dress, you know."

"Oh, it is, it is, yes…"

Interrupting, Andrea studied her watch and put the dagger in. "Well then, I'll be blunt as I have run out of time, Signora, if Bella does not come back with me now I shall be forced to dismiss her!"

"But you couldn't."

"Oh yes I could. Non-appearance with no acceptable reason."

"Oh my, oh dear."

"You do understand, then?"

"Yes, of course, but what can I do? What will my husband do to me when he returns?"

"I suggest you tell him the ultimatum I gave you and, of course, remind him of how the family will live without Bella's very generous salary and tips!"

"But…"

"…I've already said no 'but's'. Look I have to go. Decide now, please."

"All right, but I don't have the room key, you know."

"O Mio Dio! And now you tell me?"

"I just remembered. You've confused me and panicked me so much I can't think straight."

Andrea smiled inside and told herself the ruse had been a success then. "OK, OK, he must have left it at home, he wouldn't carry it around at work. Think. Think where he could hide it."

And so she did, and she found it hanging on the back door under a coat. She went upstairs, unlocked the room, told Bella to clean herself up and get downstairs. Bella looked crestfallen as she entered the living room but cheered at the sight of Andrea, "Oh Madame, what are you doing here?"

"No time now, Bella, later. Let us get back to the shop, now. I must go! Oh, Signora, don't forget to tell your husband something."

"Yes, but what shall I say?" she pleaded, with fearful tears in her eyes.

Andrea paused for a reason. She had been about to tell the mother to tell him he should be ashamed of himself, but she had the prize, she had surprisingly and successfully obtained who she'd come for, so she ameliorated. "Tell him I will personally guarantee Bella's presence in the shop, but if he so wishes he could come and collect her when we close and deliver her each morning. I believe that is a reasonable compromise, don't you?"

"Yes indeed. I will tell him that, and that you desperately needed her. I hope that will stop a beating."

"That is dreadful, but," she lied, "you might remind him that your domestic circumstances are no business of mine, but the shop is my business!" Andrea was rather proud of that quip and chuckled inside. In reality the thought of violence between man and wife appalled her and she wondered about reporting it. First things first, though.

Once round the street corner Andrea launched in to Bella, "what in Heaven's name is going on, Bella?"

"Oh Madame, I am so sorry. I tried to get word to you but my father is wicked, he locked me up and would not let me speak to anyone."

"Yes, but why, Bella? I can see all that, I am not blind!"

"He said he had just been told some awful information about Luigi and his family by a well-wisher. Not very well-wishing in my opinion. So I asked him but he refuses to divulge it. All he said is I am banned from ever seeing my true love again!"

"Oh Bella, I am so, so sorry."

"Thank you. But worse, my father is extremely traditional. He has vowed to keep the honour of my name intact and says he will shoot Luigi if he ever comes near me again!"

"Oh Lord! Will he?"

"The mood he is in, I don't doubt it, madame."

"Have you managed to speak to Luigi or get him word?"

"How could I?"

"So you know absolutely nothing about the veracity of the rumours, or indeed of your future?"

"No, Madame, I have just sat cooped up for nearly three days in my room."

"OK. Look, you hardly resemble a top ladies outfitters showroom assistant like this. Would you like to borrow some of my makeup?"

"Oh thank you, Madame. Look, I am truly sorry about all the trouble I have put you to."

"So you should be!" But then she smiled, "but actually, if I am honest, I find all this rather exciting! And certainly challenging!" And she began to laugh.

"Really?"

"Yes. Come on, you must agree it is certainly something beyond the run of normal daily events."

"True, it is. But what am I going to do, Madame, I am desolate. Luigi is my one and only true love and if I cannot be with him I will surely die. No, I will actually kill myself!" She broke down sobbing in the middle of the street.

"Now, now, there, there, it will be all right. Please don't cry, well, not here anyway!" A number of people were beginning to stop and stare.

"But Madame," she sobbed.

Andrea thought quickly, as ever. "Maybe I can help, Bella," she soothed, uncertain of making promises she could not keep. After all, how much more did she have to do for this girl? How much had she already done? She's not exactly a friend of mine, merely an employee. "But let's get back to the shop first without flooding the entire street, then we can think more clearly." Bella smiled and the flooding imagery helped her cease the tears.

"But it is our busy day today..."

"...yes, and that is why, one, I need you there and, two, why I am so annoyed having to leave the shop to fetch you."

Bella started her profuse apologies again but Andrea waved them away, "it's OK, you can sit in my office until you feel well enough to help. Leave everything to me, you little minx. But we do need to find out what Luigi has done."

And so they did.

Inbetween serving customers and running the shop Andrea tried to formulate a plan. She knew she had little time. As soon as the father appeared home the game would be up, of that there was no doubt. He would probably be so furious he would erupt volcanically and never let Bella near the shop ever again, nor anywhere else perhaps. And what might he do to me too, she worried.

During Siesta Andrea asked Claudia to take Bella home to Claudia's house, or at least disappear for three hours, just in case her father came to the shop then. Fortunately he did not; perhaps he was tied up somewhere else. Andrea waited in the shop for an hour in case he came, but then went to visit Luigi at the address Bella had given her. He did not know for certain Bella had been incarcerated and he himself was tear-ridden, even though he was loathe to admit such a failing to a woman, and he did not know Bella had just escaped. They formulated a plan, of sorts.

So half an hour before closing Luigi waited at the back door of the shop and secreted Bella away without any prying eyes. Therefore, if challenged, everyone in the shop could say quite honestly that they knew neither the time Bella had disappeared nor with whom. Not even Andrea.

And so it was. Bella's father appeared just before closing time, steam spurting out of his ears, and everyone stuck to their stories. He then raged like a bull, especially at Andrea who had guaranteed Bella's presence, but when Andrea told him what a scheming, wicked minx she must have been not only to escape but also to destroy Andrea's faith and trust in her, even the father had to concur, and he calmed down somewhat.

A week later Andrea heard from Claudia that her plan, plotted with Luigi, had surprisingly not only worked but had worked beautifully. Bella and Luigi had gone to Brindisi, found a hotel on the termination wages Andrea had been able to afford her, consummated their love and obtained a doctor's certificate of lost chastity. They had then returned home openly and triumphantly to declare "ssuta di cassa". This is how couples overcame the problem of objecting parents – they would escape the home, elope together, consummate their union and then be forced to marry, otherwise they would bring shame on their families.

* * *

30
WEDDING BELLS
1 9 5 6

Isabella still had a few twinkling embers of romance left burning inside her. Although still only in her 40s she had not known a man since Eduardo had walked out seventeen years ago. And since then she had survived a house move in the night, a complete change of lifestyle and countless crises. Andrea was now a well-established shop manageress, Pasquale was making money by means not known, and even little Maria had finished part-time school and, apart from her small sewing income, was bearing the burden of most of the sundry household drudgery. Whenever she complained Isabella always insisted that she was learning to be a housewife. But it was certain Maria would soon be ready to look for work: she was a nineteen-year-old, blossoming even more rosily than Andrea had, and oft times Maria would catch her Mama watching her in admiration, and perhaps even a little jealousy.

And sure enough, Maria, off her own back, followed the way of Andrea in Oria and secured herself a job serving behind a bar. Isabella railed, Pasquale grumbled and Andrea expressed her shock, but in the end, as Maria so forcibly argued, what else could a pretty girl with limited education do? The only amelioration was that Pasquale promised to meet her at the end of every shift and walk her home safely. This inevitably led him to realise just how much being the head of the family and the only male meant, and just how pressurising it was. Worse though, it meant he had less time to keep an eye out for Andrea.

Mama, meantime, had her own fish frying. Signore Bellini continued to call three or four times a week, ostensibly to offer assistance in any domestic matter, but in reality to continue attempting to cement a relationship with Isabella which was fictitious in everybody's head except his own. Mama did not chastise him because even his company was better than an empty house and, after all, he was the perfect gentleman. Although it was ever so tempting, she resisted reviving her rusty romance skills by flirting with him because that would have been ever so unkind to him. Also it would leave her exhausted for the main bout.

This was a less-frequent, twice weekly affair when Cosimo found time to travel over and visit the family. But he too had an alternative agenda, although just how secret it remained was less clear -- to woo Isabella. He considered fifteen years was long enough to allow her marriage to settle in the Puglian dust, and even he had not seen or heard of his friend Eduardo in all that time.

Clearly Signore Bellini was not a good judge of the wind, but Cosimo was. It only took a few weeks of gentle hinting and probing for Cosimo to go down on his knee in her parlour and ask for her hand. The children knew it was coming but were still over-joyed: their mother had had precious little life since father had left, or even precious little life before that too, truth be told. Cosimo, on the other hand, was a kind, caring, considerate man, everything their father had not been, and they wished them many happy years together. Even Signore Bellini, who had been totally oblivious to his rival's campaign, wished them every happiness with a 50,000 lira housewarming gift. However, he did enquire, almost innocently, how they were going to marry when Isabella was still officially married.

But Cosimo was always one, or even more than one, step ahead of him. He had checked it out at the Town Hall and even eleven years after the War had ended post-war Italy was still not back to normal. All Isabella had to do was to find one respectable citizen in Oria and get him to vouch for her "decency", as they termed it, for her length of stay in the town and for her property tenure. They would be happy to accept Eduardo Carone as 'deceased' if Isabella knew not where he had gone, because they had insufficient time, manpower or energy to check every town hall in Puglia looking for a record of him. And anyway, as they surmised, he would probably have changed his name immediately upon leaving so the task would become impossible. Furthermore, so many people had died or lost their identity papers during the War years that the system would take years to re-record and re-catalogue every citizen.

And so it was, in a tiny, stuffy, hot room behind the Town Hall Isabella Carone became Isabella Patisso. Andrea had managed to 'borrow' a beautiful dress for the occasion, Cosimo stayed so fit and healthy that he still managed to morph into the one Sunday suit he had owned for 30 years, just, while Maria also received help from Andrea's shop. Pasquale needed a suit anyway so splashed out on a new one for the occasion. Needless to say, therefore, the wedding photo looked splendid, a total misrepresentation of their worldly wealth, but who cared? Even the folk in the street muttered the same as the family walked past them in the traditional manner, en route for home: what middle class union had taken place? Did anyone know this prestigious couple, they all whispered and joked.

Isabella and Cosimo were finally happy. As he walked along the street proudly displaying his beautiful bride to the world all kinds of random thoughts flooded his brain. It had taken him years of low-key courtship to land his catch and every minute had been worth the wait. Well, all those except the anxious times when the Carones had upped and left Avetrana without a word. They now had a pleasant house to live in, and it would be even more pleasant when Andrea and Pasquale moved on. He could now sell his shop and the rooms over it in Avetrana and finally become a townsman. Instead of scrimping and arguing over every cent on a kilo of beans he could perhaps invest in some business or even help set up Pasquale, if only he could discover exactly what Pasquale did! It suddenly dawned on him that he had no idea what job Pasquale had taken on, who he worked for or even where he worked. He was a total mystery to Cosimo even though they lived under the same roof.

"Cosimo, please, be polite, smile and wave at Signora Ostori!" barked Isabella.

"Sorry, my dear, I was just dreaming about how fortunate a man I am," he lied.

They returned to their gaily-decorated house and found outside a feast fit for a king. A long trestle table had been covered with crisp white linen. Everyone loves a wedding and all the neighbours had adorned it with trays of antipasti, meats, pies and salads, bowls of sagna penta (square spaghetti) and fruit, plates of local favourites like ricotta asquanta, frise (crisp buns with holes in the centre), piddica (filled pizza bread) and cupeta (crunchy almond nougat), plus of course flagons of homemade Primitivo wines. Certainly many of the residents would be in need of physical assistance staggering to their doors in a few hour's time!

A local band had been engaged for a night of pizzica dancing, the energetic Puglian dance that would need Primitivo for fuelling and refuelling. Isabella still loved to perform this dance, not as energetically as her little Maria, or even Andrea, but what she lacked in energy and sheer physical exertion she by far made it up with gracefulness. Cosimo too surprised his bride, and many more from the street, with his ardent, passionate exposition, but he refused to admit where or when he had learnt all the complicated steps. However, it was Isabella's night and she was instantly everyone's choice for 'best dancer'.

In the shadows of a side alley a pair of eyes watched on all this with satisfaction. He was pleased the Carones of Avetrana had found happiness with a man his colleagues had been unable to bribe, threaten or extort. Cosimo Patisso was a worthy winner and he would leave him be.

From another alley at 10pm emerged a swarthy, muscular young buck, dressed in the latest tight jeans and abs-clinging shirt, and he strolled straight across to the wedding table in that aggressive, arrogant gait so typical of the South and demanded that Maria dance with him. How could she refuse? Already the willing recipient of three or four glasses of deep red wine, and not wanting to insult or cause offence, she rose a little slower than usual from the happy gabbling and was swept across the square by a firm cool hand. The band sensed that something special was happening, or was about to happen, so they struck up their most passionate jig. The buck responded immediately and drew in Maria to his passion. Light-headed she responded rather more enthusiastically than the watching Carones might have hoped for and other couples soon melted away, either too saturated with drink to keep up the rhythm or in due deference to the superior exposition that was beginning to enthral the crowd.

Soon Maria and her man were left alone to play out the classic story. And play out they surely did. This pizzica dance tells a story, the story of a young maiden working in the wheat fields in June who is suddenly stung by a tarantula, of which there are many in Puglia. The venom immediately drives her crazier and crazier until she is dancing like a possessed being. Along comes a man who attracts the tarantula and its poison away from her with a red cloth, very similar to the toreador and the bull, and in so doing eventually cures her. [It is said if you are ever in Puglia and are bitten by a tarantula, drink the Holy Water in St. Paul's Church, Galatina, near Lecce, and you will be cured!]

The passion of their performance had never been experienced before, a history-making coupling that made it a dance to end all dances throughout Puglia. Indeed, for many a year after the street gossip could never remember any other dancers except Maria and her mystery man. The cheering would not cease and they were compelled by shouts of 'encora, encora' to repeat the second half. To repeat all would have probably killed them and, as it was, the second half left them drenched in perspiration in a crumpled heap on the flagstones. And then, to everyone's surprise, the man picked up Maria in his arms like a bundle of sticks, carried her gently back to her table and promptly disappeared.

"And just who *was* that, Maria?" asked Pasquale, now the worse for drink.

"I have no idea, brother, maybe some customer from the bar," she wheezed breathlessly.

Pasquale needed to consider if Maria was lying or not. He always knew when she was lying, the corner of her eye twitched, but it was too dark and he was too drunk to spot it. Furthermore, everyone was crowding round her to congratulate her on her epic performance. Poor Maria was overwhelmed and merely wanted to rest with another quenching glass of Primitivo, so Pasquale and Cosimo proceeded to shoo everyone away.

"Better look out, sis, that boy meant business!"

"That kind of business would be welcome, brother," she laughed, tossing her head back coquettishly.

"Oh, and you would be happy to join on the end of his long list of conquests, then?"

"It would be worth it!" she giggled.

"Oh sis, please, you don't mean that. It's the drink talking…"

"…talking's not doing, brother."

"Maria, stop that now!" he exploded. Everyone stopped their gabbling and stared at them. "It's OK," soothed Pasquale to the onlookers, "just a bit of family bantering," and they returned to their overheated, exciting gossip. "In the morning you'll realise this was just a dream, Maria, so sit still and enjoy it now. Here, some more wine, my dearest." His aim was to make her drowsy so he could get her into the house and safely tucked away. Fortunately it worked, although he had to practically carry her in rather than just support her. Folk were starting to drift away, realising that *the* dance had been the highlight of the evening and could not be bettered. The band eased down a few notches and people staggered home happy and content that their neighbour Isabella had received a truly marvellous send-off.

Next morning Cosimo and Isabella called on every neighbour with a gift of wedding cake and homemade sweets, although truth to tell some folk failed to get to their front doors!

* * *

31

NO CHANCE MEETING

1 9 5 6

Tonino sucked in breath, eased his shoulders back and pushed purposefully through the glass door. Previously he had made sure only the owner, or manageress, was present and he manufactured his most non-masculine, sweet smile for her, which was extremely difficult for one in his profession to achieve, make no mistake. Slickly-dressed, handsome, athletically-built, with not an ounce of waste about his frame, a perfect set of pearly-white teeth, again no mean feat for a region such as Puglia in those days, how could anyone really resist him, he thought.

Well...it seemed this beauty could! She nodded politely and asked in a totally non-coquettish manner what a gentleman might desire in a lady's outfitters. He'd planned his answer for days, for as long as he had been observing Andrea and the shop, in fact. But still he was forced to improvise the first part of his response because he did not think for one moment she would have been so frank or politely confrontational, but it still brought a smile to those beautiful peachy lips.

"I am pleased you consider me a gentleman, Signorina, but I am here at the bequest of my dearest mother..."

"...so you are not a gentleman, signore? Then I will have to ask you to return when another of my staff is here to protect my honour," she half mocked.

For a second he thought her serious but suddenly his Sunday-best smile returned. "Excellent, most amusing, my dear, er..."

"...yes, your dear mother, pray?"

Oh, I am going to like you, sweet thing, he agreed internally. Spirit and humour, as well as beauty. A perfectly exquisite chase to enjoy, a phenomenal capture to visualise and an irreplaceable remedy for long winter nights, he thought contentedly.

"Yes, yes, my dear mother, bless her." Always good to show how much a man loves his mother, he had considered earlier. "She bought a dress last week and now needs to know if your shop can alter it. She has decided it is a little on the large side...er...on her large side, I should clarify," he continued, smiling as ever.

Andrea feigned a smile back, but considered this fellow to be most agreeable, unlike most she ever met. "And pray, why does she not enquire herself, or know from the outset what we can and cannot do here?"

He paused, nearly hoist by his own petard, and mumbled, "um, not very well today."

"And you, signore, you have no problem entering such an all-ladies domain?

"Not when I find such a domain of beauty governed by one equally so," recovering as he caressed in his most silky, gentle voice.

Andrea felt herself redden from the neck upwards. Blunt but romantic too. She struggled a little to recover her composure. "And how do you know I govern this domain of beauty, signore?"

"Ah, that's easy. Only the most beautiful can ever govern domains of beauty!" He was pleased by his repartee but wondered if he had pushed the boat out a little too far, and certainly too fast.

Fortunately Andrea chose to ignore that minefield and resumed, "where then is said dress, signore?"

Instead of toning down proceedings, as she had hoped, and repelling his advances, it encouraged him more, "do you think I would risk walking down the street with a ladies dress slung over my shoulder on the off-chance you might be able to repair it? Come, come, I have a reputation to maintain, fair lady!"

"And pray, fair sir, what would that be?" her mouth uttered before her brain could engage. She could not remember when she had last felt so light-headed and girly, and she reddened further. "Oh dear, excuse me signore, I am feeling a little faint. I must sit down."

Tonino rushed over, grabbed her arm and guided her to a chair. "Thank you," she said, feeling all the more giddy from his hot, gentle touch.

"Some water, Signorina. Where is your tap?"

"Oh yes please, through that door." As she pointed Andrea's assistant returned from an errand, saw the two together and thought the worst. "Signore, leave her alone!" she screamed.

"Its all right, Claudia, there's no problem. I just felt a little faint and signore, er…signore?"

"Lupo, Signorina."

"…Signore Lupo came to my rescue."

"What, from the street? How could he see in the shop?"

"No Claudia, he is a customer…"

"…what, a man, Madame? We don't have men in here, ever!"

"Well now we do, Claudia," hissed Andrea impatiently and angrily. Suddenly restoring her 'madame' voice she smiled, "just let me sit a while while you take Signore Lupo's details. His mother needs a dress repaired."

Lupo panicked, "details? Surely no need. Oh, is that the time?" He studied his pocket watch carefully, thinking fast. "I am so sorry, Signorinas, I really must take my leave: people to see, money to make." He laughed again. "I'll bring the dress soon, then. Goodbye!" And he was gone, as quick as that, floating out of the door.

"Oh my," gleamed Claudia, "what I could do with him…"

"Claudia! This is a ladies' outfitters, not a public bar. Please tailor your language accordingly."

"Tailor, Madame? Here?" She laughed, and Andrea had to agree she had made a most amusing pun as they both giggled for what seemed an artificial age.

* * *

32

NO CHANCE MEETING...AGAIN

1 9 5 6

Only three days later he again sucked in breath, eased his shoulders back and pushed through the self same door. Again he had waited outside until the shop contained only Andrea, but this time his patience was running thin as it had taken nearly two hours of customer comings and goings. He was a busy man: people to meet, money to make. It was also hot and tiring standing around in the street, as well as undignified for someone in his position. Interestingly, he had not spotted the pretty girl, Claudia, all day. Always sound policy to have a reserve, he thought. Undoubtedly, Tonino Lupo was a ladies' man, as well as a man about town. It would need a notebook to record all his female triumphs and they ranged from virginal girls to wrinkled old maids. He obviously preferred the former, but certainly the latter could be counted on for their generosity of gifts, money or experience. He was still searching for the perfect woman, in other words, the one-in-the-middle and he felt he was onto a winner with this shop lady --- beautiful, confident and comfortably appointed, but obviously still naïve in the ways of love. She was the one, he knew it, and he must proceed with utter stealth. The fox can only enter the chicken coop by day disguised, he remembered.

"Buongiorno, Signorina!"

"And to you, signore, welcome again."

"I am very pleased to see you," he said quietly, trying to avoid the leer that would ruin his chances.

"Have you brought your mother's dress to adjust?"

"Oh drat, I knew there was something I'd forgotten..."

"...please, signore, do not jest with me, this is a busy shop and I am a busy person."

"Oh certainly," he laughed, casting his eyes around the agonisingly empty premises.

But Andrea was not to be outdone. "But signore, surely you have had to wait nearly two hours to catch me alone: that's how busy we have been," she smiled wickedly.

Tonino burst out laughing and sought hard for a retort, but all he could manage was, "I would make a rather useless spy then, Signorina Andrea!"

"Oh, I don't know, you seem to have found out something..."

"...what? To put a lovely name to a beautiful face?"

"Signore, is there something you want?" she demanded in mock anger, quickly applying that great female trait of deflection.

"Err...well...yes, I suppose there is..."

"...and? I have not got all day, you know."

Tonino gulped unobtrusively and plunged in. He was not at all used to such self-assured, direct women. "I wonder if you would like to join me for coffee at lunch time?"

"Do you realise what you have said, signore?"

He panicked. Had she taken offence? Could anyone take offence at such a harmless suggestion? "Er...yes, I asked if you would join me. Is that such a problem?'

"No, no, yes. In that order!"

"Excuse me?"

"I said, no it is not a problem, no you do not realise that you foolishly asked me to drink coffee at lunchtime when one drinks coffee at coffee time and eats lunch at lunchtime, and yes I will!"

"Excuse me?"

"Yes!"

"Aah. And lunch then?"

"Yes. Anything else?"

"No." But by now Tonino was both totally confused and helplessly under her spell, so he could only mutter again, "no, thank you."

"Right, one pm, be here prompt, or you will miss me."

"Yes, good."

"Indeed, now run on, you silly man. Goodbye!" Andrea was already shooing him out of the door because she could see Claudia returning from her break.

"Hello Madame," chirped Claudia, "a man in the shop?"

"Yes, yes, seeking directions. Can you change that green dress in the window, please."

At 1.05 pm Andrea had got rid of all her assistants. Quickly she gave the street another once-over, but still no Tonino. She still remembered how strict she had been about the time, but she knew it was only to show off her domination of him. So was he testing her? Or was he waiting till the coast was completely clear? Or was he perhaps genuinely late? That he had no intention of showing up, to teach her a lesson and make the wait more delicious, had not once crossed her mind. Where was that silly but impossibly handsome man? Oh, so he was really trying to see just how interested I am, is that it, she thought crossly.

Well, we will have none of that nonsense, she thought, and she left the shop and began walking home. Then she suddenly stopped in her tracks. I certainly do not want this stranger to know where I live, she considered, although if he has already found out my name who knows what else he may have already discovered. So she veered sharp right at the next corner. This took her straight past Bar Roma, and who should be sitting there, elegantly draped across a chair.

"Ah, Signorina, I knew you would come!" he smiled courteously.

"But…but," spluttered Andrea, "how did you know I would be here?"

"Magnetism?" he laughed. But he quickly realised that Andrea was not amused and he cursed himself for being too clever. "Sorry, I got detained, but as we are now here could we eat something? I'm very hungry. Are you?"

"Could be," she replied, giving nothing away nor forgiving him.

So they sat and ate a splendid lunch. He spared no expense but she only sipped the wine; work to return to later and possible wagging tongues. As if to order, the squid was morbido to perfection, the prawns fresh even though the Gulf of Taranto was two hours away by lorry, the local breads delicious dipped in olive oil and the fresh fig desert mouth-watering. But most of all, the chemistry was electric. Andrea could not remember when she had had a more exciting time with a man. She felt like her breath was constantly being taken away and she would need to gulp huge gasps of air to stay alive. Luckily it was only a feeling, otherwise she would have been totally embarrassed. However, on the outside she remained calm, cool and sophisticated throughout and Tonino became totally hooked, if he hadn't been already. He had never met anyone quite like her before and he just had to have her.

To any bystander they seemed to be having a business lunch, with a little humorous and flirtatious posturing typical of the Italian male, and even when they left there was still no physical contact, however hard Tonino tried. He longed to just touch her arm, her shoulder, her back, in a romantic gesture, but she remained politely aloof. Even walking back along the streets and into the shop itself she managed to negotiate his wandering hand, despite her burning up inside for the wanting, and when it came time to part she resolutely refused to shake his outstretched hand, offered in a business-like sign of friendship. Tonino was desperate, but he remained ever gallant and already fuelled for the next encounter.

"Perhaps we might do that again sometime, Andrea?" he nonchalantly asked.

"Anything is possible signore. Thank you."

"I shall look forward to it, then, Signorina."

"Yes, I must now return to the everyday. Goodbye."

"Indeed, goodbye."

And that was it. Two burning fuses doused in a trice. Andrea remembered next to nothing of the rest of the day, even of the tricky lady who wanted to return a perfectly good dress, no doubt after she had probably worn it once for that all important function, and had been prepared for a mental and verbal battle, which she always enjoyed, only to find Andrea authorising it instantly with a vacant smile and taking all the wind out of her sails. Claudia stood agape, then realising why, she turned away with a wry smile on her face.

A respectable but not too lengthy three days later, a three days mind you of constant glances out of the shop window, the assignation was repeated. Same time, same restaurant, same result, the only differences being the pre-lunch flowers, which Andrea chose to use in brightening up the shop window rather than take home and raise numerous eyebrows, and the post-lunch chocolates which she stashed in her office drawer for the same reason. Soon the window became overflowing with flowers and it began to take as long to change them as it did to change the display dresses! Meanwhile the staff's diets and trim figures were also going to ruin as the chocolates became a daily complement to their coffee.

And every time Andrea held out. She did not want to but she did. Tonino became more and more desperate, but also more and more excited. Firstly, because the longer the game went on the more convinced he was that Andrea was the one, and secondly because he knew full well he had now made the mental conquest. He only hoped the physical one would come soon, even if she were to be his virginal bride.

A small part of the reason Andrea could not commit herself to him was because she could not countenance his wealth. He would only ever tell her he was 'in business', buying and selling and all that goes with that occupation. However, she well knew by now that this job description could cover a multitude of sins and/or vices. Yes, he was an intelligent man and yes, he was certainly worldly-wise, but was he good enough to respectably earn the amount of money he seemed to have? Andrea had wisely made discreet enquiries around Oria but had drawn a blank, the majority of contacts thinking that he, or his wealth, was coming from further afield, possibly Taranto. At the mention of that place, of course, she had resisted further enquiry. She had even resisted asking Tonino direct. She did not think he thought it odd that she had not asked him about his work and his obvious wealth, but who was to know what went on behind his enchanting eyes? Certainly she would have had the perfect reason to ask about Starsi, being in the same business herself, but she thought it would have been oddly random to just come out with it and ask if he had heard of Starsi and Sons in Taranto without some long, clever preamble. The very thought that Tonino might know him, or even have business with him, made her shudder in fear, but she realised she was becoming hysterical and it was all probably just a coincidence. Maybe he was not even based in Taranto anyway.

However, there was just a small part of her which was saying 'this man is not all he seems, beware', and being so very sensible and so damaged previously it was enough to counterbalance the part of her which so overwhelmingly wanted to love him and claim him for her own, for ever and ever.

Eventually she had no option but to seek help. The only person she knew who could both help her and keep the secret was her own dear brother. So that night she ushered him into her bedroom and poured out all that had befallen her. Immediately he could see her debilitating dilemma, once he had got over the shock of it, and he promised his utmost assistance. "No man is going to upset my most precious sister without reckoning with me!" he said. "I do not know the name Lupo but it is a fairly common family name, so that could be both an advantage or a disadvantage in my search."

Nevertheless he asked all around his circle of acquaintances but drew another blank. Even Cosimo had no success further west towards Taranto. How could a man with such obvious wealth and power be a ghost, they thought. It was strange indeed, unless...

Time was of the essence. Andrea could not repel the man forever and neither could she continue to feast on his undoubted hospitality. People would talk. Finally, the alarm bells began to ring when Tonino suddenly switched ploy and invited her to accompany him to the opera in Lecce by car.

"Whose car, Tonino?" she asked enquiringly in order to stall him and give her some panic time to think.

"Why, mine, of course!"

"Oh, and do you drive?"

"Of course, but I also have a driver..."

"...a driver? My, you must be a wealthy man."

"In my line of work I find it helps to enforce an image of wealth, so to speak. So, will you come, dearest Andrea?"

She did not reply immediately and he felt a rush of panic, so added, "I should be so proud to be accompanied by the most beautiful lady in the audience!"

At that Andrea had no heart to resist any longer and flattery, for once, won the day. The big occasion was for the following Saturday, nine days away. A touring opera company from Milan, no less, was singing La Traviata, and tickets were like gold dust. But Tonino already had two, courtesy of his many contacts. In the Royal Box no less, nothing but the best for his love.

So Pasquale had nine more days to come up with the goods, or... or what? Andrea felt the noose tightening as she struggled to think of a possible excuse if he couldn't. But at every attempt her brother came up against a brick wall. In desperation he asked Andrea if there was any way she could obtain a photo of Tonino. "Impossible, dear brother, how can I just ask for a photo like that? Photos are for when a relationship is cemented and the couple are in love."

"True, true, but there must be a way, surely." They sat in her bedroom and racked their brains. Eventually they devised the ridiculous plan of Pasquale asking his amateur photographer friend, who had one of those new-fangled Polaroid Land cameras that took instant photos, to pretend he was starting a new business taking romantic snaps of couples in restaurants and bars. But as it happened it did not turn out to be ridiculous, and when his friend turned up with a "free" rose as well Tonino could not refuse the lady and happily posed with Andrea for a romantic snap. Actually, when the friend used that American word "snap" it seemed to convince Tonino of the authenticity of the arrangement.

When Pasquale saw the photograph he realised two things --- Tonino certainly was a handsome devil, almost worthy of his precious sister's love, but secondly, did not that face look vaguely familiar? Unfortunately however, as such things go, the more he pored over it the more he was less sure. So he left it for a whole day and waited until the next morning before studying it again. Sure enough, there was certainly something about the slant of the eyebrows and their junction with the nose. He became more and more certain but just could not place the man. It began to drive him wild.

Pasquale warned Andrea of his nagging recognition but she felt it was not enough to make her reconsider. But reconsider she had too. In those long, lonely nights alone in her room she had thought long and hard about the whole situation: she was 29, still living at home and still, she hoped, a virgin. What had happened in Taranto still haunted her but there was no way she could ever pluck up courage and march into a doctor's surgery and ask to be examined to put her mind at rest. She would rather die of shame first. But she would be 30 next year and her life was slipping away. She had to admit also that she had not met any man who came even close to Tonino, or any man who made her feel so much in love. Yes, in love, she finally had to admit it: I'm in love with the most wonderful man! And all these years I have had to scrimp and save, slave and scrape by. And for what? For little more than a pittance. I deserve better, I really do, far better, and I mean to have it! She became quite agitated at these thoughts. Tonino has money; Tonino is rich. Do I care anymore where he gets it, or even how he gets it? Am I not entitled to some pleasure before my life is over? Where else will I get such joy? And am I not beautiful? Damn it, I am, but it will not last for ever. I deserve this now. Oh Mary, dearest Mother, please help! Yes, I will go straight to Church and plead with The Lord. He will tell me what to do.

But at Mass that Thursday evening The Lord did not tell Andrea what to do, well, not in so many words anyway. She knelt and prayed, long and hard, till her knees ached on the cold, unyielding stone floor, repeating all her thoughts to Him even though she knew there was no need as He is omnipotent, but no reply came, no feeling inside of right and wrong, no directional sign in her soul, no tugging of her heart. And still the uncertainty raged.

Perhaps a level-headed person would have interpreted "the uncertainty" as truly a sign from God to not proceed, but it did not appear to Andrea so. She was by now so desperate, and desperation makes people do the strangest things. So as she kneeled in that tiny chapel of St. Barsanofilo she made her decision.

The new Andrea chose a medium-price evening dress from the shop and after dismissing all the staff Friday night she quietly secreted it home. The next day she feigned illness at 12.30 and left the shop in the hands of Claudia for the short evening session.

At 6pm exactly Tonino appeared behind Bar Roma in a beautiful Bugatti, replete with uniformed chauffeur and all the trimmings, and the couple swooned as they admired each other. The evening was perfect: the drive appeared to take no time at all even though it was 35 miles, the opera was magical and the supper exquisite. They made a stunning couple and every head turned at each movement they made. On the imposing steps up to the theatre the press had photographed them more than any other couple or local celebrity, perfect publicity for the Milan Opera's opening night and the highlight of Lecce's annual social calendar. Inside at the interval it was the same as they struggled to find their ordered drinks, but neither could care one jot as they breathed in the heady romantic air and were caught in the moment.

And so they made their way home, finally, and it was very late. Twenty minutes out of Lecce the chauffeur saw a light in the distance on the lonely, empty road. As they closed on it they could see the light was moving from side to side. A man was waving furiously at them.

"Shall I stop, signore?"

"Yes, we'd better. He obviously needs help, but be careful."

The chauffeur got out carefully and approached the man. From his other hand hiding behind his back the man whipped out a cudgel and smashed the chauffeur to the floor with just one blow. Instantaneously Tonino's passenger door was flung open and he was dragged out by another man. But he did not reckon on Tonino's dexterity. A swift jab to the neck left the assailant writhing in a heap on the floor. The other man rushed round to help, raised his arm to cosh Tonino and took aim, but in a flash Tonino had whipped out a knife from its leg-holder, ducked away from the anticipated blow and stuck it quickly into his side. The man gave an audible wheeze and sank like a stone. Tonino rushed to his chauffeur, lifted him into the front seat and drove off at speed. The acceleration pushed the petrified and blurred Andrea back into the depth of her leather seat. It was all over in less than a minute and Tonino could see in his mirror the poor Andrea shaking and shivering on the back seat.

"Get the blanket, dearest, and keep warm. I'll stop and help you as soon as we are away from these amateurs."

"Are you OK?"

"Yes, are you, dearest? I'm so, so sorry, ruined a perfect evening."

But Andrea hardly heard as she dozed off, desperately attempting to neutralise the incident the only way she could. She awoke to find Tonino cradling her on his lap and stroking her forehead. Reflex made her jump up but she turned to him and grabbed him as hard as she could. He caressed her hair and calmed her with soothing sounds until finally she pulled away.

"Here, drink this," he asked, and he put a hip flask in her mouth. The amoretti burned but woke her fully.

"Where are we?"

"Close to Oria now, don't worry, quite safe. I stopped because I needed to see if you were all right. You slept the whole way," he smiled gently.

"Oh, you kind man." She looked into his eyes, smiled and the inevitable had to happen. How could she hold back any longer? She kissed him. Gently at first but with increasing passion as the silent, burning heat rose in her. He responded with even greater ardour and the combustion was spontaneous. "Be careful, dearest," she sighed, "this is not my dress."

He smiled back, actually glad the moment had been broken. "Soon can be, if you like. I've never seen a more fitting dress for a lady," he laughed. Just then the chauffeur groaned and tried to pull himself upright.

"Are you all right?"

"Yes, signore," mumbled the poor man. "What happened?"

"Nothing much, except the lady has finally seen the light!" he laughed.

* * *

33

BAR TALK

1 9 5 6

After the dinner in Vecchia Oria restaurant and the fated trip to Lecce Tonino pestered Andrea daily. He sensed the chase was over and the kill imminent. But she politely rejected him each time, heeding her brother's words of trepidation. At first he accepted her various excuses with typical grace, whilst all the time underneath seething with both anger and passion, but after a while even he began to realise something was wrong. He became desperate to see her and move their relationship along; why wouldn't she feel the same after her warm acquiescence that night?

Finally Andrea could take no more either; her heart and soul were breaking into two. On the one hand she knew full well she could never love, or live with, a murdering mafia boss, if that is who he was, but on the other hand the physical pull was like a thousand magnets still. She went weak at the knees whenever she saw him, worse even than a panting schoolgirl with her first crush. But it was clear this could not go on and she needed to make a decision.

So she did.

She told Tonino that, in the standard go-between situation of the classical Italian persuasion, he should only talk to her through her dear brother because it was improper of him to keep propositioning her in full view of the public at her place of work. She further accentuated her case by telling him that tongues were wagging and, when he still did not look entirely convinced, she chanced her arm by saying that even the shop owner, the revered dowager Madame Impiali, had been forced to have a gentle word with her over it. "I am sorry, Tonino, this is the only way to proceed. I'm sure you understand."

Tonino was devastated by this setback and even lost his famed eloquence temporarily, "but dearest, I, I, I…"

"Please do not call me 'dearest', 'bella', 'love', again, thank you. It is not appropriate in public."

"But…but…why do you do this to me? What have I done? Please?"

Andrea was frightened that he would fall into the grieving Latin Lover routine, all tears and hyperbole, so she had to be blunt. "Pasquale will be in Bar Lorch tonight at 9 pm. Either leave now and talk to him later, or be gone for good, please."

Some customers were just about to enter and Tonino did not want to upset her further, so he took the tactful route, muttered that he would bring his wife's dress in for repair later that day, bowed slightly and said his goodbyes.

Andrea cheered herself immediately, being so relieved she had accomplished all she set out to do with a minimum of fuss or damage, and even her regulars were hard put to understand why she was suddenly so accommodating towards them. No-one could refuse free extra ribbon on a new dress, they laughed. Andrea felt a weight lifted off her shoulders, but also a dagger pushed closer towards her heart.

At 8.55 pm, meanwhile, Pasquale sat shivering at the bar counter. "Are you cold, mister?" asked the barman.

"Er…no…er… yes. A little, I suppose. It's OK, don't worry, I'll…"

Three men had breezed in at a swagger and Pasquale paused mid-sentence. They spotted him and shouted, "hello there, Pasquale."

"Your friends, mister? What can I get you, gentlemen?" asked the barman with a slight look of worry in his eye. They were loud, flashy and possibly half full of liquor already. They looked like out-of-town trouble.

Four amaretto on ice and much lightweight chat later the two bodyguards retreated into the gloom while Pasquale and Tonino found a table. Not too far into the gloom, thought Pasquale: he wanted to be well seen by all, just in case.

"So you are the brother of the bella Signorina? How fortunate you are."

"Yes, indeed I am, she is a lovely sister and a loving daughter."

"Andrea and I have been seeing each other now for over a month and she seemed quite happy until last week…"

"Really, signore?"

"Yes, have you not noticed?"

"Well, not really. We see little of each other during a normal day…"

"…but you are brother and sister. Surely she talks to you?"

"Yes, but not about men friends. Well, actually, that's probably because she hasn't had many over the past few years…"

"…that is good to hear, indeed. So she is a good mother's daughter, perhaps?"

"Er, what do you mean? I'm not sure what you are saying. Yes, of course she helps Mama whenever she can, if that is what you are asking."

"Well, no it wasn't, but I think you have still answered my question." Tonino smiled to himself. It seemed fairly certain that his dear love had never felt a man on her. A perfect bride.

Pasquale wondered at the pause in proceedings. It would have been obvious to any chance observer that he was not enjoying this conversation, or indeed meeting, and he still had no idea where it was taking him. Tonino, on the other hand, was enjoying it immensely and was delighting in watching Pasquale squirm, deviate, deflect and deny. He actually thought little brother was quite good at it, for a peasant. After all, a peasant he must be. Just look at the way he is dressed for a start, and the way he talks.

Tonino was also enjoying it because this is what he did: it was his job to make conversation, prise out juicy pieces of information and conduct successful business, in other words, win on his terms and put the other at permanent disadvantage. This is going to be oh so easy, he thought cheerfully.

"Has she always stayed at home to help her mother then?"

"Oh, I didn't mean that. No, she has worked since she was seventeen."

"Always in the ladies fashion business?" tempted Tonino.

Pasquale was slowly becoming more confident as the 'chat' continued to be light and simple, but he suddenly realised just how cunning Tonino was being --- start with a few simple, innocuous questions and then follow them up with the knockout punch!

"Oh, a number of places, really, at different times," he fudged. "Look, Signore Lupo, apologies, but at risk of sounding blunt, I have been working all day and have not been home or had any dinner yet, and it is past 10 oclock, so…"

"Oh certainly, my dear friend, certainly. Please excuse my thoughtlessness, I did not realise. No, I must not detain you. Quickly then, how do you see the purpose of this meeting tonight?"

"Oh, I think it was Andrea's idea that the two of you should behave more traditionally and proper. After all, she is a country girl, not a city girl, and worse still she has had complaints at the shop, even from the owner."

"I did not know that. It is serious indeed and I am very sorry. Please tell her that. But if I cannot visit her at the shop how can I communicate with my dearest love?"

"Your dearest love? Do you really feel that strongly about my sister, signore?"

"Oh yes, I do. She is the one for me, I know it, my one true love for the rest of my life. She brightens the stars, eclipses the moon, completes my day…"

"…yes, yes, certainly, I can see how you feel," smiled Pasquale.

Suddenly Tonino leaned right over the table, grabbed Pasquale and pulled him right up to his face. "You do not know how I feel! You cannot know how I feel!" He let go of one hand to beat his chest, "Inside, my heart burns. You can never have loved like this, you… you…" And then he suddenly released Pasquale, brushed down his shirt and smiled that wicked, all-conquering smile. "My apologies, signore, I got carried away. My only excuse can be that this shows just how much I love your dear sister. Can you now see?"

Pasquale was quaking inside with fear, realising just how dangerous this man was, but he held his nerve and confidently replied, "yes, Signore Lupo, I can see clearly. And I think this is the reason Andrea asked you to come to me. This is, after all, the traditional way of doing things, right?"

"But I cannot contain my passion like this, I cannot continue to wait."

"But after only a month, signore?" instantly realising his mistake.

Tonino leapt to his feet, glared and wagged a finger at him, "you mock me signore? You distrust my feelings? My motives? You make fun of me?" The two bodyguards suddenly loomed behind, almost as if on cue.

"No, no, signore, I did not mean it like that," he stuttered in abject fear of his life, "it is amazing just how much passion my sister can engender in you in just one month. It speaks volumes for your love." Tonino smiled, the guards dropped their shoulders, the barman replaced the shotgun beneath the counter, everyone relaxed.

Only Pasquale worried that customers would notice the growing stain at the front of his trousers.

"Good, I think we see eye to eye now, my dear Pasquale," putting a squeezing arm around his shoulder. He then downed his amaretto and made to leave. "So, please tell Andrea I cannot wait to see her and I would love to take her to dinner next Saturday night. Bring her reply here tomorrow night at 9 pm. Julio here will take the message, I have business in Sava."

I bet you do, thought Pasquale, relieved beyond measure that Tonino Lupo, so called, had not recognised him. But he was now certain that Lupo was Paulo Sempre from the Sava SCU and he went home a worried man, a very worried man indeed.

* * *

34

ANTIQUITIES HUNTER

1953

"Boss, that idiot Pasquale is back!"

"Where?"

"Outside in the bar, asking after you."

"Hm, he's a hard man to shake off, eh? He must be really desperate."

"Nah, I think he's just simple in the head. Surely he must realise we've been ripping him off all this time?" laughed Toni.

"Precisely, desperate! Probably he does realise something's awry but he obviously needs money, any money. Ah, go on, show him in."

A very dishevelled Pasquale shuffled in, looking twice his twenty-one tender years in tramplike clothes with greasy hair and the sproutings of a rough beard.

"Hello again, Pasquale, my dear friend, how have you been?" beamed Mario Gennari.

"OK."

"Well, if you don't mind me saying you look a long way from OK."

"What? Oh, you mean my appearance? Sorry, I was so excited by these finds I hurried straight here without even bothering to change. I am sorry. Do I smell?"

"No, no, no, of course not," Mario lied. "So, what you got that can't wait, eh? Most of this stuff has waited over 2000 years so why can't it wait another day?" he laughed expansively, and surprisingly was joined by Toni too. Together they all roared in that false style worthy of the bonhomie of best mates, eagerly wondering what the other had to offer.

Business had picked up considerably since he'd last seen Pasquale and the cash flow was returning; well, to Mario's pocket at least. But Mario was keen to not let all and sundry know how well he was doing so he had kept the same dull and dingy back office for appearances, or lack of them.

"I thought I'd poke around a new area and it looks like no-one has ever come across it. In all the time I was there I never saw a soul, probably because it is way off the beaten track in the middle of nowhere."

"Sounds good," offered Mario non-committedly.

"Good may not be the word," countered Pasquale excitedly.

"Really, so where is this place, out of interest?"

"Oh, Grottaglie way", replied Pasquale, equally non-committedly.

"It's been over a year since you've been to see us, what have you been up to? Looking for this new site?"

"And I had to leave rather fast, if I remember, out of your back door, thanks to those government inspectors who…"

"…oh, yes, them. Actually I've been fortunate lately as they seem to have left me alone. Anyway, come on, let's see this exciting discovery you have made, shall we?"

Mario pulled his green baize cloth from a drawer and neatly laid it on his bare desk. After thinking how good business could be if there was no paperwork on the desk Pasquale carefully lifted a dirty jute bag from his lap onto the desk and one by one pulled out a range of items - rectangular coins, tiny oil lamps made of stone, blackened jewellery and a clay pot about 8 centimetres in diameter.

Mario pretended to give them a cursory examination but in actual fact the sly young bird was very quickly realising that simple Pasquale may have stumbled across some very valuable items. He kept his deadpan face and grumbled, "not easy to identify some of this. The coins are fairly valueless, the country is awash with ancient coins, and the jewellery is so blackened I'd need to get it cleaned up first. And that's an expert job, and it all costs money, you know."

"Oh dear," mumbled poor Pasquale, immediately reduced to misery, as Mario fully intended. "But what about the rest, Mario, surely they…"

"Yes, certainly I can take the oil lamps and pot. I'll give you a good price for those. Must be Messipican period."

"Really?"

"Oh yes, very popular now. I'll tell you what, I'll give you 20,000 lira each for the pots, that 80,000, OK?"

"80,000? Oh yes, certainly, great! And the coins?"

"Ah, the coins, as I said, not worth a lot. Shall we say 100,000?"

"Oh yes, 100,000 for the coins would be good, Mario, thanks."

"No, no, 100,000 for everything. 20,000 for the coins plus the 80,000, OK?"

Pasquale thought the coins worth more than 20,000 but what choice did he have? "Yes, I suppose so," he replied hesitantly. But the jewellery?" He had nearly forgot all about those pieces in his deliberations with the slippery Mario. Pasquale was not a complete fool: he understood how middle men tricked and fawned.

"Ah, the jewellery. Look, may I take it to a friend to get it cleaned up and valued?"

"Er...well..."

"It'll be fine, dear Pasquale, nothing to worry about. Look, if you like I can give you a receipt now, see?" He pulled out a scruffy small notebook, tore off a page and started writing. "There, '5 pieces blackened jewellery, possibly Greco', how's that?"

"Yes, but what does that piece of paper do? I give you precious jewellery, you give me a dirty scrap of paper!"

"Oh Pasquale, my innocent young friend. This is called a 'receipt'. It is proof, if you like, proof that you gave me the jewellery and proof I gave you this paper to say so. If you like, Toni can also sign as a witness?"

"Well...alright."

"Look, meet me back here in two, er, better make it three days, same time, and I'll let you know what's happened. OK?"

"OK."

"Good, a quick drink, Pasquale? Looks like you need one. Then I'll get your cash." He handed Pasquale a dirty tumbler with some pastiche. It burned all the way down. Good quality, then.

Pasquale had never seen Mario so happy or affable. He felt pleased with himself. Perhaps they *were* valuable after all. Now he might respect me a bit more, he thought.

Mario returned with the cash in a dirty brown envelope, bringing him back to his senses.

"Mind how you go; you are carrying a tempting amount of cash there... even if you do look like a dog's dinner!"

Pasquale muttered a thanks and turned on his heel, the sound of Mario and Toni roaring with laughter echoing in his head. Was that a sinister comment or a piece of advice, he thought, ramming the envelope down the front of his trousers and pulling out his shirt over the top. True, he still had no bank in which he could safely lodge the cash and 100,000 lira was a lot of money.

Three days later Pasquale found himself again in front of the counter at Mario's, in both good humour and better clothes. He had cleaned himself up, gone to Brindisi and found a medium-priced gentlemen's outfitters and treated himself to his very first suit. Dark brown with cream thin pinstripe and very handsome indeed. Even a number of ladies approved out of the corner of their eye. How did ladies not go cross-eyed, Pasquale laughed to himself. He wondered how good the news would be, for he was sure the jewellery was special. Hints of gold and silver, with corners of sparkling stone, had lain under the black of natural aging by 2000 years of soil and rain and sun.

"Boss, he's back!"

"Yeh, Pasquale, right? Thanks. Now, remember, not a word about their value."

"You sure your friend's right, boss? He ain't really no expert, you know. He grew up with me in Andrand and as far as I know never went to university or any posh college."

"Toni, knock it off. He's spent years, well, most of his life dealing with this stuff. There ain't nothing he don't know. University of life, Toni, experience beats books. He was raving when I collected the stuff yesterday. Nearly gave me an armed guard just back to here, he did."

"So it's true it's worth a packet, then?

"And some more! My friend couldn't believe it had been found locally. He's never seen it before and he's sure it's the first of its type found in this region. 'Alter the archaeology books', that's what he reckoned. 'Get a lot of people re-examining the ancient history of this region, he reckoned."

"Mama mia, boss! Hadn't we better be careful then?"

"Yes, we'll need to fence it very quickly and take what we can too. You know, all the way up the line the seller gets stuffed, the buyer always gets it cheaper than he should for a quick sale. Oh well, that's the way of the world. We stuff Pasquale, then we get stuffed. But at least we make some money along the way."

"What we talking boss? Thousands or tens of thousands?"

"Maybe even hundreds of thousands!"

"Hell! We're rich! You didn't tell your friend Grottaglie way, did you, boss?"

"Do you think I look stupid? I never reveal my source; too dangerous. Got to keep one or two steps ahead of the game. Come on, think, where would we be now if I'd told him who'd found it and where? Middle men must always protect the middle with their lives."

"Not literally, boss!" Toni laughed.

"No. Right, this Pasquale. I think instead of constantly cheating him, which I agree is so easy because he's an idiot and it is such fun, I think we should cultivate him a little now."

"Oh, you think he might find another dealer who was more scrupulous and realise what we've been doing to him, then we'd be… well, I don't know where."

"Precisely. He could. But it wouldn't be easy. You know this is all totally illegal, fencing historical artifacts, and I don't actually know many others who do what we are doing…"

"…You wouldn't. They would all be too busy like you keeping quiet, hiding and watching their backs," Toni surprised Mario with his crude insight.

"Maybe. Anyway, I am going to give Pasquale a slight inkling that he's on to something good. At least that will convince him to keep the news all to himself and realise he can't go blabbing it about."

"And make him try harder to find lots more," Toni smiled.

"Obviously. And this time I'm not going to tell him he found real treasure, either. The dog's got to chase the rabbit, not just sniff its scent. Get him in."

Pasquale walked in to a beaming Mario, handshaking and double cheek-kissing him simultaneously. "Ah, the hero returns!" he exclaimed jubilantly.

Pasquale realised instantly he must have found something valuable. "So what did your friend think of the jewellery, Mr Ginnaro?"

"My friend said it was decent stuff, yes 'very decent stuff' were his exact words if I remember right."

"And the value?"

"Ah well, now then, first he offered me 150,000 lira but I said no and managed to haggle him up to 220,000. Pretty good eh?

"Wow, for 5 pieces of blackened metal and stone? Fantastic, I'd say," purred Toni.

"Thanks, Toni. He asked if there was likely to be more, Pasquale?"

"Yes, I'm certain of it. Did he say what they were?"

"Now you remind me, yes he did. He reckoned they were brooches and clasps worn by upper-class Greek ladies."

"But," Pasquale interrupted, "they never lived round here."

"Ah yes," Mario interjected, rather impressed and quite surprised by this village idiot's working knowledge of such things, "Greek businessmen had bought them and taken them back to Greece as gifts, probably from Spain."

Toni asked, "So they are not actually Greek then?"

"Oh no, certainly not. Too ornate. My friend estimates most likely early craft work from what is now Andalusia. Brought through here perhaps for sales along the way? It's hard to say for sure. So you can get more?" enquired Mario quietly and calmly, not letting any excitement get the better of him.

"Oh yes, I'm sure. It wouldn't just be an isolated find, one businessman dropping them, would it? Maybe I've found an early trading point."

Mario confirmed, "Maybe you've uncovered an ancient settlement the experts didn't even know existed! After all, I think the semi-formal exchange point a much better idea than, say, just one merchant being robbed or losing his consignment."

"Great. I'd better get back then and start looking for more, eh." He motioned to leave but suddenly remembered, "oh, what about my money, then?"

"Ah, your money. See, you are so excited you almost forgot!" laughed Mario. "Here, I've even put it in a nice bag safely for you. Mind how you go, you'll soon be rich!" Pasquale went to leave. "Oh, just out of interest, where *are* you keeping all this money, by the way? Can I help in any way?"

"It's OK, I have it safe. Thanks. How much am I carrying this time then?" Pasquale had not even bothered to check the bag's contents.

"Er.....100,000 lira."

"But you said he gave you 220,000?"

"Yes, true, but heh, this is normal business, you know. What about all my expenses and my little bit of profit? This is risky work too. Fair's fair. ..."

"I know that, but you could have..."

"Could have what? Could have given you less? Certainly. Lied to you? Yes. But we are partners now. I couldn't cheat you. Heh, we could get very rich, you and I. What about that, my friend?"

"Well yes, true, but..."

"OK then. But promise me one thing, Pasquale, promise you won't go down the bars tonight getting blind drunk to celebrate and telling everyone where your site is."

"I won't. I wouldn't, honest. I…"

"No, you won't. Can you imagine, it would be like a gold rush, like that one in California."

"Yes, 1849."

Once again, Mario was astounded by Pasquale's knowledge and was about to ask him how he knew when he thought better of it, more time-wasting. Instead, he reverted to his earlier theme, "I mean what I said about partners, Pasquale. Not business partners, not like that, but you and me working together, and getting rich."

"Yea, right, Mario, great idea. I find it, you sell it."

"Great, great. And to help you find it I'm going to help you."

"How?"

"By investing in some new equipment for you."

"Wow, thanks Mario!"

"Yea, new equipment. But I am going to keep it very hush hush, and you have to also. Otherwise, like I said, if anyone sees it and knows what it's for, we're lost. Sccch!" He made the noise and motion of someone cutting a throat with a knife.

"OK, Mario, hush hush."

"Yeh, so when I've got this equipment I'll need to get word to you. We'll meet somewhere out of town to keep it quiet, OK?"

"OK". Pasquale moved again to leave.

"Wait, I need to know where to find you"

"I've got a few things to sort out. I'll send you a letter with the address, Mario."

"Thanks, good luck then. Give me a couple of weeks."

* * *

35

ABSENCE, HEART
AND ALL THAT

1 9 5 6

Andrea had to admit she could not wait to see Tonino again. Her passion burned on without consummation and it made her alternatingly ecstatic and irritating at work. No-one could understand or cope with her rapid mood swings as the days went by, not even her family. The kind opinion was that she was tired and unwell, the less kind that these were the first onsets of matronhood, only cured by having a man. Of Tonino there was neither sight nor sound: he had disappeared off the face of the Earth. The papers had reported the attempted carjacking incident after the opera and those at work and at home asked if Andrea had seen anything of it because she must have been on that road at that time. Her answer became a stock response: 'does a farmer see the fox take the chicken?' When she was met with stares and open mouths she changed it to 'just because we drove home from Lecce that night doesn't mean we saw the incident—would we be the only car on the road?' That received a satisfied acceptance, with no further interrogation fortunately.

A few days later Andrea read in the newspaper, 'Mysterious Death of Lecce Car Robbers'.

There was little detail as the whole piece was speculative, to say the least, but it suggested that two men had been mysteriously murdered near Napoli and seemed to be linked to the recent car hold-up. She started to worry intensely, panic-stricken that Tonino might have disappeared because he was hunting the men and, even worse, become a murderer in the process. Pasquale read it too and asked her the very same question. She could only answer, 'I don't know; I haven't seen him.' So Pasquale became similarly worried, but at least kept his thoughts to himself, well, for that moment anyway.

He had reported to Andrea that Tonino wanted to take her to dinner and she had agreed, reluctantly, but he did not tell her that the message had not got back to Tonino because his bodyguard Julio did not turn up at the bar as agreed. Maybe he had gone off hurriedly with Tonino to Napoli too?

And then, to confound all theories, Tonino appeared, as always he did, in the shop when there were no customers. "Hello Andrea," he smiled, while winking at Claudia.

"Claudia, go and hang these dresses, please," demanded Andrea sternly, obviously angry at the wink.

"Certainly, madame, straight away," winking back.

"Tonino, why do you wink at that girl? And where have you been?"

"Oh dearest, I know I said I'd see you again in the wink of an eye." He paused for her to laugh, but when she glared back even harder he tightened up. "But business came up and I had to go to Napoli at short notice…"

"Oh, and not killing road robbers then?" He looked blankly at her so she thrust the newspaper in his face so hard that it nearly knocked him out!

When he had recovered he read a little and said, "oh, great, they have caught them them…"

"…no, not caught them, murdered them!"

"Ah, probably part of some gang war then, territorial dispute, something like that. Who knows?"

"So you don't then?"

"Don't what, Andrea?"

"Know."

"Of course not. What would it be to do with me, dearest? We were just the victims."

"Yes, but you were rather adept at overwhelming them so quickly, weren't you?"

"Well, to be honest, when you have a lot you soon learn how to protect it. Anyway, I have not come to discuss murder in Napoli, I have come to apologise for my absence and…"

"…why couldn't you let me know you'd be away?"

"For the simple reason that I did not know how long it would take. There were complications and they delayed me. And anyway, if it had been the opposite way round and I'd said I would be away a week then came home early you would have been equally annoyed."

"No I would not! But perhaps next time it might be caring of you to let me know you are going away. I didn't even know you were going and you just took off."

"My, you are starting to sound like a nagging wife," he laughed, "and we hardly know each other yet. Anyway, I told your brother I was going away".

Andrea knew she had lost and she realised how foolish she had been to let down her defences so and allow him to realise just how much she had missed him. Perhaps it had always been that all along, just a ploy to see how much she cared for him. Well, she'd fallen into that little trap, fair and square, just like the fool her feelings were making her.

"And I told you never to come here again, and I would only speak to you through my dear brother!"

"I know, and I very sorry, but it has been so long and I longed to just see you again."

Andrea softened at that, inside, but she would not let him see it. "So, you have seen me; be off before there is trouble the next time."

"Oh, and I'm glad you said next time, twice in fact, Andrea, so the next time has arrived. Tonight, can I please offer you dinner?"

"Hm, where? What time?"

"Vecchia Oria? 9pm?"

"Well, if you see me there I'll be there, and if you don't, I won't, OK? Now go away, I am very busy!" Tonino was shooed out of the shop without knowing his fate, but he could guess: he knew women, and he knew the lure of the best restaurant in town.

And he did guess correctly. She walked in at exactly 9.15, enough time to let him wonder and worry but not enough time to lose him. They had a joyous meal, especially the antipasti which was always to their liking there because it was always cheese-rich and fish poor. All seemed well and he walked her partly home, only stopping to kiss passionately in an alleyway. She forced him to stop, not wanting to; after all, who was to know who might see such a flagrant exhibition of wanton desire? On arrival home poor Andrea's head was in such a flurry it was the first time she did not wonder where he actually lived and how he travelled home as she crept in her door.

Pasquale, meanwhile, had been waiting the three hours late that she was. "Have you been with him again?" he whispered.

"Yes, actually I have. We had a lovely dinner and he walked me part way home. Is that a problem?"

"Dearest sis, you know how much I love you and how much I'd do for you, but after a week away from him I was hoping you might be feeling differently."

"Are Mama and Maria asleep?"

"Of course, it is past midnight. Now look, I have been asking around again about your rich boyfriend, especially after those robbers were killed. By the way, I learned that one of them was short, fat and about 30, the other fairly tall, very thin with odd spiky hair. Would those be the two who attacked you, by any chance?"

Andrea paused to recall. It had all happened in such a flash, a continuous blur of movements in and out of headlights. She couldn't be sure but said, "it sounds like them, but it all happened so quickly. Spiky hair, yes, that could be so."

"Ah, in that case I'm more and more convinced. I've found out his name is not Tonino Lupo at all! He is actually from near Avetrana, between Avetrana and Sava, and he is not a bone fide businessman at all!"

"Oh no!" cried Andrea, clearly upset.

"Yes, and when I saw his photo I thought he looked familiar. If I am not mistaken, and I might well be because it is ten years ago, he was a member of the neighbouring SCU area group when I…"

"…SCU? Oh no!" cried his sister, aghast.

"Afraid so. He was the leader of the Sava youth group when I was deputy of the Avetrana group with Damiano. As we all got older I managed to get out, luckily, as you know, but Tonino must have progressed up through to the main SCU and by the looks of him now must be rather important and powerful, if not the leader."

"But how can you be sure, brother? Why did you not recognise him straight away?"

"As I said, it was at least ten years ago. People grow up. He did not have a moustache them. I only met him a few times at joint meetings."

Andrea was by now sobbing. "Oh, what am I going to do now? Will I never have any good fortune in this world? Why has Mother Mary so forsaken me? I have always tried so hard to be good, and this is my reward?"

"What do you mean, sis?"

"Pasquale, you fool, you absolute and utter fool. This is the only man I have ever truly loved. This is the man I had hoped to marry!"

* * *

36

DESPERATE SITUATIONS, DESPERATE MEASURES

1 9 5 6

"**A**part from protestations of love, what else did he say this time?"

"He wants to take you for dinner again on Saturday night," replied Pasquale.

They were both in uncharted territory, rudderless in a raging sea, and, quite frankly, petrified. They did not know what to do next and there was certainly no-one in Oria to whom they could turn for advice or help.

"But I can't, brother, I can't. You know I can't," pleaded Andrea as tears began to well up.

"I know you can't but I'm really frightened now. Andrea, you should have been there: so polite and charming one moment and threatening the next, a real schizophrenic. And as for his bodyguards, that is something else totally…"

"…he has bodyguards? Oh Mother Mary! What can we do?"

'I suppose we could stall him yet again and say you're not free this weekend," suggested Pasquale dubiously.

"And, pray, what might I be doing? Gardening?" Her joke was unable to break their tension, and Pasquale mumbled on.

"We could say you have a visit to a relative already planned, with your Mother and sister. He would have to believe that."

And so he did. But he was most unhappy. Suspecting that all was not well he turned up for the appointed meeting himself, instead of his bodyguard, and poor Pasquale had to bear the brunt of his railing and acrimony. But there was little else Tonino could do, except make another dinner date with Andrea for the following Thursday. Fortunately, Tonino was out of town until then so they could relax a little in the lull before the storm.

But it was only a lull, a stay of execution. Something permanent had to be concocted, but after racking their brains for two nights they could only arrive at two possible solutions, apart from the obvious but far-fetched and risky one of hiring a hitman. She could either tell him bluntly that she was no longer interested in him, or they could all leave town…yet again! Both were difficult; both had uncertain outcomes. At present they could only hope that by being out of sight so much Andrea might also become out of Tonino's mind, and then he might either lose interest or find consolation elsewhere, if he was not already doing so.

So Pasquale passed the message that Andrea would meet him on Thursday at 7pm in Bar Sedile and then go on for dinner. The bar was at the north end of Piazza Manfredi and there would be plenty of people about at that time, taking the evening air or sipping coffee. The more the better, thought Pasquale. Cleverly, by letter, he had invited Cosimo to come for the day, to see everyone and to help a little in a "tricky situation", as he called it. Pasquale thought that if he had entered into more detail in the letter Cosimo might have been scared off, but he did agree to come only on the condition that all would be revealed on arrival. Pasquale also asked Signore Bellini and his elderly friend to the bar for strength in numbers. He asked them to sit nonchalantly around him, not like bodyguards obviously as they were far too old and dignified to ever pretend that.

So when Tonino arrived without bodyguards everyone heaved a sigh of relief, but not too happily, as who was to know how many of his men were lounging outside the bar? Pasquale made his opening gambit, saying that poor Andrea was unwell and could not come. However, would Tonino like to join his friends for a drink? As anyone could imagine, he was by now at his wits end and he glared dangerously at the ragged band of old folk and peasants.

"You do not speak the truth! I am not happy at all. I am a busy man who has taken time out of his schedule to attend this agreed appointment and you have the audacity to tell me now that the appointment is cancelled? What is going on, Pasquale?" he menaced.

"Going on? Well, it is true that Andrea is unwell…"

"She managed to go to work today!"

"And how did you know?" dared Pasquale, losing confidence and Dutch courage by the second.

"I have my informants. Go on."

"As I was saying, Andrea is unwell, but not with a normal sickness. She is ill because you have made her so," he gulped.

"Me? What do you mean, me?"

Pasquale girded himself, it was now or never, no turning back, "she has wrestled with her heart and with her conscience these past days, and she has finally come to the conclusion that she just cannot see you anymore."

"Cant?"

"Er…well, won't…"

"…won't?"

"No, she will not see you again, she says. It's not that she doesn't like you…"

"…like?"

"Er… like, yes, but she feels the life and the lifestyle you might offer may be very different to what she knows…"

"…might?"

Cosimo smiled to himself: this boy has certainly come on in leaps and bounds and has really mastered the difficult art of diplomacy and tact; very impressive, he thought.

"Well, she, we, know very little about you. We don't know where you live, for instance, or anything about your family…"

"But you see me, don't you, isn't that all that matters?"

"Presumably not to a traditional girl…"

"Traditional?" Now Tonino was really angry and his temper was almost ripe for bursting.

"She is very sorry, signore, but can you not see it from her viewpoint?"

"Her viewpoint? How dare she insult me so? I am a man!" he bellowed. He raised his hand and within seconds three men appeared at the door.

Pasquale spotted them immediately, perhaps almost expecting it, and trembled as he muttered, "please Tonino, I beg you, please don't make a scene in here. It is so embarrassing…"

"…oh, and you think your sister has not embarrassed me? Not ruined my reputation as a man?"

"But it will not help in the long run, will it? It will do your cause little good."

"So? I can have some satisfaction here tonight, yes?" Tonino leered menacingly as he entwined all ten fingers and cracked them in a backwards flex.

"But how would that impress Andrea, signore?" panicked Pasquale.

"From what you say she is beyond that anyway, correct?"

"Oh signore, so hard to tell with females," joked Pasquale, desperate to restore some sensible equilibrium to the ever-darkening proceedings, "you know how they are…"

"…yes, indeed I do," smiled Tonino. He paused and thought about it. He certainly knew how fickle women could be and how some would stop at nothing to appear the dominant partner in a relationship, thinking they always had the upper hand. He remembered those before who had angered him so, and especially the two he had cut so badly their happiness had been permanently ruined. Served them right, he thought.

Pasquale, despite his continuing fear, sensed that this might be the moment and put his hand on Tonino's arm in a warm gesture, "all may not be lost, dear sir, so let us be sensible in case there is future possibility. Yes?"

"OK." And that was it, as quick as that. Tonino jumped up, straightened his back in pride, spun round, muttered 'OK' again and walked majestically out of the all-eyes bar at a reverent pace.

The others merely stared at each other in total shock and amazement. With increasing belief came the breaking-out smiles, the odd muttered words. No-one really knew what to say or how to say it, until finally Cosimo slapped Pasquale on the back and shouted in excitement, "you did it, boy, you really did it!"

Suddenly the group was re-energised and started clapping wildly and laughing with each other. "Shush, please, everyone," shouted back the numbed Pasquale, "what if he is still outside? He will come back in and kill us all!"

"Nonsense, boy, he knows when he is beat, he won't be back. You've won!"

"I may have won the battle but the war is not yet over, uncle."

* * *

37

INDECENT PROPOSALS

1 9 5 6

"Where is Pasquale?" asked Cosimo.

"He went to Brindisi in his old motor."

"Oh? Why? That's an odd thing to do, isn't it? Will that old rust heap make it? Can it go more than a few kilometres at a time?"

"You know Pasquale, dearest, "odd things" is his middle name," laughed Isabella.

"When did he leave then?"

"Crack of dawn, I believe."

"Hmm! All very odd, very odd indeed"

Isabella continued cooking while Cosimo swept the tiled floors. With three working children it did not seem fair to ask them to do all the housework when they came home after a tiring day. Suddenly the front door banged open. "Come and see, everyone, come and see!" They put down their implements and hurried to the door. Looking out they saw the square was empty, not a soul in sight.

"See what?" asked Cosimo.

"See what I've got, silly!"

"Well, what *have* you got, silly boy yourself," retorted Isabella, "I can see nothing, there's nothing out there except..." She paused, "two cars."

"Yes, the black one is? Is who's?" asked Pasquale, now rather impatient at their stupidity.

"The Mantira's at number 6, yes," answered Cosimo dutifully.

"And the blue one?" sighed Pasquale.

"Ah, the blue one, I don't know who's that is. A visitor, perhaps?" asked Cosimo vaguely, and with increasing boredom at the game. But Isabella saw the twinkle and knew her son better than his stepfather.

"Pasquale, you haven't been to Brindisi to buy that, have you?"

Her son could not contain his excitement any longer and he practically flew down the steps. "Come and see, it's a beauty, the new-style Fiat, with…"

"…but how could you afford a new car, Pasquale?" asked a concerned Cosimo.

I said the "new-style", Cosimo, not "new". Of course it's not new, but it is in such good condition and has done very few kilometres. It's a beauty!"

"And how did you get this beauty, Pasquale?" asked Isabella, becoming concerned too at the cost of it all.

Pasquale became a little less excited and more cautious now, "er… er… a friend of mine heard about an old lady dying and the family wanting a quick sale…"

"…old lady, dying, quick sale…all sounds very…um…predictable," replied Cosimo, starting to become suspicious.

"Yes, these things *do* happen, Cosimo."

"True, true; but now then, are you sure you're telling us the whole truth, boy?"

"Yes, of course, why wouldn't I?" shouted Pasquale, angry and affronted.

"And your old scrapheap?" enquired Mama.

"Ah, you wouldn't believe the price for scrap metal, Mama. Even now, all these years after the War there is still a shortage. Do you know, I got 50,000 lira from the scrap merchant!"

"Nearly all profit, then, clever boy, since you found it for nothing in that field three years ago!" admired his mother.

"Well, it looked lovely for a while but soon the rust got the better of it and it was just eating up money, you know. Come on, come on, let's go for a drive now, you'll love it…" Smiled Pasquale, regaining composure and excitement.

"…but dinner is on, silly boy!"

"Right, of course. OK, we'll go after dinner and surprise Maria coming out from the bar."

"Sounds a sensible idea, yes let's," agreed Cosimo, "and if we leave a bit earlier we can have a quick drink there too!" he laughed.

"So where is Andrea tonight?" asked Pasquale.

"On another date with her fella, I think," muttered Mama.

"What? Without asking me?" demanded Pasquale.

"Obviously!"

"Actually," interjected Cosimo, "now your Mother and I are wed would it not be more correct for this young stud to be asking me, rather than you?"

"Oh, I wish he would," smiled Pasquale, "he frightens the life out of me, especially when he has his two *friends* with him."

"Yes, I saw that last time. I wonder if he would act quite the same with me, though?"

"Cosimo, he is SCU, an SCU leader, I told you. He was in charge of Sava youth when I was in Avetrana, and I'm sure he has worked his way up. How else could he be so wealthy? I have warned Andrea but she does not heed it. She seems to want to marry him!"

"Oh dear, and when did you plan to tell us all this, pray?" asked Isabella as she collapsed in a chair and started to swoon from the news.

"I have known a while and I have just been too worried to tell you. I was kind of hoping she would get over him, but it seems less and less likely now."

"Oh Cosimo, what can we do? We can't let her ruin her life so."

"No, no, certainly not. Pasquale, I wish you had told us this earlier, I am very angry now. I thought we had dealt with it at the bar, once and for all."

"I'm sorry, I thought it best. I hoped it would go away. I said then our victory over Tonino was only a temporary one. You know what she is like, never becomes committed to any man. And, as I said, I did warn her. Actually, it was straight after those road robbers were killed…"

"…yes, I'll bet Tonino had a hand in that too."

"They attacked Andrea and him on the way home from the Lecce opera that same night."

"Pasquale, you never told us this!" Cosimo exploded, becoming even more furious.

"I'm sorry, I'm sorry," wailed poor Pasquale.

"There, there, dear, it will be all right," soothed his Mother, who was nowhere near calm herself, but always a mother first.

"Isabella, it will not! But really, there's nothing we can do now, at this minute. I suggest we wait and see what she is like when she comes home."

"You're right, dear, yes, let's see what she has to say then," calmed Mama. "Let's have dinner now and cheer up a bit, it's not the end of the world yet! Sorry, Pasqua, your lovely new car will just have to wait."

And so they did. And afterwards they buzzed around Oria in the *new* car. One or two heads even turned, as there were still not many people who could own a car in those days. They daringly ventured out into the campagna in the dark, getting up to 55 kmh under the probing headlights. The elation and exhilaration of the speed partly neutralised their depressing pre-dinner conversation; that is until they pulled up by the bar to pick up Maria. At the front door lounged the mysterious stranger from their wedding. Suddenly Maria emerged and he grabbed her arm as she pushed past him, but she wrested it away, almost expertly it was noted, and moved purposefully towards the sound of Pasquale's shout. She smiled at the new car, jumped in, again almost expertly, and said, "let's get away quick, that lounge lizard is still pestering me!"

"Didn't know he was pestering you, sis, you never said."

"And how much of your business do you tell me, then? This car for instance!"

"Touche. But if he is worrying you why not tell us?"

"Oh yes, and exactly what are you and Cosimo going to be able to do about it? He's got quite a gang of friends, you know."

"Oh Lord, not another gang!" exclaimed poor Cosimo. "Just how do you Carones attract them, then?"

At home, Andrea had already let herself in by the time the others had arrived. She was happily humming a dance tune to herself and she busied with clearing up her room.

"A good evening then?" shouted Cosimo, definite in his vagueness.

"Oh yes, lovely actually, thank you," replied Andrea in mock innocence.

"And what did you do, my dear," enquired Mama, also trying to act as nonchalantly as possible even though her heart was filling again with dread.

"Oh, we had our usual dinner, and chatted," Andrea lied as convincingly as possible.

Cosimo entered her bedroom and asked, "and was he the perfect gentleman, Andrea?"

"Of course, sir, as always," she lied again, this time slightly less convincingly.

"Did you reach any major conclusions?" interjected Maria.

"About?"

"Oh, you know, about your future with him, like marriage perhaps?" Cosimo continued, seeing that no-one was getting anywhere and the hour was late.

"Sir, it is far too premature to be discussing such things: please!" she blustered with reddening face.

And then Cosimo knew, as probably did the others too by now, that something was dreadfully wrong because of that one word. She never addressed him as "sir"; it was like she was talking to an official, or being interviewed by the carabinieri. "Andrea, please credit me with enough intelligence and respect to speak the truth!"

"Oh Cosimo, I'm sorry. You are right. You are all right," she gesticulated round the room, "I had an awful evening, actually, well, nice but awful...I know I shouldn't have gone but I just can't help myself."

"...girl, talk plain, how can something be nice as well as awful?"

"I meant the restaurant was nice, and the dinner was superb, as ever, but Tonino's behaviour in the car afterwards was not. He pleaded passionate love for me, which I knew already, but he told me he was tired of my standoffishness. I'm sure he is used to getting his own way immediately, and having his way with women too, I'm not too stupid to realise that, but my refusals really anger him..."

"...what refusal, dear?" asked Mama innocently.

"Oh Mama," they all chorused, "please! You know."

"What?"

"Andrea won't let him," Maria blurted.

"Oh!" realised poor Mama, "the scoundrel, the wretched scoundrel!"

Cosimo decided it was now timely to take the bull by the horns and, being a man, knew full well what to say, "Andrea, dearest, Tonino is a man of the world..."

"...not like you, then, dear," laughed Mama, trying to alleviate the tension.

Cosimo smiled graciously but refused to be drawn down that avenue of discussion, so continued, "unlike me he has probably had many love affairs and many different women because there is no doubt he is a handsome fellow. As soon as he is satiated he discards them - young women, old women, women with history no doubt - but you see, he has probably never ever come across a more beautiful woman than you, and one who is so pure at your age, if you know my meaning." His face went bright red when he realised exactly what he had said.

"Cosimo, do not be ashamed," continued Isabella, "you are quite right, and quite right to say it. Andrea, it is clear that it is precisely what Cosimo said that makes Tonino want you so much, and probably want your hand in marriage too. You are so different to all the other women he has met."

"Yes, but you'll see, after a while he'll become bored with you and marriage and he'll start playing around again. Men like that are like that, they never change," added Pasquale.

"Oh sis, you will end up so unhappy, can't you see?" Maria contributed.

"But I love him, Maria, I really do!"

"That is the conundrum," enjoined Cosimo, "the impossible puzzle."

"Well, someone better solve it quickly otherwise nothing but grief will follow," suggested Pasquale, tired and wanting to go to bed, as did all if truth were known.

And so it was. Everyone was at a loss, too shocked and worried to think, too tired to keep a clear head, so they all decided to sleep on it. However, at least two of the five could not, and they each spent a very restless night, separately, seeking an answer... any answer. Andrea could not; her thoughts were clouded and blinded by her love, but Pasquale may have profited from the exercise.

Next morning saw everyone dashing off on their separate ways: to the dress shop, to an early shift in the bar, and to the fields. Even Cosimo decided to join Pasquale, not because he fancied trudging across hot dusty fields holding some piece of metal and a shovel in his hands, but because he fancied another ride in the new car. It turned out to be a totally uneventful day for all, except Isabella. At 6 pm she spotted a note which had been forced under the front door. It was unsealed and its message was perfectly clear... "Pasquale, meet me Roma Bar 8 pm, T". No pleasantness or politeness: it was not a request, it was an order.

So at 8 pm Pasquale again sat at the bar, this time alone. Cosimo, though, sat within the interior shadows as the light finally failed outside. Exactly on time Tonino swaggered in with his two friends keeping close company. "A beer, and another for my friend here. Oh, and one more for dear old Cosimo hiding there in the shadows!" he demanded, laughing and slapping Pasquale fiercely on the back and revealing all his pearlies in a flashing smile.

Such a good mood could turn in an instant, thought Pasquale. Cosimo eased slightly, but was still in shock from being known and recognised so easily.

"Pasquale, we have been good friends for ages, right?"

"Well, yes, six months or so, I suppose."

"Indeed, indeed. And all that time you have known me to be honest with my word?"

"Yes.' What else could poor Pasquale say in the circumstances?"

"Well, I know you are hungry and would like to get home before the beers take over your functions, so I will say one thing to you, one thing only, very quickly. I want to marry your sister!"

Pasquale's mouth dropped and he nearly spilled the next sip of his Peroni.

"No, not a word, please. Just go please and tell her. Tell her tonight. Tell her it *will* happen, and very soon. There will be no need for me to see Andrea again before that day, nor she me, but as a sign of consent just tie a red ribbon to your front door before 10 pm. Clear? Now, drink up and go. And take old Pa with you!" Tonino and his friends laughed: they were in good humour indeed.

But Pasquale could hardly finish his beer for shaking, and anyone who did not know what had just transpired would have thought the drink was responsible for his staggering as he left the bar. Once out they rushed home to tell the terrible news. Andrea looked expressionless as Pasquale announced it to the family who had gathered in dread and loathing soon after eight, awaiting his return. Then Andrea smiled, started to laugh, then clapped her hands and finally slumped back into her chair.

"So, my darling girl, what a fine mess you have got us into now, eh!" moaned her mother.

"He was quite clear, sis, he demands his reply in the next hour or so."

"I cannot, no, I will not be forced to decide like this, he will have to wait," she uttered forlornly.

Cosimo tried to soothe her, "Andrea, think, there *is* nothing to decide. Can't you see the future mapped out before you now? This is how it will be. He will de-feminise you, he will take away all your independence, your own decision-making, your freedom even. He will rule you, dictate what you do and then waste you. Do you really want to end up a slave to him and his desires for ever?"

Silence descended because everyone assembled knew how wise Cosimo was and how right he was. The minutes ticked by and soon it came to that awful hour. They bolted the door and continued to sit, waiting for they knew not what.

But as the minutes laboured on at the slowest speed they had ever known there seemed to be nothing to wait for. There were no bullets thudding into the door, flying through the window or pinging round the room, there was no banging or thumping on anything either, or no shouting or bellowing in the street. Just an unearthly silence. It seemed they waited for ever but by 10.15 Pasquale said, "I don't know about you but I'm going to bed. There's nothing to be done here, obviously."

But Cosimo was not so sure, "don't you think they might rush in and capture Andrea, or even kill us all? Surely we cannot just calmly walk off to bed like that?"

"No, if you remember, Tonino did say "as a sign of consent" we should hang the ribbon. Obviously therefore we do not consent. So he is not going to rush in and do something foolish…"

"…oh, you think he will now have to go away and consider his next move?" realised Mama.

"Yes, correct. I think we are quite safe at the moment and we should try to get some sleep. We can then reassess the situation in the morning when we are fresher. OK?"

"Thank you, Pasquale, a wise head on young shoulders. I'm sure you're right, the more I think about it," concurred Cosimo, "come on, everyone, off to bed, there's nothing more we can do here now."

At 6 am Pasquale quietly and slowly unbolted the door, and shaking slightly he inched it open, half expecting to be mowed down in a hail of bullets or be snatched away by heavies. But nothing happened and as he looked out he could see no-one or nothing out of place. Except one thing…his car was not where he left it. Or did he leave it there? Feeling a rising flush of panic he desperately tried to unscramble the events of the previous evening in the hope that it would remind him where he had parked it. As hard as he tried he kept coming back to the same place—just outside the old Jewish synagogue house. But that space was now empty and he finally came to the realisation that his car had been removed.

They have stolen my lovely car, he wailed to himself, how dare they? They will pay for this! He was now very angry and it was this anger that suddenly cleared enough fog in his brain to allow him to formulate the plan. Continuing to seethe, it all came together in his mind so quickly that he immediately rushed back into the house, hoping that everyone would be up and at the breakfast table.

He was correct: no-one had been able to sleep and they all sat blurringly around the huge olive wood table, propping themselves up over their bowls with their tired, shaking arms.

"They did come last night and they did do something, something which was outside the house!" announced Pasquale.

"What do you mean, boy, you talk in riddles again. That we don't need now, dear," accused Mama.

"No, Mama, think, think. What do we own that is not in the house?"

"The car?"

"Yes, the car!"

"Oh no, they didn't take the car, dear?" cried Mama.

"Afraid so, Mama, they've got my lovely car."

"Oh no," cried Maria, as they all started babbling at once and glaring at Andrea.

"But don't worry, the anger at my loss has created The Plan. Listen, this is what we are going to do. First, we *shall* tie the ribbon, never mind if it is late, we can always say if necessary we did not have any at home last night. Secondly, you ladies will go to work as normal. Thirdly, Tonino should return the car then, I'm sure he will. Fourthly, I will drive and pick you both up just after 1 pm at work where you will have feigned illness and taken the rest of the day off. Finally, we shall all be at home by 1.15 and we shall pack a few things to take on a little holiday which will start during Siesta when no-one is about."

"And where might this holiday be, brother?"

"Oh, I thought we could finds some rooms in Brindisi for a while and we can hide out there."

"So again we run, Pasquale, run, run, run, always running!" Shouted Mama.

"Mama, what choice do we have? And now Maria is being pestered as well, you know," replied Pasquale, slightly annoyed that no-one had acknowledged how sensible his plan was.

"No, I didn't know, actually. Oh no, not that boy at our wedding, is it?"

"Afraid so, Mama, and I wonder at his connections too," added Maria.

"Pasquale, I think it is a sound plan, well done! But how long do you think we can hide out in Brindisi? This Tonino is extremely resourceful…"

"...I really don't know, Cosimo, but we have to move now, quickly, somewhere. Brindisi is a big place and it's away from Tonino's territory. He may not hold much sway down there, hopefully."

"True. And we do need to move now. Come on, everyone, let's find some red ribbon quick and hope Tonino does not think we value the car more than Andrea!" His joke cheered everyone and they bustled off much more positively.

"Actually," whispered Isabella to Cosimo, "maybe it would be better if he did think that!" Cosimo quickly saw the logic and smiled.

"We'll be OK, dearest, it will all work out," he replied, but she could see the lack of belief in his eyes.

And so it was. The ribbon was hung. The ladies went to work. The car mysteriously returned unscratched. A note fluttered from its wiper telling Pasquale to meet Tonino again in the Bar Roma at 8pm. The remaining three Carones kept far away from the bolted door as they went about clearing up the house and packing. At 1.15 pm Pasquale picked up his sisters and by 2.30 they were all on the road to Latiano, en route to Mesagne and Brindisi.

* * *

38

NOWHERE TO HIDE

1 9 5 6

They found three rooms in the centro storico, the old town, of Brindisi, down a side street of unnoticeable architecture - a nothing street. The old lady who lived above offered very favourable terms, even though she considered June was part of the burgeoning "tourist season" of Italy. She declared that Brindisi was becoming overrun by tourists more and more each year. Cosimo did not have the heart or discourtesy to argue with her and point out that firstly, Brindisi could hardly be considered a tourist city to compare with the likes of Venice, Rome or Napoli and, secondly, if more visitors were being seen it was probably because the number of sailings to Greece and Yugoslavia were increasing each year and those people were workers rather than tourists. Regardless, they accepted her rental terms happily: they had no choice anyway.

The sisters slept in one room, Cosimo and Isabella in another and Pasquale put up on the sofa in the living room. Unfortunately, the shiny Fiat was somewhat too ostentatious for such a part of town so Pasquale decided to park it further away in a different part of the old town, near the Greek column by the dock, and walk to the house. For him, and even Cosimo, the days were long and monotonous. At least the women had the housework and the cooking to do, but all the men could do was take the odd walk, wander about illicitly and worry. They didn't want to get noticed by the locals so they varied their pattern each day. The women could only do the shopping at night when it was dark, wearing black shawls over their faces like grandmas. After a few days of being cooped up the men started to frequent the bars more, rather than sulk in their imprisonment. A decision they were soon to regret.

On the seventh day they staggered home around nine for their alcohol-fuelled dinner. As they crashed through the door, giggling like schoolgirls, they realised something was not right, even in their drunken stupor. There was not the usual mouth-watering smell of pasta and beans, only wailing and bowed heads. Maria was bending over Mama, dabbing her forehead, the cloth blood-red in colour. And only two bent heads, not three.

"Mama, you're bleeding! What's happened? Did you fall?" mumbled Pasquale.

"Andrea, Andrea," was all Isabella could mutter, sobbing her heart out.

Maria interjected, slightly more calmly, "they took Andrea, and they said they'd got your car too!"

"Who, Maria, who? The police? We've done nothing wrong, we're respectable citizens who…"

"…what?" shouted Isabella, "respectable citizens? Just look at you two drunkards, rolling around everywhere, how can you call yourself respectable?"

"Yes, you stupid men!" shouted Maria too, "why say the police? What would the police want with us, stupid? Tonino's thugs, of course!"

"What? How dare they" screamed Cosimo.

"They dare, they dared and they did," mumbled Isabella morosely.

"And beat Mama trying to protect Andrea. Look!" Maria moved away to reveal copious amounts of blood on Mama's forehead and deep purple bruising along her arm, presumably from a stick.

"Animals!" Isabella spat, "even hit poor old women!"

Pasquale had to sit down at the sight of all that blood. "Suppose we're lucky they didn't have guns, then…"

"…oh, they had guns all right, waving them round menacingly. They forced Andrea to throw some things into her suitcase and then dragged her away," explained Maria.

"They didn't hurt my dear sis, did they? I'll kill them if they did…"

"…no, no, no," said Maria, "but they were very rough."

"And they didn't hurt you, Maria, dear, did they?" worried Cosimo, finally beginning to sober up.

"I got a lot of looks and rude comments, but no, they were too interested in getting Andrea away, fortunately."

"Cosimo, I know we have had a lot to drink, but could you go and check if they have taken the car, please?" asked Pasquale, equally sobering up.

"Yes, OK, but please, ladies, how did they find us? Did they boast and tell you?"

"Actually, we asked them that very question and they just laughed. They said they had been ready for us all along and had followed us all the way from our house in Oria on the day we escaped. They lost us initially in Brindisi but then they started trawling the bars on the lookout for you two. When they found you they bided their time until you were sufficiently drunk then rushed to our house where only we females were at home. 'Defenceless' and 'easy pickings' were their actual words, if I remember right!" explained Isabella.

"So thanks to you two fools all our covert activity went for nought," added an outraged Maria.

"Rudeness does not become you, Maria," muttered Cosimo, obviously chastened. "I'll go and check on the car now, Pasquale."

"Think I'll join you."

"Don't you two go drowning your sorrows again; we will soon run out of money at this rate," demanded Isabella. "Just hurry up back, who knows what might happen next."

Sure enough, the car had been taken and they started to trudge their weary way back home with the tragic news. A storm added to their misery because they were not prepared for a soaking from the heavens. An old man sitting on a step out of the rain muttered 'sera' as they passed by. A few seconds later he shouted after them, "are you looking for your car?" Pasquale was never ceased to be amazed by how much life is noticed by so many within the tightly-packed confines of a centro storico. It seems one cannot even blow one's nose without five people noticing.

"Well, yes, we were, but we were told some of our friends borrowed it," ventured Pasquale.

"Friends? Some friends! Don't people normally give friends a key then?"

"Oh dear, did they break in?"

"No, you were very lucky; they were pro's. I used to be one once and I was most impressed by their professionalism and tact," he laughed.

"So how did they manage it?" asked Cosimo.

"Ah, they just jemmied the window to get to the door lock and then wired the engine."

Pasquale and Cosimo had no idea what he was talking about so just said, "thank you, signore," and moved on through the rain-filled street.

'Don't you want to know where it is, then?" shouted the old man again, enjoying every moment of this intriguing encounter.

They ran straight back to him and said, "didn't they leave Brindisi in it then? Anyway, how would you know where it is, signore, are you a mind-reader?"

"Nope, but I've still got sharp ears!" he laughed. "Pretty boring here, much of the time. This was the most exciting moment I've had for ages. I just crept up on them a bit and listened in. Easy!"

"So?"

"Ah, they just wanted to teach you a lesson, really. They said they had the woman, whatever that meant, and that was enough. Cars can be traced, women can't, they said. I had to laugh: that was quite funny!"

"Did they say anything else, signore?"

"Well, yes, something rather odd actually. One said, are we going straight there now? How will we find it in the dark? We might drive straight in the sea on those sandy tracks, or even miss that useless heap of stones."

"Thank you, signore, strange indeed. We will take our leave, thank you."

"Heh," the old man shouted, "your car?"

"Oh hell yes, the car!"

"I saw it only 2 hours ago, sir…" he paused deliberately.

"And? Yes? Where?"

"Oh signore, my memory is fading with all this thirsty talk."

"Eh?" puzzled Pasquale.

"Pasq, you are slow, our poor old friend is in desperate need of a drink! Here, signore, that should satisfy." Cosimo handed him some lira notes.

"Thank you, any extra always helps," the old man smiled, "yes, I remember now. It was down on the dockside behind Restaurant Gallipoli."

"Any extra"

"Yes, always welcome."

"Extra to what, pray" asked Pasquale.

"Oh signore, the men paid me ten times as much as this to keep quiet, but I'm thinking, what the heck, I'm moving to my sister's in Rome next week and they'd never find me there!"

"But you said they didn't see you, I…I…" stammered Pasquale, very annoyed at being cheated out of Cosimo's money, something they had precious little of left.

"...actually, I said nothing of the sort. My hearing is far better than my wizened appearance. They paid me to silence me for *seeing* what they were doing, not for what they were *saying*!"

Cosimo smiled, 'sound travels well in the still of night, eh old man? Here, some more for your honesty!"

"Thank you sir," smiled the old man as Pasquale nearly turned apoplectic.

It took them less time to find the car than the walking to the port, although Pasquale argued all the way that Cosimo should not have been so generous with his gratuity. In his turn Cosimo argued most convincingly that the information they had received was invaluable and worth every lira and, anyway, it was good to help an old crook on his way when such a favour might be showered on them one day from Above.

The car was totally undamaged. They had even wound the window back up and re-locked the vehicle from inside, so no-one would be tempted to further hijack it.

Driving home was a dangerous affair as Pasquale was still officially much the worse for drink and this was peak Carabinieri time.

"Do we now take this matter to the Carabinieri, Pasquale? Surely we must report this, it is an abduction after all."

"Report it? No, no, of course not. We cannot report it. This is not a matter for those idi..."

"...but why not?" interrupted Cosimo irritably, "Andrea has been taken against her will and..."

"...and what? No, we will settle this our way, quietly. We will find my dear sister and get her back for good."

"But how in Heaven's name are you going to manage that, son? They could have gone anywhere; a million places to hide, and that wasn't much help the old man was giving us, really."

"Well, actually, that's where I hope you're wrong. Think about it: Tonino is from Sava, the area he will know best is Sava. Even you should know it well, after all you lived fairly near there for 40 or more years. Come on, Cosimo, think!"

"True, but think of what?"

"Clues! "Drive into the sea"? "Sandy tracks"? "Heap of stones"? What do all those tell you? Eh?"

"OK. They are holding her at the coast, somewhere isolated and difficult to access, and probably a ruined house or something..."

"...yes, yes, exactly," said Pasquale excitedly, "but not a ruined old house, I'll bet. When we were young we went to play at the sea along that coast quite a lot, and when we got bored with the beach we used to go and play in a ..."

"...in a ruined...oh, I know," replied Cosimo now also excited by this game, "in a ruined torre!"

"Exactly! Yes, one of those tumbledown towers built long ago every three or four kilometres along the coast to protect Puglia from raiders. Now then, in that stretch of coast, how many can you remember are ruined, or at least unoccupied?"

Cosimo thought for a moment, "in ruins? Very few. I can only think of two off the top of my head, but unoccupied? I would think most would be nowadays: they were hardly for living in, at the best of times, being only soldiers quarters, and I don't think many have been renovated into homes, although that might be an interesting idea for the future."

"Right, so all we have to do is start at, say, Campomarino and work our way north-west along the coast. Many of the towers are still the focal point of little villages, so we can rule them out. We are only looking for isolated ones."

"Right, that should be easy, OK. And then?"

"Then?" Pasquale was tiring fast, and his driving was starting to deteriorate.

"So we just walk up to the front door, say hello and ask for Andrea back?"

"Ha, bloody ha!"

"Get serious, Pasquale, this is no boys-own adventure. Come on, an SCU gang, with knives, cudgels, probably guns versus an unarmed, aging man and an angry brother. Ha! Ha!"

"OK, point taken. But surely we can wait till very late and sneak her away? They'd only have one guard awake, surely?"

"We'd have to hope so, I suppose, but if there's more than one, or if it's too difficult, we are not going in, right?"

"Suppose. Let's go and see first, eh?"

They returned home and told Isabella they had to go away for a day or two, and to prepare some food and drink. Obviously she wanted to know where and why, while Maria wanted to know why they had not yet been to the police. Cosimo warned them both to keep absolutely silent about the whole episode, otherwise it might jeopardise Andrea's life. Afterwards, Pasquale told him he thought that last comment something of a cheap trick as it would never happen, but at the time no-one could be absolutely sure of anything.

So off they drove, late that night. This was deliberate so they would be able to arrive at the coast after midnight. The roads were ominously empty of traffic and they felt very lonely in their quest. The longer they drove the more their enthusiasm drained away. All this time they had been running on anger and indignation, with all the bravado it engendered, but their personal fuel tanks were now beginning to drain low as their hangovers grew stronger. Crawling through the familiar streets of Avetrana revived their spirits somewhat and they first hit the coast at the stunning beaches of San Pietro. Then they drove along the sandy cliff tops to Campomarino, the wave crests glistening in the bright moon, and dropped to the lower beaches towards Lido Silvana. Here they saw a disused torre in the moonlight with a light at its base. They drove to within a safe distance and set out on foot. Nearing the ever-brightening light they began to hear young peoples' voices and soon realised it was just a group of pubescent youths experimenting with alcohol. They grunted their disgust and hurried back to the comfort of the Fiat as the cool sea breeze struck up and sent chills through them.

The next torre was in darkness, as was the third, but at the fourth they saw a light twinkling in the distance. They pulled off the road and bumped onto rutted, sandy tracks. "Oh my poor little Fiat!" muttered Pasquale as he inched steadily forward. Finally they parked alongside tall reed grass, locked up and started to walk. Clouds now came up and there was only just enough moonlight to guide their footsteps, so they had to slow right down and almost feel their way as they veered away from the road on a shortcut to the tower. Twice they lost the rudimentary path and ended up with sodden boots in marshy creeks, but eventually they hit upon the sand track again just 200 metres or so from the tower. They approached cautiously and again veered off at about 100 metres away to enter bushes and low grasses to skirt round the side of the building. Where they left the road they could just make out a bend and extra width. Cosimo whispered, "we could leave the car hidden here when we return for Andrea. Face it inland for a quick getaway. There won't be anywhere nearer than this."

"But won't they hear the engine?"

"No, it's a sea breeze blowing from them there towards us here, they'll hear nothing."

"OK. Let's go."

They moved closer to the sole light in a gap in the tumbledown wall. They stood still for at least five minutes but there seemed to be no guard anywhere in sight, so eventually they were able to crawl up to the gap and peep in. Originally, when the tower had been fully intact this would have been impossible because the rooms for external access were at a higher level and only accessible by a front stairway of anything up to twenty stone steps. But as the tower had crumbled into ruins the internal lower rooms could now be seen through these gaps in the normally impregnable wall.

Three men were engrossed in a game of cards and obviously had been drinking heavily, if their raucous behaviour was a clue to go by. A 5-litre pitcher of Primitivo lay seemingly nearly empty on the rudimentary table of packing boxes, and this was the presumed cause of much laughter and banter.

Suddenly a woman's voice cried out, "please, water, I must have water!"

After a deliberate pause one of the gang rose unsteadily to his feet and staggered over to a corner near the door opening. Pasquale could just make out in the shadows Andrea sitting on a chair. The guard roughly stuffed a beaker of water into her mouth, of which she spilled most in her haste to drink.

"Please, signore, can you untie my hands so I can hold the cup? I'm losing all feeling in my arms..."

"...you wouldn't in my arms, darling," he slurred, obviously the worse for wear.

"Heh!" shouted another from the table, "just you leave her alone now, you hear?"

"But she is so gorgeous!" the guard answered.

"Yes, but you won't be if Tonino hears you've even touched his precious bride, stupido! Just do as she asks and get back here, we haven't got all night..."

"...well, actually, we do, Luigi!" laughed another, and they all broke out again in raucous laughter at the thought of an all-night poker game.

Pasquale had seen enough. He motioned to Cosimo to stay for a while and observe. He then crept round to where the front access must be, under where the grand steps must have been. There was a gap to squeeze through, but only just. That was their only means of entry. He returned silently to Cosimo and motioned him back to the car. Out of earshot in the strengthening breeze he said, "basically we have two choices - either we go back now, cut her ropes and lead her out from under their noses, or we wait till they are all sleeping off the wine."

"Are you sure there are only three?"

"Seems like it."

"Well, I vote for the latter, obviously," analysed Cosimo.

"The only snag, though, is we don't know where they might put her for sleeping, or whether she'll stay where she is. Nor do we know where they might sleep. As it stands now we do know where she is, she can be got at. She is the shadows and I think I could sneak in out of their line of sight and quietly lead her out."

"Yes, OK, I can see that. Let's just hope she is fit to walk, and in silence!"

"I hope so too!"

"OK, I'll go back now and bring up the car to the bend. I'll also get the knife for you. Then you go for Andrea and I wait in the car to drive. You'll only have about 100 metres to run, if she can run, as opposed to them with stomachs and heads full of wine. Ha! Should be no contest," he chuckled.

It relieved the tension a little and Pasquale smiled. "I'll wait here for you to come back then. Good luck!"

And so it was. After Cosimo's return Pasquale crept back to the access point in the torre wall with a small sharp knife, only to find the men even more drunk and even more raucous. Ha! He thought, the element of surprise is a wonderful weapon of war. And he might not have to be totally silent either. Effortlessly he moved away from the entrance to where their car was parked and did something he had always wanted to, plunging his knife into both front tyres. That is for taking my car twice, he thought, with great satisfaction. The wind carried the wheeze of the deflating tyre away from the torre and he returned to the access point.

He waited for a particularly raucous exchange, for one that might last quite a while, then moved in. He was immediately in Andrea's line of sight, but not the men's, and her eyes boggled as she saw him, while her body tensed for action. She smiled gently as he effortlessly cut through the old ropes, dry as tinderwood, and they moved slowly, deliberately and noiselessly back to the opening. It was now-or-never time, the moment when God was on their side or when one of the men might come out for numerous reasons like checking on her, taking the air or even urinating. They both prayed and starting running, slowly at first but getting faster as downwind no noises would be heard.

Suddenly Andrea stumbled. Sitting for so long her leg muscles had quickly tired and seized, and she had twisted her ankle on a rock. The moon had kindly disappeared behind thick stratus and the way was black. Pasquale had to prop her up over his shoulder and they hobbled along at half the speed. "Only 100 metres to the car," whispered brother.

"Seems like forever," replied sister. But it wasn't and soon they saw the car, Cosimo picked them out of the blackness, started up and pulled out onto the road. They fell through the rear door together, laughing to release tension, and Cosimo eased forward.

"Faster?" asked Pasquale.

"Not yet, they might be coming and hear us. Roll down the windows and listen for shouts and look for lights."

So they did, but no pandemonium from the torre, nothing, only the sound of a disturbed seabird. Cosimo then picked up speed but could not go too fast without lights. He steered them off the sandy track twice, by mistake, and had to reverse out of the soft ground. It was touch and go, taking up precious time, but still no chase. The brow of a dune now hid them from the torre and they found the road.

"Oh Pasquale, oh Cosimo, thank you, thank you, thank you." She cuddled her brother and continued, "but how did you find me?"

"Well, we…" but there was no point. Andrea was already asleep despite Cosimo's chirpy whistling!

* * *

39

HONOUR

1 9 5 6

The two men had made up their plan on the hoof. Amazed but relieved that it had worked, they had not considered the outcome at all. So as soon as the elation of their success had abated they suddenly realised they had nowhere to go. Neither had brought much money, rushing out of the house as they had, so they could not find a hotel or a room. Anyway, it was by now past 2 am and nowhere would be open. Worse still, much worse, they had precious little petrol left! A slow, rising tide of panic began to engulf them.

"Pasquale, we have to get to the main road quickly and go either to Manduria or Taranto," argued Cosimo.

"Not Taranto, that's back towards their territory."

"Whichever, but they will be after us soon, drunken fools or not, and they will be driving like racers…"

"I think not. They won't be after us quite yet, I stabbed their tyres," announced Pasquale proudly.

Andrea was awaking, "oh well done, brother! Quick thinking."

"Yes, indeed, great, but how long does it take to change a tyre, 20 minutes?"

"When you're drunk…?" laughed Andrea, "more like an hour! And anyway, you stabbed two tyres so they can't move as they only have one spare."

"Just speed up a bit, Cosimo, but not too much. We wouldn't want to be stopped by a night patrol. How would we explain all this to a policeman?"

"Does anyone have their papers?" worried Cosimo.

"No, I left them at the house in my wallet."

"Obviously I haven't, and look at the sight of me. Explain that to them!" It was true, Andrea was muddy, barefoot, with matted hair and torn clothes. A policeman's imagination would run riot!

The main road junction loomed ahead and sure enough, their misfortune was to make out a police car sitting there watching. There was no traffic at all, worse for them, as to be expected at that hour. But would he bother to stop them? If he was awake, most definitely - it would be something to alleviate the boredom of the patrol - but if he was asleep, like most patrolmen usually are during this graveyard shift, they might creep past.

Despite all the stress of the night's activities Cosimo was the first to react, "quick, slump down in your seats, then it will look like I'm a solo driver. If he does stop me I'll just say you were not visible because you were asleep."

"Great idea! Andrea, behind you there is a car blanket. Quick, throw it over us. If nothing else it will cover up your appearance."

Cosimo eased the car down and slipped the car into neutral to coast up to the junction. They dutifully stopped, looked and gently pulled out with minimum revs, their hearts all beating furiously. But fortune once again smiled on them and as they moved past the patrol car Cosimo could make out the officer fast asleep.

They had chosen direction Manduria. On arrival they sought out a derelict back street and promptly fell into an exhausted slumber, only to be woken three hours later by a vineyard farmer growling past in his pride and joy, a new mini-tractor with an engine voluminous enough to wake the dead. Fuzzy heads were slow to clear at 6.30 am, but again it was Cosimo who was first to rationalise the situation, "where's the last place they'd ever look for us?" he asked.

"Er...home?" asked Pasquale.

"Precisely! So why don't we just go back home?"

Andrea was still sleepy and none too clear, "and where exactly is home? Do you mean Brindisi or Oria?"

"'Brindisi."

Pasquale mused, "at this minute we don't have a lot of choice. How much have we got?"

After a quick count up they could only raise 2050 lira, a sorry state indeed.

"Hardly enough to buy three cappucis," sulked Andrea.

"Priorities," rationalised Cosimo again. He certainly was a man for a crisis. "We need petrol to get anywhere, so all thoughts of cappuccis or croissant can be forgotten, OK?"

"Yes, sorry. But I am dying of thirst. Can we at least find some water?"

They found a petrol station open and the attendant looked quizzical when they asked for only 3 litres. Soon after 9 am they found themselves back in Brindisi. They parked right at the door, no time for subterfuge now, and found the amazed Mama and Maria eating breakfast. They quickly grabbed some, packed two suitcases for Andrea and set off again.

"But where are you going this time, Pasquale?" asked Mama.

"I'm taking Andrea somewhere that no-one will find her, hopefully."

"But where?"

"Dearest Mama, you know how these evil men will stop at nothing. If they get wind that we have been here and gone away again they will try their most desperate measures to get you to tell them where Andrea is. If you genuinely do not know they will not harm you unnecessarily. Do you understand?"

"I understand you are not going to tell me, wretched boy!"

"But I will return by tonight, don't worry, I'll be here, and Cosimo and Maria, OK?"

"Suppose so…"

And so it was, Pasquale took Andrea to a friend's house in Avetrana, near enough right under their noses but where they would least expect her. Alberto Benini had done well in life, unlike Pasquale, and had married a lovely woman who had borne him three even lovelier children. Andrea muttered hints about problems of passion, affair of the heart, and all that, which satisfied her hosts in the interim and they were even happier to entertain the house guest when Pasquale pulled out a roll of banknotes. The greatest bonus was that Benini had a telephone in his house, which could one day prove to be a lifeline.

Following emotional farewells, a promise from Andrea that she would not even venture out of the house, neither to any part of the garden exposed to the road, and promises from the Beninis that they would not mention Andrea to anyone, Pasquale returned to Brindisi to sit and wait. Next day, as if by clockwork, a letter appeared through the post. It would not have been Tonino's hand, he was too clever for that, but it was clear they were his words.

"Congratulations, Pasquale! I am impressed but not beaten. You have one last chance: deliver Andrea to Bar Toletti tonight at 8pm. If you do not I will have no choice but to tell the Carabinieri who killed Stefano Nania."

"Who is this man Stefano Nania, Pasquale? What is that all about?"

"Oh Mama, its nothing. He is bluffing and lying. Playing a desperate losing game, basically. I have no idea who he is talking about, honestly."

Cosimo cut in quickly, because in his experience anyone who has to say "honestly" at the end of a statement is usually lying, and he thought Mama might know that rule of thumb too. "He is just trying to make life difficult for us, Isabella," he calmed.

Pasquale feigned tiredness and went to lie on Mama's bed. He certainly had much to think about now. He started drifting off to sleep and next minute realised the image of Andrea had joined him on the bed. They were sitting in huddled whispers, "so he *is* dead, brother," wailed Andrea in his mind.

"Not necessarily, sis. Just because Tonino says so it does not mean it is actually true, you know."

"OK, but it does mean that all and sundry across Puglia know we did it though, right?"

"Again, not necessarily. What *is* a real worry is that he knows about the Stefano connection to us. I'm racking my brains to think how Tonino could have found that out. What is the link?"

"Business, as ever, I expect," answered Andrea.

"But Starsi was a respectable businessman, wasn't he? He wouldn't have any links with the SCU, would he?"

"Respectable? After how he treated me and probably lots of other girls, before and after? How could you say that, Pasquale, you unfeeling oaf!"

"No, no, I'm sorry, sis, I didn't mean that, I meant in the eyes of the public he would have appeared a respectable businessman, wouldn't he?"

"OK, yes, he would, but in truth he was not; he had his hands in all sorts of shady pies and dirty deals. Maybe the SCU even blackmailed him too, who knows!"

"OK then, so we must accept that the whole underworld knows what we did to Stefano..."

"...yes, but if that were so, why have they never come looking for us before now in order to wreak revenge? Have you considered that?"

"Good point, sis, very true. So if that is the case, maybe it *is* only Tonino and a selected few who know…"

"…or Tonino is bluffing and Stefano is fine. That would explain exactly why no-one has come looking for us!"

"And we are back to the beginning, having gone full circle. Of course, well done, Andrea!"

"…yes, but if Tonino knows, as he obviously does, he obviously has links to Starsi and so he can now tell Starsi where we are. Or maybe he has already done it!"

"Keeping Starsi up to date, you mean?"

"Yes."

It felt like they both shivered uncontrollably in the evening balminess and were hugging each other for solace.

Pasquale regained some composure first, "we must find a way out of all this mess, sis. Come on, think."

"All I know, dear brother, is that it is already 7.30 and you are due at the bar…"

"…well, at least I know exactly what I have to do now: one step at a time, one step at a time." As he woke the image of Andrea faded from his mind and he returned to the living area to tell them his plan. He felt completely energised for some reason, but he knew not why.

"I am going to sit in my car from across the square and watch the Bar Toletti."

"With a view to?" asked Cosimo.

"Do you know, Cosimo, I really do not know!" The juxtaposition of the "know" and "do not know" made everyone laugh. At least it lightened proceedings.

Pasquale continued, "look, just bolt the door after me and do not let anyone enter, OK? At least dear Andrea is safe for the moment…"

"…but what if they followed you again to your secret place? They'll have her again," asked Maria.

"I did take extra precautions driving this time. Watching all those Hollywood gangster movies finally had some use," he laughed.

"Maybe they already have her and are enticing you to this bar just to capture you, as a punishment for rescuing Andrea?" Maria persisted.

"Oh, Maria, you have an overly fertile brain, don't you!"

"I watch movies too, you know," she smiled sheepishly.

"OK, look, I'm late. I must go. Let's hope something comes of it."

"Good luck", they all chorused, but deep down they felt an impending wave of hopelessness washing over them.

He found a small parking space on Via Garribaldi and tucked well into the curb so that the small car could hardly be seen. Sure enough, Tonino and one thug swept into the bar at 8.05 pm.

At 8.07 the back door of Pasquale's car swung open, a thug leapt in and from behind and started to garrotte him on the neck with a wire. Pasquale smelt the ugly breath next to his ear, "one move and you'll be dead," he grunted.

Pasquale's eyes widened with fear as he watched Tonino and his 'friend' cross the square and move purposely towards him. It became obvious now that they were always one step ahead of him, except at that critical moment when he had rescued Andrea.

Tonino slid effortlessly into the passenger seat, like the lizard he was, smiled his perfect row of white teeth, like the shark he was, and said, "Ah, my dear friend, still not willing to play ball then?"

"With you? Never!"

"Brave words for someone with a garrotte on his neck. One slip, just one...careful, Luigi, yes?"

"Yes, you wouldn't want to do anything foolish, Luigi, eh. After all, one slip and your beloved boss would never find his true love, when I am the only one who knows where she is."

"Quite correct, Luigi, so take care, eh. Now swop seats with our good friend here and drive."

As they left Brindisi it was obvious they were on the Oria road, but as soon as the houses petered out Pasquale felt a piece of cloth whipped out and placed over his face. Blindfolded, that was the last he saw of where he was going. Only from the time taken did he guess they'd driven a long way, an hour or more, so they must have been in the region of an arc from Grottaglie to Sava to Corosino.

Suddenly they stopped, he was dragged from the car, bundled up some steps, through what seemed endless passageways, and finally thrown into a room. More hands picked him up and unceremoniously dumped him onto a chair, to which his wrists and ankles were tied. One was too tight and already cutting his flesh - was it deliberate, or purely accidental? Someone thrust back his head from behind and another pinched his nose hard and poured water non-stop down his throat. It was only a matter of time before he choked on the water and spat the residue back at whoever was pouring. An enormous thud to the side of his head followed and that was the last thing he remembered before seeing stars.

His senses awoke and told him someone was there. Tonino was muttering to his thug, "you didn't have to hit him so hard, idiot, we haven't got all night!"

"Sorry boss, but he spat all over one of my best shirts…"

"…you wear your best shirts to work?"

"I was supposed to be off tonight and taking out my girl, boss, remember?"

"What! You expect me to remember every one of you people's details and personal life? What is this, a social club? Wake him up now before I put *you* to sleep!"

The thug shook Pasquale hard and he pretended with his best acting skills to be 'waking up'.

"Right, Pasquale, you pathetic specimen, I'm gonna give you one minute to think about this - either you give up Andrea or I ask gentle Luigi here to help rearrange your private parts, OK?"

Pasquale brain was clearing quickly with this unpleasant ultimatum, 'I can't see what good any of this will do. Even if I gave up Andrea to you, how are you going to keep her? After all, it's not the Middle Ages, you can't chain her to your back door and put a chastity belt on her. You can't drag her to the altar if she doesn't love you or want to marry you."

"Shut up, you pathetic apology for a man; you've got a lot to say for yourself. Perhaps, Luigi, you could remove some of that long tongue?" he laughed.

"Can't wait, boss!"

"Anyway, she would come to love me. In fact, she does love me. It would work!"

"After all this? Please, look at yourself. Is this the life an ordinary girl wants?"

Tonino smirked, "she would no longer be ordinary. I would give her everything, anything, and make her rich…"

"… and then run to others behind her back when you became bored!"

"How dare you attack my morals, I am an honourable man!"

"But Andrea would still be a murdering criminal's wife…."

At that Tonino's patience and temper finally exploded together. He smacked Pasquale across the head hard, "you've had your minute; where is she?"

"Go to Hell!"

"No, sir, you go to Hell!" He nodded to Luigi, who licked his lips and advanced menacingly.

The next morning Pasquale found himself being propped up by one of the thugs at a countryside bus stop. To his right he saw a car crashed against the stone wall of a field and burning, or in its final stages of being burnt out. A bus pulled up and its doors opened.

"Just found this man staggering along the road. Must have come from that crash. I'm going the other way unfortunately for an urgent meeting, can you help him, please? I think he said he lives in Brindisi," shouted the thug convincingly.

Immediately two women jumped down and helped him into the bus. His face was covered in blood but he seemed able to move fairly freely, albeit at a stoop. "Sit down here, dear. Has anyone got any water? A towel or cloth perhaps?"

Three days later a letter came for Pasquale. It was from Andrea. She was well but very bored from staying indoors all the time. Pasquale's friends were treating her really well and not asking many questions except, of course, when she might be well enough to leave. Most importantly Benini's wife had asked if she knew any good dress shops and Andrea had taken the risk of recommending hers in Oria. Andrea had also asked Signora Benini to try and pick up any Oria gossip at the shop just to cheer up Andrea, but to not mention Andrea's name. The signora had entered the game enthusiastically --- much more fun than cooking and cleaning up children! There hadn't been much gossip but it did not take long for the shop girls to fathom out that the signora had a connection with Andrea. The signora gave in but did not reveal any details, merely saying Andrea had had a nervous breakdown and had left the area to recover. She was given some letters for Andrea but, more important, one for Pasquale. It appeared that the letter had gone to the Oria house so old Signore Bellini had had the initiative to bring it to the shop for Andrea to pass on. She had enclosed it in this letter for him to read.

As an aside Pasquale mentioned to the family that the Oria dress shop might still play an important part as a valuable conduit of communication in the future, as who might know what could happen next in their roller-coaster life.

The letter was from his old dealer in Taranto, Mario Gennari, concerned that he had received no business from Pasquale in a long time, especially now the antiquities inspectors seemed to have 'disappeared'. He considered this long and hard, suddenly realising that there might be an angle in it here for all of them. So he decided to reply post haste, saying he had been in a lot of bother lately and he gave a reasonably full account of everything that had transpired. He had nothing to lose now, so why not tell Mario everything? As he wrote his left ribs began to ache again. Everyone had thought he had broken some of them, but fortunately it seemed they were only bruised. He did not really want to think too much about these recent events, especially the beating he had received at the hands of Luigi, the passing out and the buckets of cold water to keep reviving him, his refusal to give up his sister and the final setting fire to his lovely car while he was forced to watch. He doubted the insurance would pay up and he worried that the police would go to the Oria house, as that was the car's registration address. 'Oh, what a mess,' he sighed, "when will this ever end?"

But Isabella had overheard and soothed him, "shortly, my dear, very shortly, I think."

"But how can you know that, Mama? It just seems to get worse and worse. I could be dead now," he started to sob.

"Yes, dear, it was wise to keep it to yourself about Andrea's location. It has probably kept you alive."

"Certainly. But how can you know what will happen next?"

"Oh, a mother knows, believe me…"

Three more quiet days passed and although Pasquale felt sure they were being watched, in the hope that the location of Andrea would be compromised by one of the family, nothing untoward happened. But Pasquale needed revenge and all he could think of at that moment was to keep sending out individual members of the family, separately, on numerous pointless errands to numerous pointless locations. At least this would be severely testing the resources of Sava SCU and stopping them concentrating on crimes elsewhere, he smiled.

Then a reply came from Mario: 'sorry to hear of all your troubles. I will be in Brindisi on Thursday. I will be in Bar Tandarti all evening if you wish to meet. Salutations, Mario.'

Wish to meet? thought Pasquale, you bet.

And so it was. On Thursday at 7pm Cosimo helped Pasquale climb the steps up to the bar, because making sure they had thrown off their tail had tired him alarmingly. With the bruised ribs pushing against the lungs he was having great difficulty getting his breath. Mario saw this instantly and uttered prophetic 'Mama Mias' heavenward.

"What have they done to you, poor friend? Mama Mia!"

Pasquale waved away his concerns and sat down. It was indeed good to see Mario again. He looked prosperous. Business must be good in Taranto, thought Pasquale, he's nearly as well dressed as that Tonino! A couple of drinks later they all walked to Restaurant Obsessione and had a fine dinner - a real treat for Pasquale and Cosimo. Mario refused to let them put their hands in their pockets after all the atrocities he had heard from them. Finally, his anger boiled over, "how dare such animals do such things to my friends!" he uttered rather too loudly. Other patrons glanced up from their meals and he quickly subsided, "Pasquale, since I received your letter I have actually been quite busy…"

"…oh dear, so you have not been able to consider our plight, then?"

"No, no, on the contrary. I have been very busy on behalf of your plight!"

"Oh thank you, Signore Gennari," said Cosimo gratefully.

"Mario, please, Cosimo, we are all good friends here."

"I would like to hope so, Mario, thank you," replied Cosimo.

"Pasquale, you know me, always ready to help my good friends. And, as it happens, there is a golden opportunity in this situation to kill at least two birds with one stone, my friends!" Mario was excited now and he cared by showing it.

"Really? I don't understand, Mario."

Mario took another long gulp of the excellent Manduria doc. Primitivo and elucidated. "We have two reasons for our course of action: one, no-one should treat someone else like this, certainly not to my friend or his family." He patted Pasquale on the back comfortingly. "Two, the Ndrangheta are very interested!"

"What? The Ndrangheta? Interested?"

"Shush, friend, walls have ears! Suffice to say, Pasquale, they are a much bigger organisation than the SCU and have much loftier ambitions. The SCU Sava area borders onto their area and they always welcome any opportunity to expand their empire. When I told them about the exploits of this animal Tonino…"

"…what? You actually told *them*?"

"Yes, certainly, why not? That was half the reason, don't you see? Anyway, after I had told them they said they'd had him in their sights for quite a while, waiting for the opportune moment. I think you will find the opportune moment has indeed arrived!"

"Why, what will happen?" asked Cosimo, fascinated but oh so totally innocent.

"Please, please, my friend, the less said the better, the less you know the better. Just rest assured that in about a week's time you will never need to fear anymore and you will all be able to go about living your lives in peace again."

Pasquale smiled for the first time in days: Cosimo slumped happily into his seat, and they all got magnificently full and drunk on a sumptuous dinner!

Exactly eight days later Pasquale received another letter from Mario. Well, it was actually unsigned and it was formally typed, but he knew it was Mario for reasons that became patently clear as he read it:

'I read in the news that an SCU headquarters in Sava was burnt down; the leader and seven others were all unfortunately lost in the fire; you will find a reasonably familiar vehicle in your street tomorrow - sell it quickly.'

"Good news, son?" asked Isabella, seeing the enormous grin breaking out on his face.

"Oh yes, Mama, wonderful news! Listen, everybody. Tonino has died in a fire at his...er...office, along with his workers. And tomorrow will bring its rewards!"

Cosimo rushed to open a fresh bottle of limocello for the ladies and some primitivo for the men. He was hopping about like an excited boy and Pasquale started waltzing round the room with Mama. Needless to say, the celebrations carried on well into the night!

And so it was: the next afternoon they found Tonino's glistening Bugatti parked in the street with its keys under the carpet. Immediately Pasquale drove it to a shady dealer on the edge of town who was so excited to receive it he asked no questions at all and gave Pasquale more than three-quarters the going rate. Pasquale didn't care: whatever he got for the Bugatti was all windfall profit to him and a king's ransom compared to the loss of his Fiat.

That night they fetched Andrea home in another Fiat bought on the cheap from the dealer and went for another sumptuous dinner at Restaurant Obsessione. But their joy was still not yet complete: Andrea had brought another letter through the dress shop delivery system to her brother. It was from the car insurance company – contrary to his opinion, a settlement cheque in full for the burnt-out Fiat. Good times, indeed!

* * *

40

ULTERIOR MOTIVES

1 9 5 7

Mario Gennari had told Pasquale and Cosimo that there had been the chance to 'kill at least two birds with one stone' when rescuing the Carones from the SCU. The Carones, in their joy at being freed from the tyranny of Tonino Lupo, had forgotten that 'at least two birds' could mean more than two.

The third, in a nut shell, revolved around the Ndrangheta itself. The leader of the Taranto division, Damiano Milone, had once met Andrea at Massimo Starsi's dress shop while picking up a robe for his aunty. Even then he knew he would never cast eyes on a greater beauty in his life...and he hadn't. Then she had mysteriously disappeared and he had employed considerable manpower and effort in trying to trace her, unsuccessfully. And then, as if out of nowhere, his good friend Mario Gennari tells him the sordid details of poor Andrea Carone's life. He was so incensed he had shown no mercy over the retribution, and his Godfather was so pleased with his actions he had offered him control of the old SCU area too.

Consolidating this new territory had kept Damiano busy for months, for there was much to do. Not all old enemies roll over when an area changes 'allegiance'. He had networks to break and re-form using his own personnel, businesses to offer revised 'protection' to now the old sentinels had been wiped out, officialdom to be reassured and re-bribed, new avenues of supply and receipt to kindle, new agents to recruit, and so on. The mazy spider's web of a Mafia organisation can only be appreciated from the inside: an outsider could never comprehend its complexity. Once all this was completed he swore he would make it his priority to re-discover this rare beauty, Andrea, and perhaps the brother who so valiantly tries to protect her. Such traditional values were certainly on the slide in post-war Italy, but still to be much admired, he thought.

After a month of rest and recuperation in Brindisi the Carones continued to discuss their future plans. Cosimo and Isabella saw no reason not to return to live in Avetrana, Maria had no particular preferences, while Pasquale and Andrea fought vehemently for a completely new start for everyone. Mama and Cosimo wondered time and time again what was wrong with Avetrana and all the children could counter it with was that 'it is such a parochial place; the neighbours will think we are running back tail between legs; it is a backward step; there are so few prospects there in such a tiny town', and the like.

In their hearts the parents had to agree, but they had seen too much excitement in their lives over the past two years and just wanted to find somewhere they could relax again in their goldening years.

Then they all considered whether Mama and Cosimo should go back to Avetrana on their own, leaving the children to forge their own lives elsewhere, perhaps in Oria again or Brindisi. This idea kept the discussion fuelled for a few more days as it had considerable appeal. The parents could have their much-desired "quieter life" and the children could forge on into whatever the modern world was likely to offer.

But then Andrea played the trump card, something they had all forgotten up to that point. "You cannot return to Avetrana, either just the two of you or all of us!"

"Why not, dear?" asked Mama.

"Because you are not legally married, silly!"

"Oh Mother Mary!" exclaimed Cosimo, "of course not. Eduardo is not officially dead."

"But he is long gone, surely, Cosimo, no-one would care now, would they?" pleaded Mama.

"But what if he suddenly showed up one day, Mama?" asked Maria.

"Yes, but why would he?"

"Who knows? Stranger things do happen," added Pasquale.

Cosimo had been thinking hard, "what if some official knew we were back and came asking the whereabouts of your husband, say for taxes, voting or the like?"

"Yes, Mama," added Andrea, "you cannot prove he is dead, you have no official death certificate, you..."

"...have broken the law, basically, by marrying again!" triumphed Pasquale, following through the argument to its logical conclusion.

"You mean we must live in hiding, in sin, outside the law for the rest of our lives?" cried Mama.

"Afraid so, dearest, until or unless we can prove Eduardo died," confirmed Cosimo. "You knew that when you married me, don't pretend now it is some huge new revelation..."

"Yes, I'm sorry, I did, you're right. I tend to get forgetful as I get older."

"Selective forgetfulness, if you ask me!" joked Pasquale, and they all laughed.

But Cosimo was not really laughing with conviction. He was angry that he too had forgotten all this in the light of all that had transpired recently. But he tried not to show it and followed up by joking, "yes, it looks like we two are inextricably bound to the rest of you for ever, heaven forbid!"

"Perish the thought!" laughed Pasquale.

And so they went on like this, round and round in circles, just not knowing what to do for the best. But it was clear that this could not go on for ever and a decision had to be made quickly. Whichever way they looked at it, it seemed clear that a new, fresh town was beckoning because they could not afford to stay in their cramped accommodation in Brindisi for ever and in Oria the many unhappy memories outnumbered the good times.

And so it was. They packed their Fiat with what few possessions they had remaining, thanked their honest landlady and drove out of Brindisi. She was, of course, extremely pleased to see them go after all the scandal and disrepute they had levied on her, her house and the street. They, in turn, were extremely apologetic, but they also knew that she could never be approached for a property reference in the future like Senor Bellini in Oria could!

Pasquale had studied a road map earlier, poring over it hour after hour, until he decided by means of elimination that Ceglie Messapica was the place to go. Why Ceglie? they all asked. For no other reason that it was north of all the places they had lived to date, it was a reasonable sized town - not too small to be gossipy, not too big, like Brindisi, to feel lost in - and because it was not a particularly popular place to live, being well inland and somewhat off the beaten track.

"Properties might be cheap, then," said Cosimo, as they bowled along the stone-wall lined road north-west. The summer breeze filled the car and their spirits with renewed optimism, and it felt like an adventure, heading up onto the low plateau after living their whole lives down on the Plain of Salento. Soon the scenery subtly changed: the soils became much redder and richer, the small and narrow smallholdings exhibited neat rectangular patterns running away from the road, the farmhouses were all painted white and were all immaculately kept, rows of vegetables and fruit trees replaced vineyards and olive groves and there was a greater air of prosperity. The road dipped and rose, sometimes alarmingly, as it crossed ancient river dissections through the pale limestone plateau, valleys sometimes narrow and deep, sometimes wider and shallower. And then as they passed through Martina Franca a trullo replaced a farmstead, then another, then a disused one, then a cluster, and they realised that it was not just Alberobello that housed hundreds of trulli but they could also be found in the countryside too. A few had been recently painted white, the stark whitewash glistening in the sun and forming a magnificently original foredrop to that beautiful blue of the Mediterranean sky. But many were still the original grey stone and in traditional design, a simple dome-shaped, small, stone house built without cement. Such dwellings can be found nowhere else in the world, they are truly unique, although some travellers argue the remote plateau-top stone huts of Lesotho in South Africa come close. The Carones were fascinated by their appearance, as are most, but agreed they would not want to live in one. They would have needed a four or five-tower trulli to give them sufficient space, but it was the height restriction they were concerned about, forever bumping their heads on the low ceilings. They were changing hands for very little money but the Carones also considered they did not have the right family balance to cope with an agricultural smallholding of four or five acres, even though Pasquale had the requisite talents.

They soon found lodgings in town and spent the first week re-orienting themselves. It seemed a pleasant, unassuming town but not particularly exciting. Most life centred around the main piazza and duomo for traditional activities, and around the small theatre, or cinema, and a few bars, for the 'nightlife' typical of most small Italian towns at that time.

Pasquale was strolling along a reasonably important street one morning when he spotted a paper notice stuck on a large shutter:

'Vendesi', for sale. It was a bar with a large apartment over and it had been closed for 4 months, said a passer-by local. Pasquale wrote a letter of interest to the address given, in Rome, and had a prompt reply to say the sale was because the old owner had died and his son did not want to carry on, preferring to stay in Rome as an accountant. Consequently it was going very cheap for a quick sale but there few with the ready cash in Ceglie to buy it. So typical of the whole area after the war, thought Pasquale. The owner did not want loans, mortgages and lengthy bank interference, he wanted quick cash to take it off his hands. He had received a number of offers involving loans, but only one for cash. Could Pasquale better 550,000 lira? he asked bluntly. The owner had also given the address of his local solicitor handling the sale, so after Pasquale had explained all this to the family they thought it worth considering and paid a visit to the bar the next day.

It was certainly in need of redecoration, but only cosmetic, so it would be cheap and they could do it themselves, but all the essentials seemed to be intact. Upstairs there were three bedrooms and a living area, plenty of space for all, again requiring minimal improvement.

The family conference considered everything carefully: Pasquale had the necessary cash from his Bugatti sale and still the savings from young, the men could run the business, Cosimo could handle the books, the girls would be the barmaids, helped by Pasquale, while Isabella could cook light meals and bar snacks. Their nearest competitor bar was over 400 metres away, ensuring a fairly large local catchment, the street's position in the town was accessible, the two stunning barmaids would soon pull in the clientele and Isabella's food would triumph over the usual cornettos and paninis.

"Could we try to offer things like homemade ice cream too?" asked Pasquale.

"Yes, a great idea, but shall we not try to run before we can walk, eh?" steadied wise old Cosimo. "We could make this the best bar in town with some innovation, but let's learn the business and the clientele first, yes?"

"Yes," chorused all, highly excited at the prospect of a totally new direction in their lives.

They took the plunge, went with the solicitor to the notaio and by putting it into Pasquale's name they found it easy to bypass the legal requirements of address, previous occupations and so on. A 30,000 lira 'ex-gratia payment' in cash to the notaio smoothed the waters enormously too, of course, plus an extra 10,000 for the solicitor. After ten minutes of form-filling the bar was officially theirs.

They rushed back, opened the shutter, found some bottles of spirits and celebrated with a toast, "to our new bar, Bar..." They paused. In all their haste they had forgotten one thing - what to call it! So they continued anyway, had a few more drinks and staggered out for a celebratory dinner. Over antipasti they debated the name. After much hilarity and jollity they decided that the catchiest name was "Bar Fortuna" because they had been so lucky to come through all their trials and tribulations...and, of course, it was going to make their fortune, they knew! For once the Carone family felt cheerful and confident about the future.

They had their 'Grand Opening' on a Saturday night with all drinks and food half price. They were so rushed off their feet that they could hardly drag themselves out of bed the next morning for the early shift. In their months of leisure they had forgotten just how early people did get up and go to work, but also demand that bars be open before them. They quickly decided therefore to split the shifts - Cosimo and Isabella doing the 5am to 2pm while the others the 2pm to midnight.

The grand opening was a huge success, not just because of the cheap prices and the twin attractions behind the bar, but because they took the time to smile and be friendly, thus grooming their local clientele, and they soon found that customer numbers remained steadily high thereafter. Indeed, it quickly became one of the most popular spots in the evening for the men of the town until Pasquale wisely hired a handsome young man to entice more female clientele, and the ladies' numbers suddenly shot up too.

They managed to obtain a music licence, with the usual lubrication of an ex-gratia payment, and Cosimo bought a second hand jukebox. Although dancing was not allowed, who was going to report them when the Carabinieri could be offered a few free drinks for their silence? Soon, Bar Fortuna became *the* place to be on Friday and Saturday nights and the profits were rolling in. Normally Isabella would cook enough in the mornings to last through the day, but even she found herself working a double shift these nights, serving up delicious bowls of homemade pastas, with either prawn, chicken, calamari or funghi, to ease the alcohol down. They even set up a separate little dining area in the corner on these evenings with gingham tablecloths and proper cutlery. Yes, Bar Fortuna was zinging!

Maria and Andrea must have received a dozen or more offers every night. They always refused so courteously and with such alluring smiles that the customers hardly ever took umbrage and they kept on returning, often forgetting previous refusals and repeating their offers during another drunken moment. Maria received the greater number, being the younger and more flirtatious, but Andrea received the more serious requests, usually from the older men. Even Pasquale had his followers too, but far fewer than the new Stud Giovani! But Pasquale was far too occupied running this far-busier-than-expected venture. He, and indeed Cosimo too, was amazed at just how much there was to do and to organise, so that as the weekends became more popular they both spent less time outside and more in the bar.

Perhaps they had all been looking for a quiet, restful backwater oasis, particularly Cosimo and Isabella, but the bar's success denied them all that and drained their life blood daily. But they battled on, largely running on adrenalin, although they would not admit, except secretly, that they were actually enjoying themselves.

After about a year Pasquale suddenly began to feel incomplete and unsatisfied. Something was certainly missing from his life. It took him quite a while to realise exactly what it was because he was so caught up in all this euphoria.

He was missing the campagna!

He was missing the wide open plains, open to a free-spirited wind, not one that had to sneak through dirty streets, cut across alleys and dodge buildings before it arrived tired and stale. The open plain where you could see forever across a multitude of vines, olives and beans. A land with dirt tracks so straight you would lose them in the distant shimmer of summer or the mists of winter. The graceful bustle of birds on pomegranate bushes, foxes slinking through crisping old vines and wasps dancing on peach trees, all benevolently overseen by the Giver of Life.

He longed to be holding his precious metal detector again. The mental agility required to find the location, the promise of the chase, the excitement of the hunt, the rewards extracted from unyielding earth. The silence, the loneliness, the self-dependence, the utter peace.

He was not made for smiling obsequiously at patrons of bars, for making endless small talk which bored him to tears, for preening at tricky customers, for commiserating with the lost souls, or for balancing complicated books.

And one day he told the family so! They were devastated when he said, "you can do without me now you know all there is to know about running a bar. I want to return to the fields."

The Carones, for once, were all sitting down together, placed around a similar great olive wood dining table at 7pm one Sunday night. They had decided to close early out of respect for an old lady across the road who had just died, and they did not want to disturb her traditional wake.

"But, Pasquale, we all need you here," enjoined the family, "please be sensible."

"I'm sorry, I've been thinking about this for quite a while and I've made my mind up."

"But how will we manage, silly?"

"Come on, you have plenty of hands, you could employ someone extra, we are making a fortune here. Maria and Andrea can lighten their load too and do the books easily. I must get back to the countryside, this is killing me!"

Cosimo added his wise words, as ever, "this is killing us all, boy, but we agreed as a family to do this together as a family. Do you realise, you might not be the only one here who wants to get out, but each one of us is battling on out of respect for the others, so you must too."

"Oh, I wish I could, and I have been for the past few months, but it is really destroying me inside. And anyway, when we started no-one said how long we were going to take on this bar."

"True, but you were the one who found it, Pasquale, and you were the one who convinced us we could do it!" aimed Isabella pointedly. It had the desired effect. Pasquale had been brought up with a moral compass but it took his Mother to remind him which direction it was pointing.

"OK," he said, "I'll carry on for now, but please bear in mind I cannot keep this up for ever!"

"Neither can we, dear boy!" agreed Cosimo.

And so it was. Pasquale continued to fight the lure of the countryside but it became increasingly hard each day. The whole family could see his heart was no longer in the bar, as it stood, and they noticed he was starting to make mistakes. They loved him too much to suggest the mistakes might be deliberate, but Cosimo never ruled that out.

One night, during a quiet moment, he sat with Pasquale and asked him outright. Fortunately, all his errors had been minor, except for one which had lost them nearly a whole day's takings, but in his state of mind he exploded and stormed out, saying, "is that how little you think of me? All of you? Well, that's it, I'm leaving!"

Poor Cosimo was left sitting there, wondering if Pasquale had meant leaving the room or leaving the job.

The next day he realised it was the latter, unfortunately. Pasquale took the Fiat, headed out to the fields and disappeared. That night he did not return, nor the next, but the Carones were not able to truly worry - they knew not where to find him so there was no point. He would return when he was ready, Cosimo told them all wisely. "He'll soon miss Mama's cooking!"

The region was new to Pasquale so he just adopted the pot luck method. He saw another man out with a detector and so he started in the adjacent field, waiting to see if the man shouted at him to get out. No shout came so he plodded on, happy as a lark. Within a few hours he had hit upon a collection of Messapican oil holders, possibly lost or dropped by an ancient trader or carrier along a road outside a Messapican settlement. He found and packed twenty-two of the tiny clay objects, drove them to Mario Gennaro in Taranto and returned with more money than the bar would make in a week! Mario was over the moon that he was back in the antiquities hunting business and only cheated him a little this time out of deference for all he had done bringing Tonino to them.

* * *

41

THE FIND

1 9 5 9

"Another couple of years like this, Pasquale, and we can retire anywhere we like!" said Cosimo one morning. "Even without your help we are rolling in the lira!"

"That's fantastic, but please be careful what you say or wish for. You know how much success breeds competition, and competition hits profit margins."

"Listen to you!" teased Isabella, "being all day out in that hot sun is obviously turning your mind. And fancy coming out with such jargon!" They both laughed at their son.

"But the boy *is* right, dearest," reasoned sensible Cosimo, "others are getting very jealous of our success and are trying to emulate us,or think of something different."

"Yes, but as long as clever Maria and Andrea keep ahead of the crowd with all those ideas they get from Napoli and Roma we shall be OK. These locals are just too stupid to think up the things we offer, or at least we always have the acumen to do it first," argued Isabella.

"Suppose so, dear. Like this thing they call a *discotheque* with its flashing lights and thumping music. Gets the people so hot they have to drink more to cool down."

"Yes," agreed Pasquale, "but a bit cynical of you to start charging for aqua when we've always given it out free!"

"But everyone kept demanding it all the time as they were so hot. Bottled water is not cheap, you know, nor are our huge refrigerators to store it in!"

"So why not just refill the empties with tap water? They'll never know!" argued the irritated Pasquale.

"What? We can't do that, stupid boy! What if customers got ill. They could easily trace it back to us," replied Isabella.

"True, but didn't I read they have made the town supply safe to drink at last?"

"Oh dear, your head is still in the clouds, my boy," said Cosimo, "that was Ostuni not Ceglie! It will be another ten years at least before small towns like this get safe water."

Pasquale realised he was beaten so countered with "ah, just watch out, popularity comes and goes quickly in this business."

"It's OK, honestly, Pasquale, we are sitting pretty. We already put more coffee powder in our cup than other bars, we always use UHT milk not powdered milk. Our fridges and drinks are colder than others…"

"…how could you possibly know all this? Heavens!"

"How?' asked Isabella, 'because our customers tell us. Simple as that. Our cornettos keep fresher, my pasta is famous and those biscuits from Britain were a real success, I can't understand why, except it was a new taste, I suppose."

"We're fine," agreed Cosimo, "just fine. Only tired, very, very tired. Your Mama hasn't taken a proper break for nigh on three years now. Never more than one or two days at a time."

"Why would I want a holiday, stupido? No-one to visit, nowhere interesting to go. I've got everything I want here," laughed Isabella, cuddling up to Cosimo.

"So there, Cosimo!" laughed Pasquale back.

"Yes, but I might want to see places before it's too late! Had you even thought of that?" pouted Cosimo.

"I'm certainly not stopping you!" smiled his wife, half in fun, half in seriousness.

"Wouldn't be the same…" he began to reply, but suddenly thought better of it. It was certainly not the moment to turn light-hearted banter into an argument.

"OK, I'm off then," chirped Pasquale bouncily, "another day in the fields, another famous discovery awaiting!'"

"Don't forget the fruit and veg for the bar!"

"Would I ever? It's in my blood to forage, you know that!" he laughed. "So, it's pomodoro, beans and water melon today, right?"

"Yes, and don't forget some extras for the old ladies over the road. Yesterday you didn't bring enough!" pouted Mama.

"Oh yes I did, it's just you had extra customers in the bar; how can I help that?"

"Must keep them nice and sweet, eh Mama?" smiled Cosimo.

"Have to, when patrons roll out onto the street at midnight waking the dead!"

Pasquale couldn't wait to get going. Already 7.15 am. By the time he was on site it would be at least 8 and the sun would be revving up. Mama surely needs a holiday, he thought, but what could he do, apart from being so selfish, he admonished himself.

He drove south to near Villa Castelli where he veered off left down a local road, then left again onto a track. The vineyards thinned until they gave way to rough grasses and bushes on a small collina. Although low, the hill was a like a tiny growth on the face of the plateau and gave a commanding view of the Salento Plains to the south, because the land was dropping as it went anyway. He could easily see Grottalgie, Crispiano and Francavilla Fontana at different ends of a star, and his heart so filled with love and joy that he just had to sit down and soak up the beauty of the vista until familiarity equalled, or was overtaken by, necessity.

He had researched hard the sites in this area and had already started on this hill, it being the most likely position for an ancient settlement. With defence the paramount priority, what better site to build? A view of an approaching enemy and a stiff march uphill to overcome before attacking. A natural routeway also, east to west, hugging the edge of the higher ground on the plateau.

He had walked slowly once round the base of the hill already, looking for the Greek village, so today he would try a horizontal band around the middle of it, a task just possible in one day if he restricted himself to three or four traverses. If nothing else it would increase the excitement of the hunt and perhaps leave the best finds for the top. If he'd have been one of those Greeks he would certainly have made camp at the top, just behind it and out of view, and he would have posted sentries on the opposite, exposed side to watch for trouble. However, one thing at a time, he mumbled happily. He had attempted rudimentary camouflage by dressing in pale brown clothes and wrapping his metal detector in same to stop sunlight reflection, for he knew only too well he was no longer the only antiquities hunter around and this was not his "patch". If he could not be the best, and he certainly doubted that, he could at least be the best prepared!

It was just after his hurried ham lingui lunch that his detector started to sing. As he moved on it buzzed louder and louder. Some coins perhaps, he thought. At least that is some recompense. He stopped as the buzz died down and he retraced his steps to the loudest point. He circled the spot gently to find the epicentre of activity and his foot tapped a rock. Or was it a rock? As he looked down he saw a smooth edge of something hard jutting out a little from the baked soil that had not been tilled for a long time. He stooped down, gently scratching at the earth. The object would not budge so he extracted a tiny trowel from his back pack, took a swig of water and began gently digging away. He would have splashed some of his precious water on it but he was short already and sensed his day might be lengthening by the minute.

His opinion was truly confirmed in minutes - it was a pot. He continued chipping away at the soil and cursed that he had not brought more water, then he could have softened it. The work was backbreaking and laborious but he could not speed up for fear of breaking something. To him this was the worst part of the job, without a doubt, but it was so necessary to be cautious and painstaking. Soon the towel for dabbing the sweat out of his eyes was covering his head as the sun blistered down, but he was making progress and he cheered up.

It became clear soon enough that a pot it was not. It was too large. He had to risk dripping some water over it and immediately the beautiful detailed decoration was revealed. Wind whistled through his lips, this might be some find! It had to be a large vase or even an urn. Suddenly, as he tired, he made one chip too hard and a whole piece appeared to break off from the rest. The air became blue from expletives as he cursed his foolishness and greed for trying to rush things. But he had never seen a find like this before and his curiosity forced him to continue. Removing the soil became suddenly easier and he laughed to himself when he realised he had not broken it at all, he had merely found the lid! Now his excitement was beginning to overwhelm him, just as a piercing whistle punctuated the air around his head.

Looking up through stinging eyes he could make out a man who had obviously found his lazily half-concealed car and was waving at him. He waved back, more out of reflex than purpose and it seemed to satisfy whoever it was because he turned and trudged away happily. As he turned, the sun picked out the shimmer of something on his shoulder: a plough shear perhaps, thought Pasquale, and if it is that's lucky because it's probably only a local farmer being inquisitive. So he

sat still, pretending to be just resting on a walk if the farmer did look
back. He did, then waved and then disappeared behind the first line of
olive trees about 400 metres away.

Pasquale had one of the most major decisions of his life to make:
leave now or stay? If I leave I must replace everything to make the
ground look natural and undisturbed in case the man comes back later.
Oh Mio Dio, he might tread on it and smash it! And it will mean much
extra work again, both ends, to extract it. But if I stay will I get it all
out? From the sun's angle it must be 5 pm already so I only have two
hours left to get it out. Impossible! Did I bring my torch in the car?
Would a light be seen and raise suspicions? Quick!

He decided to battle on and see how much more he could do in the
light. Fortune was with him for once because the soil deeper down was
softer and easier to remove. But the soil depth seemed a big clue too.
Normally on such rocky hills there was only two or three inches, then
bare rock, but here it went on for ever. He considered he might therefore
be in an ancient building, now totally obliterated, which would have had
a sunken floor dug out. On the wall-free hillside two or three thousand
years of winter rains would have washed down copious amounts of soil
and it would have filled up the void in the rooms' floors.

Finally, he was able to free the loose piece. Yes, a lid, he triumphed
quietly!

Soon after he was able to ease the urn a fraction, but only slightly,
and he wondered why it seemed heavier or less mobile than it should
have been. Had it been filled with soil over the centuries? Rejuvenated
he continued to dig away under it, carefully avoiding any scratching or,
perish the thought, cracking. Soon he could gently ease it further and
as the sun started to set it still refused to come free. He cursed loudly.
He had failed, and what was worse, he had made the wrong decision.

Still cursing, with his bare hands he hastily scooped back all the soil
he had so laboriously won from the Earth in less time than it had taken
to remove about two inches of the original. The only short cut possible
was quite a big one though; he was able to fix the lid on the urn so
that there was no need to put back all that soil he had earlier taken out
from the inside of it. That cheered him somewhat, and further cheer
was elicited from the removal of the surplus soil. He literally threw
it with bare hands all over the site, scattering it like grain seed being
sown. Next he set about laying dead bush fronds all over the urn and
its site, hoping it would appear sufficiently natural till the morning.

Surely no-one would stagger up here in the night and find this place with a torch or lantern? But old farmers are very wily specimens and anything could transpire. Panic then set in: he stripped the site of the fronds, piled up more earth on to the urn and restored the dead brush. If anyone had walked across there they would have smashed the urn to bits, of that there was no doubt, but now it still might have a chance with this protective blanket.

And then he considered, should I stay here all night anyway? Sleep out rough here, or even in the car? Oh, pull myself together, who's going to come here? I am being ridiculous now.

And so it was. He drove home, slowly at first in case the nosy farmer was abroad, then much faster to not annoy Mama by being too late.

"Where have you been this time, Pasquale? You have missed my dinner again!" railed Mama.

"Er...got a bit lost today, Mama, still learning all these new roads, sorry," apologised her son. His heart was leaping with delight and he so wanted to tell everyone, but he knew he couldn't...well yet, at least.

"Expect I can find you something, dreaming boy!" she smiled.

"Isabella, give the man a chance. He is not a boy, he is a man. And he is the man who managed to start us all off in our prosperity, remember?"

"Huh! And he is the one who has so aged us and made us grumpy!"

"All I ask is you give him some respect, sometimes."

"Perhaps I will when he gives me the fruit and vegetables he promised today," answered the wily Isabella very sarcastically.

"Oh Mama, I am so sorry, I got so carried away I completely forgot! How can I make it up to you?" pleaded her son, knowing full well that if everything worked out he could buy her enough fruit and vegetables to last for the rest of her life.

But Isabella was not to know that and wanted to protract the argument, "I don't ask for much here, but..."

"...Isabella, please leave it now. Just give the man some food, please."

With a grumbling undertone Isabella turned to the big aga-like cooker and dished him up a delicious prawn pasta with lemon juice. Pasquale should have slept well that night after such a repast and such exertion, but he lay awake for long periods praying for his find to be safe and worrying about the farmer beating him to it. I should have slept there, he grumbled to himself, I'll never forgive myself if...if...if...

Heavy-lidded, he returned to the collina before sunrise. He had to beat that farmer: they were not ignorant in these matters. Maybe it was possible they found even more antiquities than the hunters…and probably unintentionally smashed more too with their ploughs. He was so engrossed in these nightmare thoughts that he raced straight through a 4-way stop junction. The police car watching never moved and Pasquale thanked God that the fat, lazy carabinieri was most likely asleep at that time of the morning.

With butterflies gnawing his stomach he parked in the same semi-concealed spot and emerged from the trees to cast a panoramic view of the scene. Sure enough, in the increasing daylight he could just make out the wretched farmer halfway between him and the urn, moving slowly but purposefully up the collina. Damn! Quick, run! Beat him! He thought, all in one action, but he did not countenance the rough, rocky ground in the half light. After two twinges to the ankles he had to slow down, but even as he did he could not think for the life of him what he would say when he arrived!

"Signore, signore, please stop!" he shouted into the morning breeze.

The man continued trudging ever higher. Pasquale shouted again, this time twice as loud and the man heard him. He stopped and allowed Pasquale to catch him up; just enough time to think.

"Oh, hello again. Back for some more?"

"More what?" asked Pasquale, trying to be as calm and friendly as possible.

"Some more walking. But isn't it a little early? Are you that keen?" he squinted and pinched his enquiring face meaningfully.

This old man is extremely wily, thought Pasquale, but countered immediately, "walking? Oh no, signore, you are mistaken. In fact, please do not walk another step forwards, not one!"

"Heh? What do you mean? Are you telling me what to do on my own land, young man?" His eyes narrowed as Pasquale thought he could just envisage a thin sneer starting to form.

"Your land? Is it, signore?"

"Indeed it is young man, and I…"

"…well, not according to my Government department," he said as he pulled out a small card and flashed it in front of him so quickly the poor farmer could not even read it. "Your land, and any of the other farmers' land around, would actually stop at the base of this hill. These hills are never owned, they always belong to the Government."

"I didn't know that. Are you sure?"

"Absolutely, signore, that's why I am here and feel comfortable on this hill."

"Well, no-one ever comes around here, it's a desolate spot, and you just imagine it belongs to you, know what I mean?" conceded the poor man.

"Oh yes, indeed so, of course," conceded Pasquale, knowing that it was 'Round One' to him. But there was still much to do to win the bout.

"So exactly who are you then, young man?" asked the farmer as he made to rest on a large rock.

Pasquale rushed forward to stop him, "no signore, please don't!" he shouted.

"What do you mean, you young fool? Can't I even sit and rest a minute on Government land?"

Pasquale smiled broadly to ease the tension, "of course you can, as long as you know it is just rock you are sitting on."

"Now what do you mean?"

"Well, you see this machine I have here…"

"…yes, yes, a metal detector, like those wretched antiquities hunters carry," he said meaningfully with a sneer, "so is that what you're really up to? You telling me a pack of lies, boy?"

Pasquale felt a wave of panic rising but kept sufficiently calm to reply with a smile, "of course not, signore, please dispel the thought. No, I have been sent here by my ministry, the Ministry of the Environment, to check that people like you do not sit on, or kick, or dig up…",he paused for effect.

"What, young fella? Eh? Antiquities? Eh?"

"No signore," stated Pasquale most sombrely, "bombs, signore, bombs! Unexploded bombs, no less!"

"Nonsense! Ain't no bombs round here!"

"And how do you know?"

"Never seen one."

"Oh, have you been looking, then?"

"No, why should I?"

"Precisely!"

"Eh?" That had truly confused the farmer, but he battled on, "I've been walking on this hill for years and ain't seen a single specimen!"

"Well, all I can say is that the dear Mother Mary has been working overtime to protect you, blessed man!" smiled Pasquale, realising the conversation was starting to drift at a tangent and he needed to go in for the kill. "How long have you lived here?"

"Came in 1948 to stay with my daughter and…"

"…precisely, signore, then you wouldn't know…"

"…know what?"

"Well, to cut a long story short, the Italian Air Force wasn't that great and when they had to bomb Allied troops they often got the wrong target…"

"…wrong target? My son was a pilot and he died for his country!" said the farmer with vehemence, advancing slightly and flexing his hands.

"I can only say what we were told, signore. I am so, so sorry for your loss…"

"Huh, wasn't the best son to me, as it happens. Go on."

"Yes, OK. You see, we know the planes tried to bomb an Allied convoy a few miles away, that way," flinging his arms about haphazardly, relieved that the farmer had not come here before the War and didn't seem to know much about any of this, "but it appears they got the wrong hill and dropped them somewhere else…"

"…but there are a number of collina around here, young man."

"Precisely, that is why it is my job to check them all!"

"Oh, so that's why you have that detector."

"Yes, indeed! Now do you see? Some of the bombs did not go off, probably not well made, and I have so far checked four hills over there without success and I am now here. Every hill I check narrows the field, as it were!" They both laughed at that weak excuse for a joke, but it did serve to clear the air.

"Must be a boring job."

"I thought farming was!" Pasquale countered and they both laughed again, easier this time.

"Ah, now I understand; that's what you were looking at yesterday, then?"

"Quite. I thought I may have found something but it was too late in the day to begin. You have to be so careful with these bombs…one mistake and puff!" he gesticulated an explosion which nearly made the old man jump out of his skin.

"Oh my, you scared me, signore."

"Apologies, signore, but you have to be ready at all times."

"Are you trained?"

Pasquale thought this might be the last question before he sealed his victory, "only in the rudiments of bomb disposal. The easy ones I could attempt if they were life-threatening, but I prefer to leave it to others."

"Which one is that then?" he asked, pointing up the hill.

"Don't know yet. Don't know if it is a bomb yet, but I think so. If my detector is anything to go by. So, I must now ask you to go back and not come near this hill again until I can give it the all-clear. Do you understand, signore?"

"Oh, most certainly. I will go and tell everyone around here not to come near..."

"...er...I would prefer if you did not, er, Signore...?"

"Peschici, signore. And you?"

"Agent Scarpone. No, please do not tell anyone. Please keep this to yourself. It is a secret for the time being."

"But to warn people away?"

"Yes, but I thought you said no-one ever came here?"

"Well, sometimes they do..." he admitted, defeated.

"...look, we tend to find our job hampered by interested onlookers once word gets out. Then children do not understand if they come, do you know what I mean?"

"Oh heavens, they might trespass and get hurt!"

"Precisely; blown to tiny pieces!" he pretended to shiver.

"OK, OK."

Sweet victory, but such hard work, requiring mountains of patience for a small molehill. Pasquale smiled to himself; rather amusing idea I came up with on the spur of the moment, that! "Now, it is quite possible I may have found something yesterday and I will have to remove it."

"You mean take it away? Down this hill?" The farmer was confused.

"Please don't worry, I am very well trained. If it is small I can disarm it, as I said, and just carry it to my car."

"Oh agent, you are a very brave man!"

"Well...er...thank you, signore, just doing my job..."

"...but so dangerous, after all. So you won't need any help then? Or can I come and watch? From a small distance, that is."

"Thank you, but no; insurance and risk and all that. Surely you can see that?"

"Yes, yes, of course." But Pasquale could see the old farmer was agitatingly excited: obviously nothing like this had happened to him

ever before. He would still need to be firm and nip this renewed interest
in the bud, quickly.

"OK, I must get on…"

The farmer made to go, then stopped and swung round, "thank you
again for saving my life, I'll leave you to it."

"Indeed so," answered Pasquale. It came out more condescendingly
than paternally. "Goodbye, signore, I will be in touch later."

"Good. First house where the track joins the road."

"Thank you." Oh please just go, thought Pasquale, this has taken
for ever and I just can't wait to see what I've found before it gets really
hot. He smiled and marched off up the rise in elation. He'd certainly
fooled the farmer and had made up the whole yarn on the hoof. On
the hoof! He laughed uncontrollably. Luckily the old man was now out
of earshot. Then suddenly he stopped. Don't get carried away, the man
is not a fool. It may not be all over just yet. Beware. First house, eh?
He must have heard me drive past, along somewhere no-one normally
goes, then got suspicious. He will hear me come in and out every time
if this site proves to be valuable. How will I be able to fend him off for
ever and stop word getting out? My Ministry cover will not last long,
not long at all. Still, one thing at a time, let's just concentrate on the job
in hand, otherwise everything else is lost.

He found the spot easily, as might others in daylight, and was glad
he had got here early. Surreptitiously he watched for the farmer to
disappear out of sight before attacking it. Soon he passed the point of
status quo and had the urn out of the ground. It was truly magnificent,
even covered in dirt and slightly stained by water/soil interaction. But
it was so heavy!

So, carefully he started to scoop out the interior, hoping no
tarantula, red ants or scorpions had made their nest there in the night.
His thoughts were soon confirmed because instead of removing totally
soil he started to hear "chink's". Soon he was pulling out coins in the
soil, some bronze, some silver, but then came a gold one. He laughed
for joy, this was an incredible find!

He would have danced a jig of delight but maybe the farmer was
hiding and still watching, so he kept as much movement as possible as
close to the ground as he could. As more bronze, silver and gold coins
emerged he couldn't help joking to himself that maybe he'd stumbled on
one of the sites of the earliest Olympic Games. But then he remembered
someone had told him that in those days there were no prizes, only the

glory of victory. Well, this sure was a prize and a victory for him and he determined to let no-one steal it from him.

To be safe, he decided to role-play the sequence of bomb disposal events as far as he could remember it, in case the old man had by chance a pair of old wartime binoculars or something. So he wrapped everything in a large cloth he had purposely brought, replaced the soil and started his next search. Soon, more scattered coins were added to the collection, but little else. Enough for one day, he thought, musn't be greedy. He needed to get the urn away as early as possible but he did not want to arouse suspicions. Surely if the bomb was defused there would be no need for him to go racing off with it in his car straight away. The farmer would expect him to complete a day's work. But every minute he waited was pure agony and in the end, by lunchtime, he could bear it no more.

It took two trips to the car and a weight of perspiration to get the urn and all his equipment down the hill. He deliberated over boot or rear seat and decided on the latter for greater softness and protection. Not ideal, but beggars couldn't be choosers, and slowly down the bumpy track he drove.

The old man was sitting by his gate and could clearly contemplate the slowness of the car. Pasquale had no option but again to brave it out, so he pulled up a tactful distance across the track and said through his driver's window, "I was indeed right, signore, we have a bomb! Please do not go near that hill. I will return with all the necessary warning signs in a few days."

"Oh dear! No, I will certainly stay away. But can I ask just one favour? Could I take a peek at the bomb? Was it heavy?"

"Not a heavy one. Certainly you cannot see it."

"Not even one little peep?"

"Have you never seen a bomb, signore?"

"Well...certainly, but..."

"In that case I would have thought your generation would never wish to see a bomb ever again! Goodbye, signore."

"Yes, goodbye, drive carefully."

"Oh, it's quite safe now I've defused it." Pasquale had finally managed it.

That last exchange had been very risky and indeed touch and go, but he had been obliged to stop, it would have looked most suspicious if he had not.

He hit the tar toad, he was free, away with the most precious thing he had ever found. Now what? Ah, what the heck, I am going to celebrate. His singing still failed to raise the snoozing carabinieri at the crossroads and Pasquale wondered if in fact he was indeed alive or had he been shot by the Camora and just left there. Again, Lady Fortune smiled down on him: he would not have wanted an officious policeman inspecting the large lump on the back seat of his car.

It was quite a long drive but he took his treasure to a secret hiding place he had purposefully prepared, cleaned it up as carefully as he could and stashed it away safely. The coins, meanwhile, he soaked in a bucket and they looked splendid. He would take those with him and go home. He couldn't wait to see their faces. All the criticism he had endured after leaving them to fend for themselves, all the jibes: he could now sell the bar and buy them a luxury villa with this urn windfall, he was sure.

Back at the bar everyone was slaving away over the pre-dinner aperitivos, so many fussy little plates to clear and wash from the tiny, delicate portions of pizza slices, prosciutto crudo buns, cold noci, assorted cheeses and finger sandwiches. No-one had a minute for his news, that was clear, so he casually parked himself at the bar and started on orange liqueurs. Eventually, he managed to pull Cosimo aside and ask, "I really could do with your help tomorrow, and…er…maybe a few more days too, I'm not sure yet. Any chance, please?"

Instead of the expected polite rejection, for he felt it politic to approach Cosimo first, he was taken aback when Cosimo replied, "Oh Pasquale, thank you, thank you. I really need a break from all this; it's such hard work for someone my age."

"Can't you afford to hire younger legs, like I said?" replied Pasquale. "And more handsome?" he added for good humour.

"Ha ha! Yes, but they are so unreliable it is hardly worth it. At least when I know I must do it I do it, but I've been forever taking staff's places who have cried off for the most ridiculous excuses. It can get chaotic sometimes."

"I know, Cos. Look I'll ask Stud if he can work some extra shifts or if he knows someone reliable. This is important, or I wouldn't ask you."

"I know. But I keep forgetting I'm the manager here, not just bar staff, because it's too busy to even draw breath. And now we have all that lovely homemade gelato to make every morning, O my!" He rolled his eyes heavenward.

"Just get more staff. You'll be able to soon anyway."

"Oh, why?"

"Tell you later when it quietens down. But tomorrow, early, I need a big wooden sign made, OK?"

"OK. And?"

"And you may have to sleep out rough tomorrow night!"

"Are you sure? I don't think I am up to that kind of thing anymore."

"Oh please! There is no-one else I would want to ask to do this."

"Really? Will you be there too?"

"Might have to be. I'll let you know."

"Heavens, Pasquale, just what are you up to now? Though I must admit it all sounds rather intriguing…"

"Do you still have your shotgun?"

"Yes."

"Is it serviceable?"

"Yes. More and more intriguing! You'll have to tell me now. Quickly, mind. Isabella will be shouting for me any second, if I know her."

"Cosimo, what if I told you I may have found the biggest, most important site of my life?"

"I'd say "wow"! And then I would say 'may have'?"

"OK then, I have found it. But there's a problem…"

"…oh, there's always a problem!"

"Shush, the problem is that there lives nearby a nosy farmer."

"Young or old?"

"Fortunately old, but he is so wily. Look, I'll explain everything later, but I have found something that I believe is worth a fortune!"

"You see? I knew it would bring us luck."

"What?" asked Pasquale, mystified.

"Bar Fortuna, stupido!" laughed Cosimo, shaking him by the shoulders and then embracing him enough to squeeze the breath away. "There's my boy!"

"Actually, Eduardo's boy, unfortunately."

"Let's not split hairs while we are celebrating. Right, I will be ready before dawn. Let's have another cocktail, eh?" And at that Cosimo went off dancing and singing.

"Not a word, mind, Cos!" shouted Pasquale.

Cosimo held his finger to his lips while he poured with the other hand.

And so it was. Next morning dawned bright and clear and they made a rough sign with a sheet of wood, a pole, some nails and old red paint. They took it to the collina, driving fast past the farmer's, and hammered it in.

'KEEP OUT – DANGER' it read, and underneath, 'BY ORDER, Min of Environment, Roma'.

A few metres away, behind a large rock, Cosimo set up his temporary camp. He covered the food, water, blankets and toilet paper with a waterproof and readied to repel all invaders. Meanwhile, Pasquale had convinced him that he would be better employed if he were the mobile one, and when Cosimo saw the site he lost all anxiety about defending it.

"There's absolutely no-one living around here! This will be easy," he boasted.

"True, but remember as soon as gossip starts the onlookers come. Now remember clearly the bomb history and story I told you; we don't want old Farmer Peschici comparing notes, do we?"

"Certainly not. And I am employed by the Ministry too, right?"

"Yes. Now, have a real good rest, keep that hat over your face for the sun, and I'll be back later. If you hear the detector beeping, cheer loud, but only inside your mind. OK?"

"Good luck!"

So Pasquale resumed his search on the circumference of the hill, halfway up, walking round and round and round, each time leaving a marker to see where he was. At 5 pm he returned to the snoring Cosimo and woke him with the sight of two more smallish Greco vases and some Messapican lamp holders.

Instead of being thrilled to be woken by such treasure Cosimo grunted, "Is this it? Doesn't seem much for a day's work under this hot sun!"

"Not much? Has the sun driven you mad, Cos? This is brilliant, truly brilliant, I'm telling you!"

"Brilliant?"

"Huh, just proves how little you know about antiquities."

"All I want to know about antiquities is their value. The money. So, are you saying these ugly things are valuable?"

"They are certainly not ugly and, put it like this, I've never seen vases like this before so I reckon they are really valuable."

"OK, well done!" chirped Cosimo, still not convinced, "can we go now?"

"Go? Have you seen anyone?"

"Not a soul."

"Is that because there has been no-one here, or because you've been asleep all day?"

"Sorry, probably the latter."

Pasquale considered for a while as he watched the sun dropping faster and reddening up. "OK, we'll take a chance on it tonight and leave. It certainly seems very quiet."

"Good! A decent supper and bed!" laughed Cosimo.

"Trouble is, I need to get these to Taranto as soon as possible but I can't be in two places at once."

"Well, tomorrow, drop me off here, go to Taranto and come back to pick me up. I should be OK."

"Are you sure?"

"Yes. It was certainly very hot, and I'm no longer used to that, but it was so peaceful and beautiful I'm sure I can manage another day."

"OK. Let's bring a big sheet and some poles, or something, and make you a sort of canopy structure to stop the sun."

"Great!"

The next day, after dropping Cosimo at the deserted site and then fetching the large urn and coins, Pasquale motored as fast as he could to his friend Mario Gennari. Mario was delighted to see him after such a long time and after the fretful Lupo affair. They took coffee and almond cake, then Mario inspected Pasquale's treasures. His sucking in breath between teeth told all, "wow, good friend, you have certainly done well this time!"

"Thank you. Just what I thought too."

"You're not going to disclose the location though, eh?" he laughed.

Pasquale had learned to know Mario over the years: all sugary and friendly, obsequious even, if necessary, but above everything else he was still a businessman. More polite than Tonino, certainly, but little different underneath. "Not going to have me followed either, Mario?" he laughed back.

Each knew that the other was serious, despite the laughs, so they cancelled themselves out.

"Touche, old friend. Look, I'm certain I can move the coins and the two vases, but the urn is far too big and heavy."

"Really? But is it valuable, Mario?"

"Oh yes, I would say so, certainly. Well done!" he said slightly enviously. "But you know how these things are, it's far too big for me to move, value-wise and literally." He laughed.

Pasquale did not, "So what am I going to do?"

"There's not much you can do here. Any other middleman will tell you the same. You know the risk we run. It's easy with the small goods, but this is hard to hide."

"So?"

"So, all I can suggest is that you drive it yourself all the way to Napoli, a big showroom. They should be able to help you…"

"…but…but…"

"Look, don't worry, here are some of my trusted contacts up there, they will help you." Mario gave him two business cards, and the discussion had ended. "Now, for the rest I can offer…hmmm…let me see."

He buried himself in figures on a notepad for what seemed an age, "er…400,000 lira."

"Sorry, Mario, this is real treasure, that's not enough. 600.000."

"500,000, no more!"

"Done!"

Cosimo was fine when Pasquale returned, and he also reported no sightings. Had he pretended to look for bombs, as Pasquale had suggested. Indeed he had, walking across and up the hill holding the detector, just in case the nosy Peschici was still snooping. And no, he had found nothing. But yes, it had been rather fun even though that could not have been envisaged. And yes, how amazing it was that Pasquale had got so much money for the treasures. And no, he didn't think he could stand another day on the hill -- what could be beautiful one moment could become so boring the next. Pasquale resisted the temptation to draw the parallel with marriage, to help illustrate why he was still single. And yes, he certainly was ready to go home and celebrate. And no, he did not think Isabella would agree in a million years to close the bar for the evening so they could go for a celebratory dinner!

※ ※ ※

42

ERUPTIONS GREATER THAN VESUVIO

1 9 5 9

Pasquale had never been to Napoli. To be honest he had never been further than Taranto. He had consulted his worldly-wise bar customers on the best route and all except one had advised him to go up to Bari and then across the Apennines. It was a better road than to Taranto and then up to Potenza and Sorrento, although this would take him past the beautiful Sorrento Peninsula, Herculano, Pompeii and Vesuvio. He reckoned it would be better to go the boring route via Bari and then if his visit was a great success he could stop for a little holiday break on the way back at Sorrento or Amalfi on the other route. Whichever, it was over 300 miles and a seven or eight hour journey each way. However, *faint heart never won fair lady*, he argued, and so *in for a penny in for a pound*. His customers also worried him with two more warnings about Napoli driving --- the drivers were the worst in the world, more frightening than even Parisians, and second, 'once lost in Napoli, forever lost' was not just a traveller's tale, there were few road signs and fewer ways out, leading to rapid confusion and a longer than expected trip.

So with some trepidation he entered the largest city he had ever seen with the most precious possession he had ever owned. He had made a rough wooden crate, filled with packed straw and he had cleaned up the urn before resting it in it. The crate was sat on blankets on the back seat and wedged in tight by various boxes to avoid shifting around. It was the best he could do and although the road was rough in places he hoped the urn would survive. The crate was draped with yet more cloths to avoid prying eyes. The urn had looked magnificent once the caked earth had been soaked off: a series of hunting scenes revolved around it, embossed with bulbous juicy grapes and slender girls carrying jugs, presumably of wine.

Surprisingly the citizens of Napoli were friendlier than his bar patrons had suggested and he was directed to the antiques showroom very efficiently. Without Pasquale's cognisance Mario Gennari had telegraphed ahead to his showroom friend to 'expect a country bumpkin, easily cheatable but honest and true'. Following gentile introductions Pasquale watched carefully the crate being carried into a rear workroom, for this was his baby and he trusted absolutely no-one. The weary traveller was feted with a temple-cooling glass of amaretti and ice as the urn was delicately extracted. Suddenly "ooh's" and "aagh's" filled the room. The experts walked round it, huddled, muttered, walked round it again, nodded, tiptoed to check inside, executed the 'chink test' to authenticate the ceramics, then finally whispered again. It was an extremely hot room, Pasquale's head was thumping from a stress-related headache and the second glass of nectar was starting to kick in.

"Signore Carone, this indeed a worthy and rare find, we all congratulate you! After our consultations we are sure it is an early Greek urn and we believe it could be worth in the region of..." the senior partner coughed, probably for effect to heighten the drama, "... probably worth upwards of two and a half million lira. And maybe much, much more now that rich Americans are puncturing even our humble little market again."

Pasquale stared transfixed at the man, his brain unable to engage his tongue. As he tried to form a reply the senior partner continued, "however, we are unable to give you this amount."

Ah, thought Pasquale, here come the usual sales tricks, but he was in no way prepared for what was to follow and it finally stunned him totally.

"In fact, we are unable to give you anything at all for it: I am deeply sorry, we cannot buy it off you!"

"Cannot...buy...it...?" mumbled Pasquale, his brain totally befuddled now by the heat, the drink and the partner's rejection of a priceless object.

"No. You see, in such a fine city as ours there are many strict laws and as dutiful citizens we are bound to keeping these laws for the good of all. Perhaps in the countryside where you come from the law is more lax or remote and you find ways round things, yes?"

"Not really, well, yes, maybe, but…"

"…now, as an antiquities house of great distinction and reputation we find we cannot just trade any item…"

"…but this is not just any item, signore…"

"…precisely, that is my point. If it were just any ordinary item we could easily make a deal with you and no-one would even notice or be the wiser, but because this is a piece of such beauty and rarity it would be the talk of the town within hours…"

"…great, so what would be the problem? Its value would rocket and you'd be even richer, right?"

"Wrong, young sir, we would be…er…we would have a problem."

"Problem?"

"Most certainly. Signore, my partners feel we cannot discuss this any further. We are humbly sorry." He got up to walk away.

"But signore, please, what can I do with it then?" responded Pasquale, unwilling to be cut off like that.

The partners went back into their huddle, to emerge with the advice, "it appears the only solution is for you to go direct to Napoli's branch of the National Museum."

"What? And give it away to some fuddy-duddy? No, signore, no, no!"

"Sorry, I do not mean you to just give it to them. They are able to buy such items, we are not."

"But they would not give me much for it…"

"…I hate to interrupt, but wrong again, signore. They would be the end-owner, we are only middlemen: they would probably offer you even more than us!" he smiled and turned away.

"Truly?"

"Truly. Look, I will give you the name of the Head Curator of Greco objects…"

"…signore," someone called from the huddle, "we could phone now for an appointment for Signore Carone?"

"Excellent idea, excellent. Come, let my staff re-pack it for you and we will take refreshment outside."

Still with great suspicion, despite all these pleasantries, Pasquale said, "er, I'd rather stay here, if you please."

"Certainly you may. We will bring you food here then," agreed the senior partner, wondering if this country bumpkin was not quite as bumpkin as he looked. The assistant flashed a look at him, which Pasquale unfortunately missed, and said, "you are in luck, signore, you can be fitted in today at 5pm."

Even the partners were impressed and wondered if the assistant had mentioned what the piece was to get such a rapid viewing. They sometimes had to queue up for weeks!

Pasquale too was most relieved because he would not have known what to do with the urn for the night. Sleep in the car with it? Heaven forbid! Get robbed as well as shot or stabbed? Find lodging and leave it unattended in the car? Worse! Take it to his room? Impossible to carry; with the crate it was now a 2-man lift. Too many questions. His mind raced on. "Oh thank you, signores, so helpful," was all he could manage.

"A pleasure, signore!" bowed the senior partner obsequiously. "Any friend of Mario's is a friend of ours!"

"Oh, you know Signore Gennari, then? Did he say I was coming?"

"Of course. He telegrammed us that one of his most worthy suppliers wished to see us."

Pasquale wondered about that: was it all so gentlemanly and businesslike? Or was there more involved? He knew of Gennari's connections with the Ndrangheta only too well: they had helped him get rid of the Lupo problem, God, how does the man know everyone?

At 5pm he found himself in Signore Marcuni's office, just as the two men who had carried it up five floors carefully opened the crate. "Oh my, it is exquisite, signore!" cried Mancuni, in ecstasy, "remarkable, what a stunning piece."

"Yes, indeed it is," replied Pasquale carefully. He was learning fast how to measure his conversation.

"And where, again, did you say you found it?"

"I didn't, actually."

"Well, little clues like that help us in our underststanding, signore... perhaps?"

Pasquale was also learning to think fast on his feet with all these experts, "actually, it was not I who found it, it was a friend who passed it to me. He never told me where he dug it up."

"Oh, what a pity! A pity indeed. You see, when we exhibit any such piece we need to state where it was found. Well, I can tell you it is an extremely valuable piece. Did it contain anything or was it empty, do you know?"

Pasquale considered this question: was Mancuni fishing in the dark, thinking an urn must contain something, or did urns like this always carry something? Whichever, why was he asking? he thought. Another rapid decision: "I believe it held a substantial number of gold, silver and bronze coins."

"Ah! And where are they, pray?"

"No idea, signore. I did not see them. Is that an important clue too?"

"Hmmm, most certainly." Pasquale started to fidget and yawn. "Well, I don't normally like to give estimates quickly, I usually need to consider and consult, then write to the client..."

"...oh dear! And I don't like to let antiquities of such value out of my sight, either, signore. I cannot afford to stay in Napoli more than two days: important business calls me elsewhere, I'm afraid." Who was tricking who in this game, he thought.

"In that case, as a rough estimate, I would value this beauty in excess of three million lira."

By this time Pasquale did not even blink because he was becoming used to these totally unreal numbers, and Mancuni was a little taken back that the man had shown no emotion at all. "Does that not surprise you at all, Signore Carone?"

"Indeed, signore."

"And if I told you that price would rank it within our top ten objects in the entire museum?"

"Really? How wonderful," trying a little enthusiasm.

"So please, can you give me some time to complete my evaluation and consult with our finance department? Say two days? Could you come back on Thursday at, say, 11am?"

"Certainly signore, but the piece?"

"The piece will be as safe as houses here. Look, I will give you a receipt for it now."

"Ah, then that will be OK. Thank you." Pasquale took the receipt and did not walk out of that office, he floated out. It was all he could do to stop himself dancing all the way back along the dark, fussy corridor. I'm rich! I'm rich! He kept screaming to himself. Three million lira? I could buy 10 bars for that, or 2 villas in Roma and a boat in Lido di Ostia for that, or...oh, how his bumpkin head spun!

After two whole days of sightseeing and sumptuous dining, after sailing across to magical Capri, strolling the rich, tree-lined avenues of majestic palazzos owned by Napoli's upper-crust, he was well rested and even a little prepared for his new wealthy lifestyle. What a time he'd had. He'd even soaked up the rotten-egg stench of the sulphur vents in the ancient crater of Solfatara, as well as trudge for five hours up and down the scoria-covered slopes to peer into the mighty crater of Vesuvius.

He knocked on the door. All he could think about as he waited was the worry of having a cheque. He'd always hated banks and only dealt in cash, keeping it stashed away in secret places, like his very first loose tufa block in the Avetrana kitchen. Indeed, despite Cosimo's protestations, all the Bar Fortuna profits were in banknotes, hidden away in his secret location. Now he would be forced to open an account in Ceglie Messapica and, whatever the banks say about confidentiality, tongues would soon wag and everyone would know he was rich. It would be impossible. Would they have to move towns again? "Come in".

He walked into a room full of people. He only recognised Signore Marcuni sitting at his desk. Flanking him on his right was a photographer with an enormous flash bulb on his pedestalled camera, but on his right a Carabinieri. In an arc around the sides of the room must have been at least eight others, presumably museum staff. What a reception, thought Pasquale proudly, an official handover ceremony with photograph in the Napoli newspaper. In the centre of the desk was the urn, shining in the soft morning rays beaming through the window. A perfect moment. He was so excited.

"Good morning, Signore Carone. Pasquale Carone, correct?" asked Marcuni.

Why ask that, he thought, he knows my name perfectly well, he wrote me a receipt. "Good morning, Signore Marcuni."

"Thank you for returning after out meeting of Tuesday, 11 July 1959." Again, Pasquale thought it odd that the man was being so formal and that another man was writing everything down. "Please be seated."

"If it is OK I'd rather stand, signore."

"No, we'd rather you sat. Please. Captain?" He motioned Pasquale to the chair and suddenly there was a hand on his shoulder forcing him down. Pasquale had not seen the other policeman in the arc. He was confused. What a fuss.

"Now, on Tuesday you told me you did not find this urn, but a friend did and he gave it to you. Is that correct?"

"Yes, signore," answered the confused Pasquale. Should he stick to this story or the truth? Why would it matter?

At this point the Carabinieri took over.

"And did you pay him anything for it?" he boomed imperiously.

"No."

"Are you sure?"

"Yes."

"Why then would he give you something so precious?"

Pasquale was dumbstruck. He had no answer. He must stall. "Why is this so important? Why I gave him money or not?"

"Can you name this so-called friend?"

"Why? Do I need to?"

"Have you done this before for him, or for any other friend?"

"No, sir."

"How many years have you taken an interest in antiquities?"

"Quite a while, but what is the point to all this, please?"

The policemen totally ignored him and didn't seem to care whether he answered or not. Everything was being written down anyway, either way.

"And you said you did not know where your friend found it?"

"Yes."

"Would it have been in a farmer's field or on wasteland, do you think?"

"The former, probably. How do I know?"

"And you took it to others but they refused to buy it, correct?"

"Yes."

"And they told you to bring it here?"

"Yes."

The carabinieri then turned and said to the arc, "well, there you have it, judge." One of the men stepped forward and peered right into Pasquale's face. He was now so confused by all this questioning. Was it the normal procedure perhaps, or was there something wrong? He soon got his answer.

The weasely judge said, "I believe you to be a liar, signore, and a scoundrel, and probably a thief. Officers, take him away!" Still reeling from the bad breath and the spittle, poor Pasquale was dragged to his feet by unseen hands, handcuffed and marched away. The carabinieri thrust him into their waiting car and took him to the City Gaol.

"So, signore Marcuni, I trust you will get this on display as soon as possible? Isn't she a beauty?"

"Certainly, and yes, in that order. We are so happy to have it. It will be one in the eye for Museum Roma, ha! But, I suppose…"

"…yes? Is there a problem?"

"Well, I suppose we shall have to put for location, 'Puglia' until the court case. It won't matter too much, I suppose."

"Detail, merely detail. Do you have enough security, signore?"

"Oh most definitely," he smiled happily. His career would be made, but inevitably he would have to show his gratitude to those down the line in the usual manner.

Pasquale was left in a hot, fetid cell for a week. His family knew nothing of his whereabouts, but of course worried increasingly as each day passed.

Then came the day of his trial. The affair had attracted considerable attention because the museum, in order to gain publicity to increase visitor numbers, had declared the enormous value of the urn. The police were happy too because they were forever on the lookout for ways to cut down antiquities' trafficking. So Courtroom 3 was packed with a wide cross-section of the general public, as well as officiario and politzi, but there was no-one supporting Pasquale. He could not afford a barrister so he was given one pro bono. Finally, from this barrister, Pasquale discovered why he was there. He was being tried for dealing in precious antiquities, and he also added that the courts were meting out progressively harsher sentences to try and stop it, so he should not raise his hopes. There would be three judges: chief judge Alduni from Napoli, magistrate Prellori from Brindisi and magistrate Starsi from Taranto.

It was clear from the outset that the Prosecution certainly did want a stiff sentence, as the barrister had warned, because Pasquale was classified as a dealer. His barrister countered that it was in fact he who had found it and he had lied out of fear earlier on, but that defence soon fizzled out when Pasquale refused to give up the location, or any details of the find at all, so it appeared obvious to all he was not the one to find it. Pasquale had his reasons, mainly that he was confident that one day he would make even greater finds there. They also argued that he had found it on farmers' land so it was a legal find and he had done the right thing to bring it to the museum. However, he refused to reveal the farmer's name to the Prosecution so that argument too was nullified. The Prosecution then called the Napoli dealers as witnesses who confirmed he had tried to sell it to them but they had quite rightly refused. They then were forced to give the name of Mario Gennari and the whole trial was held up four days while he was 'escorted' from Taranto.

Mario was forced to admit that his friend had first brought him the urn and he had indeed refused, being the legitimate trader he was, and instead referred him to contacts in Napoli for assistance. At this point Pasquale's case crumbled.

One evening Mario had asked to see Pasquale in his cell and he was so apologetic. He never realised how much trouble all this would have landed on Pasquale's lap, and they both wept man tears. At that, Pasquale had no reason to doubt him. Pasquale asked if it was the Starsi of dress shop fame, because he had never actually seen the man before, and Mario concurred. Pasquale was dumbstruck. Mario explained that it was normal to recruit two judges from other regions, to show fairness to all, and as Starsi was the rising star he had been top of the list to ask. Then Pasquale lowered his voice and told Mario how upset he had been with all this, being tricked into thinking he would get 3 million lira, and his family probably berserk with worry. Mario felt obliged to help him and promised he would telegram the family immediately and then he would contact the Ndrangheta. Pasquale had asked why and Mario whispered that they were still in his debt from the Lupo incident and they in turn could contact the Camorra in Napoli to see what was to be done. Both left the meeting much relieved and more confident.

But the trial disintegrated into a farce. It was patently clear Pasquale had no chance, despite continuing to plead he had done the right thing all along by approaching the proper authorities and not trying to sell it on the Black market. The judges only took an hour to confer.

"Pasquale Carone, we find you guilty of the crime of being an illegal, unregistered antiquities dealer. However, in view of what can only be called your naïve attempt to sell to the Napoli Museum and not to the Black Market we have agreed to reduce your sentence."

Pasquale lifted his head and looked meaningfully at his family in the Gallery, who had now arrived from Ceglie, willing it to be a light sentence for their sakes.

"We therefore sentence you to five years in Napoli Gaol."

Pasquale's mouth dropped, his head bowed again and he shouted, "no, surely not? I have done nothing wrong. I am not a dealer!"

"Take him down," ordered the judge, "before we increase it for contempt!"

Pasquale openly wept as he was led away. Cosimo wept the most because only he knew how innocent his 'son' was. Andrea wept under her shawl because she had nearly died when she had spotted the evil Starsi presiding. She wondered if he had put two and two together and realised this was the self-same brother of hers, but she personally thought it had been so many years ago, and did he even remember her family name anyway? Mama wept buckets, as mothers do, that was a given.

They were allowed one brief family reunion before Pasquale was taken to the gaol, and it was an emotional, if empty, meeting. After all, what could be said really? What could be done? Pasquale could only mutter, 'ask Cosimo', when they inquired the details, and the look he gave him was very clear: say as little as possible and remember the future.

And so it was. Pasquale began the lowest point of his life and the Carones returned home on the long bus ride to Ceglie Messapica. With what little joy they had left they tried to continue running the bar but it soon became obvious that their hearts were no longer in it. A new bar-cum-trattoria opened up nearby and within weeks many of their customers had osmosised across, enjoying the new idea of a man playing records while they drank and ate. Someone said he was called a disc-jockey.

But Cosimo refused to give in. He knew something of Andrea's pain in Taranto from Isabella, but it was after seeing that bastard Starsi deliberating in judgement on her dear brother, like the hypocrite he was, Andrea finally disclosed more to him, but not the worst parts. Understandably, Cosimo was totally outraged and, knowing how the rescue he and Pasquale had engineered had impacted on Lupo and the demise of his SCU gang, he decided to find Gennari.

Certainly Mario was pleased to see him and asked after Pasquale with genuine interest. In turn, he graciously accepted Cosimo's thanks for brokering the solution to the Lupo Affair. Cosimo wasted no time in pleading Pasquale's unjust treatment, but Mario quickly stopped him by saying it had been troubling his conscience ever since, as he had been the one who had sent Pasquale to Napoli, and if there was anything he could do please ask. He pointed out too that he had even racked his brains to help but nothing had yet presented itself; it had been such an indefensible defence of Pasquale's.

Suddenly Cosimo decided to take a chance and risk this smooth businessman's promises, as he had little ammunition left with which to help Pasquale. So he told Mario the basic details of the Starsi Affair and how could he be such a hyprocrite, sitting in judgement of others. As Mario listened his outrage grew too. He had seen what a beautiful woman Andrea was and how dare anyone treat women like this. He had heard many rumours about Starsi but never this one. The man had shot to power and influence very quickly in recent years but was very clever to hide any impropriety.

As Cosimo talked Mario knew this was something else his friend, the leader of the Ndrangheta, would love to hear about Andrea. Oh, it will make me even more in favour with him, thought Mario greedily.

Suddenly he stopped Cosimo and said, "could you bring Andrea with you for a meeting on another day? I have people waiting to see me now, unfortunately." Cosimo nodded. "Good, I will write to you when there is a suitable time etc. Please give me your address."

And he did. A few days later Cosimo received an invitation to bring Andrea to Taranto to meet some friends. At first, Andrea was nonplussed and when she asked the reason she screamed, "no... never...never ever!"

But Cosimo reassured her that she would be doing it for the dear brother who had once rescued her, and she would be safe amongst friends, he would guarantee it. They left Isabella and Maria out of it and quietly disappeared to Taranto on the bus.

At 3pm were seated Mario, Cosimo, Andrea, the Ndrangheta leader and a Camorra conduit. The last they had managed to attract because of the increasing "cooperation" between the two rival mafia groups. It was becoming increasingly difficult to safely bring ashore contraband, especially cigarettes, in the ports around the Bay of Napoli, like Pozzuoli or Sorrento, and even further north of Napoli around places like Castelvolturno, owing to increased customs vigilance. The Camorra had therefore struck a deal with the Ndrangheta to import them through small Reggio Calabrian ports not policed by customs, and then drive them north by unmarked vans at night. This conduit was proving to be increasingly successful and profitable so that the Camorra, in return, was being asked favours by the Ndrangheta, such as liquidating certain enemies of their group. As if in rotation, the Ndrangheta were again in position to ask a favour of the Camorra, and so it was going on.

Mario opened proceedings and introduced everyone. But the two mafia men instantly lost all hope, and all their manners too, in the presence of Andrea as they stared uncontrollably at her beauty. Damiano Milone, the Ndrangheta leader, smiled masculinely as he was introduced, then reverted to jaw-dropping worship, while the lieutenant from Napoli showed slightly more resolve, mouthing "an honour to be in your presence, Signorina!"

Damiano was enthralled: this woman was far more beautiful than the girl he had seen in that shop all those years ago. How could no-one have claimed her for his own, he wondered. Equally, Antonio the conduit had fallen in love within seconds of seeing her and wondered if she had this effect on the others in the room, who had all ceased to exist in his mind as soon as he had seen her.

As the story unfolded of Andrea's captivity and rescue the men's rage mounted, so that by the end they were raring to cut Starsi's throat. When Mario had calmed them with refreshments they continued by putting their heads together and devising a simple but devilish plan. Pasquale's lawyer was asked to make an urgent and immediate Appeal to his sentence. As soon as the new Napoli judge was known he would be compromised. He would be taken to a bar, slipped drugged drinks, driven to a hotel of low repute where he would be semi-woken to perform indecent acts with three coquettes, filmed, and driven away under a hooded cloak to his point of release. The films would be sent to the police and the legal authorities if he did not severely reduce the sentence. Meanwhile, Starsi would be taken care of locally now that it was clear how he made so much money in the vice trade.

And so it was. Cosimo read in the Mezzogiorno newspaper the following week of the shooting of eminent businessman Massimo Starsi. Two men had allegedly waited at the gates to his mansion and machine-gunned the car as it pulled in. His driver, Stefano Nania, was also killed. Condolences to the family during this rising tide of mafia-related crime in Italy, it said, and what kind of country was it becoming when law-abiding, respectable, hardworking businessmen were being executed by such rabble.

"Andrea, come here, you might want to read this," smiled Cosimo.

Although she knew she shouldn't she could not stop herself dancing for joy around the room, while Mama wailed tears of joy and relief, as mothers do.

So we did not kill Stefano after all, she mused, and felt another huge weight lift off her shoulders.

The new judge was indeed 'new', as judicial shelf-lives were short in places like Napoli, and he decided to steer a middle-course. He determined not to give in completely to the Camorra but to show who partly was boss in his court. So he "re-balanced" the evidence regarding the 'naïve Pasquale' and reduced his sentence, as requested, but by not as much as he was asked. He awarded him 18 months instead of the five years, thinking he had offered a sweet deal to satisfy all. But his decision did not please the Camorra, although they would have accepted it just this once, as he was new after all, if it had not been for insistence of the Ndrahgheta. Again they reminded the judge of the photos they held and demanded he reduce it to 9 months, as Pasquale had already served 3 months. He refused point blank and drew their bluff, saying it was impossible for a judge to keep changing his mind: he would be in deep trouble. Two nights later a masked gunman scaled the judge's drainpipe and machine-gunned him in his bed while his wife was in the bathroom and his 3-year old twins slept soundly next door.

Pasquale was released after 8 months for excellent behaviour by a 'sympathetic' parole board. Awaiting him at home was a hand-delivered envelope containing a banker's draft for 2,000,000 lira!

A week before, the Napoli Museum had had a break-in. Only one piece was stolen. It now lodges on the vast oak desk of a Wisconsin industrialist.

* * *

43

PLANS CAN CHANGE QUICKLY

1 9 6 1

Only Pasquale, and of course Cosimo, knew where the 2 million lira had come from, and amidst the jubilation of the Carone family he tried to recount to them everything that had happened to him since digging up the urn. Spellbound, they listened for over two hours, despite the odd knock at the bar door. It seemed some customers could just not understand what 'closed for business' really meant.

They then discussed what could be done with money. The ladies wanted to put half into re-imaging the bar with modern décor and facilities, Cosimo thought it should be put into a savings account in a safe, respectable bank, while Pasquale was all for buying a new Audi or BMW. Certainly it was a colossal amount of money!

For want of a determined plan they therefore decided to bury their heads in good honest work and try to regain the bar's former glory days.

So they introduced a new range of cheap cocktails, imported some foreign bottled beers to compete with Peroni and Nastro Azzurro, and they upgraded the bar snacks to meals-in-one. It had the desired effect for a while, especially as Pasquale stayed to run the business. He had rightly tired of antiquities-hunting in the wake of his prison spell and he had also become much more serious and withdrawn.

In prison he had certainly had a difficult time - shocking living conditions, appalling food and the most dubious of company. But above all, the injustice of knowing he was innocent: finding and handing in antiquities was legal, trading them was not. And although he was classified as a 'soft criminal' there was no real differentiation within the prison walls and he had been forced to mix daily with the 'hard criminals'. Fortunately, he quickly found his protector, a local mafia employee doing time to protect his team's credibility, or to be exact, the protector found *him* when he realised that Pasquale may not be just a simple country peasant and may have assets to his name. Thus he remained relatively safe during his incarceration, although not without the occasional worrying threat. However, to achieve this level of safety he did have to make certain promises to the protector, such as lies about large reserves of stashed cash awaiting his release. In reality, Pasquale was hoping Mino Orsini might be a useful man to know in the future, being a fast-rising captain in the Camorra, but it had never been made clear to him how important the role of Mino had been in obtaining his early release. Nor did he know fully just how much Mino had respected Pasquale for not disclosing key information during his trial despite offers of leniency - he respected a man like that.

Inevitably, keeping the bar ahead of the street competition took a toll on all of the Carone family. Although they regularly hired staff the new youth of the 60's did not have the same work ethic or loyalty, so employees came and went in rapid succession. This made customers somewhat unhappy: they liked to meet and greet the same friendly face when they walked in. Young bucks like to show off to their girls or boy gangs just how important or well-known they are to the staff, old timers just want to continue their never-ending stories, while flirts cannot cease flirting. Often the Carones had to work double shifts when an employee sent a message saying they were sick, or had a headache, neck ache, backache, or were facing family problems. Isabella suffered the most and her aging continued unceasingly, but hardly noticed by the family under the camouflage of their fast-paced life.

Pasquale and Cosimo agreed in the end to put the windfall in the bank. They reckoned, as it happened, accurately, that if their customers saw him driving around in a new Audi, or spending a fortune beautifying the bar, they would either be jealous or they would think he was making a fortune at their expense. The customers would conveniently forget, of course, that Bar Fortuna's prices were still lower than others. However, what the customers did not know was that the Carones were making considerable profits in less obvious areas, like acquiring the sole rights and becoming the only concessionaires in town for the new national lottery tickets, or taking percentages from the drinks and snacks companies' regular promotions of new products, even in this quiet backwater of the region.

Then Mino Orsino came out of prison. After a month or so re-energising with his family he decided to pay a visit to his friend in Ceglie M, so one fine day he strolled into Bar Fortuna unannounced. The first person he saw was Andrea, and he stood transfixed. Four weeks of good food, sunshine and fresh air had repaired his physical condition, and there was no doubting he was a fine figure of a man—-twenty-nine, unmarried, companionable and ready. But would she remember me? he wondered. Andrea noticed him immediately: he stood out from all the locals, that was for sure. But she gave nothing away and continued to observe him out of the corner of her eye, like all professional barmaids do. From the door Mino thought she had not noticed him and even by the time he had gently swaggered across the floor to the bar she still made no sign of acknowledgement. He was more than a little put out, but took it on the chin like the tough man he was. Perhaps she meets many, many men, he thought, so why would she notice me? Deliberately, Andrea continued to work on with her head bowed, pretending to be washing up cups under the counter, until he spoke. "Café, per favore, Bella."

Hmm! 'Bella', she thought, another gigolo from out of town, and she grunted quietly in disdain. But she had noticed he was neither dressed as a salesman, coming to try to sell her a new range of nuts or coloured serviettes with 'Undulations' printed on, nor as a field worker traipsing dry mud and sand across her sparkling floor. Even beneath his demure casual shirt and slacks she could sense the rippling muscles and she had to admit to a tiny female fluttering, even though it was not like her to do so normally. "Certainly, signore. Aqua?"

"Grazie. I am looking for Pasquale, please," he added.

"And who may I say is asking?" Andrea fluttered, somewhat taken aback.

"Oh, just tell him an old friend from Napoli."

"I do not believe my brother has any friends in Napoli, signore!" she said most coldly and dismissively.

"Your brother?" feigning surprise. "Lucky brother," he muttered under his breath, but Andrea heard.

"My dear brother had no luck there either, signore. Perhaps you should pay and leave?"

Mino reached out gently and took her arm, "look, I'm sorry, I meant no harm. Just tell him I'm here, would you?" he pleaded.

Andrea felt a rush of electricity which calmed her rising anger. "Excuse me."

She went to the back and found her brother. "Pasquale, there is a very handsome man, if I admit it myself, at the bar saying he is your friend from Napoli. Is it safe? Would you know him?"

"Oh. Really? Who is he? Young, old, what?"

So Andrea described him, this time omitting the handsome part, but as she did so it began to sink in that she knew this man or had met him somewhere before. It must have been when she was in a fog, under great stress a while ago, she thought.

"Oh yes, that will be Mino. Yes, wonderful! Thank you, Sis, you've made my day!" He put down the huge tub of gelato he was making. "Could you carry on with this stracciatella, please, just for a minute?"

He whipped off his apron and went out into the bar, "Mino, my friend, oh you do look so well!"

"Better than you, bar boy," he laughed.

"A man has to make a living somehow. So, how are you?"

"Very well thanks; better now I've seen you are OK again, old friend."

"So, let's have a celebratory drink, come on." They sat at a table, then Pasquale fetched one of his better bottles of Primitivo. "So, what brings you here, eh? It's a bit out of the way for someone all the way from Napoli."

"Oh, nothing special. Just come to spend all that money," he laughed.

"Pity I don't have the time to help you," Pasquale laughed back.

"Seriously, Pasquale, it is good to see you, and to see you're back on your feet."

"Too much on my feet in this job." He laughed. "And to see my dear sister, perhaps?"

"Oh, why?" Mino pretended to act innocent.

"Well, she had certainly formed an opinion of you by the time she came out the back to tell me you were here!"

"Really? A favourable opinion, perhaps?"

"Now that would be for you to find out, dear friend," Pasquale laughed again.

"Well…I have the time if you have the money!" he joked back.

They accommodated Mino in a spare room. He made little fuss and few demands and soon all the Carones fell for his easy ways and polite charm. Andrea and Maria suddenly realised as the days went by that they were starting to fight over him, but soon after it became obvious whom he favoured, even though he acted as a perfect gentleman to both. He insisted he was single, and as free as a lark over a spring wheat field (even his reading of English poetry impressed them!), and Pasquale had to concur that throughout all that awful time in prison he had never heard Mino tell of a wife or children. A wife one might forget, miss or want to avoid, but children never. But then in an instant he was gone, like a puff of wind on dust. Business in Napoli, he had said, and could Pasquale please drive him to the station at Grottaglie for the Taranto to Napoli train. He brushed the backs of all the ladies' hands with his lips, French-style, and double kiss-hugged the men, Italian-style.

"I shall return, thank you," he uttered as they ran to the car.

"Must be really urgent business," said Pasquale.

"Yes. You know, if I told you what it was I'd have to kill you!" he laughed.

"But you will come back and see us, won't you?"

"Most certainly, dear friend; wild horses would not keep me away from your sister!"

"Which one?"

They were at the station drop-off point and Mino leapt out of the car seeing the train pull in, "no time to talk now, must dash, goodbye... and thank you so much!" And he was gone.

Unfortunately, his return was for a tragic occasion. One morning Cosimo could not stir Isabella and the doctor pronounced her dead in the night. Overwork... tragic... he had said. For a few weeks prior to this they had found her doing odd things. She would leave the chicken out of the chicken pasta, she would sit behind the bar for ages watching the others rush about, yet handle no money or serve no drinks, and she would stand at the top of the outside back stairs with a bucket of water so that if children playing nearby became too noisy or started kicking a ball against the wall she would throw it all over them.

Everyone was shell-shocked and the bar was closed for more than a week. The family was inconsolable from disbelief and from the knowledge that they had driven her to her death and not even noticed the warning signs. But they had thought, as do we all, mistakenly, that mamas do not drop dead, they live for ever. It was also such a shock for many to discover Isabella had been only 54, two weeks shy of the

55th birthday party the Carones had been planning. Cruel fates indeed, everyone agreed, and a jet-black blanket descended on that part of town. The funeral was held in Avetrana, of course, so Isabella did get to go back there in the end. People travelled from far and wide, from Ceglie Messapica in the north, the Bainsizza folk from Oria in the north-east, even some from Brindisi in the east, but the greatest turnout was from her home town. No expense was spared, now the Carones had wealth, and a private chapel was born in the town cemetery. Throughout the day itself the family braced itself for one special visitor who might have had the decency to see her off, but he did not materialise. They ventured he was either dead himself, or he had not heard the announcements, or, heaven forbid, he did not care even to see his wife for one last time. They hoped the former, but years later found out it was the last because it would have exposed his new illicit life.

After three days of ceremony the Carones drove back in Pasquale's lovely new Audi in almost complete silence. They did not know what to say or think, and if they did they wondered why it was worth saying anything. Only one thing could they agree on, when it came to discussing future plans, and that was that they just did not know what to do! Clearly the bar would never be the same as it would hold too many memories, but on the other hand they could not forever keep moving on, running away from problems or responsibilities. So they all just sat at home and did nothing, except feed and clothe themselves. Cosimo took it very hard but he was also the first to snap out of it and become both philosophical and practical. With the accepted 'life-must-go-on' outlook and the mature views of a sensible middle-aged man he began to entice the others out of themselves by finding them small errands to run, jobs to do, things to think about and future activities to plan. The family did not know it yet but one day they would be forever grateful for what he did for them then.

But there was no doubt Isabella's passing became a giant watershed in this family's life. The bar was never re-opened and it was sold on for a substantial profit. They split it four ways and each invested it in a bank. They were allowed to carry on living above and behind it until they could find new accommodation and were given six months to do so. How else could a decent person treat a family which had befallen such tragedy?

And life went on. It had to. It has to.

* * *

44

NOSE TO THE GRINDSTONE AGAIN

1 9 6 2

Pasquale was the second person to snap out of it. His dear Mama had passed on and that was how it had to be. He had to admit to being pleased that not only Mario Gennari had been sent to the funeral but also Mino Orsini too. It showed he still had standing with the Mafia, and although some of the mourners may have had their suspicions it was never overtly obvious that he 'had connections'.

He also knew only too well he could never find peace in the town again, so he had no option but to return to the countryside. For the first few weeks gentle sorties were the order of the day: a few limited opportunities for the uninvited taking of the fruit and vegetables offered by the land. In his mind he still maintained that he was merely helping the needy and therefore not committing a crime, or if it was, then only a 'social crime', as he called it. But now that he had a police record he should have been more careful.

Amongst the bric-a-brac in the garage he re-discovered his metal detector and this gave him a great boost of energy. Therefore, one hot sunny morning and cheery, rushing cumulus clouds found him once more at the foot of the collina. The old farmer's house now had a fading 'VENDESI' sign at its front, but who would want to buy an old, run-down farm building with no infrastructure or facilities in a hostile farming landscape on the edge of wasteland? Maybe apart from him, that is. Then he found his temporary 'Keep Out' sign lying in the grass and nearly totally faded by the sun and the rain, and it then became increasingly clear that very few people, or indeed perhaps no-one, had ventured past it in his two-year absence.

He spent two happy and invigorating weeks systematically exploring the complete hill, but if it did have further treasures to reveal it was not going to give up its secrets easily. The sum total of his efforts was three small vases, two plates and some more coins, apart from the odd broken small vase which was worthless unless he could be bothered to find the missing broken-off part.

He sent a pleasant, chatty letter to Mario in Taranto and he asked if he could bring the pieces to show him. The reply he received startled and disappointed him. It was brusque and business-like, 'Friend, for that is what you are and shall always be, we cannot accede to your request at this time owing to your and our reputations being out of alignment. We suggest you take your wares to No.6 Via Ceramica, Grottaglie for satisfactory intermediacy. Ever yours, M.'

So even Mario wishes to cut me off, he thought. How tragic after all these years. And telling me to take my pieces to a common or garden pottery maker in Grottaglie? That is an insult, as well as an extra fuss and bother.

Neither had things gone quite so well lately with Mino either. He had made two more visits, for obvious reasons, and on the second Pasquale decided to show him how he operated, for he was convinced Mino would be fascinated. How wrong could he have been! All through the day, almost non-stop, Mino complained about the heat, the dust, the boredom and the loneliness. At first Pasquale thought his friend was just joking with him but he soon realised the extent of the complaint. He took it in good heart, explaining that this occupation was not for all and there were those, i.e. Mino, who preferred the town, the cleanliness and the cool. They mutually agreed it had been a 'different' day and they should both cut their losses. Of course, Mino was also disturbed that he had had to endure such an anguishing day and still learn nothing of Pasquale's fortune. Time was moving on, as he needed to, and he looked forward to results. Poor Pasquale just thought him an excellent friend in whom he could confide most things. Mino just wished that list included the whereabouts of his stash!

Mino did admit, however, that Mario's evasive tactics were rather uncalled for and he promised to help Pasquale by being his go-between. He would act as a direct intermediary with Napoli and cut out Mario completely, and as he too owned a car now, a symbol of his rising importance in the Camorra, he could ship the artefacts very carefully and discreetly. This worked very well on three separate occasions, although Pasquale did think Mino took a little more commission than was proper. However, he was really past caring: he was still on auto-pilot and hunting was just something to do, the money meaning little to him now he was rich. But on the fourth occasion Mino reported that the arrangement was no longer viable as his contact had been arrested for very much the same crime as Pasquale's - trading illegally in ancient artefacts. Just think, he reminded Pasquale, if he had not told that very first lie about the friend giving it to him to sell, he would have only received a fine for illegally removing a relic from the ground and/or not taking it straight to the authorities, rather than a prison sentence for trading. But Pasquale then reminded Mino that in that case they would never have met and a glorious friendship would never have blossomed. Mino gulped. He could not point out that, apart from Pasquale's stash, a certain sister was the real reason he kept returning.

So with every visit the bonfire sparks being ignited in the cooling autumn winds flew ever higher. And then, one delightful russet day with the vine leaves curling into yellow and orange and terracotta hues, the sparks finally ignited the touch paper and fireworks flew upward. Mino was a caring, gentle wooer, knowing for certain she was the one, while she played the sweet, dark-eyed damsel, knowing truly too that he was the one. Cosimo tried his hardest to put a wet blanket over both bonfire and fireworks by reminding her that Mino was a Mafia captain, someone with not just a killer streak inside him but also someone with a limited shelf-life, probably, liable to be terminated by any one of police, his enemies or prison, leaving her a widow in every sense. She was not foolish; she knew all this, but she had lost much of the will to resist Fate after what had earlier befallen her, and losing her mother too. In short, there grew inside her such a sadness and such a willingness to accept the tranquillity of life that she not only gave up on religion and the Church but also on any expectations of long-term happiness.

Better, she told Cosimo, to enjoy a few passionate, deliriously-happy years with a gangster than a lifetime of dull acquiescence. Being nearly 35 years old Andrea now demanded something back of Life.

And so it was. Andrea and Mino's was a quiet Town Hall wedding in the autumn of 1962, with a honeymoon up the coast at Barletta. No-one knew the reason for that choice of town, except Barletta has a most attractive harbour and beautiful architecture around the Duomo, until Andrea explained, laughing, that she had just dropped her finger on a map of Italy to see where it would land! On their return the Camorra provided a pleasant, but fairly small, villa in the suburb of Herculano, once buried by Pompeii in AD79, and within days Andrea had left the Carone's life for a new and exciting start in Napoli. As the 'technical' head of the family Pasquale was well pleased that Andrea had finally settled and found happiness from a disjointed, eventful and ultimately unhappy life to date, but he was also sad that he would not be able to see his beloved Sis very often, the Sis he had helped through thick and thin: Napoli was a long way away, even in 1962.

So the year had certainly been one of fractionation. When Cosimo also decided he might like to return to a quiet life in Avetrana, surrounded by familiarity, there was little objection. Again, Pasquale and Maria were tragically sad to see him depart, for they had learned so much from his calm, careful stoicism and his unswerving loyalty to their dear departed Mama. But in their hearts they knew it was for the best, as eventually where would he be able to go, and who with, when it was too late for him to gain some last few years of enjoyment from life? Pasquale and Maria would have, hopefully, forged new trails through life and would have been indebted to care for him if he asked but that would have been unfair on all. Cosimo now had no financial problems, none of them had, Pasquale had seen to that, so it made sense for him to return to his roots.

The greater surprise to Pasquale was that his little Sis did the actual 'forging' straight after these events, and so quickly. However, when he sat quietly one day in a field and banished all other thoughts he realised she was already 25 and a most eligible beauty. How time flew for poor Pasquale! One day Maria announced that she would go mad if she did not escape the small-town South. She had money, thanks to her brother, and this could make her independent in the modern world. He was loathe to believe she would do anything, being hot-headed and irrational, but that worked in a contrary way and made her even more unstable. And sure enough, the very next day she packed just one bag, jumped in a taxi to the nearest station and headed for Roma.

"Don't worry, dear brother, look at me, it won't take me long to find work!" she said. "Even in a decent hotel I can train as a receptionist - they always want beauty before brains on the front desk!"

"But you have both, dearest, you will bowl them over."

As soon as she was waving goodbye he was already starting to worry. He said an infrequent prayer and asked God to protect her from the evils of the capital.

And suddenly, just like that, he was alone, very alone. The Carones were now scattered to the four winds like dandelion spores and they would unlikely ever bear fruit again together in the same place. He moved to a single room in Ceglie Messapica so that all ties were released with the bar and a great depression rose over him. He had money but no real skills. He had family but was unlikely to see them much ever again. At 30 he had his years still but nevertheless he felt as old as that hill he kept fruitlessly searching.

What would he do next? For days he sat in his room, sat in a bar, sat in a restaurant, sat in the Square, pondering the realities of Life and the next direction to take.

He finally chose Grottaglie and gained a reprieve, though he did not know it then.

* * *

45

THE POTTERY SHOP

1 9 6 3

"Buongiorno, Stefania, a beautiful morning, yes?" shouted the old man of rounded back, born of a lifetime of bending over wheels.

"Indeed it is, Luigi," replied Stefania as she went to unlock her door. The ancient lock almost refused to comply but eventually allowed the old, rusty metal door to swing open with a complaining high-pitched squeal.

"Like me, nothing that a little oiling won't fix," he laughed.

Entering into the spirit of the moment she quipped back, "at least you don't squeal".

"No, my wife does enough of that for two of us!"

Stefania realised this game of verbal comedy tennis could proceed indefinitely and she really needed to get on before it grew too hot. Inside, the cave was at least ten degrees cooler than outside and most refreshing to enter every morning, even at 10 a.m. The shops were all carved into the solid tufa rock face and were literally rock-lined caves. Should she work inside or out today, she pondered. Inside costs electricity but outside will be hot, even in my shady spot under the tree, and competitors might get free previews of her wares. She decided to start off indoors and see if a breeze sprang up later to act as a natural fan. She would fire up some unusual bowls she made two days before, then paint the jugs that the restaurant had ordered.

Luigi's wizened frame suddenly appeared in the doorway and she jumped. "Stefania, I appear to have run out of sepia, again. You couldn't lend me some, could you?"

Stefania was tempted to recommence the banter again with something like 'how can you appear to, you either have or you haven't', or 'how can I lend something you cannot give back, silly?', but she refrained and merely mumbled, "yes, dear friend, certainly." As she went to retrieve some from her workshop at the back he cast his admiring eye in two directions, first at her fine rear disappearing, he being still an expert Italian judge of fine quality, and secondly at her fine quality of pottery ware on the shelves. This is what Grottaglie needs, a brave new spirit producing both modern and original products, displayed in fetching ways, he thought. I'm too old for this business, it's definitely time to get out. And doesn't my back ache all the time.

"Here, Luigi, is this enough?"

"Oh yes, plenty thanks. I'll return the pot refilled tomorrow."

"Don't worry, I have plenty". Beautiful *and* generous, he thought, but mumbled 'kind, honest girl' as he walked out.

Stefania's shop was in the middle of a row of pottery shops which had sprung up at the foot of the castle in Via Ceramiche, old Grottaglie. The tradition had been there for hundreds of years, based on local fine-quality clay and long-serving artisans, making the town a famous market for everyday pottery goods, but what with the steady growth in national wealth and the odd visitors starting to come from further afield the town was starting to acquire a reputation for finer quality decorative pieces. Its hinterland was now all of Puglia and even beyond. So Stefania tried to concentrate on both the past and the present ---her reproductions of fine Grecian wine urns were eye-catching and her modern take on the traditional rooster design for kitchen crockery, pots and small vases was winning many new customers. As to be expected, within days the designs would be copied all along the street, but no-one could create so beautifully as Stefania.

The old, open door jingled as a young, wealthy-looking customer brushed through the chimes. An open door always looked more welcoming, she considered, and sure enough, within minutes she pocketed another 8600 lira in sales. "Yes, Luigi, it is going to be a beautiful day," she hummed.

Stefania was seldom known to be wrong, but this was going to be one of those occasions. The very next customer turned out to be her father, accompanied by two less-than-honest-looking men in worn, shiny suits.

"Hello daddy," she greeted him brightly. It was always lovely to see her father finding time to visit her in the premises he had bought on her behalf, but for some reason today she felt was not going to be one of those occasions. He moved forward gracefully and embraced her fondly, double-cheek kiss and a squeeze, whilst looking appreciatively over her shoulder at her blossoming talent on the shelves.

"Signore, you are right, your daughter certainly has great potential as a potter," said the taller man admiringly.

The other weasel-faced man peered beyond to the workshop and added, "oh yes, just as you said. Perfect."

"Perfect for what, Daddy?"

"Come, Stefania, let us take coffee. Please close the shop for a minute…"

"…but Daddy, I've only just opened up."

"Doesn't look too busy to me, dear, just a few minutes is all we need."

"But I never get to see you as much as I'd like, Daddy, can't you stay longer?"

"Sorry, these gentlemen are very important, busy people. It wouldn't do to keep them." Stefania certainly agreed with that, they looked extremely off-hand. She moved to the door and looked out. There was no-one in the street except Luigi and one or two of the other potters.

"Alright," she agreed half-heartedly. "I'll ask old Luigi to keep an eye on things for a while. He can often be a wilier salesperson than I," she laughed. "What can be so important for all this rush?"

"Coffee, my dear, coffee," laughed her father, and his two friends concurred.

* * *

46

HALFWAY HOUSE

1 9 6 3

The jukebox record was just finishing, Pattie Duke maybe, but oddly there was no-one left listening to it. The table football lay dormant, the cigarette machine silent. So the back room of Bar Roma was ideal for the meeting as they carried their coffees through. Stefania had asked for a cappuccino to make it last longer. She was in no need of an adrenalin rush so early in the day and hated the men who kept running in to bars all day, gulping back the tiny cupful in seconds and promptly carrying on with their business fuelled by the caffeine. Of all the Italian customs she thought that was one of the saddest, yet funniest to watch. However, in this case the men invited her to sit down, so it must be something important.

"Darling, we are wondering if you can help us a little?"

"Of course, Daddy, anything. You know that," she smiled.

Cheered by her positivity he continued, "so you are really pleased with your little shop?"

"Oh Daddy, you know I am, and…"

"…and you seem to be doing very well, we hear," interrupted Weasel-face, his friend also nodding and adding, "we've had little chats along the road and everyone reckons you're a real acquisition to Via Ceramiche."

"I don't know about that, but yes, business is good."

"I expect it is your creative and inventive products, dearest."

"Maybe, Daddy, but it helped that you put up the money to make the shop look lovely inside," she thanked him.

"Well, my dear, you will be pleased to hear I have now gone one step further."

"Really?"

"Yes, I have bought the shop completely for you now!"

"Oh Papa, thank you, thank you!" jumping up and embracing him, caring little for what the present company thought. This was a genuine moment of joy, a family moment, so what if Weasel-face scowled. But Weasel-face did not scowl, nor did his friend; they beamed too, if that was possible from their gangster-marked faces. Unfortunately, though, they were smiling for a different reason. But Stefania was not into reasons at this moment, she could only think in terms of gratitude and love.

"OK, OK, steady, don't squeeze away all the little breath I have left in me! And, more important, dearest, it is in your name!"

"My name? Really? You mean I am the new owner of this shop?"

"Yes, indeed. I have lodged the property deeds at the bank. All finished."

Stefania sat back down stunned, the excitement almost too much for her. Shocked beyond words, she just sat there smiling foolishly like a five-year-old just given a lollipop.

"But now your father asks something of you," interjected Weasel-face, bringing the conversation back down to the ground.

"Yes, my dear," murmured Eduardo. "You see, my friends here represent huge business companies around Puglia, and even beyond, and I myself do considerable business with them…"

Weasel-face could not resist butting in; he was the short, chip-on-the-shoulder type who just had to feel important all the time, a real 'Pugnacious of Puglia' character. "Nearly all our business, import, export, trading, etc, is totally legal, but er…let us say 1% of it is not quite…"

"…not quite? You mean 'illegal' then?" asked Stefania, her grin dissipating by the second.

"No, no," answered the other, "certainly not illegal but, could we say, operating in that grey area in between?"

"It used to be legal before the War," answered her father, "but since then the laws have been altered slightly, if that clarifies it more."

"Papa, I do not like the sound of this at all, in fact I…"

"My darling, please be calm. What we are asking you to do is not illegal, especially if you do not know about it."

"How can I not know about it: you have just told me!"

"Actually," continued Weasel-face, "we have told you but we have not told you."

"I don't understand…"

"What he means is, Stefania, although we have asked if you will do something we have not actually told you what it is. Do you see?"

"Oh yes, I suppose so. So do you mean if someone comes checking up I merely plead ignorance, Papa?"

"Precisely," squealed Weasel-face, almost lasciviously. "You merely pass on the goods for us…"

"What goods?"

"Ah now, if we told you what goods, then you'd know, wouldn't you. Do you see now?" grinned the friend.

"Stefania," said her father a little more authoritatively, "all we need you to do is accept the occasional envelope or packet and pass it on when the time comes."

"You mean?"

"Yes, someone comes to your shop with a packet, you assume it to be craft materials, then you let us know and we send someone to collect it and he gives you an envelope. Then the first man returns and takes away the envelope…"

"Money, you mean, presumably?" asked Stefania.

"Er….yes. Now, that couldn't be simpler, could it?" demanded Weasel-face. "You are just doing your daddy a favour or two, right? Eduardo shifted uneasily but Stefania did not notice it.

"So what is in the packet?" asked Stefania, "is that illegal?"

"No, the packet is legal, you could say the money was not. Understand?"

"I think so."

"So will you do it, my proud owner of a pottery shop, just for me? asked Eduardo.

"I suppose so, but only because it is you." Again, Stefania missed the almost-audible exhalations of relief.

* * *

47

THE GO-BETWEEN

1 9 6 3

A thin, clingy mist hugged the plain as he drove slowly west the twenty kilometres to Grottaglie. After stopping three times for directions he thought he had been sent to the wrong place because Via Ceramiche was not a domestic road but a row of pottery shops. Why did I assume it would be a house anyway? He thought. He drove past number 28 and noticed immediately that it was better presented than its neighbours. He drove on and parked in a nearby street to avoid unnecessary attention. Approaching the premise gingerly seemed excessive when there was no-one in the street either way, but who knew where prying eyes might be lurking. After all, it could have been some sort of a trap; but, chuckling to himself, he wondered why he would be considered sufficiently important to be laying traps for?

'Tinkle, tinkle.'

"Good morning, sir, do come in and have a look round."

"Thank you, signora…"

"Signorina, signore."

"Apologies, Signorina, he stressed the second word amusingly, "as much as your products are truly beautiful I'm afraid I have not come to buy." He glanced around, through to the large workshop behind and to every darkened nook and cranny at the back of the old cave, but there was no-one else in the shop. "I have to deliver something to you," he muttered hesitantly.

Stefania added, "for Taranto, perhaps?"

"Yes, yes, for Taranto."

"Fine. Please wait there." She disappeared into her workshop and returned with a large brown envelope. "Will this be big enough, signore?"

"Oh yes, no problem," as he handed her his packet.

"Any message?"

"Ah, message, yes, in my haste I forgot. Thank you."

She handed him a scrap of paper and he scrawled furiously a note to, presumably, Mario before tucking it into the packet. However, he was no longer certain he was still dealing with Mario after that final letter he had received: it could have been any one of a number of dealers in Taranto.

"The earliest you should return is," she paused, "er, Friday. Is that satisfactory?"

"Oh yes, Friday. Friday is fine. I will see you then, about six o'clock." It was all over in a few minutes and Pasquale emerged into the sunlight with mind and sight blurred. He could not even remember what the girl looked like to whom he'd entrusted his coins, but vague images of a Puglian beauty sat in the back of his brain.

* * *

48

HIS DATE

1 9 6 3

Pasquale concentrated more and more of his time hunting voraciously for new antiquity sites and valuable finds. He didn't need the money, obviously, but he needed to do something to raise him from his lethargy. He even risked driving his expensive car to the library at Lecce, a pleasure he had to finally admit after a few visits. Lecce's golden limestone buildings were internationally famous, 'Baroque masterpieces', one newspaper had called them, especially during that special hour of the day when the light was just perfect, around about two hours before sunset. The library and the palaces and the amphitheatre glowed in these lowering acute angles, while new-formed black shadows crept up their walls like a temporary sickness. In the library he would search through huge tomes for any ideas as to where ancient Mesopotamian, Greek or Roman sites might be found around this Puglian 'heel'.

Oria itself had 15 known separate sites scattered around the newer, urban expansion outside the town walls, and he had even tried to work on two of them at night - Via Tote and Via Frascata -but with truncated success. The former lay at the foot of a gentle slope, right on the edge of town, without any houses too close, but the land had been hardened by years of children playing football and he had insufficient tools to chip through the sun-baked mud. Via Frascata was at the junction where the market was held every Wednesday and, again, feet and vehicles had regularly compacted the ground till rock-hard. He had actually found the handle of an Etruscan vase there but in his attempt to remove the whole piece it had shattered into useless fragments as he tried to disinherit the baked earth of its treasures.

Hence he preferred to find rural sites where the artefacts had been disturbed and brought nearer the surface by farmers constantly tilling the land. In such circumstances you could say goodbye to porcelains and pottery, pulverised by the plough shear unless remarkably lucky, but it made the discovery of coins and jewellery much easier to extract. Olive groves he hated the most because for over five hundred years, in many cases, the roots of the trees had been steadily intertwining themselves around other roots and the precious artefacts he sought. Imagine his annoyance when his 1933 Gerhard Fischar metal detector, which he had miraculously spotted in a Taranto second-hand shop window all those years before, revealed metal but he could not dig down to it through a tree root as thick as a man's upper arm. But in a grass field he would sing the praises of Alexander Bell for ever for inventing the wondrous device that could locate metal underneath a waving green or a wind-scorched yellow anonymous sward.

Therefore, by stepping up the level of his antiquity hunting he naturally increased the frequency of his visits to Via Ceramiche in Grottaglie. Of course, he would try to persuade himself that the two were mutually exclusive but he knew in his heart that one was causing the other. Only on his third visit did he realise why his footstep became lighter and his heart rose nervously - it was not the thought of all that lovely money but the thought of seeing the vision in the shop again. To have said he was developing an affection for Stefania would have been understatement. It was instead becoming a burning passion.

But was it reciprocated? he thought. She would smile when he walked in, but was it more than a smile, was it a lingering of those beautiful creased lips perhaps? Or was she merely being polite in acknowledging him in this way, as she would to any regular customer, as it had already been the fifth time she had seen him there in as many weeks.

He wondered too when he might be able to pluck up enough courage to ask her for a coffee or aperitivo. He cursed to himself, 'nearly thirty-two years old and still totally gauche where women are concerned!'

Yet strangely that was exactly the same question Stefania was posing herself as Pasquale walked through the door - when will he try to invite me out? After all, it is clear he likes me; he seems unable to hide his feelings like a mature man of the world could, but anyway I wouldn't want such a man of the world, she thought pensively. On the contrary, he appears an honest, genuine, sincere person who would be open and kind towards me. So why would he be mixed up in these 'not-quite-legal' activities? That would be an important, if not *the* important, question to ask, but how?

"Hello, Signorina...a..beautiful, er, morning, er, as ever," he stammered shyly.

"Yes, signore, welcome...again, do come in."

"Again, er, yes, that is certainly true. I must not come so often perhaps? Does it concern you? After all, this is not your normal business, is it?"

"No, sir, it is not, but your business is your business," she laughed. He paused, trying to analyse where the humour was, and his brow knitted. She felt his obvious unease and mumbled on, "oh please come as often as you like!"

Was that a sign, he thought.

Was I offering an invitation, she thought.

Both their thoughts were disturbed by the tinkling bell and the door swinging open. An old couple hobbled in and Pasquale glided gracefully to a table covered in exquisite breakfast bowls, all plain cream-coloured with the Grottaglie cockerel in the centre. The couple soon departed unrewarded and Stefania continued, "the usual large envelope?"

"If you could please."

"One moment."

Oh, take as many moments as you want, please, he thought, watching her poetic motion move to the rear of the shop. He sighed.

"Are you alright, signore?" she asked with concern.

"Perfectly." He forgot that in these old caves the acoustics were superb, but he was pleased that the lighting was not good enough to expose his reddening face.

"Any message?"

"No, just put 'Pasquale' on the packet; they will know."

"OK, thank you."

"Goodbye, Signorina, have a lovely day," he smiled, and he tried to fashion a small nod of the head but its success was questionable.

Two souls would not meet, it seemed. Poor Pasquale went back to his fields and poor Stefania buried herself in a new project making ashtrays for bars. But they did promise themselves one thing, each totally independent of the other: he would ask on Friday, and she would accept if he asked on Friday.

And so he did. And so did she. It had been so easy, after all, and they both wondered why they had sweated over it so much. But undeniably it had been helped by a third party, a dilettante who had pranced around the shop ostensibly seeking a present but who really wanted to get Stefania to attend some ball with him. Pasquale had watched firstly with anger but then with increasing amusement from a darkened corner, pretending to be a simple customer, so that when the fop eventually retreated tail between legs the obvious opening line came to him immediately, "that was such thirsty work watching you make that poor man suffer, I think I need a coffee, do you?"

"Oh yes please." She tried not to sound too enthusiastic, but inside her heart was finally singing.

They chatted for over an hour until she suddenly realised it was not even siesta time and she may have missed a number of customers in that time. Pasquale gleaned that she was from a rich family whose father had set her up in this her first venture. They lived in a big house halfway between Grottaglie and Brindisi and she had a brand new little red Fiat car. It was clear to both that they were worlds apart - class and perhaps inherited wealth-wise - when Pasquale told her he lived alone in a small central house in Cegli Messapica and worked the fields for antiquities. He did not tell her, of course, that he stole fruit and vegetables from different farms at every conceivable opportunity to help feed the poor of the old town. He did however tell her that he had lived in a number of different places once his father had walked out on them and that he had not seen his father for near twenty five years since.

At this admission Stefania warmed to him even further and, like many a female, she wanted to take him firmly under her wing... and immediately. Unintentionally Pasquale had played the trump card - the little-boy-lost - which few women could ever resist, even those as young as Stefania.

Back in the fields he strove even harder to find some more of those Roman coins. They not only paid well but they also gave him the chance to return to the beloved shop early the next week. And so he did. And she had no problem at all saying 'yes' when he asked if she'd like to go to the cinema.

It was fortunate they went on the Friday night after he had received his coins payment from Taranto because she could then see he was able to afford the customary late supper afterwards without knowing he possessed a huge fortune. No-one in Grottaglie knew them so they were able to relax and crunch contentedly on the fresh king prawns, skewered in basil and tomato sauce, and fresh, hot pizza bread which flew straight from the restaurant's oven.

But the more she talked the more he realised how out of her league he was. The more he talked the more she realised he needed to be guided into a bigger, safer arena.

Pasquale drove her back to her shiny red Fiat in the battered old jalopy he'd borrowed so that she would not see his Audi. They said a semi-formal, polite 'goodnight' and drove home separately, and in different directions, wondering what direction the future might take for them, together or apart.

***

49

SECRETS ABOUND

1964

"How are you, Helena, dear?"

"Very well, Papa, thank you. And you?"

Eduardo had to think about that. To most people his reply would have been an automatic 'musn't grumble' but with Stefania he'd always tried to be ultra honest and sincere. "Musn't grumble," he replied. "Now, show me where you have been 'sleeping'."

Stefania led him to her workshop so he could see the camp bed. "There."

"Is this it? You sleep here? So where do you bathe? Eat?"

"I have a big basin of water; there is a small toilet, remember? You said that was so important when you bought these premises. And I eat at the restaurants down the road."

"So how many more days will it be before you come home?"

"Hard to say, Papa, it really is a huge order. Maybe three or four."

"Well, OK, but we do miss you so, and we do worry about you, you realise."

"Certainly, Papa, but I couldn't refuse this order, it's a quarter of a year's income in one fell swoop!"

"I know, I know, and we are very proud of you! But you must be exhausted?"

"Yes, but happily so."

"Good. Now, while I've caught you in a good mood I need to ask a favour."

"Anything, Papa."

"OK. Look, you know you have a secret room at the back of the showroom…"

"…do I?"

"Obviously! Otherwise I would not have said it, silly."

Stefania clapped her hands with delight and skipped off to look for it. She moved quickly along the back wall and her shelf displays but saw nothing amiss. Then she did a second run, this time much more slowly, tapping and listening as she edged along. Suddenly the dull thud changed to a hollow echo and she could make out an area of slightly lighter-coloured blocks of tufa, each with slightly newer cement. It had been a good job, an attempt to blend in the stones, but newer slabs can never stain fast enough to compare with old slabs and thus will always deceive. She had never noticed it before because she had never been looking, and of course the lighting was very dim at the rear of the cave.

As Eduardo approached he smiled and said, "I see my clever girl has not lost any of her powers of attentiveness during this fatiguing period."

"How big is it, Papa? Do you actually know? How did you know it even existed?"

"My dear, it was open when I bought the premises and I had it blocked up again almost immediately, waiting for such a moment as now."

"And why is this the moment, Papa?"

"Because I need to store some boxes here now, if I may?"

"And I am not to ask any questions, correct?"

"Yes, because what you do not know cannot harm you," he laughed.

"So, will it be temporary or permanent?"

"Probably fairly permanent, if that is OK? As long as we don't forget them if and when you move on!" he laughed again.

"Well, Papa," she hesitated, "as you know my designs are proving rather popular at the moment and I am starting to get interest from further afield."

"Where? Taranto? Brindisi?"

"Oh no, Papa, Napoli and even Roma!"

Eduardo whistled through his teeth. "Oh my, that is fantastic, well done!" and he gave her a huge hug, something he was usually very reticent over.

"And it seems the general consensus of opinion in the street is that one does not continue designing and manufacturing here for such big markets, but one moves to those places to be on the spot," she added hesitantly.

"But Helena, you are only a youngster, my darling baby, how would you cope in that cut-throat world and…and…live safely. You are a beautiful young lady already," argued Eduardo, almost passionately.

"Yes, I understand all that, Papa, but it might not be such a problem as you think."

"Oh? Why?"

"Well, maybe I have a protector?"

"What? What do you mean? Me?" he laughed nervously.

She really hesitated now. This was definitely not how she had planned to introduce the topic. It has all gone wrong, she panicked. She had meant to be far more subtle about it and also take it one step at a time, rather than like a bull at a gate. But she realised it was too late, her father was no fool and she had ruined it. "Well...er...I have been seeing this lovely young man for quite a while now...er...obviously in a light-hearted manner so far, and we are very happy...er...I mean comfortable with each other."

"Do you love him then?"

"I think so, Papa, we are very, very happy."

"Who is he? Why have you not told me before? Why have I not met him?" Clearly, Eduardo was totally stunned by this bolt out of the blue.

"Well, normally it would have run the fullness of time, Papa, but I suppose with such offers coming in I cannot refuse them otherwise they never ask again, so it has all rather precipitated a quicker conclusion..."

"...conclusion? What do you mean exactly? Marriage? Heaven forbid!" Eduardo suddenly felt a great need to collapse on the nearest seating receptacle.

"Oh no, Pa, nothing like that, but if I had to move to Napoli I would want Pasquale to come with me..."

"...what! Live with you? Live in sin? Over my dead body, Signorina!" interrupted her father, nearly reaching apoplectic boiling point.

Just at that moment the door bell tinkled and a couple of tourists entered the shop. They were in no hurry, just welcome to escape the burning sun. It was amazing how cool the Grottaglie caves could be in summer. They fussed happily from one table to the next, obviously highly appreciative of Stefania's work, and seemed not to want to leave. Eduardo started to become most impatient, agitated almost, and he began coughing and scraping his feet as he moved around behind them. Then they asked him in English about a particular adaptation of the Grottaglie cockerel design, the famous trademark logo of the town, that Stefania had made and he was forced to direct them to his daughter. She in turn seemed to talk for hours about its history, its significance and her adaptive instincts, making Eduardo even angrier. Was she doing it deliberately as a punishment, he thought. But what punishment? Why? He was perplexed and that made him even more annoyed.

Just before the dam of his anger was about to burst they finally bought two plates, a bowl, a large vase, a set of tea cups and a matching teapot. Each had to be carefully wrapped, individually, which also seemed to take forever, especially as the couple insisted on chattering on in that happy euphoria which always comes when one has chosen something nice to buy. The bill came to 93,000 lire, with a little discount, and Stefania smiled broadly after they had gone.

"Why did you take so long? You know I am a busy man," demanded her father.

"Long? That was not long, in fact it was fairly fast as choosing pottery goes. Papa, it is not like buying a kilo of tomatoes off a market stall, it is a careful and delicate decision-making process!"

"Yes, but…"

"…No "buts" please. Actually, I could shut up shop now. That single sale is more than I usually take in a whole day of fussing customers. They were rich Americans looking for something really unusual. Now do you see what I mean? They said they had looked in many other of the Grottaglie galleries and had not seen anything as nice as my work. In fact, Papa, they were thrilled!"

"Mm, happy for you then…"

"…and they said they lived and worked in Napoli and they will send their friends to my shop when they in turn come visiting. How about that?"

"Hm, excellent. As is your English, by the way. Where did you learn that?"

"On the job, Papa. This is not just pottery design, I need to learn languages to speak to tourists. It's just great!" and she danced off round the room.

"Heh, slow down girl, let's get back to the issue in hand here. Now, who is this boyfriend of yours?" relaxed Eduardo a little, obviously extremely proud of his daughter's achievements but not so willing to say it.

"Pasquale is one of your package customers who…"

"…what! A thief and a vagabond? Oh no, Mary Mother of God!" he exploded.

"No, no, no, Papa. Not all of them are criminals, I am sure of it. Pasquale earns an honest living seeking antiquities in the fields and he sends them through your network to Taranto for sale."

"So he is a peasant - impoverished, uneducated and uncouth. Certainly not suitable for you, my dear!"

"No, Papa..."

"...and may I remind you your mother is a Countess and we are a titled family!"

Finally Stefania snapped too and bit back with vitriole, "Yes, an impoverished countess with a divorcee for a husband who deals with... with all kinds of ...of odd people!" She just could not force herself to say 'criminals'.

"Enough! That is quite enough!" Eduardo screamed. "I have rescued that title and that castello with the sweat of my brow. Oh, and just remember who put you here too!"

"I'm sorry, Papa," pleaded Stefania, now applying all her little-girl-loves-Daddy tricks, "I am ever so grateful, you know that, but having this business means I meet a lot of people and I have even learned English," she laughed, "and I can tell you now, quite categorically, I have not met a nicer, kinder, gentler man than Pasquale."

"Hm...well..."

"...and he is not just a village dolt, he is clever, quick-thinking and very knowledgeable, so there!"

"Hm...well....I ..."

"...I would like to meet him, right? Shall I bring him home for pranzo on Sunday then?"

"Well....I suppose we could all meet this fellow, if you insist, though I don't know..."

"...oh shush, Papa, you'll adore him, you know you will."

"All right. I'll tell Valeria to inform cook. I must go now. I think I have had to absorb more than enough for one day - boyfriends, moves to Napoli, secret caves, successful daughters. Hm! Goodbye." And he pecked her on the cheek lightly, as was always his want.

From that she knew she had won the battle, but certainly not the war...yet. Oh thank you, Mother Mary, she mumbled to herself, those American tourists were a godsend. And then she laughed when she realised what she had muttered, 'Mary' and 'godsend'! It might have been very different without their intervention.

Just then the door tinkled. "Has he gone yet?"

She giggled, "yes darling, come in, the coast is clear and it is plain sailing again!p";

Oh how they laughed, hugged and kissed at that.

* * *

50

CEMENTING

1 9 6 4

"It still drives so well, doesn't it?" said Pasquale, as they headed for the cinema in Manduria. They liked to do the rounds of the cinemas, one town at a time, then fewer people would get used to seeing them together. But why they were being so secretive they were not entirely sure. Perhaps Stefania was still afraid of her parents' ire, though the cinemas they frequented were a long way away from the castello.

But they did so love the little town cinemas, the new centres of life for the young and middle-aged folk alike. Oria had a lovely but tiny cinema in a corner of Piazza Manfredi overlooking the bars and restaurants, Sava's was tucked away, Grottaglie's was big and plain, but their favourite was always Manduria. The Cinema Grand Teatro held a dominating position facing the Town Hall in the main square and was always a hub of lively activity. In the daytime the old men would line the benches along the edge of the road and swop reminiscences or argue politics non-stop, at aperitivo time the married couples would push their babies swiftly into the film, knowing full well they were on a limited time span, while the evening show belonged to the young who would mill about for an hour before and an hour, or more, after the show, spilling over the pavement and forcing the busy night traffic to detour. Clearly, everyone wanted to own a bar in this square with such non-stop patronage and profit!

Tonight was the opening of a new film from Britain, a James Bond film, 'Dr No', and the square was packed with excited anticipation. Pasquale and Stefania had made sure to get there early for a seat, and that ploy had certainly been proved correct. The film was so exciting and fast-paced they had little opportunity for canoodling and they emerged at the end in near ecstasy. Over drinks in a backstreet bar they agreed that they couldn't remember a more action-packed, jaw-dropping thriller, and the ending had been out-of-this-world! The escapism of James Bond's fantasy life had penetrated the parochial, quiet Heel of Italy and they were still zinging from the adrenalin rush.

True, they'd had American films imported since before the war but it wasn't till post-war that the real advance of American globalisation had started, flooding their world with "movies", music, jeans and language. So tonight had been a relief, a respite, with a British film more exciting and well shot than ever Hollywood could fabricate, for all its money, and although they would never admit it Pasquale secretly wanted to be James and Stefania Honey Ryder!

Being an expected sell-out, the cinema had put on three shows every night that first week and Pasquale had opted for the 5.00pm one. So at just after 7.00 they were free for the night. Neither felt hungry after all that excitement so they returned to the car where they squeezed hands and kissed passionately in the fading light, not caring who passed by.

"So what shall we do now, darling?" asked Pasquale, head in a spin.

"Do you know, I feel so happy and I do love you so much that I want to jump out of this car and tell the whole world!" she whispered throatily.

"An admirable sentiment, dearest, but I'm sure the world doesn't really want to know…"

"…but I know who might!"

"Really? Who?"

"My parents!"

"Oh no, please no, banish the thought, Steph, you are joking aren't you?"

"No, I'm not. Come on!"

"Stop teasing, Steph, you know it is impossible."

Stefania suddenly became serious, "I've had enough of all this, Pasquale, I love you, I want to tell the world, I want my parents to know. Simple!"

So Pasquale decided to play along with it; just to humour her, not to admit she was more persuasive and powerful than he. He knew once she got near the house she would back out of it. "OK, come on then, otherwise it will be too late."

She drove like a whirlwind to cover the windy 30-or-more kilometres to the castello, but it was still after 9pm before they arrived. Pasquale was wrong; she did not back out of it but drove straight down the cypress-lined driveway right up to the front steps of the imposing structure. Although it had once been a castello the renovations had sensibly converted it more into what a Georgian country property would look like in England.

She jumped out gleefully, or in a thinly-veiled attempt to hide her nerves, and bounded up the ten marble steps. She took a deep breath and pulled the huge bell rope. Pasquale was still in the car, still somewhat in shock from this tempestuous turn of events, and he was able to see just how quickly the door opened. His heart missed a beat and his mouth a breath, but it was only Davide the butler.

Helena, good evening, but no-one is home," he trumpeted good-naturedly.

"Oh dear, where have they gone, then?"

"They never tell me, Signorina, but I would guess to another of those parties."

"That means really late then."

"Oh, to be certain, madame. The master told me to retire at 10 and not to worry."

"Damn, damn it, damn them, damn everyone!" Stefania was raging; Pasquale was celebrating.

He called out from the car, "no point waiting, Stefania, come on, let's go!"

Stefania hesitated. She wanted to leave a message. Pasquale sensed as much and shouted, "not really much point in leaving a message, dearest. They'd think you a little odd for coming over at this time of the evening, and unannounced at that. Let's just go. We can always come back and do this properly another day."

"Yes, but if we wait for them now they might be in a better mood from the drink. Davide, was Luigi driving them?"

"No, madame, the master wanted to drive."

"OK, Stefania, let's go. Now! No good will come of this."

"Er…excuse me, madame, but does this man know you?"

"Yes, of course, he's…"

'…but he keeps calling you "Stefania" and "dearest"!"

Stefania finally burst out into fits of laughter. The mood had been broken, finally. They sped off in fits of infectious giggling, but Pasquale was unsure why he was laughing so much.

By the time Pasquale had been driven back to his car in Manduria, where they had met, and he had covered the miles back to Ceglie Messapica it was well past midnight. He survived one near accident when a typical Italian driver cut a corner and nearly ran him off the road, but he also escaped injury when he dozed off on a straight stretch, one of the many left in Puglia by the Roman road builders emulating the Appian Way, and the car awoke him by bumping along the rough verge. Could Stefania have really said all that? Did she really tell him she loved him? He was so very happy as he thought the night's events through, for he too knew that she was the one. He'd known since the beginning but did not want to tempt Fate. He'd done that too many times already and look where it had landed him. But was Stefania the proverbial light at the end of the tunnel? The beam of light to radiate his life and his world for ever? He was sure the answer was 'yes', but he had no-one waiting at home to tell, unfortunately. He could not sleep either, how could he?

Two days later Stefania's letter arrived, 'meet me tomorrow at 7 pm at the usual junction. We are going to see my parents! xxxx S.' Pasquale began his flutters again.

By the next day his flutters had turned to panic and then to total dread. Could he go through with this? He wanted to marry Stefania more than anything but he knew her parents would never agree to it. He sighed. Oh how his life had been a constant battleground. He'd never really had more than a moment when it had been easy, he surmised, and he wondered if he ever would. Was he fated for continual unhappiness?

But on the other hand, such constant adversity had also trained him well for tough battles and he had experienced much satisfaction from turning defeat into victory. This final thought cheered him and gave him a modicum of comfort, so that his panic attacks began to subside slowly but surely as he drove along into the setting sun, although the glare was replacing them with an increasingly throbbing headache.

That is, until he approached the junction where they always met, and his fears began all over again. They decided to take Pasquale's car this time to at least show he was not a completely poverty-stricken peasant. Furthermore, if a quick getaway were to be required he could impose the roughness of the road more onto an older car than her new one. She immediately calmed him with a full-bodied kiss, proof she had not paled over the past three days, and Pasquale drove on with delight. For the first time he felt utterly sure this could all work out. The headache went into remission too.

"Are we turning up again unannounced?" he asked timorously.

"No, I told them on the telephone I wanted to bring you, and to behave."

"Well, that's a start, at least."

"But the funniest thing was, Davide had told Papa you were a stranger because you did not know my name."

They both laughed. But suddenly Stefania became serious. "Pasquale, if you need to call me by name please say Helena not Stefania. OK?"

Davide opened the door to them but Eduardo, Countess Valeria and Fabrizio were standing just inside, in the centre of the enormous entry hall, all in a line like a dam wall. Pasquale was so taken back by the size of the interior and its grandeur that he forgot to take off his hat, despite the delicate, tactful cough of Davide. Only Stefania's gentle and unobtrusive kick to the side of his ankle brought him to his senses.

"Darling!" exclaimed Eduardo, advancing with open arms to greet her. Was this too good to be true, considered Stefania as she ran toward him. Valeria she double cheek-kissed and Fabrizio she grabbed by the hands and twirled him round and round like a fairground ride, thus eliciting squeals of joy from the little boy. Finally she said, "this is Pasquale" and as he stepped forward Eduardo countered with "at least you know *his* name!"

Stefania was not sure how to take that, but at least she always had an answer. "Oh Papa, please don't go on so. Everyone in Via Ceramica knows me as Stefania for the simple reason that ancient Luigi next door mistook my name at our very first meeting, passed it on and it has just stuck really. Pasquale met me for the first time there too and thought I was Stefania, so he got into the habit too. He does know my real name. Pasquale?"

"Yes, signore, my beloved is Helena Pinto."

"And you, signore, just who are you?"

It was the 'just' that immediately caused Stefania to rankle, though probably Pasquale was too tense to notice the subtlety, but she was determined to be civilised and suggested, "come on, everyone, shall we go into the drawing room; it is the coolest at this time of the day."

Valeria was relieved already: she could sense the tension building up, so like a good hostess she affirmed, "what a good idea, yes, let us. Davide, refreshments, please as discussed."

"Certainly, Madame," smiled Davide, relieved to be escaping what he considered impending doom.

Eduardo considered there was no point in beating around the bush and if he got straight to the point he might be rid of the fellow the quicker. From the outset he had taken an instant dislike to Pasquale, or was it for what the man he symbolised? He couldn't be entirely sure yet, but the decision was immaterial really: whichever he thought, he would still be rid of him quickly. "Now, young man, what is it that you actually do?"

Stefania and Pasquale had pre-prepared his answer and, true to form, Pasquale pulled himself together just as the amaretti biscuits and limoncello arrived. "I am very much like you, signore, but just starting out. I am a dealer."

"Oh," Eduardo was taken off guard, so the Countess continued on his behalf.

"And what exactly do you deal in?" she asked pleasantly.

"I deal in a most valuable commodity -- antiquities."

"Oh, do you have a shop then, or shops?" The countess' eyes lit slightly.

"No, not yet, I'm afraid, but I hope to one day. At present I actually find and distribute the goods."

"And have you found anything valuable yet?" asked Fabrizio innocently.

"Well, yes and no. There are many sites, and many more to be found. I am actually researching new sites all the time."

"This sounds illegal work to me," queried Eduardo, recovering his position, "and if so that would make you a criminal, right?"

"Certainly there are some grey areas."

"Where?"

"Mainly over ownership. Most of the ancient sites are on land which is owned by someone or some company."

"So do you give the artefacts to the owner?" asked Fabrizio.

"I give them to the museums at Taranto and Napoli."

"How?"

"Through my trader contacts."

Stefania saw the right moment to step in and turn the conversation, "that's where we met, Papa,"

"Oh really?" Eduardo glanced quickly at Valeria, hoping she'd missed that, but unfortunately for him she had not.

"What does she mean, Eduardo? Does Helena meet such people in her pottery shop? Is she involved in illegal trading?"

"No, no, not at all. Helena?" His eyes pleaded for her to rescue him. But Pasquale, suddenly sensing that his interrogation was over, for now at least, and the finger was now pointing at his beloved and her father, quickly interjected.

"No, Countess, apologies, you misunderstand. Yes, I do send the artefacts to Taranto through Via Ceramiche but not through Steph... er...Helena. No, no, it's another shop further down the road. It was just that one day I had some time to spare and I needed a birthday present for my dear, dear Mother so I went browsing and met your wonderful daughter."

"And where do you hail from, Pasquale?" asked Eduardo, anxiously relieved to move on the conversation and away from him.

"I was actually very fortunate to be born in Avetrana, signore, and when my father went away to better himself I was forced to grow up very quickly."

"So you had no schooling, Pasquale?" asked the Countess rather viciously. She had seen and heard enough and wanted this nightmarish charade to end quickly.

"You could say the world has been my school," answered Pasquale, well aware that although everyone was being edgily polite and pleasant his exit was nigh.

Eduardo, meanwhile, was trying to maintain a neutral visage, but inside his mind and heart were churning. Avatrana? Could this possibly be? Or was it mere coincidence? Pasquale, my son Pasquale? Not even changed his name. But why should he? He had done nothing wrong, but I had: I left him. Does he recognise me? Doesn't seem to. But why should he? He was only seven when I left: seven-year-olds don't remember much. Suddenly he could feel beads of sweat breaking out on his brow and his stomach now joined the fray. He needed to sit down, rather quickly, on the nearest chair.

Fortunately, no eyes were on him at this moment because the Countess had already turned to Stefania and said, "my dear girl, such a headache has come on, I fear I must take to my bed. My apologies, Eduardo, but I am really in pain. I must go up now, goodnight."

"Yes, goodnight, dear," acknowledged Eduardo rather vacantly. He was so relieved because this meeting had certainly not proceeded as he thought. In fact, in many ways, it was far worse than he could ever have imagined. Throughout, Helena has maintained a radiant smile and a glow of fulfilment and his heart wept for her predicament. And if this man was who he thought he was he could not believe how small the world was and how cruel the Fates could be. Already business was bad, very bad, Valeria was keen to know more of his dealings, and he was finding it increasingly difficult to hide them from her, Fabrizio was becoming the typically annoying young boy, and now his lovely, lovely daughter was in love with…his own son? God forbid, if it were so.

Pasquale and Stefania departed ambivalent, soon after, but on balance thinking they had done a good job of presenting their case.

✳ ✳ ✳

51

POST MORTEM

1 9 6 4

"As expected, darling?"

"Afraid so. But it could have been worse," suggested Stefania.

"Really? It was exactly how I imagined it," replied Pasquale, "total disregard for our seriousness and total opposition to me."

"Fabrizio liked you," proffered Stefania.

"Ha ha! Very droll. Your mother was such a stuck-up snob and…"

"…well, you can now understand why I wanted…"

"…yes, but she is no longer a grand lady from a grand family. Sorry, darling, but she is hardly a countess today, is she?"

"Technically yes, by title, but certainly no longer by wealth. But you know how such people hang on to their historical rights."

"Yes, it is all rather pathetic in a way, and so sad to see. And did you notice just how unhappy your parents are with each other? Did you pick up the tension?"

"True, there was much coldness between them," agreed Stefania.

Pasquale was unsure which way to go: criticise her family more or commiserate? He did not want to upset his love and had to tread carefully.

"Do you think they had argued about us before we arrived, or was it just part of something more symptomatic?"

She pondered awhile. "Hard to say, but I think the latter."

"Why? Because they don't think I am important enough to bother about? I'll be gone tomorrow?"

"We'll never be allowed to marry, do you mean?" cried Stefania.

"Please don't worry about that."

"Why not?"

"Well, we don't really need your parents, do we? You have done fantastically at your shop and you could move to Napoli. I have saved up quite a lot over the years, actually, and am worth far more than I look." He laughed. She did not.

"Pasquale, are you saying we should ignore my parents, move to Napoli and even, dare I say it, get married?"

"You took the words straight out of my mouth, sweetheart!"

Stefania gave a huge sigh and collapsed into Pasquale's arms across the front seats of her car.

"When shall we leave?" he asked.

Three days later two letters arrived at Stefania's shop. One was an offer of an appointment in Napoli as Assistant Head Designer for a large ceramics company. The other was from her father:

'Dear Stefania,

Apologies for the truncated visit the other evening. I do not know how to tell you this, except in plain words, YOU CANNOT MARRY PASQUALE, EVER. To do so would be to deny God.

Worse still, your Mother and I have finally decided to go our separate ways. Marriage is no longer an option. I have many problems, personal and business. I do not wish to burden you with them. I hope you can continue our arrangement in Grottaglie.

Until we meet again,

Your loving Father.'

Stefania had to sit down in case she swooned, but her brain raced into overtime. How could two letters such poles apart, arrive together? Why could she not marry Pasquale? Was her father just trying to frighten her? What had God to do with it? Why were they separating? Should she accept the post? Why had this offer come today?

Her head began to spin and next thing she knew she was being carried to an armchair by old Luigi. "Luigi, what are..."

"Hush, hush, child. I found you on the floor. I'm not too old to carry you still. Rest," he smiled. He brewed her a really strong cup of coffee, which was as good as smelling salts. She sat bolt upright straight after.

"I must go, I must!" she muttered, but promptly collapsed in a heap on the floor again as she tried to walk.

"Go where, child? You are not fit to go anywhere at this minute, look at you!"

Yes, rest, she mumbled, half awake, half asleep.

She awoke three hours later to gaze into Pasquale's deep, full eyes. Was it a dream? How could he be here? Are we in Heaven?

"Hello, darling! At last. You had me worried for a while." It *was* Pasquale, holding a cool, damp cloth which had been dabbed all over her face and neck. "How do you feel now?"

"Er...fine, it must have been the heat." She quickly glanced about and could see that Luigi, or someone, had returned the letters to their envelopes and put them on her workbench. There was no way in the world she could ever tell Pasquale about her father's comments and she only hoped it had not been him who had tidied up and been tempted to read them. It is only human nature to pry, she thought, and feared the worst. "I had a letter from Napoli today. They offered me that job!"

"Oh darling, that's wonderful news. What did it say?"

❊ ❊ ❊

52

THE NEXT MOVE, NORTH

1 9 6 4

Stefania refused to heed her Father's bizarre letter. She was already sufficiently upset both by the news of her parent's break-up, a rare event in the Catholic Church, and the absence of any forwarding addresses so that she could contact them, and perhaps knock some sense into their heads. The business of God and Pasquale was too much of a mystery to think about in the circumstances, so she did not.

"I just cannot understand what he is talking about, darling," Pasquale answered when she had eventually considered all the possibilities and risked asking him about it. "Anyone would think I am already married, or something," he laughed. Stefania did not.

She loved him so much she had not even considered that argument and she certainly would never have asked him that. However, she did ask something else. "Is there anything you have done in your past that would have been against God's Laws and hence make me unable to marry you owing to conscience?"

"Oh, Stefania, how could you ask such a thing? Don't you trust me?" replied a hurt Pasquale.

"Of course I do, darling, but let us be fair and honest here. I have only really known you for a short time and you have lived life much more than I, agreed?"

"True, true, but an exceedingly boring one too, for the most part, unlike you with your countess Mother, rich businessman Father, intensive education and a pottery business."

Stefania ignored the obvious slight, and refused to let the argument slip by countering, "so there is nothing?"

"No. There is nothing, there can never be nothing. And there is certainly nothing your family would know about me."

"Fine then. But who else would know this 'nothing'?"

"Eh?"

"Who else would know what else?" she repeated, collapsing in fits of laughter at the ludicrousness of the sentence construction.

But Pasquale was not laughing. Instead he felt honesty to be best, so he said, "when I was much younger I rescued my 18-year old sister from an evil shop owner in Taranto and in order to escape we accidently pushed her guard down some stairs. We thought we had killed him but found out many years later he had survived."

"Oh Lord, that must have been frightening for you both. You must tell me the whole story."

"OK, I will one day. And I also got tricked by the Napoli police and was wrongfully found guilty of illegal trading in antiquities, when all I did was find them and sell them. I got 9 months in prison for that."

"Oh you poor thing. I thought it was legal to find antiquities?"

"Yes, but illegal to trade in them or not hand them over to the proper authorities."

"Wait a minute, then, what you have been doing here in my shop all these months was actually illegal, then?"

"Yes, but I kept it to a minimum. Surely you noticed?" I actually sent most of my relics direct to my brother-in-law in Napoli. He married my older sister Andrea so I felt I should. The Taranto traders got wind of this and told me to stop dealing with him and go through them again via your shop. I only partly agreed, obviously, to keep them happy."

"And so I was breaking the law too by handling the goods?"

"No, not really. A good lawyer would have argued that you had no idea what was in the packages and you were only acting on your Father's instructions."

"Ah, so my Father was a criminal then!"

"Precisely. He knew all about it and set it up. He would have been found guilty…"

"…fortunate then that we were not caught. Thank heavens we are leaving and ending all this deceit."

"Oh, that's wonderful, darling! So you *have* finally decided, right?"

"Yes, dearest, I *am* going to accept the job in Napoli. I'd be a fool not to!"

"And we will go there together to live?"

"Yes, but we will have to be careful tongues do not wag: we are not married, dear heart!"

"Who cares!" He whooped and danced around the shop until he knocked a bowl off the display case, smashing it to the floor. "Sorry, darling, but I am so happy!"

When he had calmed down, he asked, "but what will you do with all this? So many happy memories for us. Will you take it all to Napoli? It will need two trucks!" he laughed.

"No, I think I will keep the shop and ask Luigi to find someone reliable to manage the sales for me."

"Make sure every item is recorded and the price paid for each, then."

"Yes, of course I will. Luigi has a certain acumen, he will find someone with integrity."

"And he could get in an apprentice to use your wheels and oven?"

"That is a splendid idea, thank you, dear!"

"You see? A great team! But will we have enough to live on in Napoli? I might not find much work and it a very expensive city after all."

"My new job is going to pay handsomely, don't worry. But if you feel the need to be productive by day I am sure there are jobs abounding for willing hands."

"My darling, at this present moment my willing hands are only willing me in one particular direction...!"

"Pasquale!"

And so it was. In the Autumn of 1964 they sold Pasquale's lovely Audi, being too unsuitable for city driving and too tempting for thieves, drove to Napoli and settled in to the beautiful apartment the company had found for them and had paid two-thirds of the rent for. It comprised the whole third floor of one of those imposing palazzos along Via Cavallo, overlooking the port from the side of the hills. The views from the lounge and bedroom were spectacular - the whole of the Bay of Naples in one long sweep, the Isle of Capri, and even a part of Vesuvius in the southern corner. The company also provided a cleaning lady three times a week, plus all furnishings and fittings. The latter was a godsend as they had no furniture of their own and Stefania had been unable to go home to collect any treasured belongings. They had certainly fallen on their feet this time!

A few days before they had departed Pasquale had been tying up some loose ends and had perchanced to re-visit Oria. He noticed the place had not changed one jot as he took a nostalgic walk around Piazza Manfredi and then exited the Manfredi Gate into Piazza Lorch. He saw his sister's old dress shop and paused outside. One of the assistants inside waved at him, presumably remembering and recognising him. He waved back, smiled and walked on. Then he walked down Via Torre Santa Suzanna to his favourite bar where one or two recognised him, shouted greetings and stood him a Peroni or two. Suddenly there was a tap on his shoulder and the shop assistant smiled and asked, "welcome back, signore, how is Andrea?"

Rather taken aback Pasquale muttered, "oh, very well and married now. In Napoli no less."

"Ah, we always knew she would do well. Not that Signore Lupo, is it?"

"Er…no. He died, didn't he? Some fire, I recall? No, no, a very nice man from Napoli. And you?"

"Oh no, signore, not yet anyway. I came to tell you…"

"…look, please excuse my manners, would you like a drink, er…?"

"Alicia. Yes, that would be nice, a coca cola please. I came to say that a while ago, well, actually a long time ago, well I can't actually remember when, you know how it is, time stands still in a small town like this, right?"

"Very true. Nothing has changed: it seems only yesterday I was here. You were saying?"

"And why have you returned, out of interest?"

Pasquale began to get frustrated. He did not wish to spend ages reminiscing about Oria with someone he did not even know and with someone who was obviously a gossip with little else on her hands but time. "Just a flying visit, really. You were saying?" he tried again.

"Oh yes, anyway, a solicitor came to the shop and left a letter for your family, asking if we could pass it on if we ever saw any of you again or found out where you were, as presumably you left no forwarding address."

"Yes, we were in a bit of a hurry to leave, as I remember. A letter, you say?"

"Andrea just upped and left, you know; not a word, signore, not a word! I was left to fend for the shop and take charge…"

"…and what a fabulous job you have done, Alicia, well done! Now, a letter?"

"Well, it was kept by the till all this time, constantly gathering dust. In the end it became something of a talisman and as such a precious object it achieved revered status!" she laughed heartily and one or two men flicked their heads towards her. Pasquale merely smiled, taking the visual accolades, for Alicia was a fine-looking woman to be sure.

"And so?"

"Yes, I remembered it, followed you down here and have brought it: voila!"

Pasquale took the fading, grubby envelope and thanked her. "Must dash now, got to get home to my sick mother, 'bye!"

"But please, stay and have another drink, it's the least I can do?"

"Love to, sorry, got to dash. Va bene!" A number of male heads admired the swaying hips and confident gait as she swung out of the bar. A few whistled. She tossed her head back and smiled seductively.

"Missed your chance there, Pasquale," said a friend.

"No problem, I have a steady girlfriend now."

They laughed. Pasquale with a steady girl? Whatever next?

"Farm reject, is she?" another quipped.

"'Baby-plucking from mama, eh?"

"I'll have you know my Mother died a while back!" replied Pasquale angrily and he stormed out of the bar. It'll never be any different, he thought, his misery sweeping back over him, they'll never respect me. Always the agricultural clod.

He stormed off back up the hill to the piazzas and paused on a bench in Lorch. Already the two's and four's of girls were perambulating around the perimeter, either followed by equal numbers of boys or ogled at by boys sitting on seats such as his. Suddenly he felt an intruder. Heavens, would someone think he was a paedophile? He moved quickly and found another bench out of sight of the young peoples' courtship ritual.

He took out the even-more crumpled letter. Solicitor? Formal then. Trouble? Usually is. How many laws did we break in Oria? Me? The family? What could it be?

Finally, he could not contain his curiosity further and he ripped it open. Heavens, it was from Signore Bellini!

'My Dear Carone Family,
I will be brief as I am most unwell, probably dying in fact.
It was so sad you had to leave so suddenly but I do understand the reasons. Wherever you are I wish you all God's good Grace.

Becoming ill soon after you left, I was unable to re-let the house, so I decided to sell it and be done with it. You know we were unable to trace the former owners and on checking the law I found that you, being the last respectable and longstanding tenants to live in it, therefore inherited it as your house.

The sale is lodged in your name in Banco Stella del Sud, a/c number 0183730548, in Via Militia. With interest accruing the money should make you most comfortable.

I took only 55,200 lire for legal expenses, some of which was for my funeral fees. I hope you didn't mind the latter. I had no need of more.

So if I do not see you again, can I say it was an honour to know such a kind, loving and friendly family. May we all meet again some day in God's good Heaven.

Your good friend,

Alphonso Bellini

(transcribed by D. Minaro of Minaro & Son, Solicitors, 12 Via Militia)'

Pasquale could not believe what he had read. Their house? Sold? Money? Oh, poor Signore Bellini dying like that and us not even saying goodbye to him. How cruel we were. How cruel life is.

He looked at the angle of the sun. About 12 noon, he considered, still open. So he rushed to the bank, offered the letter and his Identity Card as proof and waited in expectation. After a seemingly endless time the manager himself called him into his office. "Yes, Signore Carone, we can verify that everything in the letter is indeed correct. The account is here and, may I say, somewhat healthy." He smiled that smile bankers use when they are feeling benevolent, or perhaps when they sense there may be a little 'ex-gratia' for them too.

"I am most relieved, signore. One cannot be too careful these days. May I have a settlement banker's cheque, please?"

"Certainly, signore, made out to whom?"

"Oh, P. Carone, please. I am the head of the family now my Mother has passed on."

"My condolences, signore. I will arrange the cheque now. Five minutes?"

"Many thanks."

He returned in seven minutes - when could bankers ever be relied on to tell the truth? He handed Pasquale the cheque. He had been standing but suddenly he collapsed into the chair, "4,005,600 lire? What? Is this correct?"

Misunderstanding him, the manager backpedalled with platitudes, "I can assure you that is correct, signore, if you think it should be more. We have included the interest up until last week. If you come back on Monday we can give you the rest, only a few hundred liras I can assure you…"

"…but 4,005,600?"

"Signore, please be our guest if you wish to examine the books. I can assure you it is all there." He looked crestfallen and somewhat worried at his client's doubts over their propriety.

"Oh please excuse me, signore, no, no, no, I am not questioning your honesty, far from it. It is the size of the cheque: I cannot believe we own this much money. It's just amazing!" And he burst out laughing, finally releasing all the tension. The manager joined him, laughing even louder when Pasquale began one of his common indulgencies - dancing round the room - and all the staff outside in the banking hall wondered just what was going on. Of course, what was running uppermost through the mind of the manager was how such common riff-raff could walk in off the street poor and re-emerge a few minutes later rich. Such is life, he sighed, out of Pasquale's range of vision.

"Can I take this to my bank in Ceglie Messapica?"

"Oh, you have a bank account then?" insinuated the manager slyly.

"Certainly I do, and there's probably far more in it than in yours, signore," replied Pasquale, the manager's sarcasm not lost on him even in his high state.

"Well then, excellent. You can take it to the Moon if you want, anywhere is fine."

"The Moon it is then," he laughed.

"Yes, but before you go, remember to give one of my many clerks your details. Good day signore, a pleasure doing business with you."

"Even though your branch no longer has 4 million lira in it, ha?"

Pasquale returned to the street and continued dancing down Via Militia oblivious to whoever wished to stare.

He wondered why he rushed to his bank in Ceglie, deposited the cheque, but never said a word to Stefania. She assumed he was in high spirits because they were about to depart on their great adventure: he knew otherwise.

After some rather cumbersome correspondence and a lengthy time period Pasquale managed to transfer 1,000,000 lire to each of Cosimo,

Andrea, and Maria. Cosimo had a considerable problem with this because he had never had a bank account in his life as he did not believe in them, but he was ecstatic because the money would pay for all the repairs his house needed. Andrea was ecstatic too, because with twins on the way she needed every cent to bring them up in a manner befitting Mino's status. Maria's letter was the shortest - "many thanks, it will solve the rent problems, love to all, M" - and of course worried Pasquale no end. I do hope she is safe and well, he wondered, but he could not share his concern with Stefania as it might mean disclosing the reason for the letter. For his part, he left his share of the money in Ceglie Messapica, gaining steady if unspectacular interest in the bank. My nest egg, he thought, in time of trouble or dire need.

Certainly he had no need of it in Napoli. Stefania was being paid a generous base salary and was also receiving commission on her own sales or on orders she attracted for the company. By careful husbandry and a far from exotic lifestyle they were able to accrue sufficient cash to even nearly buy their own showroom after a year.

"Just a few hundred thousand lire more, darling," encouraged Pasquale.

"Yes I know, but the perfect opportunity has already arisen in the Jewellery Quarter, a lovely building, perfect for a showroom and for entertaining clients."

"Really? But must you entertain clients too?" he twinkled.

Laughing, she knew what he meant, "no silly, but you must have a comfortable room for them to sit and contemplate the work. You know, dainty finger food, fine wine, relax them and encourage them ..."

"...yes, to cloud their judgement," laughed Pasquale.

"No, to enhance it," she smiled back seductively.

"Soft music, attractive assistant..."

"...no, I shall be busy!"

Stefania leapt out of her chair, jumped on him and started tickling his ribs. He wouldn't stop so she grabbed his fruit, hard. "Stop now! Or I'll squeeze harder!" she promised.

He would have loved it to play out but there was no time, "OK, truce then." But she still squeezed harder and he was even more excited, "promise!"

"OK, that's better, bad boy!"

Back to seriousness he asked, "you really want this place? Give up your job?"

"Yes, I know I can do it now. People know me. I have a reputation. Look at this month's magazine." She waved her smiling front cover picture at him.

"Yes, it's fantastic, you clever girl! But how short are we, then?"

"By my calculations, including start up expenses, only about 300.000 lire."

"Is that all?"

"All?" she asked, "all? That's a lot of cash dreamland boy!"

"Well, not really, actually. If it is really what you want to do and think it will work I can find that. I have some savings, you know…"

"…really? That much?"

"Yes, savings from my dubious past!" he laughed.

"Oh yes please, darling, yes! Let's do it or be damned. You make me so happy!"

"Your turn now then," he smiled as he led her towards the bedroom.

And so it was. Stefania gave her company one month's notice and bought the showroom. They were most upset, of course, but admitted it was going to happen sooner or later, the talent she had. She filled the rooms with all her new creations, advertised the Grand Opening, particularly around the top Napoli hotels and the trade journals, and she proudly produced her first Catalogue. They must have launched their very own company, Pinto-Carone Ceramics, on an obviously auspicious day because the rooms filled to bursting with local experts, rich tourists and ordinary Neapolitans and she took over 300,000 lire in sales and orders in a few short hours. Stefania Pinto Creations had truly arrived!

The next day being a Sunday they continued the celebration at home, devouring any uneaten delicacies and gulping the remnant bottles of champagne. At the opening they had been far too busy and nervous to partake, so there was much catching up to be done. That evening, when both were truly over-imbibed and exhausted there was a knock at the door. The new apartments' janitor stood holding a very expensive-looking envelope. "A courier has just delivered this, saying it was extremely urgent, so I hurried upstairs with it now, signora."

"S…hank you," giggled the inebriated and assumedly married Stefania.

She tried to open it once she was safely indoors but just couldn't match fingers to brain. "Pasquale, can you pleesh do the honoursh," she garbled, falling gracelessly into a chair.

He managed to open it with some effort and little dexterity. "Shall I read it to you, my inebriated queen?"

She nodded, or moved her head as best she could.

'Dear Signora Pinto, the delivery of this letter is stated as "urgent" because I leave Napoli in two days. I am Sir Arthur Bellinge of Dover Court, Knightsbridge, London, and I own a number of galleries around Europe. I am opening a new ceramics gallery in Paris in two months. I am astounded at the beauty and quality of your work and therefore I wondered if you would like to stock it and also manage it as your own? It will be 1200 square metres in Rue de Versailles at the heart of the Artisan Quarter. The small details we could iron out later but as a start I would suggest these terms: I pay for all rents and overheads, we split the profits 45/55 in your favour. Please, I do need your decision before I leave. In hope, Arthur, Hotel Grand Bay, room 1307.'

"Is this a joke? Are you trying to amushe me?" said a fast-sobering Stefania.

"No, no joke, it would seem."

"Why?"

"Well, for a start it looks and feels very expensive paper, second it has been embossed with the hotel's stamp, third it shows his crest of arms at the top, fourth it has his own seal at the bottom. Enough?"

"OK."

"I mean, if this is true, wow! What a fantastic opportunity, eh? Paris, Paris, Paris!" He was so excited he had to run to the bathroom. He shouted on from there, "'all, I have had a number of undulations in my life but this High would have to be the highest High of the Highs, if you see what I mean. Oh, you clever thing, Stef! Well done, old girl!"

He returned to find her fast asleep across the chair, snoring like a female pig. Or had she passed out? Better not wake her. Two days is plenty. Surely she can't refuse this offer?

The letter still read exactly the same in the morning. Stefania was due in the gallery at 10am but struggled to meet that deadline. If Pasquale had not driven her she would have been late for her first official opening day, but fortunately too her efficient assistant Genny was waiting at the door and busying herself with opening procedures. Stefania had time to take a blearily-eyed look through all the well-wishing letters and cards that had arrived in the post. Amongst them were some cheques also so she had to work slowly and carefully. This did not improve her mood and headache, but then she spotted some more orders in the pile and that cheered her. Then she started to panic: how can we get organised this quickly, get everything made, packed and shipped in time, write up the books, deal with new customers? Should I take on extra staff, she thought. And what about Sir Arthur? She had to sit, calm down and ask Genny to make coffee so thick she would have to spoon it out, like in the London coffee houses of old!

Genny was clever, that is why they had hired her. "Madame, may I suggest you leave all this paperwork to me and you just do front of house? After all, it is you they want to talk to and negotiate with, not me."

"What a wonderful suggestion! Just what I was thinking. Oh, and tomorrow, when you are ready to process, I will ask Signore Carone to come in and help you."

"Yes, Madame, a good idea, there is so much here to do. A bit of muscle around the place would not go amiss either!"

"'I beg your pardon! Please do not refer to my partner as 'a bit of muscle', he is a highly intelligent and sensitive young man!"

"Apologies, Madame, I did not mean it like that…"

"…yes, all right, I know what you meant, but please control your tongue in these premises."

"I'm so sorry, Madame."

"Yes, and I have a flaming hangover, apologies." She tried to smile, but even that hurt like hell.

Pasquale picked her up for siesta time at 1pm and they drove to the hotel. They found Sir Arthur just commencing a grand pranzo in the dining room and when two chairs were added to his table and introductions made they sat to share the feast. To their surprise Sir Arthur was neither old nor stuffy, quite the contrary, he was a dashing young member of the aristocracy who spoke tolerable Italian after studying for four years in Verona. So when Stefania began to add sentences in English he was even more impressed with her and wondered how she could have picked that all up in the Heel of Italy. He himself agreed that he was no expert in ceramics, but he knew enough, and as a back-up had sought professional advice. He told Stefania that no-one he had consulted had doubted in the least her future potential in ground-breaking ceramic design, and Pasquale added that he was pleased it was only ground breaking and not crockery breaking. Everyone laughed politely.

He said he was only too happy to let her have the Paris gallery. The city was the centre of chic so why not put Italian chic at the centre?

That raised more than a polite laugh. His lawyer, seated with them, agreed the terms of the letter, which the two of them had drafted the day before in Sir Arthur's room, but Stefania and Pasquale held out for 60/40, as they had planned before arriving. Sir Arthur, ever the pragmatist, but also an acute businessman, said 'yes' but countered with the new condition that she pay all advertising, all catalogue production and all catering. They needed to consider this further and politely excused themselves. They considered that if the products were so good they would sell themselves, so minimal advertising would be necessary. Secondly, a simple catalogue would be sufficient for the same reason, and thirdly if the works were so attractive customers would not need time to make up their minds so would need little hospitality.

So it was agreed at 60/40. Everyone was extremely happy, and perhaps not a little flushed with fine wine and food, so they felt like being a little cheeky and asked politely if he could finance their airfares to Paris and up to 100,000 lire for shipping costs of those pieces presently in Napoli which would suit a Paris clientele. Everything had been such a whirlwind, they explained, and even two months to make new pieces was a very rushed time span. And they would also have to make careful arrangements for their Napoli showroom too.

"Gladly," he replied, knowing that by obtaining the services of Steph Pinto he was indeed the one who had obtained the real bargain.

True to his word, the next day the lawyer came with the papers to sign and within a few more days they were applying for passports. Also, they had never ever flown in a plane before and were therefore doubly excited. Equally good news too was that Genny had agreed to stay on as manageress of the showroom until all the pieces had been sold or Stefania could re-stock remotely. Meanwhile Pasquale busied himself with the complexities of personal administration and the delivery of existing sales. Stefania buried herself in the back room working feverishly to complete existing orders, design new pieces for Paris and even make a few new ones for Napoli. Soon she became exhausted and fell sick with a fever, which put even more pressure on her schedule. There was little or no time for each other, certainly not for love and affection, and soon even their relationship began to fray at the edges. Stefania faced few daily problems, apart from ever-tightening deadlines, but Pasquale battled all kinds of bureaucratic nightmares in keeping the business running. Even the efficient Genny could not help. But the worst problem was his trying to get something as simple as a passport. He had no birth certificate, all his previous addresses were rented not officially owned, the bar did not count being both workplace and home, he had a prison record, his parents were deceased and disappeared, and so on. As the days rushed by their prospect of moving from Napoli to Paris began to look less and less certain.

And then, out of the blue, there came a letter. Stefania recognised the handwriting immediately and took a deep breath as she opened it. With all this going on she'd had no time to even think about him, let alone do anything about finding him or seeing him. Earlier she had been writing once a fortnight to the castello but she had never received a reply so she discontinued it. She couldn't be sure but she presumed her Mother was not passing them on to wherever her Father was, and then she realised that her Mother might indeed be opening them and reading them, so she tailored her comments accordingly.

With hands shaking slightly she slit open the envelope with a letter opener. 'Dearest Daughter,' it read, 'I continue to exist in health but not in happiness. Fabrizio thrives but your Mother, I understand, ails. I see from your last letter, grudgingly passed on by your brother and much against your Mother's wishes, I believe, that you are now in Napoli. Well done! But it seems you did not heed my warning about Pasquale. When you both visited us I sensed it then, so I had detectives check his past. Again I tell you, more fervently this time, you cannot marry him: he is your half-brother!

E Carone/Pinto, once of Avetrana 1939.'

She collapsed into a chair. "No," she screamed, "no, no, no! Impossible! Evil man. Why does he do this to me? How could he? Must he make us all unhappy with his ridiculous games just because he is living in misery? Liar, coward, bastardo!" As she screamed the last she felt she was strong enough and angry enough to even kill her father. "How dare you try to ruin my life, and now, at this critical time? How dare you?"

It was indeed fortunate that Pasquale was out on some errands. She would not have known what to say to him, or how to react.

If there were any truth in this it would be the end of her world, her life, her happiness. Why would Papa do this to me? He has always loved me and doted on me, maybe at the expense of his own wife, so there must be a strong reason why he now suddenly wants to ruin my future. What if it is true, she thought. Maybe he *is* desperately trying to save me from incest and permanent Hell. Oh Mary, Mother of God, what *is* the truth? Please help me!

Think! Pull yourself together and think! I haven't seen him for ages: he has made no attempt to contact me. That is not the sign of a caring, loving father who wants to protect his daughter. This must be all false, malicious lies. Could it be those Ndrangheta who he deals with in Taranto? Could they be putting pressure on him for unpaid debts, perhaps? But why? How could it involve Pasquale anyway, he is only a small-time hunter to them, and anyway, they like him, don't they? He is their friend, surely? Or has taking business straight to the Camorra annoyed them? Surely not?

Stefania screamed again. None of this makes any sense. How can he be my half-brother? No, no, no! Her head began to swim and the next thing she remembered was Pasquale leaning over her whispering, "darling, darling." Or was that a dream too? She felt she was sinking into madness.

* * *

53
TWO STEPS BACK
1 9 6 5

The familiarity of the scene thrust a little warmth through his chilled bones. But how long would the warmth last? Long enough to reach the square? The next single room? The next drink? Numbed to the bone he had driven on auto-pilot the six hours from Via Cavallo and darkness was now blotting out that last bewitching 'sunset half hour' - the absolute best of the perfect Mediterranean light of painters and photographers. Ceglie was certainly no Napoli but it was comfort, it was the first place to run to, the simplest place to lose himself, but the most foolish place to hide.

They had had everything: the whole world had been near their feet, the promise of a lifetime far beyond the wildest dreams of an Avetrana peasant boy. But the Avetrana father had to go and wreck it all, snap it in an instant, cast it onto an ocean of misery so black that even a night moon would not reflect on it. He himself felt like a pine needle floating away into an inky nothingness, while his one true love was the flickering and fading lamp at the end of the harbour wall. And then the light died as quickly as had their love when he read the letter.

The knowing, the guilt, the shame would have destroyed their union far quicker than any priest's mumblings or Hail Mary's in a confessional box. Staunch Catholics were they neither, but their love even opposed Natural Laws that can never be cracked asunder.

Even if the letter had been a lie, to either taunt them or to test them, they knew they could not continue because there would always be that element of doubt and uncertainty about an incestuous union. It would have nagged and torn at them constantly, wreaking its own powerful destruction inside their minds.

Pasquale had been the first to acknowledge it and be positive. While Stefania sobbed uncontrollably for hour after hour he quietly packed his bags, moved to a hotel and made plan upon plan for the future. He knew life and happiness were at their end but they had to continue somehow.

He stopped at a different neighbourhood of Ceglie and soon found a room where no-one knew him. But in less than a few days the tongues were successfully wagging and everyone, it seemed, knew that the golden boy was back, tail between legs. Ten per cent felt genuinely sorry for him but kept quiet about it, twenty per cent revelled in his misery and let everyone know their feelings, but the remaining seventy per cent just carried on with their own small, humble lives, regardless of Pasquale and his pain.

A few weeks later whilst in the post office, Pasquale chanced upon a board which daily displayed unaddressed letters and packets, merely addressed to 'Signore A.N.Other, Ceglie Messapica'. It horrified him that there were so many people who did not know each other's addresses and wrote in hope that one day their letter would get through. Then he spotted one addressed to 'Sig. Pasquale Carone' and instantly recognised the handwriting. It began, 'I have sent this same letter to about ten different town's post offices in the hope it may someday reach you.' He paused and checked the date stamp on the envelope: it was two weeks ago. 'I am very sick now and indeed failing fast, but I wanted you to know two things before I pass on - 1. although I did leave you and the family when you were seven I never stopped loving you in my heart; that is why I had to tell dear Stefania about you. I am so sorry it all turned out so wrong for you.' Tears welled in Pasquale's eyes, but they quickly turned to anger - how could he say he never stopped loving us? He never did one thing to help us after he left, bastardo!

He read on, now furious with his father. '2. I wanted you to know that Stefania arrived safely in Paris and her showroom is 6, Rue de Versailles, Montmartre, Paris 0612. If I never see you or hear from you again that will be my just desserts, love Papa.' Pasquale wept openly and everyone in the Post Office from the ten per cent clucked soothingly, those from the twenty per cent sniggered and muttered 'I told you so', while the rest continued their business in an embarrassed fashion.

In complete desolation and fury he went back to stealing fruit. He could not understand why and he could not explain it: he just had to do it. Now he had a car he could use its headlights at night to good purpose and also transport vastly greater quantities. In blind rage he would often randomly choose a whole street upon which to bestow his bounty, and at dead of night hang a bag of mixed fruit and vegetables on every door knocker. As can be imagined, it soon caused quite a stir. It even reached the front page of the local newspaper when an urban farmer complained that he had found delivered to his door the very same fruit he had planted and had hoped to pick himself later! He could prove it too because he had been the only farmer in the whole district to try out Spanish melons that summer. Up until then Pasquale had had no fear of being caught because his random selection of beneficiaries was just that -- random. No-one could predict where he would 'strike' next, or on what night. However, he did cease his activities after the newspaper report for fear of being caught, but while it lasted its excitement had been most therapeutic, almost like electric shock treatment, and he did begin to feel a little less lost and hopeless.

Knowing no other way of keeping himself, and still wishing to share his misery only with himself, he next reverted to his trusty metal detector. Hours of solitude became days; days became weeks; and weeks became months, staggering across thick, roughly ploughed autumn sods and wild, degenerate scrub. He did not even care if he found nothing, the thrill was in the chase and he realised he just needed to do some chasing.

* * *

54

A SISTER'S PLIGHT

1 9 6 7

'Dear Brother,
        You don't know how difficult it was to get this letter to you.
I really hope you receive it. Please, I beg you, come to Roma and rescue
me! My pimp never lets me out of his sight and I had to ask a client to
secretly post this to you. I'm afraid I have got into big trouble. Please
meet me in Via Tratelli, San Marco any time after 9pm. Pretend to be a
client. Must finish, another one waiting. Please help me!' *Maria*

Pasquale stared at the letter, read it again and then re-read it. But each
time it never changed; Maria was a street-walker, it said, a lady of the
night. Impossible! He refused to believe what his eyes clearly saw. He
read it again: 'pimp, client, street. It must be. But, my dearest beautiful
sister, how could you? Why did it all go so wrong?

He had earlier heard that she had secured a temporary job only days
after she arrived through one of those 'new ideas' companies called a
job agency. They had offered her a position as a receptionist in a 3-star
hotel, nothing special but a start at least, and after the one-month trial
they had taken her on permanently. He had then heard no more for ages
until occasional short letters arrived once every few months. She had
sounded content and at ease with the world, had gained a promotion
to receptionist in a 4-star hotel, with better clientele and fatter tips,
and she had even found a steady man to walk out with, rather than a
hinted-at succession of flirtatious encounters. But then Pasquale had
heard no more; nothing for eight months. However, existing in his own
silent world of gloom and despair he had not realised it had in fact

been that long until he had checked the date of the last letter. Yes, it was July 1966, now in fact nearly nine months hence.

The overnight train to Roma had been freezing: the carriage's heating system was faulty, explained the sour-faced guard at Potenza Station. Pasquale felt like he was aching in nearly every bone from trying to sleep doubled up on the firm second-class seat. He did have plenty of money to afford a first-class seat, or even an entire compartment if he'd so chosen, but his parsimonious past always prevented him from wasting money on unnecessary frivolities. But as he tried to extricate his frozen bones from the locked position, he truly wished he had. He stumbled along the train's swaying passageway like a hung-over drunkard to relieve himself in the rather smelly toilet, but he drew the line at splashing ice-cold water all over his face to engage with what was promising to be a most difficult day, or days. However, he did finally allow his money to make one concession and he lurched into the first-class dining car looking somewhat the worse for wear. Despite the frowning looks from the elite travellers, and in one or two cases outright glares, he ordered a breakfast that would have cost five dinners in Ceglie. Embarrassingly however, he was asked to pay up front as the waiter did not believe he was of sufficient means. But oh, it was buono! Buonissimo even, with lashings of scalding cappuchino, crema cornettos, cereal with warm milk, a meat bun and fresh fruit. At least he felt more human and he certainly creaked less internally as the train finally crawled into Roma's Central Station.

He had not really formulated a plan even though he knew he ought to have done, but how does one plan for this kind of bizarre situation? He had merely brought a good deal of money strapped to his waist in a pouch. Cash usually talked in such situations, he assumed, though he was not entirely sure. Indeed, in these days of abject depression he was never really sure about anything anymore. He had told his landlady he would be away only a few days, but of that too he was not really sure either.

Next, he needed to find accommodation in Roma, and fortunately two factors proved to be in his favour: it was February and there were next to no tourists about, and he had cash, lots of it, and he could walk into any hotel he chose. He was so pleased it was not summer because he had been told that summers in Roma were now becoming intolerable and all the locals were trying in reverse to get out by taking their own holidays in August. The city was being inundated by a new wave of richer visitor, feeding off the publicity generated in film and in music on both sides of the Atlantic. The 'New Italy' was now the place to be: 'Roman Holiday', 'Three Coins in the Fountain', Frank Sinatra, Dean Martin, Gina Lollobrigida, Sophia Loren, and even Cliff Richard's 'Summer Holiday' had immortalised such treasures as the Trevi Fountain, Spanish Steps and Coliseum.

He took the underground system to Coliseum, then changed to the other line and carried on three stops past San Marco, alighted and found an unostentatious but clean 2-star establishment aptly named Hotel Hope. He spent the next day resting, actually huddled to the radiator, as he so much needed to be mentally alert for his meeting with Maria, despite feeling great guilt that every day extra was another day of pain for his dear sister. The next night, with great trepidation, he asked the taxi driver to take him to Via Tratelli. He thought the driver smiled quietly to himself as he said it but could not be sure, like so many other things these days. He alighted at the corner, paid the man a handsome tip and started walking. It was a freezing cold night with overhead light drizzle, certainly not a Mediterranean night to be proud of, rather a Manchester or Goteburg one. The street was not particularly well-lit and what few pedestrians there were about hurried by, heads down into the biting wind. An occasional car headlight or even less-frequent street lamp illuminated the dreary scene, but only temporarily. Pasquale could make out some girls along the side walls, spaced regularly and conveniently every ten to fifteen metres apart – far enough apart to let clients choose comfortably but never too far to suddenly gang up on a drunk or a garrulous customer. How they survived this weather he knew not, with their uniform so necessary for their trade totally at odds with the elements– flimsy short skirts to show off their legs and skimpy tops to emphasise their busts. Smoking and chewing they looked a sorry bunch of humanity, and tears welled in his eyes when he remembered this was now Maria's new life. Oh Mary Mother, will I even recognise her, he worried, as he moved along the winding, narrowing street. But he needed to rub away such confessions and think positively: he needed clear eyes and brain to help her, not guilt or pity.

Indeed, he did not recognise her, she did he. Startling him alarmingly she morphed from the shadows of a doorway, "good evening, signore, what would you like?"

Automatically Pasquale replied, "no thanks, not tonight."

"Then what are you doing here, signore, having a bit of fun at our expense?" said Maria clearly, but afterwards muttered under her breath, "brother, it's me, Maria."

"Well, I… I…I could be interested if the price is right," he recovered smartly.

They continued their hurried play-acting until Maria coquettishly took his arm and led him towards a dark door. "You'll have to come to my room," she murmured again, so they entered the building, and had to brush past a huge ugly man who put out an arm to inspect the client's credentials. They received the accepting nod and ascended two flights of stairs to Maria's business premises.

"Oh Maria, is this where you …er…live now, dear Sister?" he uttered in amazement, once they were inside.

"Sssh, don't call me 'sister', the walls here are paper-thin."

"Yes, sorry."

"How did you end up here? What happened?"

"I had some bad luck, OK? Now, you'd better take some clothes off at least, quickly, and I must too, if you can bear to look, in case he comes to check."

"What? Clothes off? Check?"

"Yes. When I passed that man I muttered a code that told him what service I was providing, so firstly he knows how long I'll be and, secondly, how much money I'll be collecting. If we exceed that time he will get worried and come to check. Things happen to us kind, you know, we need protection."

"And he makes sure you don't pocket something on top for an extra service, right?"

"Yes, true." She smiled.

He undressed a little and asked, "do you have a plan because, as yet, I do not?"

"Yes, but not a great one. Quickly. You come back tomorrow at 10pm exactly, in a taxi, stop here, its number 52, I come to your window to negotiate but you drag me in as loudly as you can and roar off before they can do anything, OK?"

"Sure. So you are not allowed to go in vehicles or leave the street?"

"No, never. Rule number 1. Hence we are total prisoners. Look, I'm going to make some suitable noises now otherwise someone might get suspicious. You might care to do the same…"

"…but Maria, that's terrible!"

"I'm sorry, but it is just as embarrassing for me. Life is at stake here, these men do not play around for fun, you know. We are nothing to

them, just money-earners. You should see how some girls are treated!"
She shivered.

Soon they were ready to leave but Pasquale pulled her back from
the door and whispered, "but what if you are not there at 10pm? What
if you are with a client?"

"Yes, true. Look, if you cannot see me just drive away and return at
10.30 in a different taxi. OK?"

"Yes, but similarly engaged at 10.30, heaven forbid?"

"You will just have to return every half an hour and hope for the best.
Pray that Thug Man doesn't get suspicious. Look, we must go now. Can
you give me some money? I have to slip it to him when we leave."

And so Pasquale stumbled out of number 52, past Thug Man and
into the street, his brain in a daze. Poor sister, this is even worse than
I thought. In a blur he managed to hail a taxi and returned to the hotel
to relive the evening and the escape plan. The taxi driver was critical; he
would have to be bribed as it would look like kidnapping and someone
might take his taxi number. Otherwise, it seemed easy enough. But
if so why didn't more do it? Or did they not want to escape? Were
they content to live a protected life earning far more than they could
anywhere else? Or were they subjugated by evil force, frightened to an
inch of their life? He fell asleep not caring to think on it any more.

Next morning he was already taut, taut with fear of the evening's
escape and taut with the thought of having to sit all day in that 2-star
room just waiting. Indeed, he had never ever visited Roma in his life so,
despite the continuing cold weather, he decided to take his mind of the
coming events. He would play tourist for the day.

He returned on the underground to Coliseum, paid his entry fee
and duly enjoyed walking round the impressive edifice for an hour. The
weather started to brighten and warm up so that everything looked
more attractive and positive in the crisp winter sunshine. A group of
German tourists moved slowly around with a guide, followed by a
Japanese one. So there were a few tourists about, he smiled. As the
German group passed some of the ladies smiled at him somewhat
positively as he sauntered by. When he met them again in the crypt
area two of them deliberately emphasised their walking posture for his
pleasure. He smiled and lingered, admiring appreciatively. Then one
secretly beckoned him over and whispered, 'follow, outside,' and went
on her way with the straggling group. He knew no German and smiled,
trying to understand her request. As they walked she hung to the back,

kept turning and beckoned him on. He understood and, with little better to do, continued to follow. They exited the Coliseum, crossed the road and began to ascend into the old Roman city opposite where the guide issued maps, gave them a brief lecture on the attractions and the route to follow, and warned them that they had two hours to walk to the other end and meet the coach at the statue of Caesar on the roadside. The two ladies lingered, waiting till the rest had moved onwards and upwards out of sight, then dodged away to the right. They beckoned Pasquale who sauntered over and smiled.

In German, one asked, "do you speak German?" Pasquale continued to smile and shrugged his large agricultural shoulders. "Obviously not," she muttered to her friend and then she moved nearer and stroked his arm. Her friend snuggled up the other side and motioned that they had two hours free and would he like to go anywhere with them. He continued to smile, amused by their antics, but they took that as a sign of acceptance and spun on their heels and walked him back to the Coliseum. Chattering happily they walked all the way round to the other side into a smart avenue of restaurants and hotels. At the third they stopped and motioned to him that they would like him to come in with them. Finally, it dawned on him what they wanted and in a flash he had to make a decision. He had hidden most of the cash at the back of his sink so there was no problem of being robbed of his wealth; he was feeling very depressed and worried; this might be quite an interesting distraction as long as he kept his head; they were fairly attractive ladies probably in their forties, well dressed and fun. There was no decision necessary. He nodded and smiled. They gesticulated room 41, told him to wait five minutes and then enter the lobby and go up. He walked calmly past the unconcerned receptionist to the lift, found the room and knocked.

One had opened a bottle of wine from her suitcase while the other sat demurely on the single bed. Pasquale was by now certainly excited; this was far more than the diversion he had imagined two hours previously. He took a swig from the bottle, went to the bathroom to freshen up and returned to find both ladies seductively beckoning him from the bed. Once there they became wildly animated, kissing him and caressing him all over. His long-lost passion arose immediately and both ladies dealt with it in different but exciting ways. One tumultuous climax led to another, for all, and for over an hour their passions were satiated in different combinations. And then it was over.

An hour later found the ladies dressed, freshening up and smiling again at poor Pasquale. He thought to reach for money in his pocket but was flabbergasted when one took her handbag and counted out a wad of lire notes and gave to him smiling. He looked embarrassed and confused and they sensed this, so they gave him a peck on each cheek and guided him to the door. One pushed him gently out while the other patted his backside, and it was over. Dreamily he returned to the street where he realised he had just been given 50,000 lira! Surely a mistake, he thought, and counted again. No, he had just earned 50,000 lira in an hour or so for doing something which normally men would have to pay for. No wonder the Germans lost the War, he laughed, as he almost skipped back to the underground. He needed to re-group, clear his head, get ready, so he returned to his depressing little hotel room and lay on a bed similar to the one he had earned money on an hour previously.

Yes, earned money! He sat bolt upright as the significance suddenly hit him---he had just done the same as his dear sister; he was no better than she! He had offered his body for money. This realisation brought him to his senses: it was like he had been hit by an icy-cold facecloth on a steaming hot day. He began to break out in a cold sweat but jerked himself out of it. Rationalise, idiot, think clearly! I am not the same as my sister, I did not know what was going to happen, she does. I do not have a pimp, I am not forced into it, I can refuse if I want. At worst I am a gigolo, at best a playboy. This is not my job. But it could be, maybe. Now there's a thought. There must be worse ways of making an easy living, and a lot of money at that. Oh, dismiss the thought, idiot! You have far more important work to do tonight: focus, rest, sleep.

A car horn woke him. It was 9.05pm already. He had not eaten all day, nor showered or changed. But he had to go, and go quickly. Revue the plan. Hurry. It's simple. Surely too simple? They must have fall-back mechanisms, one cannot just drive off with a prostitute, surely? 'Prostitute'? Even the very word horrified. What if they were constantly watching? Had a monitoring system? Worse, what if they followed his taxi? Ridiculous! But was it? Better to be safe than sorry? And would they hunt for Maria all over Roma? Or would they just accept she'd gone and forget about it? Surely there would be plenty more girls coming to Roma, like Maria, looking for the bright lights and ending up fueling the obsessions of men? But Maria was not just any girl, she was truly beautiful and presumably much desired in this line of work, a valuable commodity, an invaluable loss. Keep calm, think through the plan. Where will we go after? Back home? What if they know where she lived? Forced her to tell? Simple torture even? Stay in Roma? How? Where? So much not known, so little time to think.

But he did know one thing: this was no amateur outfit, they were professionals, well-organised and no doubt bribing public officials too. He would have to be so careful.

Fortunately, on the way he saw a street vendor, grabbed a panini, raced into the underground, caught a taxi at Central and arrived finally in Via Tratelli... late! It was 10.20 and no sign of Maria. He told the driver to drive round and return at 10.35 but there was still no sign of her. A little anxiously he paid off the driver at the far end of the street, walked around a bit and then returned by walking down the street again. At 11.05 Maria was there, but he had no taxi and had to walk on, head down, ignoring her. He felt eyes watching him at every turn. It was a quiet weekday night, few on the street. He resisted the urge to speed up or break into a jog and finally reached the lower end of the street in a sweat. He moved quickly and tried to procure a taxi. There were none about. Then two came but they were occupied. 11.35pm. Very late now. Ten more minutes and an empty taxi came and he drove round again. No Maria! Too late? Exhausted from the day's events and all this stress Pasquale decided to direct the taxi all the way back to his hotel. After all, his immoral earnings could pay for fifty taxis! He would have to try again tomorrow. Maria would understand.

Next morning, taking cornetto and cappuchino in a street bar, he reviewed the situation. Another day to kill, what to do? Reverting to tourist mode he decided to view the Trevi Fountain, Spanish Steps and Baroque Roma. The weather had changed and it had become unseasonally warm and sunny. Pasquale sauntered, as ever, along the narrow streets in tight T-shirt with jacket slung over his shoulder. His agricultural biceps bulged, his abdomen rippled and the tight jeans accentuated his lower manliness. With his swarthy tan he could have been taken for a sailor. Certainly a man in his prime, 35, commanded lazy lingering glances along the jostling streets from ladies of all ages, and even some men, truth be told. Unfortunately it was not long before he found himself in a similar situation to yesterday and as he rested at the foot of the Spanish Steps, underneath Keats's House, he found himself being admired by a distinguished lady walking with a young boy and a man in uniform. She smiled as she passed and Pasquale offered a nod and a wink as reply. The lady stopped at the first shop window and looked back, tossing her head. He heard her instruct her driver to take her son to the waiting car and drive him home. He should return in three hours and pick her up from shopping. As they left she walked purposefully down the street to a cafe offering all-inclusive lunches for tourists. She sat at a table in the window, it was early, and gazed back down the street. Pasquale, believing himself to be encouraged, entered the café, paused and looked around. With her eyes she beckoned him to her table.

"Buongiorno, signora," he mumbled sweetly.

"Pranzo?"

"Grazie."

It was indeed early and there was no delay with the 'menu touristique'. A simple but surprisingly delicious lunch of mussels in white wine, prawn pasta and tiramisu was washed down with a Montepulciano red. Not a word was spoken throughout the meal, but much was said in other ways. Her refined and elegantly treated features paid homage to a fading beauty which must have been truly stunning, and her immaculate clothes clearly indicated considerable wealth. Pasquale made to pay but she would have none of it, paid the waiter, left a handsome tip and muttered 'come.' She led him through a maze of tiny but expensive streets to finally knock a door. A maid answered, the lady gave orders, the maid grabbed a coat and made off down the street. "My friend's apartment," was all she said, and she headed straight through the elegantly decorated ante rooms and lounge to a bedroom, where she quickly pulled the curtains and started to undress. Pasquale moved to her and helped speed the process, she knowing instantly his passion. She ripped off his T-shirt and began to kiss his chest. He swung her round, bent her over and entered, instinctively knowing she did not need to wait any longer.

An hour later, 70,000 lira better off and a promise of a repeat tryst seven days hence, Pasquale found himself once again at the foot of the Spanish Steps. The low February sun dropped behind the buildings and he shivered. Was it with cold? Was it with delayed pleasure? Or was in trepidation of the night rescue? But whatever it was he knew there were certainly many worse ways to make good money, and he finally realised he was again performing a valuable service.

* * *

55

ANOTHER RESCUE

1 9 6 5

He dared not fall asleep this time so he hoped the three newspapers he'd bought would keep him awake. Then he visited a quality ladies' outfitters and purchased a thick winter coat of inconspicuous hue, long skirt, woollen jumper and brimmed hat, all in what he hoped was Maria's size. Initially he caused quite a stir with these requests until he chose the assistant closest to Maria's build and told them it was a surprise for his sister returning from the Equator. He then took an early, but splendid, dinner in the most expensive restaurant in the street and returned to his room by 9.00pm. He told the desk man that he had been pestered by men in the street and if anyone should ask for him he should telephone a warning up to him in his room immediately, no matter what their story. He added that he had no relatives, business or personal contacts in Roma so no false story of theirs would be relevant. Settling the bill in full and adding an extra 5000 lira helped the understanding considerably.

Maria was waiting this time. It was that easy. No dangerous taxi chases through slippery, cobbled Roma backstreets, no shooting of guns out of vehicle windows. An hour later the desk man nodded understandingly as they entered the lift to the 6th floor room. Collapsing on the bed they hugged as if they had invented this age-old social convention. Then Maria shivered, whether out of cold or relief, and her brother put her in the hottest, most perfumed bath he could arrange. Her singing soon testified to her pleasure. She clapped her hands at the clothes and the fact that Pasquale had even thought of it. They fitted beautifully even though she had lost considerable weight during her street ordeal. She grabbed his hand and danced him round the tiny room as best she could and they laughed so happily with the release of relief and adrenalin that always follows a caper. Suddenly the room phone rang,

"Signore, two men just asked for you and they threatened me. They are entering the lift!"

"Oh Mother Mary, we *were* followed. I knew it was too good to be true. They're in the lift, come on!"

They ran out the door, leaving everything and yet nothing, and dashed down the corridor to the emergency stairs. Just as that door closed the lift door opened and the thugs advanced slowly on Room 66. The siblings raced down the six flights as noiselessly as possible, through the foyer before the desk man could emerge from his office, if he dared anyway, and out into the now quiet, darkened street. Pasquale looked for the compulsory car with getaway driver keeping the engine ticking over and they were in luck because it was in front of them and he could see the exhaust smoking. They had five seconds to decide. Pasquale risked it. Holding Maria's hand he advanced quickly up behind the rear of the car, hugging the wall so the driver would miss them in his rear view mirror. He grabbed a loose brick on the crumbling wall, crawled under the back of the car, wrenched open the driver's door and smashed him on the head with it before he could even move.

Fortune favoured them because the blow instantly knocked him out. Pasquale dragged him out, threw him on the pavement and jumped in. Maria fell into the back seat and they raced off.

"Ping, zung," thudded two bullets into the back of the passenger seat after smashing the rear window.

"Maria, are you OK?"

"Yes. Just showered with glass on your lovely hat!"

"Well, literally hold onto it, it's the end of the street!"

The thugs continued firing but Pasquale screeched the car round the bend and out of sight. He immediately eased off the pedal so as not to attract any unwanted attention and they drove on directionless. After five minutes they pulled up and Maria jumped into the front seat. They sat there hugging each other, even tighter than before, shaking from post-fear trauma. Onlookers would have assumed them lovers, if there had been any, but it was already past midnight and raining again. They needed a hotel and Pasquale had the cash, grabbed from behind the sink earlier. But where at this time of night?

"We can't check in to a big hotel, too many questions, and small ones will be closed now."

"Yes, I know where, the airport!" shouted Maria.

"Of course, the airport, late flights and all that."

"Now all we have to do is find it sitting here in the middle of Roma past midnight in a car with no window," she laughed.

"Could be worse, dear sis," he laughed back.

"But would they think to look there?"

"We'll use false names if we can. Let's go."

✽ ✽ ✽

56

SWINGTIME

1 9 6 5

Over the next few days in the airport hotel room Pasquale learned the full story of Maria's plight. It had coincided with the onset of the Swinging Sixties in Britain which slowly but surely reached out to the rest of the West European countries, albeit in a much more hushed up form owing to the still-strict stranglehold Catholicism held over morality and lifestyle. Pasquale, in the spirit of full disclosure, even revealed his two sexual adventures and he wondered why such ladies could be so free and easy with their wantonness.

"I had no, er, no protection, sister, and they did not raise the matter either," he admitted.

"Oh you silly peasant boy from the campagna, they were probably on the Pill!" she laughed.

"The Pill?"

"Oh dear, my little big innocent brother! No wonder the ladies love little-boy-lost you!" and Maria had to give him a brief lecture on the wonders of the new form of contraception. All he could answer was 'wow!' and 'amazing!' Poor boy. And all he could think was, this world is certainly changing fast and what a sinful city Roma is.

Maria's plight had been all too simple and, sadly, quite common. She had first boarded in a guest house until she had been offered live-in accommodation with the permanent hotel receptionist's job. She had learned well and had taken up English in an adult class, finding the rudiments to be quite within her grasp. She even found a tutor for two sessions a week of scenario-playing hotel English, so with her great charm and rustic beauty there was not any way she was going to remain long where she was. Sure enough, she had attended an interview for the same role in a 4-star establishment and she had obviously attracted the attention of the personnel manager. A week after her appointment he was courting her around fashionable restaurants, theatres and cinemas, generating considerable gossip of nepotism amongst the staff, and worse of course. Maria hadn't minded, naturally, as the country-girl in her was head-over-heels for the big city lights. He had even persuaded her to feign marriage by buying her a cheap wedding ring so she could get a prescription for the Pill from the doctor. He paid. Then he had begun to feel sufficiently comfortable with the time span and the gossip to start taking her to parties. At the start they were fairly innocuous dinner gatherings or closed cocktail parties, but with the ever-increasing import of western methods of 'having fun' the parties began to get heavier. Hash and 'Peace, Man' to start with but soon graduating to the more dangerous hallucinogens like LSD and cocaine. Inevitably they would arrive together for the parties but more and more they would change partners before the end, so that very soon she found herself in one of the most extreme hedonistic groups in Roma. At first she could just about pull herself together for the next shift at the hotel but as the weeks went on and the drug habit accumulated she could hardly remember which shift she was on or not. Consequently the inevitable happened: two warning letters and a final dismissal with no reference.

Finding a new position was impossible on both counts: hung-over permanently from drugs and having no references. She slipped even more into the lifestyle and was only rescued by a hippy group living in a drop-out condemned apartment. Well, she thought she had been rescued but they only wanted the money she constantly boasted about when high. So paying for drink, drugs, wild hippy clothes and utilities for the group drained what little savings she had left in a few short weeks, with the inevitable result that the group drove her in their flower-power dormobile to a lonely spot and threw her out, literally. For two whole days she wandered aimlessly, clutching all her possessions in a tote bag, until a man in a car pulled up and asked if she had any problems. Blurry-eyed from lack of sleep and a hangover she nodded and when he promised he worked for a Christian group set up to help such women she naively believed him and got in the car. She was taken to a huge terraced house near the city centre and given food, warmth and a room of her own with many other women like her. She thought she had turned the corner and recuperated happily for a few days while the kind people there nourished her back to some sort of health. But when she was moved to another room in the house she quickly she realised all was not well and in fact the other women there were nothing like her at all. "Dear Brother, you know the rest," she sobbed.

"Merda, Maria, what a disgrace!"

"I'm sorry, Brother, I really am."

"No, sis, not you, those evil men."

"Yes, we were like prisoners the whole time."

"But did they pay you?" he asked angrily.

"Huh, we got only 3000 lire a client, regardless of what they wanted."

"Oh no! So they were pocketing a fortune…."

"Of course. But the other women told me I should be grateful as we were fortunate to get even that considering they housed us, fed us and clothed us. And of course protected us and gave us medical help when sick."

"Mio Dio! So everything was brought in, you were not allowed to go out, or shopping, or the cinema…nothing?"

"Nothing! They even had a cook on the premises to prepare our meals in a dining room. We ate in shifts, would you believe? They did also provide a lounge for the daytime but we never went there, having to sleep owing to exhaustion."

"Oh you poor thing. But are you OK now with the drugs and the alcohol?"

"Yes, we were never allowed anywhere near any of that, we had to keep a clear head for the customers."

"And are you OK with…with…er…you know?"

"Disease? Babies? I think so. A doctor came every four weeks. I'll spare you the details…"

"…yes please," hurried an embarrassed Pasquale.

"So there you have it. You know everything now really. So what are we going to do?"

"I'm hungry. Let's go down to dinner and discuss it there."

"OK, I'll dress nicely for you again. Thank you for buying these clothes…"

"…well, airports are not just for aircraft anymore," he laughed.

Over a pleasant and civilised meal in the airport's top restaurant they formulated an outline plan, after considerable deliberation. Maria obviously wanted to leave Roma immediately for fear of being seen by a client or the brothel workers, or being caught again by her previous 'owners' in a street sweep. She explained to Pasquale that, although it was not at all obvious, it was highly likely that the whole operation would have to be overseen or be blessed by the Mafia, and the police of course, and they would have far-reaching tentacles throughout most of the city. Who knows, if she tried to get a new job or accommodation someone somewhere would report back, perhaps. Pasquale was more of the opinion that her previous 'employers' would not be too bothered, plenty more girls where Maria came from, not worth the trouble of setting up a large-scale manhunt, or even woman-hunt, he joked.

"I suppose you are right, brother, I am a little fragile at the moment and perhaps I worry too much. After all, you are the clever Big Brother," she joked, poking him in the ribs affectionately across the table. "So what should we do, Mr Know-it-all, eh?"

"Maria, to be serious, I do have a lot of money, as you know, and so do you if you had bothered to access it. Incidentally, why did you not bother to use it and avoid all this trouble you got into?"

"It was difficult to access, I didn't know how to get it," she sulked.

"Weak excuse, Sis, you only had to write to me and ask," he countered crushingly.

"Suppose so. But also I didn't want others to get their hands on it. They would have taken everything I had. And would it have changed much anyway? It was a progression of events I just could not extricate myself from."

"True, I suppose. Anyway, I have lots of money and what I thought was, I'd like to stay in Roma for a while."

"Really? Why indeed?"

"Actually, I find it all really exciting here and to be honest I am totally fed up with living in Puglia in a small, boring, parochial town where nothing ever happens, everyone knows your business and there is nothing to stimulate me."

"Or to invest in."

"Or to invest in. Here there is so much life and so many possibilities. It's wonderful!"

"So?"

"So I thought we could rent a nice apartment in the rich northern suburbs…"

"We?"

"'Yes, you and I. We can have a bedroom each and keep ourselves to ourselves. Come and go as you please, obviously. I don't think those evil people would go that way, it is very exclusive there, you know."

"But, would we fit in?"

"Who cares? We have money and money talks."

"Yes, certainly, but what will we actually *do* in Roma?"

"I'm not sure yet but there must be endless possibilities for a handsome pair such as us!" They laughed and toasted each other with their fine Montepulciano wine of that same town, not the cheap d'Abruzzi red from further north. Their plans were interrupted by the pasta with black squid and fresh crab and the secundo piatti of seared chateaubriand with baby shallots. Then Maria continued, "do you know, I think I would still like to work in the hotel business. It is so lively and fun, yet serving people."

"Never a dull moment, eh?"

"Yes, people to greet and tourists to help.'"

"And thugs with guns racing up the lift to the rooms!" he laughed.

Pasquale sent Maria back to intensive English tuition; two hours a day with a very expensive Englishman who also tutored rich children. She even tackled rudimentary French and German too. They had found an exquisite apartment overlooking the Parco, but still extremely quiet and unobtrusive. The agent had doubted their credentials until Pasquale pulled out six month's rent in advance in cash, plus the deposit, from his pocket with a cheery smile. The papers were signed on the spot and the agent beat a hasty retreat, muttering something about them being some new pop band's manager or similar, and why it was so unfair that decent, hardworking folk would never be in possession of that kind of money.

Meanwhile, Pasquale took to the streets of a Roman spring in all its blossom and fresh-leafed glory, and he trolled the bars with a few well-placed lire notes to ascertain the name of someone expert at forgery. He found the statutory crinkly, wizen-faced old man in a statutory back street and asked him to produce an officially indented, letter-headed reference from the 5-star Seine View Hotel, Paris, recommending the abilities of one Maria Carone of Avetrana, Italy. He dictated the wording, a few alterations were agreed and 3000 lire later Maria's perfect introduction was ready. She was thrilled when he showed it to her and they agreed she should absorb two more week's lessons before seeking employment.

Maria found three suitable positions in top hotels and applied for all. Two gave her interviews and were most impressed with the Paris reference. A week later she received what she had been waiting for, the offer of a position as trainee secretary in the prestigious 5-star Vatican View Hotel. She hugged and danced Pasquale all round their grand lounge and his failing spirits were once again lifted when he realised what he had been able to do for his little sister.

For Pasquale had experienced little success in any new direction in life. For weeks he had drifted around the bars and hotels, meeting people and making new contacts. He had spruced himself up with new clothes and hairstyle and was still attracting a sizeable number of women. It was so easy. A drink or two in a hotel bar and then an invitation to their rooms. He learned quickly the different types of ladies he could target, usually lone women on business or visiting the city for a multitude of reasons. Single or married was not considered, they just needed to be on their own, or with another woman, as he did not need the extra complication of meddlesome husbands. He perfected rapidly the knowledge of their different approaches and needs and was always the perfect gentleman. He smiled to himself; he could now be officially classified as a 'gigolo' of Roma. Certainly the money over-rode some of the less pleasurable encounters and he began to be less and less discriminate as the weeks passed. Some of the women even told him about Roma's budding reputation in Europe, and indeed the world, for handsome studs such as he, and the city became one of the first ever venues of 'sex tourism' before it was even termed that. But he still lacked direction and purpose and saw this only as a pleasant money-making diversion in his life.

Meanwhile Maria was ploughing a similar furrow as before but being much more careful about it. After she had regained her health from the good living of her brother's money she also regained her magical Mediterranean beauty. Consequently she still received many offers whenever she manned the front desk, but she had by now cultivated many more airs and graces, assisted by her greater composure. Accepting invitations from guests was much more difficult anyway because it was frowned upon greatly in such a superior hotel and so if she did she had to do it very surreptitiously and only to the theatre or opera with dinner, and only with men on their own and of a certain standing. She drew the line at the inevitable physical contact from the outset, and that wheedled out a good many of the propositions straight away. Pasquale never once pried into her private life but he did finally enquire as to any budding romantic entanglements after a few months, especially as she had never brought any man home, to his knowledge anyway. She explained her rules and modus operandi and he said, "so you are basically a social escort, right?"

"Is that what they call us?"

"Yes, I read about it somewhere. It is becoming a huge business in places like London where commerce is flourishing and executives need to be entertained."

"So why don't we do that here? Look, in my hotel there are always men asking for a companion. You should see how many I refuse and I am only one of five pretty girls behind Reception. Multiply that by all the requests the concierge receives and again by all the hotels in Roma and …"

"A great idea, yes, Maria, let's look into it. I too will go and chat to some concierges. For 500 lire they'll even tell me where their aunty lives, you see. I will find out how many organisations exist doing this kind of thing and we'll go from there.

And so he did. He discovered quite quickly that there were one or two fledgling companies setting up but they were not really popular because most of their girls were just not suitable. "Prostitutes?" he had asked. 'Basically yes,' was always the answer. Most concierges agreed there were two basic scenarios – men who just wanted a prostitute to come to their room and men who needed attractive and intelligent companions for the evening who could make suitable conversation or impressions at either a dinner table or at a gathering or an opening ceremony. Sometimes they needed to pretend they were not escorts but someone else for authenticity. But more intriguing to Pasquale was the suggestion that it was not just women escorts who were needed: an increasing number of ladies were discreetly asking for male companions too in an equal-sex society fueled by women's liberation. He did not tell the concierges that he already had proof of that, of course.

Then Pasquale met with a sensible businessman he had befriended earlier and they discussed the best ways to attract such suitable women to join their agency. Ivano Fantini had made money in the entertainment business running a small agency for models. His partner Rene Marsillo had recruited a few people as actors for advertising, but they had both reached the limit of their endeavours because essentially they lacked the finance to expand, and the banks would not help, it being a high-risk business in their opinion. Their true assessment was, in fact, that such agencies were merely brothels without walls, but they would never reveal that openly.

"I have money," said Pasquale after considerable thought, "what say you? Let us set up Roma's first modelling/advertising/escort agency! Whoever we decide to recruit as an operative can choose to be one, two or all of those, as they like."

"Great!" replied Ivano, "we can advertise discreetly in all the local Roma newspapers and especially those in the surrounding provinces…"

"…and with TV, films, magazines and advertising starting to boom we can offer attractive rates for the best models," suggested Rene.

"And the best way to raise more start-up cash is to charge every applicant a small fee by making them agree to us taking their first five publicity photographs, here in our studio, whether we accept them or not," contributed Pasquale.

"And who said you were not a businessman, Pasquale?' Ivano and Rene laughed. "Isn't it called a portfolio or something?"

"Is it? How much money do you think I would need to put in?" asked Pasquale.

"Always it's the problem of money, or lack of it, eh?" reflected Ivano, "I have a little cash to put in it…"

"…no, Ivano, I have the cash, no problem…"

"Yes, but that *is* the problem, Pasquale, don't you see?" replied Rene. "No money, no partnership. Think about it, if you are the only one to invest in the company it will become your company alone. We would just work for you!"

"And only on a salary too," added Ivano. "You see, unless we put money in we cannot be co-owners and hence take a share of the profits."

"That's right, it would not be worth it for us. And remember, we already have a business each which is making money, nothing fantastic but good enough, as far as it can go, so you can see we are in a quandary."

Pasquale considered this for a minute. "OK, why don't I just give you a personal loan, then you put that money into our new company and you can then share the profits?"

"And who said Puglian folk were all ignorant peasants?" They all laughed and toasted each other, and the new company, with champagne. Pasquale paid the bill.

* * *

57

CARONE'S

And so it was. Carone's Agency soon took off and within a month they had enticed Maria away from the hotel at quadruple the salary. She was appointed Personnel Consultant with the job of vetting all the initial applications and then following the chosen ones through. Essentially, she was the nuts and bolts, the heart, of the business because she knew exactly the demands and could spot the perfect applicant from the rest. It was not the same ingredient throughout either, obviously: for escorts she could sense if the girl could maintain the man's interest, bear herself confidently and smile at the slightest hint, while for advertising she could sense the ideal father, boyfriend, daughter, bike rider, dog walker, you name it. For the modelling she attended their first photo shoot, sorted the carthorses from the thoroughbreds and helped put out the perfect portfolio.

For months, as Pasquale had predicted, they made a lot of money out of the portfolios alone, and they never ceased to be amazed at some of the impossible hopefuls who came forward. However, at the business end take-up was slow initially, but when July and August arrived and the hotels were bursting with tourists they suddenly found themselves overwhelmed. They had taken on an excellent lady as office manager to arrange all appointments and movements, but she could not cope and three more clerks were employed. Soon the office was jammed with ten staff fighting over five desks and six phones. Compliments were also pouring in from concierges and advertising companies to further boost business by word of mouth. Pasquale, in his daily 9.00am staff meeting. constantly called for quality not quantity, but it became increasingly hard to deliver.

He wrote telling Andrea of the booming success. She told Mino and within days over 100 young ladies' names, addresses and details arrived from Napoli. In an instant their prayers had been inadvertently answered and within a week twenty-one new girls were taken on, thirteen as escorts and eight stunning models. Pasquale phoned Mino to thank him personally and before they knew it they had set up a regular corridor of personnel movement from Napoli to Roma.

And then in September Maria took a call from an Italian television producer. He had heard off the success of Carone's and requested ten actors for a TV serial.

Maria replied politely, "we do not have actual actors on our books", to which he replied, "precisely! That's why I am asking. We have a strict budget on this new daily domestic drama so cannot afford many known stars. Can you have a look and see what you can offer for the parts? I'll send a man over with the details tomorrow." And so it was. Ten of their fortunate clients ended up on TV every night at 7pm. But more important, 'Carone's Agency' was clear for all to see on the credits each night too!

Mouths talked, suits conferred, and soon more phone calls came in: another TV drama, an agency making TV adverts, two magazines wanting models for a clothing shoot. Carone's was forced to move to a bigger office and employ another ten staff. But Rene defaulted three months running on his loan repayment and Pasquale was forced to take him to court to reclaim the principal. Rene also lost his partnership therefore, under the terms of his contract, but Pasquale did not mind in the least as he could now take two-thirds of the profits. The cash was rolling in! He made Maria a partner too and appointed her General Manager. This freed him totally, and after a year of hectic activity he could finally rest on his laurels.

Then the icing on the cake finally materialised. A Hollywood film company, International Studios, phoned to say they would be in town in three months time and they needed an Italian chief of police, a detective, his attractive girlfriend, three waitresses with speaking parts, a taxi driver with over 50 lines and about one hundred extras for varying crowd scenes, plus costumes. "They told us you were the best in Rome and you certainly checked out, so can you do it?" asked friendly Ed, the third producer.

"Absolutely, sir," replied Maria in a perfect but sexy Italianised English accent, "we can give you what you want and more, no problem. Just send the details and your fee expectation and we'll take it from there."

"You sound a mighty fine young lady. Where did you learn to speak English like that?"

"Oh, you'd be surprised, sir. This is Rome!" And Maria hung up.

"I've gotta meet that chick when we get out there, Helen," he muttered to his secretary. "Don't blow the deal, offer them 10% over the usual rates."

When the details arrived Maria and Pasquale were flabbergasted. The fees the studio was offering their actors were astronomical and after they had converted the US dollars into lire Carone's percentage was well over 3 million lire, plus a 500,000 lire finder's fee on top. When they had finished dancing round the office Maria gasped, "they're on a different planet in America, aren't they?"

"Different solar system more like! Heavens, that's what they mean by 'big bucks'. The phone rang and he listened, then said, "lovely, OK, 8 o'clock Restaurant Giraud. Ciao Bella!"

"Another of our ladies, Pasq?"

"Afraid so, sis, but I'm not telling you who!"

"And I'm not going to play guessing games. There have been so many I can't keep up!"

"Oh, be fair, not *that* many."

"Enough. And I wish you'd be more discreet; not good for business."

"Just the odd photo on the Celebrity Pages, what's the problem?"

"Odd photo? Its nearly every week now in one newspaper or magazine, 'Fashionable owner of Carone's with his latest date seen leaving Restaurant Another,'" she mimicked.

"Just a bit of fun, sis, nothing serious."

"Yes, but expensive fun!"

"Agh, we're making a fortune here…"

"…yes, but our overheads are getting ever higher too: it's not all profit, you know."

"Oh stop being a nag, I'm off."

"A round of golf? Drinks with the boys? Then a wild night with Miss Floosy?"

"Could be worse, dear Sister!" he replied, waving as he breezed out of the office.

Two months later International Studios arrived amidst a host of publicity and hoo-hah in the trade journals, the press and even local TV. Roma itself felt the need to keep the cash cow fully fed and to keep its name in the forefront of world cinematography. And this certainly was an event to celebrate after a certain lull in shooting schedules for nearly a year –a projected ten weeks of filming one of Hollywood's latest blockbusters. In their slipstream Carone's had certainly come of age and the newly-heightened publicity was more about them than the actors they had put up for the auditions.

"Everyone's a winner," agreed Ed Weaver as he eyed the majestic Maria Carone from the other side of her desk. It was not love at first sight for the simple reason that he had fallen in love with her that very moment she had taken that first telephone call. It had been fate, and he had known it, but he still could not believe his good fortune on seeing that she was even more beautiful, and fun, than he could ever have imagined. Maria, in her turn, was not totally disinterested either because she had to admit to Pasquale that he was a fine looking 30-something rather than the 60-something one assumed all Hollywood producers to be. He was also American, with all the excitement that country generated in a person's soul, and presumably rich enough to boot.

Production started after minimal auditioning, Carone's making excellent initial casting decisions, and as per the contract they had to pay the actors first before receiving their fees at the end of shooting. These salaries certainly drained the reserves of the company Pasquale had just said was 'making a fortune' and Maria certainly wished that her brother had been a little more circumspect about asking for staggered payments from the Studios in the contract.

Meanwhile Ed wasted no time wooing Maria, who quickly allowed herself to become fair game. They made another beautiful couple for the gossip columns to photograph and speculate over. Three days before shooting and wrap-ups were due to end Maria confronted Pasquale with some astounding news.

"Brother dear, I do hope you agree you have not seen me this happy for a long, long time, so you will be the first to hear. Ed has proposed to me and I have said yes, assuming I have your blessing. I leave in four days and we will be married in Los Angeles as soon as it can be arranged."

"Oh, I am so happy for you, if that is what you really want," replied Pasquale despondently. "So, does that mean you will live in California?"

"Yes.'

"'Forever?'

"Yes, I suppose. He is fabulously rich and has shown me photos of his home. It's got twelve bedrooms and an indoor as well as outdoor pool, a gym, a ballroom and three lounges. The gardens are so big you can't see the front fence! It's halfway up a mountain with fabulous views of the city and the sea. The climate is the same as here, of course, so that will no problem either..."

"...oh, please don't go on, I get the picture. Sounds absolutely fabulous. But will little Maria from Avetrana be truly happy there?"

"Sure. Obviously I will miss you but how can I refuse this opportunity? I have you to thank for it, you know."

"Me? Why?"

"Because you rescued me from hell and then paid for all those English lessons."

"So?"

"Well, it will make my life so much easier over there if I can speak English, silly!"

"True."

"And another thing. He has promised to get me into the movies. With my beauty and charisma and his connections he reckons he can make me a big movie star!"

"Really?" Pasquale feigned surprise and adulation, knowing how many others had fallen for that line. Up to that point he had been willing to give Ed the benefit of the doubt, even if he could carry pictures of some movie star's house in his wallet to impress girls, but he felt the man had gone too far with the movie star promise. It came straight out of a Hollywood movie itself and rang false.

"Well, even if he can't manage it, Hollywood? California? America? Yippee!"

"Yes, fantastic, well done. But do take care, sis, and tread carefully. Do you really know that much about this man? A lot of Americans, especially in that industry, are terrible braggarts and show-offs, you know. Is he all he seems? Is he too good to be true?"

"He's great, and I love him. Pasquale, don't spoil my happiness, please."

"No, I'm sorry. I really, truly am happy for you. Congratulations!"

"Thank you."

"Will he pay for me to come out and give you away?" he laughed.

"Of course he will. I'll make him! Dearest brother, why ever not?"

And four days later she was gone. The apartment felt like a tomb, International Studios had gone and Carone's was on its financial knees. It had not received a single cent in payment yet.

Pasquale phoned the company in America and eventually got through to the Accounts Department. Sorry, they said, they had still to receive formal approval that the project had concluded satisfactorily. That would only occur after a full debriefing of the personnel involved once they returned. Some were now taking a week's vacation and that meeting was not scheduled for another ten days' time. So Pasquale, continuing to struggle with the language, asked if the man could speak more slowly and simply and if some money could be wired on account in the meantime. He was shocked to be told that was not how things were done in America. After the debriefing the Accounts Department would need to receive instructions for payment, and then with such international payments as these there were many rules and regulations to negotiate. By now Pasquale was in a rage and demanded that the man 'cut the crap' (he thought it helpful to use their language which he had learned off the movies) and tell him when he would get paid. He collapsed in his seat when he was told that with these kinds of deals with overseas suppliers it could take three months or more! In desperation Pasquale threatened to sue them. The man replied laughing, "oh yes, in which country –Italy or USA?"

And so it was. Pasquale tried to get a bridging loan from a number of banks and lenders but the amount and the risks were far too huge. He tried to delay payments to all his own customers but being close on hand they could put pressure, sometimes ugly, on him and he had to continue paying them promptly. One bank did make encouraging noises but just at the crucial moment all the banks went on strike. There was just no way out. Within six weeks Carone's was put in the hands of the Receiver and declared bankrupt. It was as if Fate had been given the deciding hand and Pasquale The Born Loser had lost again.

Ironically, too, the money from America did arrive after only two months but it was too late and it was 25% less than agreed because of certain trumped up "operational difficulties and disappointments". No-one was in a position to argue over this, or try to sort it out, and so the Receiver just used what was there to pay off all the debts. In effect, it worked out that both Pasquale and Ivano just about broke even in the end, but neither had the heart or will to risk starting again. They shook hands in the emptied, cheerless office, signed the papers and wound up what could have been a highly-successful company. No-one could believe it: it was the talk of the town for ages in both business and social sectors. Both Pasquale and Ivano made one statement only –the truth—and tried to quietly disappear off the scene. That was not so easily done when the press railed against foreign involvement and whipped up anti-American sentiment at every available opportunity, but fortunately the Government intervened and cracked down on all such comment because it was damaging to promising and growing European-American relations. Soon other issues took centre stage and Carone's had had its 'fifteen minutes of fame'. Other companies quickly grew to fill the vacuum and made sure to demand staged payments from foreign customers!

Of course, by now Pasquale was accustomed to setbacks. After all, his life to date had been one huge roller-coaster ride of up's and down's. So this he categorised as a lesser down and in his heart secretly he had to admit that he would not have wanted to have continued in that glossy high-life style of living for ever anyway. He did not have to feel guilty over his staff either as they quickly procured new positions in the other growing agencies, most in some form of promoted post no less. He too still had his precious cash: the Receiver had not got his grubby hands on any of that.

So he went back to drifting again, moving from bar to hotel, hotel to disco, disco back to bar. He was seldom recognised after his temporary fame, maybe because he operated in night light and because he changed his hairstyle, but he still had his looks. The ladies still knew that and continued to cooperate, so he was never short of money or time. Once he was most amused when one lady expected him to pay her but he let her off on the basis that she was much younger and prettier than the usual rich dames. The tight young flesh had made a pleasant change so he had offered her quadruple if she would give up the game. She promised she would, took his money and a week later he saw her still doing the same. Oh well, God knows I tried, he thought, resisting the urge to go up to her and jokingly ask for three more sessions free!

He had no problem with God, and he hoped conversely God had no problem with him, because he did not consider he was doing anything really wrong, merely providing a valuable, safe and comforting service to his ladies. Meanwhile they afforded him cosy escapism into a world of opulence and charm. They were always so pleased with his service that not once did they threaten or cheat; they were always ladylike and grateful, so grateful that they often added a little gift to their bundle of lire. For fun he started to keep them under his bed in a box. One day a dear repeat client gave him a small, but dirty, stone oil lamp.

Anyone else would have shown insult but he proved his class by being most appreciative. "Etruscan, very rare, thank you," he exclaimed, and she was so highly impressed that he picked up three more of her friends' custom from her recommendation. However, he did stop short of telling her it was probably he that had found it in the first place at Ausentium near Avetrana all those years ago and it had finally made its way to Roma, doubling in value at each exchange!

Then he met Paola and he did not know what to do with himself. Paola Zecca was unlike any other woman he had ever known. Thirty-one, crew-cut hair, boy's physique in dungarees and boots with a belt of tasseled threads. She looked as his dear Mama would have said, 'as common as muck!' Little did he know she was one of the richest countesses in Lazio province and so for absolutely no known reason he fell hook, line and sinker for her. Together they embarked on the most crazy, hedonistic ride of their lives. Even when sober Paola was totally uninhibited and never was she at all predictable. Drunk she was outrageous and a danger to all within thirty metres! Quiet, shy, unobtrusive Pascale suddenly metamorphosed into wild, risqué, partying Pasquale under her spell, and together they left a trail of metaphorical destruction. With no Maria there were no boundary markers for his behaviour and he degenerated rapidly: alley sex, group sex, same sex all became de rigueur, psychedelic parties consumed more heroine than a pharmaceutical factory and the countess' supplier regularly ran out of champagne. Paola had to find a contract cleaner because no local women dared come to clean up the excesses!

One 5 am they both lay asleep at the foot of the statue in the centre of St Mark's Square, totally oblivious to the world. Two opportunist thugs robbed, stripped and beat them as they lay in their stupor, well before the Vatican guards spotted them in the rising dawn. The robbers had received something of a shock, however, thinking they had attacked two men but they were well rewarded by the booty they had discovered.

The couple were rushed to the Hospital of the Angels where Paola died soon after arrival –a cracked rib had burst her lung and vital arteries. Pasquale too had complicated injuries which took three separate days of surgery to aright and a bill in excess of 300,000 lire. The hospital had to wait until he had recovered as he had no next of kin and indeed not even a document with his name on it, only to find he had no insurance anyway. When he was able to walk again after a month of intensive physiotherapy an administrative officer and security guard accompanied him home in the taxi to ensure he could pay the bill in cash.

Two days later his bank statement arrived. His balance was 13,300 lire. Head in hands he sat on the bed staring at it. So 13,300 lire, plus 20,000 remaining cash behind the bathroom sink, was the sum total of his wealth. He was penniless yet again. This definitely had to be the lowest of all his lows! He drowned his sorrows in a 5000 lire bottle of brandy and collapsed on the bed with only 28,300 lire left.

* * *

58

ROOTS

asquale steered the last corner of the road from Manduria especially slowly because one of his favourite local views had to be savoured: rising above the low-slung terracotta roofs of Avetrana stood the outline of the familiar church and round castello. As he entered the centro around the ninety-degree bend the main street had also remained timeless. Half way down the street the same café's tables and chairs as always jutted out defiantly into the road itself. On the left the town square and spitting fountain were still the same discoloured tufa and cement, and old men still sat on benches passing their time on fruitless gossip which they called serious business matters. Only the new Second World War memorial at the end of the street was an alien reminder of an alien conflict already being swallowed up by the history books.

He drove on through, along the street that eventually led out to the low plateau top and the Gulf of Taranto's calm azure waters beyond.

There was a certain beauty to it all, he had to agree, but he soon came back down to earth on viewing all the modern concrete block houses being thrown up by the seemingly bottomless funds of the government's Mezzogiorno Project – staving off poverty, keeping families in The South, offering new improved living conditions and jobs. The aim was laudable, the end-product ugly. To replace the tiny tufa abodes of his childhood they could not even use new tufa still in the quarries; they had to resort to concrete because that was one of the new, burgeoning industries deliberately placed in Puglia by the Project to offer new employment.

Worse still, when he came to his old street he found it had all gone, even the house he had grown up in, to be replaced by two rows of faceless, grey, concrete terraces. But they did keep the street's name, at least. He did a U-turn and made for the nearest bar, carefully remembering he had little to spend on anything, let alone alcohol. "A coffee and a room to rent, per favore," he smiled to the wizened old bartender.

"The first is easy, the second is not," replied the barman, "a large tufa quarry has just opened up nearby and the workers have taken all the free rooms in the town."

"But all I see is concrete houses."

"That's as may be, but there have been so many complaints that the new policy is now concrete blocks on the inside, tufa on the outside."

"Typical! But didn't the company build their own houses for the workers?"

The barman laughed, as did a couple of bystanders. "You must be joking. They didn't think the quarry would last long and so they saved money by just offering rental allowances. But the joke is the allowances are so generous they have forced up property prices throughout the area…"

"…exactly what the Project did not want to do."

"Precisely. And more, the jobs were supposed to be for Avetrana men, so they go and employ workers from other towns!" The barman grunted and spat on the floor behind his bar. "Bastardos!"

"OK," muttered Pasquale, concerned that he had lit a blue touch paper, "so I won't find a room in Avetrana, right?"

"Yep, I know of none."

"But I do,' squeaked an old man sitting in the shadows of the corner. "My sister's lodger has just left and she hasn't advertised yet, as far as I know."

"Thank you, signore, can you give me the address please?"

"Come here then young fella."

"I'd buy you a drink to say thanks, signore, but I haven't…" Pasquale tailed away, feeling most embarrassed.

"Don't worry, young fella, I know what its like to be short. Now then, don't I know you? You look familiar, you know."

"Not unless you have lived here all your life."

"I have, cheeky brat. Look at me, where else do you think I would have been, eh?" the old man laughed.

"Then I'll give you a clue, well, two clues, Via Ardania and beans."

"The old street they just demolished?"

"The very same."

"Via Ardania and beans, eh? Hmm, I wonder..." he muttered as he walked out.

"I won't frighten your sister by turning up unannounced, will I?"

'Nothing frightens my sister, you'll see," he chuckled and carried on.

Signora Matera was a kindly old soul living in an old farmhouse, once in the fields but now threatened to be engulfed by development. She had refused to sell so many times the builders had given up and were carrying on building all around her instead. Pasquale quickly realised why her brother had said that no-one could frighten her. She had converted the outhouse into a tiny apartment, which suited Pasquale admirably as he could come and go as he pleased and be at no-one's beck and call, or constant scrutiny. The first month's rent he could just about manage but being almost double what he had expected it nearly cleaned him out. He would certainly have to do something quick to feed himself and buy petrol. There was no doubt he could no longer afford to drift; he needed a plan, or at least some help.

And then it came to him, in an instant, just like that, out of the blue.

His request was answered immediately. By return of letter he found 50,000 lire in big notes from his sister. She would never turn her back on him, he knew that, but he also knew how much it would have grieved her to hear that he had almost thrown away his life in a whirling cocktail of drugs and sex in Roma. So he could not tell her, ever.

Andrea had also given him her telephone number and told him to open a bank account there in Avetrana.

He desperately needed to hear her voice, Andrea his beloved sister. As for Maria, she was on the other side of the Atlantic and had always been the world's worst communicator anyway. He had not heard from her since receiving one postcard of Rodeo Drive with the Hollywood sign on the hill beyond when she had first arrived in Los Angeles. He had lovingly kept it as a prized possession to prove one Carone at least could be successful.

"Pronto?"

"Ciao, is that you, Andrea?"

"Pasquale? Oh how wonderful to hear from you again!"

"Yes dearest sister, va bene?"

"Yes, oh yes, we are all fine, thank you. Mino is now a..."

"Can you phone me back? I have few coins, sorry."

"No problem, hold on."

Pasquale waited for the ring: it seemed for ever.

"Pasquale? Yes, I was saying Mino has been made a lieutenant and you'll notice from our address we have also moved to a new house twice the size."

"Does it have a pool?" laughed her brother.

"No, but we'd like to put one in, for the kids. Flavia and Pinuccio are shooting up now, nearly to my waist…"

"Oh how the years go, sister…"

"Yes, indeed. And why have you never visited us?"

"Well, why have you never visited me, sister?" he tried to laugh it off.

"Maybe it's something to do with there being four of us to transport to one of you?" she laughed back.

"OK, OK, maybe I'll come soon, then?"

"Oh please, really. We'd love to see you."

"OK, I will then. Oh, by the way, some very sad news."

"Pasquale, I hate bad news…"

"…as do I. I have just found out from bar gossip, Cosimo passed away just last year."

"What? Didn't you know?"

"No. Did you?"

"You wicked boy! We came all the way down for the funeral, and neither you nor Maria were there. We were extremely upset but said nothing at the time. We didn't even know where you were to get in touch. You both seemed to just drop off the planet!"

"I am so, so sorry, sis. It must have been after the agency collapsed."

"It was in October. And Mino helped you so much with that."

"Yes, he did, and we were ever so grateful, but we fell foul of the usual cash flow problem when International Studios took ages to pay us…"

"…is that when Maria took off to Hollywood then?"

"Yes."

Pasquale knew how badly this conversation was going and he felt an absolute heel. He had to end it quickly before more revelations could occur. "Look, sis, I really have to go now, sorry. Can I call you again, please?"

"No!"

"No? What?"

Andrea laughed, sensing his horror, "no, don't call, come and see us!"

He laughed back, rather relieved by the joke, "OK, thanks, bye". That had been a worrying moment, because if ever Andrea turned her back on him he would be totally lost and rudderless, no one left of the family at all.

The cheap little Fiat had managed to stagger the 600 kilometres from Roma to Avetrana in two days, so Pasquale reckoned it could manage the 450 kilometres back up to Napoli. Like most things in his life he was wrong, and it gave up the ghost halfway up Potenza hill in The Appenines. A garage finally pronounced it well and truly dead, scrap value only, and he had to board the bus for the rest of the journey.

At Napoli Central he phoned Andrea, who was overjoyed to hear him. "That was quick, Brother, we didn't expect you this soon!"

'No time like the present, sister," he laughed.

'Wait there and Mino will come to collect you."

On reaching their lovely house in the suburbs Pasquale had a lump in his throat, and when he finally embraced Andrea again after nearly five years he could hardly contain his tears of joy. "You don't look a day older, sis, in fact even more beautiful."

"Oh brother, neither do you!" she replied, lying for all she was worth. There was no doubt Pasquale's life of debauchery, of which she knew nothing, had aged him more than ten years, gouging great furrows of depression across his forehead. Mino too had aged, although his rugged good looks still lingered along with a side-dish of white hair, but for other reasons. He had just cause to worry on a daily basis in his line of work: the more senior you became the greater a target you presented.

"Come children, come greet your Uncle Pasquale!" Andrea shouted to Flavia and Pinuccio, but instead of approaching with a run and a skip like the old days they shuffled cautiously across the wide kitchen floor. "Your uncle has been away, you've forgotten him, it's OK, give him a big hug."

"We will if he has something for us," replied Pinuccio cheekily, laughing.

Pasquale felt devastated. He had rushed from home and not even thought of the simplest thing, a gift for his nephew and niece. As he cursed himself inside Andrea immediately felt his anguish: the sixth sense of a really close sibling, one could argue. "Uncle's car broke down in Potenza and he had to finish his journey by bus. He wasn't able to stop to buy you something so he told me he wants to give you a treat in town instead. Is that OK? Yes?"

"Oh yes, they chorused, "the zoo, the zoo, uncle, please, please?"

"Yes, the zoo, that will be great. This weekend then," enthused Pasquale, smiling to Andrea and mouthing a 'thank-you'. Then he got the biggest hug in the world and he felt wonderful again.

"That's great," chipped in Mino, "I have to go to Roma so you can take over, Pasquale. I'll get you a car, a nice big one for the weekend, OK?"

And so for a week Pasquale played the dutiful uncle and brother in a lovely happy family. Although it constantly reminded him of what he had never had it did do wonders in repairing the mental damage of his last year or so, and when it was time to leave he felt almost fully healed. He realised just how much even simple, daily family life could be uplifting to the human condition and he ached to have it himself one day.

On top of all that Mino had been able to 'procure' a very clean, nearly-new Fiat for next to nothing and gave Pasquale the keys. "But I can't pay for this, I don't have enough money."

"Never mind, pay me something later if you feel like it, or don't bother, as it suits you. I'm sure its last owner won't be needing it any more," smiled Mino with a wicked giggle. It didn't take a graduate brain to work out what Mino was insinuating.

Meanwhile, Andrea too had agreed to send him some money monthly till he got back on his feet. Pasquale felt the need of a confessor and finally did not hold back on the events of the past five years. She had listened with sisterly sympathy at everything that had befallen him since going to Roma and blamed it all fairly and squarely on Stefania, not him. When he got to the business of Maria and Ed Weaver she became utterly incensed and decided immediately to open written correspondence with both Maria in Hollywood and Stefania in Paris now she had their addresses. "I refuse to let the Carone family fall apart just because our dear Mama and lovely Cosimo have passed on. Families are the cornerstone of our society and we *shall* be healed. And if this Stefania is indeed family, and my step-sister to boot, which I still very much doubt, and if Eduardo is indeed our father, we are going to get this mess sorted out once and for all!"

Needless to say, Pasquale was mightily impressed by this show of family and filial solidarity and he was fully re-invigorated for his return to Avetrana. Andrea had actually asked too why he needed to return at all. Sadly he told her he believed there to be too many unhappy memories in Napoli and he really wanted to get back to the simple rural life again after the excesses of Roma. For once, Andrea had nothing to argue.

* * *

59

LETTERS

1 9 7 0

'Dear Edward,
If I am unknown to you I am Maria's older sister, Andrea. I trust this letter finds you both well. Please excuse me writing such bad English but I got a friend to translate for me.

Also please excuse me writing to your workplace but we have no home address for you. Apart from one postcard to Pasquale, Maria's brother, our family has heard no news from her for quite a while. Presumably she is very busy?

Tell Maria we are all well here but dear Cosimo, her step-father, died last year.

Do let us have your news soon, thank you,
Andrea Orsini (Carone)'

'Dear Helena,
If I am unknown to you I am Pasquale Carone's sister, Andrea. I live in Napoli with my husband Mino and our two children. I trust this letter finds you well.

Please excuse me writing to your workplace but I have no home address for you. If indeed you and Pasquale are half-siblings then I am too your half-sister, as is younger Maria now in Los Angeles.

I personally do not believe this and I think your father has concocted the whole story to stop you marrying Pasquale, who he thinks is beneath you and your countess mother. I hope I would know my father better.

Any news from you would be welcome.
Yours,
Andrea Orsini (Carone).'

'Dear Andrea,
Your letter came as a tremendous surprise. Yes, I am well, successful and even a little famous here in Paris. Yes, I am your half-sister. Our father is very ill in hospital in Brindisi. I have no other news.
Apologies, in haste,
Helena.'

'Dear Edward,
Perhaps you did not receive my last letter of 20 August? I am Maria's older sister and I hope you can let us know soon how she is.
Thank you,
Andrea Orsini (Carone).'

'Dear Helena,
Many thanks for your reply, however short, as we know how busy you must be. My brother has had many ups and downs since you two parted so tragically, but at present I need to inform you he is most depressed, even to the point of suicide. He has returned to Avetrana. His mother died two years ago and his stepfather more recently. He feels there is little point in living since you two parted.
Regards,
A.'

'Dear Pasquale,
I hope you are well.
I have heard from Helena but not Maria. Helena is very successful, famous and rich in Paris. Our father is very ill in Brindisi hospital. She has given no other news as yet.
Sadly,
A.'

'Dear Andrea,
Thank you for the news about Steph. Perhaps I should find my father?
P'

'Dear Personnel Dept, International Films, Los Angeles,
I write after being unable to successfully trace one of your producers, Edward Weaver. My sister Maria Carone returned with him from

Roma last year to get married, after your film shoot, but we have not
heard from her since. Can you help?
(please excuse the poor English – my friend translated it)
Andrea Orsini'

'Dear Pasquale,
Perhaps you should wait before you try to find your father, in case I get
more news from Paris. Give it 2 weeks or so?
Love,
Andrea'

'Dear Andrea,
I am so sorry for my curt note previously. My only excuse was a big
order from Harrods of London and I had to fly out to Zurich the
next day. As you can see my life is rather hectic, but that should be
no excuse. I am indeed well, as I trust you are, but you are right. I too
never got over my parting with dear Pasquale and I have stayed single
ever since. Work seems preferable to the obsequious men I meet here in
Paris. And I too can never forgive my father, and that is why I refuse to
visit him in hospital, even though he is now in Intensive Care. Perhaps
P might find it in his heart to? Please give him my fondest regards,
H'

'Dear Mrs Orsino,
In reply to your letter re the whereabouts of a Mr Weaver, may I inform
you that he parted company with this Studio over one year ago after
certain "irregularities" were discovered.
We believe he found a lower position with Santo Films, address below.
I trust this helps,
Yours sincerely,
Bruce Daymon,
Personnel'

'Dearest Pasquale,
The news from Helena is not good ---your father is now critically ill in
Intensive Care. I think you should visit quickly. Helena is refusing to go.
She is still single, by the way, and never got over you! I still can't trace
Maria, or Ed Weaver, and she has still not written. Beginning to worry,
A
xxx'

Three days later Pasquale jumped in his car and covered the 55 kilometres to Brindisi in record time, for a Fiat that is. The hospital was easy to find, there is only one in Brindisi, but the ward was less easy. After seemingly endless bureaucratic delays he ascertained which Intensive Care ward it was and he rushed through the brightly-lit but badly-painted corridors with ever-increasing trepidation. When he finally found him and was 'suited-up' to enter the germ-free room he was shocked to find him so infirm and emaciated. He could hardly recognise him, in fact, but he reassured himself that it had been all of 31 years since that fateful day Eduardo had walked out and never looked back, a handsome, proud, upright man facing a better future but leaving a desolated family. And it had been almost six years since that fateful vetting session at the castello, much of which Pasquale had gone through in a fog-like blur.

Eduardo, in turn, although sedated recognised he had a visitor but not who the visitor was. "Hello," he mumbled from between the tubes.

There was nowhere free for Pasquale to kiss him, except on one hand, so he did, crying, "Papa, Papa, it is I, Pasquale."

"Ah Pasquale, where have you been? Off duty for two days?"

"No Papa, I am Pasquale your son…"

"…my son? No, you are my male nurse, don't trick, fool!"

"I am your son, it is me, after 31 years!"

"No, not 31, I saw you on the bus in Brindisi and helped you with the police…"

"…so it was you, Papa, I knew it!" he smiled happily.

"My son. You came to our house too with Helena, of course…"

"Yes. How are you, Papa?"

"How do you think?"

"Sorry, Papa."

"Isabella?"

"Passed away a few years ago, peacefully."

"My wife is sick too, evil woman," he gasped, tiring by the minute. "Why?"

"Tried to divorce me!"

"Succeeded?"

"No!"

"Papa, am I really Helena's half-brother?"

At the mention of her name Eduardo suddenly became rejuvenated and animated, "ah, yes, when I wrote to her I believed so, obviously.

Thinking of her constantly. She was born seven months into our marriage, bit embarrassing actually, but Valeria always insisted she was mine. ..."

"...but can she be trusted Papa?"

"I thought so..."

"...but didn't you know dear Helena was the one true love of my life? And why do you keep using the past tense?"

"Yes, I knew," spluttered Eduardo, starting to choke. Pasquale grabbed a glass of water and helped him. "I use the past tense because the last time I saw the witch she took great delight in telling me she had lied all along, all these years, Helena was not mine!"

"Not yours? So she's not my sister?"

"Yes, another man's, she said."

"But was that true, or was it just another way of trying to be mean to you, Papa?"

"Yes, I thought that too."

"So?"

"So what?"

"Is it true or not then?" Pasquale could not bear this waiting game any longer, he just had to know.

"I do not know. I hear she is dying. Go and ask the bitch yourself if it helps!"

"Where?"

At that moment Eduardo gave an almighty groan and tried to turn over. His tubes came loose and he was gasping.

"Where, papa, please, where?" Pasquale pleaded, wondering if this would be his father's last moment. As he waited he shouted for the nurses to come quickly.

"At the castello, she never moved out," he muttered as he fell into a deep sleep.

"Is he dead, nurse?"

The nurse checked his pulse and looked at the equipment, "no, not yet, but I can't think it will be too long."

"Thank you, Papa, please get better. I will come back, promise. And you can come and live with us, really, I mean it!"

There was a slight flicker of an eyebrow but Eduardo was dropping into a kind of comatose state. Pasquale waited a while and then rushed out.

As Pasquale drove out of Brindisi on the San Michele Salentino Road the journey started coming back to him. How would he ever forget it, all those years ago? The expectancy, the love, the embarrassment, their arrogance, his politeness, the inevitable defeat. The memories flooded back as he drove that familiar road up to the house, or more properly the castello. The building looked sadder than it had ever done, even before the Pintos took over the renovations, and he wondered just how run down it might be inside. He was soon to find out.

Fabrizzio himself opened the door, "well, well, never thought I'd see you again."

"You remember who I am? You were only a boy!"

"Hah, biggest excitement this house ever had, well, until my parents separated. Do you think I would forget that?"

"And you are now the butler also" Pasquale quipped in jest.

"Ah, lost all our servants and most of our money…"

"…never found that family heirloom, then?"

"What heirloom?"

"The Pinto treasure, just joking!"

Fabrizzio was partly puzzled, partly annoyed, partly amused, "are you here for a reason or just a nostalgic trip down memory lane?"

Pasquale smiled to himself and muttered "touché". "Yes, I was hoping to see your mother."

"And why would she want to see you?"

"Confidential!"

"Oh, whatever, I care little now. Come in, see her if you can stand it and then disappear again, please."

And so Pasquale mounted the stairs he had never been allowed to mount and he tried to enter a bedroom he had never been allowed to enter. Certainly the place was now bordering on derelict ---cold, bare, crumbling and musty. They must have progressively sold everything to stay alive, presumably. Fabrizzio blocked his entry and called out, "hello, Mama, pleased don't be shocked to death," he paused at his idea of an amusing joke, "but we have a most peculiar visitor."

"Yes?" muttered a croaky, straining voice.

"I don't mean peculiar in appearance or character, I mean peculiar in circumstance."

Get on with it, thought Pasquale impatiently.

"What?"

"Do you remember that awful youth Helena brought home once, years ago, well, he's here, now. Pasquale."

He walked into the chokingly-cold bedroom and took her hand at the bedside to receive the limpest of handshakes.

"Pasquale? Oh yes, Helena still talks of you in her letters, young man."

"Really? You are in touch?"

"Of course! She sends a little money each month. Good girl. How do you think we can survive?"

"Sorry, I didn't know. I lost touch with her."

"Her father said."

"Really?"

"Yes, told me some nonsense about you being half-brother and sister."

"Yes, Eduardo is my father too!"

"Ah," she choked, gasping for breath, "he wasn't lying then? I thought he was deliberately trying to hurt me when we separated. He did say he had been married before and never got properly divorced. I didn't believe him, of course. Then he reminded me of you and why you didn't marry Helena. He said he had told you both about Helena." Again she choked, the excitement was obviously too much for her and she had to lie back on her pillow and take a drink.

"Are you very unwell, countess?"

"Yes, dying, actually, or so the doctor says, cheerful man! Anyway, the man's a fool!"

"Who? The doctor"

"No, silly boy, your father. You are as ignorant as he!" she smiled.

"Why is he a fool?"

"Because Helena..." She paused to see whether Fabrizzio was still in the room, "is not your father's!"

"Truly?"

"Why should I lie?"

"No reason. Whose is she then?"

"Stupid boy, that will go to my deathbed!" Pasquale thought to himself, well you're close enough to it now so why not tell all?

"Have you told Helena?"

"No, why should I? You had gone. No need. Didn't want to stir up unnecessary heartache just for the sake of it."

"Would you tell her now if I said we still loved each other and it's not yet too late to get married?"

Valeria paused to think. Certainly this inspirational conversation was making her feel a lot better. "Don't see why not. Why should I care now, I'm nearly dead."

"Can you tell her then?"

"Suppose so. Get me a pen and some paper, I can still write, just about!"

And so the Countess Valeria scribbled a hurried note to her daughter laying out the facts, while Pasquale paced the room in utter heaven. He was overjoyed. Finally, my last chance, he thought.

'My Dearest Daughter,
Pasquale called today and told me what awful things your father had said about you and your parentage. It is not true. You <u>are</u> my daughter, but he is not your father. You were conceived before we met. How it embarrasses me to say all this. But please, never ask me to reveal your true father, he is now a <u>very</u> important person in Brindisi.
So go ahead and marry your Pasquale if you want, you have my blessing. I get worse by the day. Please visit me before I go, please!
Your loving Mother
Xxx"

'Dearest Helena,
I had two visits from a surprise person today --- my son! He misses you so. My wife has told you the truth now, I believe. I am so sorry I was the cause of your break-up with him. At the time I thought I, and the facts, was right. There is no end to the treachery of women. I cannot be blamed for being tricked so. If you still love my son, please marry him,
Your dearest stepfather.'

'Dearest Stef,
By now you should have received a letter from each of your 'parents'. We have been treated so cruelly by this world, is there ever any chance we can still be together? I love you so dearly still, perhaps even more so, but I fear it may all be too late. At the very least, please visit your parents. It will probably be your last chance so hurry.
Your ever-loving P.'

'Dearest Darling P,
Yes, the fates have been cruel indeed. I never stopped loving you too. I have made a new life full of success but empty of love and companionship. If we could ever blend both again I would be the happiest woman on this Earth!
I will come to see you and my parents on Tuesday, and I must also resolve Papa's secret in Via Corniche. Can you meet my flight from Roma at 2.40pm at Brindisi Airport?
All my love for ever,
S'
xxx

Pasquale got to the airport with over an hour to spare. He had been a cat on hot bricks all morning and just couldn't find enough things to do to stave off the time before their joyous reunion. He had changed his clothes three times, and in doing so had gone through his whole wardrobe! He had washed and polished the little Fiat till it reflected everything in the bright sunshine. He had bathed and shaved. He had tidied and cleaned his rooms. What more could he do, he thought?

Then he had heard on the radio thunderstorms were spreading west from Napoli and he didn't want to get stuck on a flooded road before he could reach the airport. So there he was, sitting in the little café in the Arrivals Hall far too early still, feeling both butterfly nervous and ecstatically happy. Despite his new jacket, bought with Andrea's money, and his clean shave he knew he could not throw off all the years that had passed so quickly under the Tiber Bridge, but Helena, dearest Stef, would not look a day older as she walked through that Arrivals door opposite him.

At 2.30 precisely the airport tannoy crackled, 'we regret to report that the 2.40 flight from Rome has crashed in a thunderstorm. It appears there are no survivors. Please check at the Information Desk for further news. Our deepest condolences to all.'

❊ ❊ ❊

60

VICISSITUDES

1 9 7 0

Pasquale awoke with a start. The man's foul breath must have been the catalyst. "I've brought you croissant and coffee, you must eat."

Pasquale eyes slowly cleared. Was it the old man who had witnessed their car theft? Surely not? I must be having the most weird dream, he considered.

He sat up with a jerk, nearly spilling the coffee, and his head began to immediately split apart. He howled in pain. "Hangover, I expect," grunted his saviour.

He looked round a small, dark, stuffy room with only a tiny rectangle for a window. Or is it prison, he thought, quickly trying to get to his feet. The old man sensed the situation and gently pushed him back onto the bed, "it's all right, young man, it's my bedroom."

"Where?" asked a bewildered Pasquale.

"Brindisi, of course. You used to live round the corner."

"So what am I doing here?"

"To be honest, I don't really know. Yesterday your car careered into my road and you fell out and asked me to help you. You were mumbling something about 'air crash, loss of your life'. You obviously needed sleep so here you are."

Pasquale started to regain some sense, realising it was indeed the old man from Brindisi. "I am so sorry, signore, how terrible of me! I just had nowhere to go and couldn't drive any further for grief. It's a wonder I got as far as here."

"But why here? Me?"

"I'm sorry, I knew no-one else in Brindisi but I knew you would be on your step...and you were." The old man laughed, at least he could still make a joke.

"Stay as long as you like, I'd welcome the company, young fella. But sleep now, looks like you need it."

It wasn't till a week later Pasquale felt well enough to go back to Avetrana. A week of fitful sleep, nightmares, fevers, sobbing and tears. A week of regrets, lost opportunities and misery. A week railing at The Fates. There could be no lower Low. Countless 5-litre glass pitchers of San Marzano Primitivo could not help either. It was the worst week of his life, worse even than Napoli prison. But as is the human condition he eventually felt the unquenchable need to pour out his troubles to another, first to the old man in brief, maybe as a practice run, and then in full spate to Andrea. She had known from the passenger list on TV that a Helena Pinto had been on board and she had guessed it had been Pasquale's Helena, but she waited dutifully to hear anything from her brother himself. He in turn could not bear to talk about it, and would not have had enough coins to feed a public telephone, so he decided to write to Andrea so that he could more carefully measure his words and his thoughts.

She replied immediately, saying how words could not express how they all felt in Napoli and how their thoughts were with him every minute of the day. Unfortunately, however, Andrea had to add more fuel to the fire. He read, 'Dear Brother, I have some more tragic news for you too. I do hope your heart will be sufficiently strong to bear it. Fabrizzio had found our address and wrote to say that your Father has finally died in hospital. It seems he left no will but mountains of debts, and these are being passed on to his wife, the Countess. Also by law all Helena's considerable assets will go to her mother who, even after paying Eduardo's debts, would still be a rich countess again if she survives her latest illness. Of course, if she dies Fabrizzio will inherit the lot!'

Indeed, this was nearly too much for Pasquale to endure and it took him another four wine-soaked days to muster enough strength to reply. And then he could only manage a 'Dearest Andrea, thank you for this terrible news. I am mourning but am still alive. Will write when more able. Love, P'

But he was not given the time to be more able. By return post Andrea sent a woeful plea, 'please phone me as soon as you get this, I am desolated.'

He rushed to the town's phone box, waited impatiently in a queue of four and finally got through.

"Oh Pasquale, we are undone. Mino has been shot!"

"Oh no! Is he alive?"

"No, no, shot dead!" Andrea shouted angrily, not at him but at it.

"Dear Sister, I am so sorry. What have we done to deserve three deaths in weeks?"

"No, five in three years, brother! The children are beside themselves. I told them it was a car accident. They will never learn the truth of their father, promise me that, Pasquale."

"Shall I come for the funeral? I cannot bear to go to Father's and it is tomorrow, I think."

"I cannot go."

"What? Not to your own husband's funeral?"

"No, idiot peasant, cannot go to Father's!" But it did make them laugh a little, or at least ease some of the tension.

"So when *is* Mino's?"

"Oh, next week, I think. But that's it, don't you see? I just *can't* think. The Camorra head is visiting tonight so I'll know more."

"Look, you must try to rest now. I'll come as soon as I can. Have you help there?"

"Yes, Mino's family are being wonderful. They will take the children in the meantime."

"OK, be brave, Sister, you must have known in your heart this may have happened one day…"

"I know, but it doesn't make it any easier," she sobbed.

Seven days later Pasquale was holding his sister in his arms. They both wept uncontrollably. But she maintained her dignity for the funeral later in the day and everyone agreed just how strong she was. The funeral was an enormous affair: it seemed a quarter of Napoli's entire population turned out. Everyone who was someone in the Camorra made an appearance, surrounded by battalions of security, and they each donated cash in the time-honoured way. Indeed, Pasquale was appointed 'chief cashier' and he soon began to panic before they entered the joyless crematorium chapel room when he realised just how much he was carrying!

"Don't worry," laughed one bodyguard, "you're surrounded by Mafia and no-one would dare to rob you here!"

"But after?"

"Again, don't worry, all is in hand. We will drive you on a detour to Andrea's bank so you can deposit it. But hurry, you must walk with her, you're her only family now, right?" Pasquale fought back the urge to start crying again, but it was true, the two of them were all that was left now that Maria was totally off the scene. But it did help him forget his own troubles for a while as he guided Andrea through the service, then along to the cars and back to the house. She could not have done it without him, that was clear.

Back at her house a buffet fit for a king, not a dead man, appeared out of nowhere and that strange Italian mixture of regret and celebration at such occasions began to manifest itself. Pasquale quickly found comfort in the food and drink until he was suddenly drawn aside in the lounge by a very important-looking man, dressed impeccably and with great bearing. With a calculated but subtle swagger he quickly guided Pasquale through the double doors and out into the garden, followed attentively by his two bodyguards.

"Boss," said one, "not too far out into the open. These is critical times and we are overlooked by that bedroom." He pointed to the neighbouring property's upper rooms.

"OK, Luigi, sorry. Now, Pasquale, isn't it?"

"Yes, signore, why are we here?"

"I don't want to worry Andrea at this time so I will fill you in, OK?" Typical of a Head Man he gave Pasquale no time to reply, but just continued, "Alora, Mino was one of my best men, in fact if he had had a little more experience I would have said my *best* man. He could even have taken over from me one day, you know?"

"Was that why he was killed, signore?"

"Of course," replied Head Man, rather surprised to be interrupted when he was speaking, "the poor man didn't have a chance, surrounded by shooters with machine guns. The undertaker did a remarkable job!"

"And it could not have been avoided?"

"You *are* an outspoken man, eh? Hm, I like that...sometimes," he said rather menacingly as he pointed a finger right into Pasquale's nose. "No it couldn't, essentially it goes with the job, I'm afraid. But please, do not mistake me, I too am devastated. And please, rest assured I *will* take reprisals, oh yes, I sure will! The Camorra rules this city, has always ruled this city and will continue to do so. How dare they think they can intrude on our rights?"

Pasquale took one step back as Head Man continued to get agitated. He saw this and quickly turned off the rhetoric. "Are you the Pasquale in Roma we once sent young ladies to, by any chance?"

"Yes, signore."

"And where are you now?"

"My agency collapsed because an American film company paid us far too late..."

"...bastardos, I hate Americans, braggarts and cowards." He spat into the flower border with feeling.

"And I!" Pasquale repeated the mouth exercise and they both laughed and cleared any foul air.

"You know, we could use a man like you here. Now that we have ascertained it is indeed you, I have also heard other stories about, how should we say it, your abilities."

"Thank you indeed, signore, but no thanks. I feel my future will be destined to be quiet and peaceful down in Avetrana. I have had enough of the world to last one lifetime."

"As you wish, but you always know where we are, and if you ever need help. Now, to business. Unfortunately Andrea's house does belong to us and we shall need to take it back. But we can wait, say six months, till she has got herself straight. Do you think that will be acceptable?"

"Oh, I am sure so."

"Now, whatever people say of the Camorra and its wickedness we do treat our own well.

Apart from the little donations you received today to help pay the funeral expenses we shall be making Andrea considerable compensation for her loss."

"Thank you, signore."

"Yes, considering poor Mino's rank and lost promise it should be in the region of half a million lire. Is that enough?"

"Oh certainly, signore, many thanks."

"Good. Now, I am not at my best at funerals so I shall go and find Andrea, give her my condolences and depart. Anything you want...you know where to come. Arrivederci!"

He swept off the lawn and back into the house before Pasquale could reply. Owing to etiquette no-one could leave before Head Man did, so as soon he departed there was a mass exodus. It was only after the very last guest had left did Andrea break down in tears.

Pasquale waited three more days before he felt Andrea was able to even think about the future, as well as him. For much of the time she had been sedated from shock and Mino's mother had somehow kept the house together. Eventually, and totally against Mino's parents' wishes, Andrea decided she wanted to get away from Napoli and all its agonising memories and return to Avetrana. Pasquale suggested they buy a house there together and she agreed readily. How strong is the bond of the early years in our lives? she considered.

And so it was. Everything, and hence the associated memories too, was left in Napoli and they returned to the town of their birth to repair the damage of the old and start afresh the new. At least it was something positive and mind-occupying and they were together again like the old days. Flavia and Pinuccio took to it immediately for so many reasons, not the least being the lack of need for a constant bodyguard restricting their every action.

But there was still no word from Maria.

***

61

NO FREEDOM

1 9 7 1

Nothing in the town was sufficiently spacious so they were forced to buy a masseria, a grand farmhouse complex, four kilometres out on the plateau top, with those self-same magnificent sea vistas to the south and the skyline of Avetrana to the north. Andrea considered that in a few years, with the new tourism boom and the free cash still being handed out from the Mezzogiorno Project, she could convert the copious stables, barns and outhouses into luxury rooms for sunseeking Germans and Dutch. After all, it was only three kilometres down to San Pietro beach with its crystal-clear waters and sandy beach, or only seven kilometres to Campomarino's longer beaches and pristine diving beds.

"You will have get used to topless holidaymakers around the farm, then," quipped Pasquale when the children were out of sight.

"Oh? And how would you know about that?" smiled Andrea.

"Er," panicked her brother, caught out, "oh, the men in the bars sometimes talk about the adult films, I think they call them, yes, adult films, they have seen in Taranto or Napoli..."

"...and you haven't, dear, sweet, innocent Brother?"

"Of course not!" he enraged, half in jest.

But they both thought the idea of a holiday guest house or apartments a fine one for the future. They could even be trend setters and both meet their guests at the airport and give them a hire car, all inclusive. Only the better clientele would be personally invited, of course. But they did not go so far as to determine how they would be able to recognise such persons from an advert reply!

But first they invited builders to tender for the primary job of converting part of the barn for Pasquale's residence, and only then would they enquire as to the bigger job. Most important, the whole concept excited them and helped take their minds off past events.

The children too were most excited about the masseria. They loved the freedom and safety of the countryside and the small nearby town, and they flourished on the healthy sea air and local produce. Within months life went on. It had to. It always does.

Andrea encouraged her brother to go back to doing what he loved best: antiquities hunting. She was sure there was still much to be discovered and, anyway, he had no income and she could not feed him for ever. Even after buying the masseria outright she had still been able to save some of the Camorra money and could just about live off the interest from these savings, if necessary, but Pasquale needed to be doing something to keep his mind alert and away from lost chances. He reluctantly agreed and thought it might be an acceptable diversion to re-discover his old collina near Villa Castelli, so the very next day he set off before sunrise heading north-west.

After an hour he reached the old farmer's house, as the sun came up behind, but to his dismay he found it abandoned and derelict, yet another victim of economic forces and hereditary disinterest. The track to the hill was even more rutted than he remembered and the fields all around were overgrown with weedy grass and gnarled bushes. So much for Mezzogiorno money, he muttered, people are still leaving in droves. He trudged to the top of the hill with deepening gloom and as he surveyed the panorama he felt no surge of enthusiasm, no love of discovery, no thrill of hunting. Andrea would be mortified, he thought, as he skulked back down to his car; all things die eventually, he considered sadly.

Andrea meanwhile had received a letter from the head of the Camorra, pleasantly thanking her for providing her new address and enquiring as to her health. He had also enclosed a small document for Pasquale with the cryptic note, 'this is not yet public but our contact in Roma Museum smuggled this copy out. It might interest you, or perhaps even allow you to get even with your incarcerators! Regards PD.'

Pasquale was surprised, to say the least, but he eagerly grabbed the sheet from a bewildered Andrea. It was obviously a copy written by hand of a new report just filed by a translator in the museum. He read, 'Tablet 74D-B-2 translates that in AD12 a settlement was created at the end of the Appian Way to handle provisions for the nearby garrison at Brindisi and to create a more pleasant place for the merchants to live away from army disturbance. It is a fine, small town with market place, wells, villas and merchants' houses like Herculano in Napoli.'

The attached footnote stated that the tablet was recently dug up in some excavations near the entrance to the ancient Hippodrome in Roma and appeared to be a kind of 'newspaper' stone placed for public view.

Immediately Pasquale was excited. He had never heard of such a settlement, he knew of none that had been discovered, and he was sure no-one was looking. Why would they? This was secret information not yet released to the public, maybe never ever to be released to the public. After all, why should today's public of Roma be interested in an ancient settlement site in Brindisi? But he did know two things, firstly the curators would soon send investigators to look and, secondly, it would not be easy to find. But they would not be familiar with the area or the terrain: he would. They might only make a cursory reconnaissance in the fierce heat of the summer Puglian sun: he was acclimatised. He decided instantly that this was a project to behold, no more Villa Castelli collinas, no more scratching around farmers sun-baked fields with a metal detector, this was the queen of projects. He knew it.

After asking Andrea to write a kind reply to the Camorra he sat down and thought long and hard. He needed to put his mindset into the situation at hand, in other words become one of the original engineers back in AD12 and use the kind of logic they would have used in order to locate the settlement. He quickly grabbed a pencil and some paper and started to make a Locational List:

1. The garrison would have been positioned on a fortified site protecting it from invaders from the sea,
2. so the civilian town would have been close,
3. but it would have been inland for even greater protection,
4. presumably on a hill or rise for views and cooling sea breezes,
5. but not visible from the sea
6. near a winter stream in the limestone plain or next to natural wells
7. with gentle gradient to the garrison for moving goods not entering by sea
8. ancient place names mentioning vineyards, farms, crops, or Roman names.

Oh, how he was enjoying all this! He could feel fresh blood coursing through his veins, his foggy brain clearing fast and his whole being suddenly alive again. I need a topographical map of Brindisi, quick, he muttered.

He warned Andrea he would be away a few days in Brindisi and was surprised to see she was not sad at all.

"I am so happy you have a project again! Go, and stay away as long as you like. Here is some money to help."

'No, Sis, I cannot."

'You'll need funds, silly boy. Now go!"

'But will you be OK with all those builders around?"

'I refuse to answer," she laughed.

He drove like a demon, again, to Brindisi and with his newly-purchased map sat at a café in the main square, recalling old happinesses and tragedies. Over croissants and coffee he pored over the map. The ancient Roman garrison was clearly marked just to the north-west of the present port on a small rocky hill, which made sense, so the town must have been within a five-kilometre radius of the garrison in the inland sector, but where? It could have been anywhere in a 25 square centimetre area of the map. Ah, he thought, just the size of a piece of toilet paper! Returning from the toilet he placed the see-through tissue over his square and started crossing out every isolated house and farm, on the basis that some remains would surely have come to light in foundations or by ploughing. He then shaded all areas that were low-lying or in natural dips, all slopes that faced the sea and all zones alongside roads or the railway line, for the same reason as previously. To his delight, and relief, the only small areas remaining were three patches: all collina where farmers might avoid cultivating, just like his Villa Castello hill.

He chose the most likely, being closest to the garrison, and drove there during Siesta. Being closest to the big modern town today the area was more populated and he had to be careful not to be noticed as a 'suspicious person', especially during this quiet time when everyone was home traditionally. So he systematically strolled through each parallel street pretending to be purposeful, but all the time scouring out of the corner of his eyes for any tell-tale signs of ancient foundations.

His search yielded nothing. But nothing a hearty dinner and a few drinks in a bar couldn't put right. At 10 pm he was on his fourth Peroni when a hand slapped him on the shoulder, "Pasquale, ciao!"

Oh no, he thought, turning, but to his great surprise it was Fabrizzio. He was a man already and Pasquale could see something of his father, and perhaps even himself, in him. "What are you doing here, Brother?" shouted Fabrizzio, above the booming of the jukebox.

"Oh, just visiting. Are you well?'

"Great, thanks. It's my birthday and we're on an all-expenses evening, funded by my dear late Mama's money!"

Obviously he had had a few drinks himself already so he missed, or totally ignored, Pasquale's reply, "Helena's money, you mean!" deliberately shaking free of the shoulder grip.

"Heh, don't go already, have another drink. Barman? Peroni's all round, per favore!"

"You said "late" Mama?"

"Yes, she died a few weeks ago. It's just little old me and all that cash now," he giggled.

"Don't you need to be careful shouting that comment all around, Brother?"

"Nah, everyone knows I am rich!"

"Well, you won't be much longer if you adopt that attitude."

"Ah, plenty more where that came from. Heh, big brother, I never really found out how you met my sister. No offence, but you *were* both from different sides of the road, really."

"Yes, no offence taken, it's true. Actually we first met in her pottery shop…"

"…oh, the one Papa bought her in Grottaglie to get some men off his back from trading problems."

"Really? Is that what happened?"

"Yes, really. Papa never stopped talking about how wonderful she was…"

"…she was," agreed Pasquale, by now beginning to be choked with memory and emotion.

"…and how clever he'd been to pick that shop…"

"…pick it, what do you mean?"

"Well, it wasn't all for Stef, you know, however good a potter she was. I can remember him telling me he was having problems with his business and he needed more storage, or something."

"Storage?"

"Yes. He described a secret room at the back but I don't think he ever got the chance to use it. It was a long time ago and I was only a boy. Most of what he said was gibberish to me at the time."" "I expect so. But what actually *was* his business?'

"Do you know, we never really knew! All he would ever say was 'import and export'. That could mean anything …"

"…and everything!" They both laughed. "Fabrizzio, you said Helena and I were like chalk and cheese…"

"…yes. So?"

"So were our parents, you know."

"Our?"

"Of course, we are half-brothers now, have you forgotten?"

"No, of course not, stupid! But does that mean you can have half the money, then?" he added worryingly.

"No, please don't worry, it is yours. But please don't drink it all away, be sensible."

"OK, I'll try. It's just, I've never had money before and Mama really scrimped and saved. You know? We always acted as if we were destitute."

"You probably were, at the time. Papa was a peasant labourer from Avetrana, didn't you know?"

"No, really?"

"See, we have so much to learn from one another."

"Right, let's drink to that!"

"And all that talk about the Pinto heirloom, the family fortune?"

"Never found. Anyway, I don't believe it, not one jot. Never did. It was never mentioned in Mama's will, either. Pure family gossip. Another beer?"

"Please. And get your friends over, they are looking thirsty again."

Next morning, with fuzzy head and blurry vision, Pasquale attempted Hill Two. In a short while he made an important find. And then another. And another. He plotted each one on a larger scale map and continued to find evidence. By the end of the day a definite pattern had emerged and he jumped for joy. A fairly oval-shaped site, at least 20 hectares, seemed to have been laid out over the small collina and down its eastern and southern sides. Under bushes Pasquale found remains of ancient walls too, to add to the foundations scattered all over. He could hope for little more surface evidence, but only excavation through nearly 2000 years of soil and loose rock would yield the real proof. So had he in fact found the ancient town of Brindisia?

Everything moved so quickly from there: it had to. Those bureaucrats in Roma Museum took months to deliberate on most things, and probably more so in this case with no-one else knowing about it, but someone there might finally realise the significance of that ignominious little tablet and bring it to someone else's attention.

Fabrizzio gave him, not lent him, sufficient money to buy the wasteland site and to hire ten freelance archaeologists, with all their equipment, to make an initial reconnaissance. Seven men and three women duly set up camp out of sight of the small, local road running past and began their digging and scraping. As the weeks went by news of the find leaked out and Pasquale had to hire an expensive security team to keep TV, radio, reporters and souvenir hunters at bay twenty-four hours a day. They were all reporting it as 'the find of the century' and as each new day revealed some further discovery or other the Press fever grew. Pasquale had to leave Andrea's and move to an apartment in Brindisi owned by one of Fabrizzio's many friends. Andrea did not mind, she was happy that her brother was more like his old self again. And she was even happier when he eventually told her he had a 'kind of arrangement' with one of the lady archaeologists. They had made a connection right from the start on a lonely, strangers-in-the-night basis, but as the weeks passed so their affection grew. Livia was North Italian, from Turin, and her fair skin needed protection from the Puglian sun. She wore a wide-brimmed hat around which she fixed a Juventus football team banner. That was actually the first thing Pasquale had spotted and it was a wonderful opening gambit that they were both supporters of such a prestigious Serie A Turin team. Fortunately too, it was one of the few years that Bari had made it to Italy's premier league and they were able to go together to watch them thrash Bari 4-1 in Bari. Livia was everything Pasquale needed, although he did not necessarily realise it at first, and her playful, youthful, extrovert outlook to life pulled him quickly out of his depression, as also did Brindisia, of course.

But first and foremost his priority was to the Dig. As these weeks passed it became patently clear that a reasonable size town, by ancient standards, was resurrecting from under the soil. Where there seemed little of sensitive value, such as pottery and coins, larger scrapers could be employed, and they quickly revealed a whole network of streets and house foundations. It was not the same as Pompeii or Herculano, nothing could be, because it had never been buried under huge quantities of Vesuvio's soft ash and cinder to leave almost fully intact homes, temples and theatres, but it was a substantial find worthy of visiting. He decided that all of the less valuable artifacts could be displayed in cases at the house where they were discovered, using new Perspex plastic. He announced this at a staff meeting one morning.

"Oh dear, does that mean we will be opening the site to the public?" asked Julio, the chief archaeologist.

"Sorry, did I not tell everyone this?" replied Pasquale.

"No," they chorused.

"Scusa, I have so much to think about, I thought I had told you. Yes, we are destined to become Puglia's number one tourist destination, I will see to that. We will open the whole site with proper walkways and direction signs, we will have a permanent funfair for the children and young people near the gate, with a Roman theme of course, we will have a restaurant, snack bars, guides and maps. There will be short, medium and long walks laid out with different coloured markers and we'll have self-guide programmes in at least five languages. I plan to keep entry fees down. Under-16's will be free and there will be special rates for schools and groups. We will advertise in every school, travel magazine and newspaper, though I think the Press are doing enough free advertising for us already."

"My, you *have* thought of everything," purred Livia appreciatively.

The other staff shot meaningful glances between each other, mainly in protest, but what could they do? They were only hired to reveal the treasures of Brindisia; what happened after that was out of their hands.

And so it was. Brindisia opened with fanfares of trumpets, actually local marching bands to be precise, two years after its discovery. Pasquale organised a parade which marched from the outskirts of Brindisi to the gates of the site. There were bands, flag-throwing troupes, a hoard of Roman centurions in full marching dress, flame-throwing performers, stilt walkers, jugglers, copious residents encouraged to dress in togas, some camels, elephants and tigers from Oria Zoo, and they were all headed by a Roman Emperor and his entourage of beauties and advisors. Pasquale had thought about taking the part of the emperor himself, with Livia as his empress, but shyly backed out at the last minute.

It was fortunate he did because he was needed everywhere to organise, cajole, troubleshoot and smile. The first problem was the turnstiles - they were just unable to cope with the crowds. Then the car park became fuller quicker than expected and cars were lining the small approach road and even the main road into Brindisi. Then the funfair suddenly stopped and it took a while to work out that some meddlesome youths had thrown the too-easily accessible main electrical switch.

Without panicking Pasquale told the ticket office to open all the gates for free entry in order to clear the growing queues. They put up hasty signs apologising and saying that patrons would pay half price on exit and those already paid should keep their tickets as proof for a refund. The latter was unlikely to be any problem as they were special first-day tickets and perhaps collectible souvenirs one day. So the pressure was relieved within minutes and the Chief of Police could relax a little. He too was on display, of course, because the national television channel, no less, was covering the Grand Opening, as well as Press and radio from all over. It was the biggest day in the history of Puglia for a very, very long time.

At 3 pm, exactly as scheduled, the Chief Minister of Puglia arrived with the Italian Minister of Culture and Antiquities, leading a huge entourage of lesser bureaucrats. From a hastily-erected stage each was to give a fitting speech. Pasquale too had to make a speech and he began to shake with fear. He had earlier sought help from both Livia and Andrea, who was also a guest of honour with her children, but he was still uncertain as his moment approached. He could also see Fabrizzio beaming with pleasure as he serenaded the dignatories. No wonder -- Pasquale had asked him to be a primary stakeholder to finance the development of the theme park, and he was beginning to realise that his investment could skyrocket into infinity if this was any measure of the park's popularity. It would come as no surprise that another major stakeholder was PD from Napoli (in his own name, of course, not his company)!

And then it was Pasquale's big moment. Shaking, he told the watching world how he had developed his interest in antiquities and archaeology from boyhood [the first true, the second not, of course] and after thirty years he thought he knew all the existing sites in Puglia. But this find really came out of the blue, thanks to a dear friend in Napoli. He had been fascinated with the rumours of Brindisia all his life but believed them to be just that, rumours, until one day it dawned on him that such a town would have had to have been close to the garrison. Along with other locational requirements, upon which he did not broach, it merely became trial and error on the three possible sites thrown up by his theory. This was the second site. He still didn't know what was at the third. [that caused quite a long bout of laughter]. He

then finally wished everyone a happy, enriching day and asked the two
ministers to formally declare the park open.

After what seemed minutes of thunderous applause the crowd finally
hushed for the Chief Minister. He expressed his tremendous gratitude
to Pasquale for finding this wonderful ancient site and for the much-
needed boost to tourism it would give to not only Puglia but also to
our proud country, supplying work and putting the province back on
the map. More cheers.

Finally the Italian Minister, who ranked most important of all
present, thanked Pasquale again and reiterated just how important was
this find regionally, nationally and internationally. It too had been a
dream he had cherished, finding the site of the mythical Brindisia, and
he believed its true importance to Italy had not been completely revealed
yet. Finally, he hoped that when the time came for Signore Carone to
return the site to the nation as a national treasure he would feel the
compensation worthwhile [barbed criticism of both Pasquale and the
Law]. In the meantime if it could enthuse a whole new generation into
wanting to reach out to more of our history and culture then it would
be a job well done and a project's aim well achieved.

Ribbons were cut, handwaves were exaggerated and a Roman
dance show ensued. Meanwhile the official party was guided to the
exit and whisked away in official cars to a grand outdoor banquet
overlooking Brindisi Harbour, hosted by Puglia's chief minister.
No expense was spared and still the TV cameras followed them.
Gastronomia and Primitivo gave way to dancing under the stars, and
finally Pasquale felt a sense of purpose and peace. Livia accepted his
proposal willingly and happily.

* * *

62

WEDDING BELLS AGAIN

1 9 7 1

"Hello Andrea, it's been a while!"

Andrea nearly collapsed on her front step seeing him beaming at her. Although more than ten years on he looked not a day older, and he certainly appeared to be better presented than ever. "Er... hello to you too. How did you find me?"

He just stared for a short while and then broke out into a smile, "remember who I work for?"

"How could I forget?"

"Yes, but those days are long gone now, Andrea, it's a new world order."

"I suppose so," she tried to reply politely and non-committally.

"Look, I am so sorry to hear of your loss..."

"...thank you," again with little emotion.

"Are you OK?"

"Yes."

"Well, aren't you going to invite me in? It's taken a while to get here."

"Oh, sorry, excuse my manners, please. A drink of something?"

"Some cold water would be very welcoming, thanks."

The children came running into the kitchen on hearing a man's voice, but they were disappointed to see it was not Pasquale returning in triumph. "Where is Uncle Pasquale, Mama, is he OK?" asked Flavia.

"Has this man brought more bad news, Mama?" added Pinuccio.

Andrea laughed, "no darlings, we have had enough bad news to last us a lifetime!"

"Can I offer any good news, then?" asked their visitor charmingly.

"How so, signore?"

"Well, for instance, how are you coping?"

"Well enough, signore," replied Andrea haughtily.

"But where are you getting money from to live?"

"Is that your business, signore?" demanded Pinuccio defiantly, fast assuming the role of little man of the house in the absence of his father.

"That depends on you, I suppose," he smiled, taken aback somewhat by the boy's forwardness.

Andrea chose to ignore this remark, well aware that her 'Camorra' funds were running down faster than she expected. Instead she attempted to change the subject entirely. She half mocked, "does your wife know you are here?"

"My wife?"

"Yes, what would she say if she knew you were calling on strange ladies?"

But he was not easy to fluster. He smiled again and replied, "strange? Hardly, I think."

"You know what I mean!" smiled Andrea, even if the tension was still running high.

"Do I?" He was beginning to irritate in his attempt to humour her and to be friendly, and when he saw her face darkening he realised it. "Andrea, so sorry, just a bit of fun. Actually I am not married, never did marry, and I'm still waiting for the right lady to come along."

"It will be a very long wait, then!" laughed Pinuccio. Everyone burst out laughing too, unable to believe that one so young would dare to offend an adult like this.

"Oh Pinuccio, you cannot say things like that to a grown-up," smiled his Mother in fun.

"It's OK, Andrea, quite the little comedian, what fun! But seriously, I have despaired about this for so long, year after year has passed me by and I suppose I had got used to the situation."

"You said 'had'. Has something changed then?" asked Andrea.

He fidgeted uncomfortably. "Yes, well, maybe. When I heard of your tragic loss I thought maybe I could..." He paused nervously.

"...could what?" demanded Andrea.

"Er...could maybe..."

Just then the front door slammed and the children jumped up, clapped their hands and ran out screaming, "Pasquale, Uncle Pasquale!"

Andrea leapt up too, much relieved to not have to hear what she had been dreading, "you must excuse me, my brother is home from his wonderful opening of Brindisia."

"Yes, absolutely amazing! How far he has come in ten years."

"Oh, you remember him then?"

"Of course, how could I forget? I shall be happy to see him."

"But will he you?"

"Certainly. We have happily…er…done business together."

Pasquale staggered in, towing a giggling child on each leg. "Oh, Damiano, what a surprise! Where have you come from?"

"The past, dear friend, the past!" he laughed.

"Hoping to catch up with the present it seems?"

"And meddling with the future, perhaps?" added Andrea sarcastically.

"And you say you do not know me, Andrea!" Damiano laughed.

"Huh, I have known plenty like you. Too many, actually."

"So you will be used to our type, then," he countered.

Pasquale felt he needed to intervene, wondering what had transpired before he had arrived home. "Excuse me, when you two children have finished playing, shall we all have a drink?" Flavia and Pinuccio looked confused. "No, not you two, the grown-ups here," he laughed.

"Great! But what are we celebrating, then?" asked Damiano.

"Pasquale has plenty to, and maybe you do too, Damiano?" said Andrea, attempting to stir the pot again, maybe for fun. "Children, please go and play, we need to talk."

"Look, Pasquale, well done with Brindisia, long may it satisfy you after all your troubles," said Damiano with genuine feeling, "but I did not come here today to say that, however important it is, I came here today to…"

"…yes, why exactly did you come then?" demanded Andrea.

"Oh Lord, does everyone in this house interrupt so?"

"So sorry, please continue," said Pasquale.

Damiano realised he had had the wind taken out of his sails, deliberately, and he now understood that the stories about Andrea being a handful were completely accurate. It excited him even more, even though it castrated his lengthy introductory words. He just had to blurt it out now, otherwise he would appear foolish, because it was now clear to all why he was here. "I have come here today to offer a service…"

"…a what?" both siblings spluttered and laughed. "Have you come to sweep our chimneys? Or unblock the sink? Maybe to re-polish the floor?"

Poor Damiano. He knew he was defeated and he felt like crawling down any available hole. But he puffed up his pride for one more go, "although it may not seem so at present, perhaps with time respect could grow, and I would do my utmost to help it."

"What *are* you blathering on about, old friend? You have totally lost me," said Pasquale, more quietly and seriously.

Andrea butted in. "Brother, foolish Brother, this oaf has come here today to ask me to…"

"…marry me!" interjected Damiano triumphantly.

"Oh Mary Mother of God," cried Pasquale, collapsing into a chair, "how wonderful! Now, *that* calls for a drink. Prosecco everyone?"

"Hold on, Brother, what do you think you are doing? Drink? Such a gesture acknowledges a celebration of some kind is in order. Don't you think you have jumped the gun a little?"

"Oh, didn't you say yes earlier, then?"

"No!"

"Why not?"

"Why not? Because he is a …"

"…er, excuse me, I am still in the room," smiled Damiano nervously.

"Now look who is interrupting!" said Andrea with feeling.

"Yes, sorry, but look, Andrea, you can tell me to my face your reply, you don't need to use your Brother as an intermediary. I *am* here, you know."

"Oh, can I? Are you sure? How silly of me. What a pathetic, subjugated female I am," she smiled, curtsying and touching her forelock in mock acquiescence as she spoke. "Damiano, nothing would give me greater pleasure…"

"…oh thank you, dear Andrea," said Damiano, grabbing her hand and kissing it, "thank you…"

"….than to refuse you!" Andrea snatched her hand back and stood full square, glaring at him, hands dangerously on hips.

"What? No? Are you saying no?"

"Yes… I… am…saying… no," she repeated slowly, stressing every syllable as if speaking to a baby.

"But, dearest Andrea, I have come to rescue you…"

"…from what, pray?" enquired Pasquale, keen to register that he was still here too, and in the conversation.

"From despair, poverty and …and…"

"Precisely! And that is why I am saying 'no'. It is no basis for a marriage."

"But, Andrea, I love you. You are still the most beautiful woman in these parts. That is why."

"Huh, easy words. Do you think I want to be in debt to a man all the rest of my life?"

"Or until you get shot, friend?" posed Pasquale.

"Insensitive and unkind as ever, dear Brother?"

"Sorry, Sis, but its true."

"Of course not," continued Damiano, "look Andrea, I have loved you all these years, before even that time we met, and I have never taken a wife because of you."

"Huh!"

"Seriously, ask anyone. Ask Mario in Taranto if you like. Pasquale knew him well and he was never a liar. Ask…"

"…you lie, signore," countered Andrea.

"No, my dearest, I could never lie to you. My passion for you has burned like an unlit flame all these years and…"

"….how can a flame burn if it is an "unlit flame", you oaf!"

"Well done, Sister, you tell him!" cheered on Pasquale, enjoying every minute of this amorous warfare. "But seriously, you could do much worse. Not everyone is willing to take on two near-teenage children these days, you know…"

"What? Marry into another Mafia organisation and have my life ripped apart again? I think not."

"But, Sis, think for a minute, if it had not been for this man standing in front of you, you might *still* be running away from that evil Tonino today! Or, even worse, married to him!"

"Ah, Pasquale," mumbled Damiano, rather worried, "I *was* hoping you would not mention that little piece of history today…"

"…you mean it was *you* who killed Tonino?" demanded Andrea.

"Er…in a manner of speaking, I suppose so," he replied hesitantly.

"I'm speechless!"

"Oft considered the best state for a woman and a wife!" laughed Pasquale.

"You horrible Brother! This is the 70's; we have electricity, flush toilets, The Pill and Women's Rights, so be mindful!" she laughed.

"Pray, a moment's silence for the wonderful Mezzogiorno Fund then," he quipped. They all laughed and the tension was broken at last.

"But in all seriousness, how could I marry a man who badly let me down all those years ago in Taranto? It was you, wasn't it? Asked Andrea.

"Heh, Sis, how did you know it was Damiano that failed to turn up in the car? I never told anyone!"

"Oh yes you did, Bruv, in your sleep that night we had to take shelter."

"And you kept quiet about it all these years...?

"...excuse me, I *am* here, you know! Yes, that was one of the worst things in my life; that car I borrowed broke down on me and I never got to tell you because you disappeared for ever the next day. I am so truly sorry for..."

"...ah, water under the bridge now, but I did always wonder why you let us down."

"So now we know the truth," exclaimed Andrea, "but as Pasq says its not important any more, and certainly your rescue of me from Tonino and the elimination of Starsi more than made up for that, dear."

"You called me dear..." perked up Damiano.

"...just a figure of speech, I can assure you!" she countered. "Pasquale, are you marrying your wonderful Livia, then?"

"Yes, I think I'd better, before life is too late..."

"...then I'd better marry this fellow as well then, and we can save money by having a joint wedding!" she announced.

Damiano rushed forward to hug her but she pushed him away most rudely and shouted, "take care, you are only marrying me. I did not say anything else!"

They all collapsed in laughter on the chairs and Pasquale reached to open the prosecco.

And so it was. One month later the double wedding was cemented in Brindisi Registry Office. It was a low-key affair: there were no parents for Pasquale and Andrea, of course, Damiano's had 'died' in a house fire many years previous and Livia's mother was 'too ill' to make the journey from Parma. She did send a huge tin of ham though. Damiano's best man was his Number Two, while Pasquale's was Fabrizzio. However, they did manage to fill the reception ballroom of the Grand Hotel with employees from Brindisia, a few selected local dignatories and the smarter members of Damiano's "organisation". Considerable celebrating took place on the no-expense-spared tariff befitting two important businessmen, albeit one legal and one not.

Damiano's family of four flew to Tenerife for their honeymoon and stayed in a new luxury hotel with pool, courtesy of the 70's boom in package tour holidays from Europe. In contrast, Pasquale and Livia spent an exhausting week traipsing through the Roman remains at Carthage and the coliseum at El Djem, in between reviving dips in one of the two pools of the brand new Sousse Palace Hotel in Tunisia. Two things they did agree on were that El Djem's coliseum was better than Roma's and that the Sousse Fez was magical. On the boat back to Sicilia Pasquale finally felt content.

* * *

63

THE FILM

1 9 7 2

Two weeks later one of Pasquale's managers was getting married and the groom's friends had organised a stag night for him. Pasquale was cajoled to join in, much against his better judgement, and after hours of trawling the bars and dancing with less than respectable ladies the staggering, noisy group found themselves between bars on a dubious street near Brindisi Docks. A small window was filled by a poster advertising 'adult films for discerning gentlemen' and a small voice ushered them towards a door. Stumbling in they found themselves in a dingy, dimly-lit corridor policed by a man at each end standing very upright with legs apart.

"Good evening gents, six tickets is it, then?"

They mumbled their assent, more out of fear than longing, and were 'pushed' through another thick door into a smoky, blacked-out room. Another man with a torch bundled them into seats and told them to be quiet or their throats would be slit. Incentive enough to drunks. They waited but nothing happened. Pasquale suddenly jumped to his feet, sobering up faster than the others, and whispered, "let's get out of here, we have been duped, we're going to be robbed, or worse!"

Just then, however, a screen began to flicker on one side of the room and music started to crackle through poor-quality speakers. Everyone looked at Pasquale and one dragged him back into his seat. "shush, shush, its starting!" they laughed at him and started guffawing at the screen. For 'adult film' it certainly was, even for such a Catholic country. Certainly not one of those pseudo-arty nude films from Scandinavia where naturists parade unconvincingly along sandy beaches in gale-force cold winds, but a really hot American XXX-rated movie. The story was certainly unmemorable but seemed to involve an Italian brother and sister emigrating to America in the late 50's. The acting was ham, the sets cheap and the cinematography puerile, but Pasquale's friends were so drunk they could not care as within ten minutes the brother met a girl who began to take off her clothes.

After fifteen minutes the brother introduced his sister to their landlord because they were facing difficulty paying the rent, being unable to find work. This was the first scene to show the girl fully and Pasquale nearly fell out of his chair. He uttered a gurgling kind of truncated scream and all his friends laughed and cheered. All he could hear was, 'what a beauty', 'wow, can't wait to see her strip off' and 'look at her curves, she'll get them free rent!' He could not bear to look at what happened next to his sister, but the friends' last suggestion turned out to be the correct, if trite, outcome. Fortunately, it was so dark in there that his friends could not see him closing his eyes and blocking his ears every time Maria took off her clothes. He so desperately wanted to rush out and vomit, but realised he could not. What would they all think? What would the bouncers do? How could he explain it? He knew he was there for the duration and would have to grin and bear it. Not the best expression to use, he thought, trying to humour himself. If he could last out till the end and see the credits, he might be able to get the name, or even address too, of the film company that put together this disgrace.

To pass the time he tried to plan yet another sister-rescuing act, this time across the Atlantic in a strange and different place. All he had to go on was the little he saw of Los Angeles on various movies; not much he agreed. The one big difference, apart from the language, was that everyone there had guns and such a rescue was a much more dangerous escapade.

The film's graphic content certainly shocked and aroused the men so that they quickly sobered up on exit. Consequently they were more than shocked when Pasquale's vomit blocked the gutter, but it did give him the excuse to blame bad beer and to get on home quickly, and they accepted that excuse as they went merrily singing on their way to the next bar.

Livia lovingly tucked him up and his last memory was of his sister chained to her landlord's courtyard wall. In the film he could see her wrists were reddened and sore and he wondered if it was just makeup or whether she was made to do the things she had to do in the film against her will. He hoped not, but it would explain why she had not written for years.

* * *

64

FINALLY FOUND

1 9 7 2

Livia helped him to the wedding next day but he cried off the reception, saying he was too old for stag nights and wasn't feeling his best after the bad beer. The bride worried but nothing was disclosed to her of the evenings' activities. And, indeed, Pasquale could not work for the three days following that Sunday, and even on return he could think of nothing but his sister. Worse, he continued to wonder if his nightmares about the chains had a ring of truth. Surely she must have been forced into making such a film, no normal woman does that voluntarily unless their circumstances are rock-bottom. Surely Maria's circumstances were not so? Or had that Ed Weaver deserted her and left her destitute, a stranger with no real vocational qualifications and only basic English in a foreign land? Maybe Weaver had forced her himself to do it? And why did she never write? Was she a prisoner somewhere to some crazed sex-fiend? The longer time went on the more his thoughts tormented him, continually twisting themselves into ever-tightening scenarios. He began to make mistakes at work, take bad decisions, argue irrationally. People began to notice, as did Livia, but he could not bear the shame of ever revealing it, not to anyone, not even Andrea. Must have been really bad beer or seafood, his employees continued to debate.

Finally, Pasquale could not see any other way of dealing with it. It was impossible for him to go to Los Angeles and try to find her. How could one man accomplish such a task in such a hedonistic place? He had no choice. He would involve the one man who belonged to the one organisation that might easily do the job – Damiano. If he and they could not find and bring back Maria, no-one could. And if they could not administer 'justice' to those who had so vilely treated Maria, no-one could. For once Andrea did not even argue against Damiano's involvement and threw her hat into the ring with force and anger.

Two weeks later Damiano phoned him. Yes, Weaver was a crook. Yes, he had used her to further his own ends and then dumped her. Yes, he had died in mysterious overdose circumstances. Yes, she had had nowhere else to turn to stay alive but to perform in those films. And yes, they had found her, suitably punished those who had kept her in house arrest on a constant cocktail of drugs, and yes, she was now well enough to be flying back to Italy in a few days.

And then the next day, after years of silence, a letter came from Mario in Taranto. To be accurate, it did not come from Mario but was about Mario. It appeared he had been very unwell for a long time and was asking to see his old friend, maybe for the last time, the writer added. Pasquale agreed at once, especially as a nice sunny drive to Taranto in his new bigger Fiat might cheer him up a little and perhaps help clarify his thoughts on Maria and the plans he was going to have to make.

It was a beautiful, sunny Wednesday and he decided to detour through Oria. Nothing had changed as he visited all the old haunts. Even Bainsizza seemed not a brick out of place. Timeless, yet of time, he mused.

Onwards to Francovilla and Grottaglie, where he just could not resist stopping for coffee in Via Ceramiche. Still a romantic at heart and full of memories he gazed lovingly at the shop where he had first met Stefania. Again, nothing had changed except one slight difference - there was a notice on the old glass door: "Affittasi". He peered in and, sure enough, the place looked cavernous in its emptiness. It was up for rental. He wondered if indeed anyone had occupied it since he and Stefania had left for Napoli all those years ago. Surely someone must have? Papa had purchased it and so it must have been sold with the estate when he died, and maybe it had had at least one more handover after that, perhaps. Oh, how time cruelly marches on, he pondered sadly, as the tears from past happiness began to well up in his eyes. Did God's plans have to be so complicated?

But he suddenly pulled himself together and returned to the present when he remembered that odd thing Stefania had written in her very last letter to him about her father's secret in Via Ceramiche. What on earth had she meant? Secret? In the street? Inside the shop? This intrigue animated him: what secrets could Papa have had, he thought, and why might they have been so important? He turned away from the door to go and find the letting agent's office, but just then a car pulled up at the curb and three men stepped out. One carried a huge bunch of keys and a long cardboard tube, while the others looked from their dress to be businessmen.

"Here is the shop. Please, this way," said the agent politely.

Pasquale hurried across to the opening door, "excuse me, are you showing these gentlemen around?"

"Yes, and what is it to you, pray?"

"Oh nothing particularly. I was just passing and wondered if I could have a look too? I don't come from round her and caves into the hillside turned into shops like this is quite novel, well, fascinating to me actually." Pasquale stopped there because he didn't want to overdo it, if indeed he had not already.

"With a view to?"

Then the other two men intervened, "excuse me, we were here first, signore."

"Yes, yes, of course. Do not worry, I am not interested in renting the property, I just wanted to take a look inside, if that is OK?"

"So again I ask, with a view to?" repeated the churlish agent, fast running out of patience.

Pasquale smiled and replied, "OK, I will be truthful. It's just that this shop has great sentimental value," and he went on to explain how he had met Stefania and so on. The truth never fails, he thought, why do we ever lie?

"Signore Pinto's daughter? Oh yes, remember her well. Tragic loss in that plane crash. You poor man, yes, please, do come in. I would be honoured to let you browse around again. Please." And he beckoned Pasquale in while the other two nodded soberly with condoling eyes.

It was quite upsetting to be back inside, even though there was no pottery on the shelves and no potter at a wheel, and Pasquale had to rest against a convenient ledge for a while to regain his composure. The agent laid out the plans on a trestle table next to him, they studied them for a while and then went off to the workshop. For want of anything more positive to do in his grief Pasquale studied the plans from where he sat. It all looked simple enough as he looked down, looked up and looked down again. Suddenly he noticed on the plans an indentation on the back wall: instead of being straight there was definitely something extra there, although it would probably go unnoticed except to the keenest eye. He looked to the wall. From where he was it seemed straight. Odd, he thought, jumping up quickly. He knew he didn't have long but he also knew old tufa-walled properties: they often concealed hidden gaps, holes and even in some cases whole rooms behind a false wall. In their house in Bainsizza, Oria, for instance, he had found a small, concealed extra room off the kitchen which was not even on the plans.

He ran to the left-hand end of the wall and started moving along it as fast as he could, tapping as he went. Sure enough, as he approached the centre, the sound changed from a deep thud to a hollow knock. There *is* a nook behind here, he muttered triumphantly. The men were returning, he hastily thanked them for their forbearance and marched purposefully out the door. "Full of grief still, I expect," said one.

"Overcome, no doubt, and who came blame him."

But Pasquale did not move so quickly that he did not notice the type of lock on the chained front door.

At 2 am he returned and with the crowbar he had found lying in a building site he easily broke the padlock. He had also found a kind of mallet there too which came in very handy for pounding the tufa wall without making too much noise. Twenty dust-filled, choking minutes later he was able to reach inside the nook. His hand felt a cold metal box. He did not stop to look at it but exited as quickly as possible and ran for his life to his car.

A few streets away he pulled up under a street light as his interior light was not working. All he could see in the box was wads of paper, no money. He wondered if he had wasted his time and risked all for some sheets of paper, and cursing his luck he drove slowly out into the countryside to find a quiet track to park and sleep till morning.

He slept fitfully, that was guaranteed. An uncomfortable seat, cold night air, no coat and a brain full of imponderables assured him of nothing and he woke more confused and upset than ever. The trip to Taranto would make him feel no better, either. Why was life full of so many ups and downs?

He found Mario as the letter said, extremely unwell. Hardly recognisable from loss of weight and pain, he had been diagnosed with cancer. Mario could hardly speak and when he did it was almost unintelligible. The only words Pasquale heard were "Brindisia, well done". The meeting and the parting were emotive to say the least.

Pasquale needed to hurry back to Brindisi and some kind of normality, swearing never to come this way again. He could have called on Andrea but she had just given birth to her third, aptly named Eduardo, and she would have her hands full. I'll go for the one-month celebration, he thought, but now I must get home.

Finally, back in his study, he was able to extract all the papers and study them carefully in proper daylight. Flabbergasted, he immediately realised what they were – hundreds of German bearer bonds, dated before the war. As he reached the bottom of the box his suspicions were confirmed -- whose they were and where they had come from. The proof was undeniable. He laughed with joy. The two bean seeds he had planted there in 1948 were still there! They had been a joke really, a bit of fun, and although they were now shrivelled and gnarled they were still unmistakably bean seeds. The bonds were the old farmer's that they had robbed when in the youth gang and somehow they must have ended up with Eduardo. And then he saw the scrawled note from the farmer Lorenzo to Eduardo – 'This is all I have got left of any value. Please take it in lieu. Never blackmail me anymore, I have no more money!' Oh, so was this the Pinto Secret Treasure? The family heirloom for 25 years? It depended on whether the bonds were still worth anything, he decided. Although they were, all those years ago when he had consulted Cosimo and Mario, probably now they were worthless, knowing my luck, he thought. But what 'blackmail'? And what had Lorenzo to do with Eduardo? There was so much I never knew about my father, he mused, and probably never would. How strange that even within a family so little is known of the past by the children.

He posted one of the bonds to PD, the Head Man of the Camorra in Napoli. After all, he had told Pasquale at Mino's funeral if he ever needed help just ask. Brindisia was yielding great returns for the Camorra so one good turn deserved another. The reply came immediately by telegram, no less!

'Very valuable. Have you more? Collectors desperate. Won't ask their origin. PD'

Pasquale telephoned him at once and after some brief calculations found that the Pinto Treasure had a black-market value of around 180 million lire! The Camorra could quietly dispose of it for 110 million, if he was agreeable. Agreeable? He was rich beyond dreams, who cared about agreeable?

Livia came in hurriedly from Brindisia with news of a huge new find of houses in the north-west corner. Pasquale grabbed her and waltzed her round the room. "What? You have better news than that, Pasquale?"

"Yes, today we are 110 million lire better off!"

"Wow! Bet you I can beat that though."

"Bet you can't. Couldn't. 110 million lira? Never. No-one could!"

"Yes I can," she laughed, "I went to the doctor today..."

"...so what?"

"So, we are soon going to have an heir to that 110 million!"

THE END

Lightning Source UK Ltd.
Milton Keynes UK
UKHW010622020420
361230UK00001B/61